STARGÅTE SG·1™

OCEANS OF DUST

PETER J. EVANS

FANDEMONIUM BOOKS

An original publication of Fandemonium Ltd, produced under license from MGM Consumer Products.

Fandemonium Books
United Kingdom
Visit our website: www.stargatenovels.com

STARGÅTE
SG·1

METRO-GOLDWYN-MAYER Presents
RICHARD DEAN ANDERSON
in
STARGATE SG-1™
MICHAEL SHANKS AMANDA TAPPING CHRISTOPHER JUDGE
DON S. DAVIS
Executive Producers BRAD WRIGHT MICHAEL GREENBURG
RICHARD DEAN ANDERSON
Developed for Television by BRAD WRIGHT & JONATHAN GLASSNER

WWW.MGM.COM

Print ISBN: 978-1-905586-53-0   Ebook ISBN: 978-1-80070-026-0

To Nicola

For research, for coffee, and for being able to
put up with me.

Author's Note:

This story takes place in Stargate: SG-1 Season 4, between the episodes 'Upgrades' and 'Crossroads'.

Thanks to everyone who helped me out on this one, especially Sally and Tom at Fandemonium for letting me write it. Large and expensive drinks go to the informational James Swallow and the inspirational Heather Wallace, without whom this book would have been a far lesser thing than it is. And high-fives all round to the Pubmeet crew, for recharging my enthusiasm batteries on a monthly basis.

Chapter 1.

TERMINAL FROST

LAURA MILES saw a dead man on her way to the dig site.

He appeared to her like a vision, out of the golden dawn haze, by the side of the El-Fayoum highway. Kemp, who was driving, must have seen him too, because Miles didn't even get time to shout before the SUV was lurching to a halt.

The vehicle had been moving fast. Miles had to brace herself against the back of Kemp's seat as the brakes came on, and Andersson, who had been dozing in the front, was thrown forwards into the dashboard. She yelped, the seatbelt yanking her back.

Miles, startled by the sight, barely heard her.

Kemp reversed, slowly. The SUV pulled up close to the dead man and stopped, the engine idling.

Miles sat quite still, one hand against the back of Kemp's seat, the other over her eyes to block out some of the glare. The sun was coming up, a molten crescent against the desert's black horizon, and shafts of harsh light were cutting towards her across the sand. They outlined the dead man, making a halo of his white cotton headscarf, and forced Miles' eyes almost closed.

Inside the SUV, no-one spoke for a long time.

The dead man was sitting by the side of the road, his back against an upturned cart. He must have been driving it along the edge of the highway when some speeding vehicle had collided with him, hurling his body into the sand. He'd lived for a while, Miles decided, after the impact; long enough to drag himself back to the cart, to prop himself against it, maybe to wait for help that never came.

Miles shivered, feeling queasy and strange. She had seen dead men before, many times, but they had been changed by the hot sand of the desert: their skins dry paper, their skulls hollow, their hearts black wisps clinging to the insides of canopic jars. This man might have been asleep, save for his one open eye and the swarms of flies already feasting on his tears.

"We should call somebody," she breathed.

Kemp shook his head. "We probably shouldn't."

"What?" That was Andersson, quietly aghast. "We can't just leave him out there!"

"Yes we can," said Kemp, his voice a flat whisper. He was looking straight ahead now, through the windshield, not at the corpse. "It's a highway. Someone will see him."

"But—"

"Anna, I'm sorry. But if we call this in we'll get involved, and Harlowe will throw a fit. You know what he's like."

Miles knew that arguing wasn't going to do any good. Not with Harlowe visiting the dig. "He's right," she said. "I hate it, but he's right."

"*Så jävla typiskt!*" Andersson hissed, sitting back with her arms folded. "All right, if you're so frightened of Harlowe. Drive on."

"I'm—"

"I hope he haunts your dreams!"

"Kemp, just go," Miles snapped. "Before somebody drives past and thinks we killed the poor bugger."

"I'm sorry," repeated Kemp. Then he turned the wheel and brought the SUV around in a sharp turn towards the east. Miles felt the tires leave tarmac and bounce solidly onto packed sand.

Andersson reached up for the grab-handle above the window and held on. "I hate all these secrets," she muttered.

"Not long now," Kemp replied. "Things will be back to normal soon."

Normal. He'd been saying that for a week, ever since they had first struck stone.

Miles risked one more glance back as they drove away. The dead man sat as if content, his one open eye gazing out towards the dig site. He was looking at where she was going.

Miles didn't like that. It felt like a bad sign, an omen. As if the dead knew more of her business here than the living.

Around her, the desert grew hot.

Deserts are defined by their extremes. In western Egypt, it is not uncommon for daylight temperatures to peak at a searing fifty centigrade. At night, frost can form, in those scattered places where moisture remains in the air.

This is the rhythm of the place: roast and freeze, over and over, forever. It is a brutal process, a ceaseless hammer that turns mountains into hills, hills into rubble, rubble into fine sand that heaps into wandering, wind-scoured dunes a thousand kilometers from end to end. It is erosion, it is demolition; it is the way the desert remakes itself.

Earlier that summer, the process had focused its might on a rock formation some twenty kilometers south of the Giza plateau. The formation was strange, but not notably so — it was a low inland cliff, crescent-shaped, its concave, north-facing side curled over as though a perfect surfer's wave had swept in from some unimaginable sea, reared up and then frozen hard into a wall of pitted yellow stone. For thousands of years the crescent had been filled with sand and largely hidden, but the complex vagaries of wind and weather had, over the previous century or two, conspired to scoop it clean.

The movement of dunes is impossible to model precisely. In another century the crescent might well have filled again, but it never got the chance. It was too exposed to survive. Robbed of its supporting mass of sand, it fell prey to the remorseless battering of daytime heat and night-time cold: together they beat at that perfect wave until, one night in early June it cracked, and split, and tumbled into a thousand pieces to litter the desert with its ruins.

No-one saw it happen. But hours later, high above the clear Egyptian air, eyes that owed nothing to evolution noted the change in terrain. Had the machine that owned them been on its normal flight path the collapse might well have gone unremarked, but there had been a minor, yet unexplainable malfunction in its navigational systems earlier that day. So it saw the collapsed area of rock, then looked more closely, and detected something from which a certain select group of human beings might be able to profit.

Which is how, four weeks later, Professor Laura Miles found herself standing at Cairo airport with a small information pack, a non-disclosure agreement from Parker-Lexington Holdings and the fattest bank balance she'd seen since she retired.

It took another two hours to reach the dig site. The terrain made for slow going, the SUV's big tires slipping and skittering as sand gave way to broken stone, stone to gravel, gravel to scrub and back to sand again, sometimes within the space of a few meters. After ten continuous days of travelling to the site at dawn and back to Cairo again at dusk, Miles thought that she really should have been getting used to the jolting.

She wasn't. Every time she got out of the SUV her left hip felt like a fire had been lit within the bone.

The sun was well above the horizon by the time they got to the dig. A sharp dip in the terrain brought the site into view; a long, shallow crescent stretching away towards the Nile. The northern face of the curve faded out, merged back into level desert in the space of half a kilometer, but the southern edge was a jagged line of hard shadow.

As the SUV rolled closer, Miles found herself picking out details of the excavation itself, trying to see what had changed since the day before. The ragged trail of flat-roofed tents had extended overnight — there were six of them now, plus the flapping ribbon of camouflage fabric that hugged the shadowed edge of the crescent and concealed the main find. Someone had parked a flatbed truck over by the spoil heaps, and Miles saw figures clustered behind it. With luck, they would be unloading the extra *sibas* she had asked for.

Otherwise, the place was much as it had been; a random scatter of shadows cast onto a curve of bright, hot sand, dotted with robed figures. Not much to look at, considering how much it had occupied her body and mind for the past ten days.

The SUV slowed at the edge of the crescent, then tipped down into it. There was a slightly hairy moment when one of the tires hit a patch of sand that was little more than powder, and spent a second or two flinging it up in a great yellow roostertail while the other wheels juddered against the dune, but in a second or two the crisis had passed and the vehicle was rolling down into shadow. Kemp pulled around left, under one of the big camouflage tents, and killed the engine. The SUV shuddered and became still.

Kemp let out a long breath. "Everyone okay?"

Andersson didn't speak, just hauled open the door on her side and jumped down onto the sand, slamming the door behind her. Miles watched her stalking away, long angry strides that carried her fast across the site, her pale skin already blotchy in the heat.

"Anna!" Kemp was out too, standing next to his open door and shouting across the vehicle's roof. "Wait!"

"Let her go," Miles told him. "It's not you she's mad at."

Kemp made a helpless gesture in Andersson's direction, then slapped the roof angrily. Dust rose to settle on his black shirt. "Ballsed that up, didn't I?"

"I told you, it's not your fault." Miles opened her own door and got out, putting her weight on her right foot until she had retrieved her cane from the seat. "She's been trying to call her husband for the past four nights, but Harlowe's done something to the phones."

His eyebrows went up. "Really?"

"Him or someone from PLH."

"Bloody hell."

"What, you've not tried to call Sarah?"

"Ahh…" Kemp looked embarrassed. He hadn't, Miles realized, with some amusement. Harlowe had told him not to, so he hadn't.

In truth, she couldn't blame either of them. Harlowe was only following the instructions from his superiors, and Kemp didn't want to risk the other half of his money. Geophysics wasn't a field that was going to make anyone rich, even with the reputation he had built for himself since leaving Glasgow. With a new wife and a baby on the way, there was no way he could pass up what Harlowe was offering.

There was nothing between Kemp and Andersson of course: not romantically, anyway. Maybe a slight crush on Kemp's part, at worst. But it was natural for friendships to blossom in circumstances like these, and it made the work easier if people got along.

"I'll talk to her," Miles said.

"You don't have to."

"Somebody does. Better me than Harlowe." Miles had noticed the company man's jeep parked under the new tent. Sooner or later she would have to go and give him a status report, but she still felt unsettled from the morning's sights. Better to spend a few minutes trying to mollify Andersson, before she attempted to deal with Harlowe's demands.

"Look, just get the geophysics rig sorted out, okay? Once we get that roof slab out of the way we'll need another sweep."

"Fine," he replied. "Hey, give me a yell if there's any coffee on the go, okay?"

Miles gave him a tired wave of assent, then turned and began to make her way across the site, leaning heavily on the cane. She still didn't feel right. There was an oddness here she couldn't identify, a strange sense that the ground she walked on wasn't entirely solid. The scene around her looked unstable, as if painted on flimsy backdrops. Everything seemed unreal — even the Egyptian workers, walking past her with their wheelbarrows and shovels and measuring lines, were ghosts, kin to the dead man by the highway.

Their robes hung low. She couldn't see their feet, couldn't judge where they ended and the desert began.

In the distance, voices rose. Miles cupped a hand over her eyes, looking back towards the curving stone wall. One of the new *sibas* had already been raised, and a knot of men was hauling the second into position. The *sibas* were lifting devices, three-meter tripods of stout wood, fitted with winches. One could lift half a ton of stone, but when she and Andersson had finished uncovering the roof slab they had realized just how massive it was. Two *sibas* would never have been enough to move it.

"Professor?"

The voice startled her. Lucas Harlowe had been standing next to her while she was watching the Egyptians.

Damn, she thought sourly. "Lucas! It's good to see you."

"You too."

"So when did you get in?" she asked. "Is everything okay?"

"Flew in last night. And yeah, everything's fine." Harlowe was American, but Miles couldn't quite place his accent. "Mohammed was just saying you'd cleared a new layer."

There were at least four Mohammeds working at the site, but Miles knew Harlowe was talking about Mohammed Rashwan, the Conservation Director. "That's right."

"Find anything?"

He wasn't going to wait, she could tell from his voice. She would have to postpone her peacekeeping duties for a while.

"Follow me," she said. "I'll show you."

Over by the spoil heaps, one of the tents had been set up to shade a long wooden bench-table and several folding chairs. It was here that the most painstaking work on the site should have been done — the cleaning and cataloguing of small finds, the translation of hieroglyphs, the careful detailing and mapping of every artifact found in the excavations. On all of Miles' previous digs, the table tended to be a major focus of interest, but after a few days of finding nothing in the sand but random fragments of uniformly dull pottery its original purpose had become almost forgotten. Now it was just a convenient place to sit.

There was one item on the table that was still used. At one end, a poster-sized sheet of printout had been carefully taped down to the wood, sealed on all four sides so the wind couldn't lift it and bear it away. Miles picked up one of the folding chairs, shoved it hard down into the sand next to the map and sank down into it, stretching out her left leg and leaning the cane against the table. Harlowe took up position next to her, peering down at the print-out and the sprawl of hand-drawn details and notations that covered it. "So what am I looking at here?"

The answer to that, Miles knew, was rather more complex than she could easily explain.

The printout was a topographical map of the site, showing the long curve of the wall and its complex patterns of elevation and ground composition. It was clearly generated from satellite data, but any hint of where that data had come from had been carefully excised.

At the very centre of the map, surrounded by Rashwan's impossibly precise notes, lay a small area hatched in blue. Miles found herself staring at it, at the tiny shaded shape that had drawn her back to Egypt in midsummer, had led Kemp and Andersson and Rashwan out to this nameless patch of desert and kept them here while the sun beat down and the secrets mounted up. A rectangle of blue ink that no-one would have known existed had it not been for the satellite and its thermal eyes.

The shape was not a measure of topography. It was a temperature reading. Something bounded by that hatched area was ten degrees cooler than the surrounding desert, and no-one could work out why.

"Okay," she forced her attention back to Harlowe. "How much had we done last time you were here?"

That would have been five days ago. "You'd gone down a meter," Harlowe replied. "Found a lot of broken columns, some pottery…"

"Right. Well, the supply of columns dried up pretty fast. We found twenty, all damaged." She picked up a nearby pen and used the end of it to indicate a double row of circles on the map, surrounding the shaded patch. "We think they bordered a short processional, like a pathway with columns either side."

"Leading to what?"

Miles shrugged. "I don't know. We were expecting to find evidence of a roof, but so far all we've got is one slab." She traced a rectangle between four of the circles, each corner at the centre of one column. "There should be another eight, but either they're a long way off the main dig or they're gone completely."

"Nothing in any of the other trenches."

"No. The one we've found is good quality stone; solid, well-carved. A lot of what was here might well have been stolen, hauled off to build other projects."

Harlowe made a face. "God dammit," he muttered. "You know what I think we've got?"

"What?"

"A well." He picked up one of the finds from near the map, a totally unremarkable shard of pottery. "Maybe ceremonial, healing waters or something… There's a chunk of water table under there, and the local bigwigs put a roof over it." He waved the shard. "Probably charged for jugs of the stuff."

Miles had heard crazier theories than that, and from people with a lot more archaeological knowledge than Harlowe. Some of the stuff poor Daniel Jackson used to come up with… Underground water could have explained the site's temperature, if it was contained in a small area rather than leaching out into the surrounding desert.

If it *was* water, Miles thought, Harlowe wouldn't have been entirely displeased. When PLH had started funding this dig they had been banking on the temperature anomaly signaling either a buried structure of much denser material than the surrounding matrix, or an as-yet undiscovered segment of water table. Miles had never been able to determine exactly what kind of deals PLH had done with the Egyptian authorities for control of the site, if any, and she guessed that the dig was only being allowed to continue because no-one was fully aware of it yet. Still, if there was water this far into the western desert, no doubt the Egyptian government would look kindly on PLH for discovering it for them. Likewise, if a new tomb complex lurked down here, sucking heat from the ground, that could be made to benefit both parties too.

To Miles, neither explanation seemed very likely, but her job was to dig the site, not fret about PLH and their machinations. That's what Harlowe was for.

"There's something else. Those pillars didn't just fall down. They were knocked down."

"How can you tell?"

"The fall pattern. And the way that somebody chiseled every name off every section before they flattened the place."

Harlowe frowned. "Okay, I'm no expert. But didn't the Egyptians used to do that when someone had really pissed them off?"

"Yes, or if they wanted to take credit for a predecessor's works. But it looks like malice here, all right."

"So there's this tiny structure, out in the ass-end of nowhere, and somebody vandalized it and stole most of the stone…" He gave her a grim smile. "Guess they got charged too much for the water."

Miles could tell he was joking, but it made an odd kind of sense. She was about to answer when someone called her name.

Andersson was running towards her, holding a sunhat down onto her head with one hand. She went light and dark like a slow strobe, between the tents and open sand, and Miles found herself envying the younger woman her easy stride. It had been a long time since she'd been able to run.

"Anna?" she asked, as Andersson halted in front of her. "What's wrong?"

For a moment Andersson could only shake her head. Then she got in a couple of good breaths. "We found something," she gasped, then pointed back towards the pit.

"There's something under the slab."

Raising the slab high enough to see that what lay beneath hadn't taken very long at all. Shifting it completely out of the way took a lot more time, and the strength of every worker on the site.

It was immensely heavy, a flat rectangular block of something that looked like smooth, dark granite, at least two meters across and three long. The previous day, Miles had asked Rashwan to get the thing up as quickly as possible, so that a new geophysics survey could be done of the pit's bed. In response, Rashwan had assembled the two existing *sibas* before dawn, and the new pair as soon as they had been unloaded from the flatbed. While Miles and Harlowe had been poring over the map, Rashwan and his men had been dragging at the winch chains, determined to do as much heavy work as they could before the day's heat became too intense.

As soon as someone had looked under the slab and reported what was there, however, Rashwan had called an immediate halt.

Now that the slab had been taken the rest of the way, Miles could see it for herself. They all could. Almost the entire work-force was either in or around the pit.

Kemp was kneeling close to where the slab had lain. He was peering down into what it had been concealing, aiming a big flash-light into the darkness. "Goes down about ten meters, maybe more."

Miles peered over his shoulder, watching the light skating off polished surfaces, picking out corners that converged dizzyingly below her. It was a strange sight, dark and frightening and wrong in a way that she couldn't quite define. "Can you see the bottom?"

"I think so. Just about." He sat back on his heels, a baffled expression on his face. "Laura, just what the hell are we looking at here?"

"I don't know. I swear, I've never seen anything like this in my life."

Laura Miles had been excavating in Egypt for thirty years before she had retired. She had assisted on dozens of digs, had been Finds Supervisor on nearly twenty and Field Director on nine before this one. And while she had seen plenty of tombs and structures that could only be accessed by narrow stone tunnels, never in all her days had she seen a shaft like the one concealed beneath the roof slab.

It was deep, but she had seen deeper. It was narrow, but she had scrambled down tunnels barely wide enough for her narrow shoulders. It was dark, but they always were.

No, what unnerved Miles was the shaft's perfection. The dense, polished granite cladding its sides was entirely unblemished.

Carving and smoothing the stone with such precision must have been an awesome feat of engineering for a people whose most sophisticated masonry tool was the bronze saw. Fitting the slabs together so that not a single seam had cracked or warped or let in moisture after thousands of years was a task that Miles simply couldn't comprehend.

It was said that the burial chamber of the Great Pyramid was lined with granite so expertly carved that a razor blade couldn't fit between the blocks. But time had made its mark even on that astounding monument. This structure, buried under unstable sand in the middle of nowhere, could have been put together the previous week, for all the wear it showed.

The shaft was not only disturbing, it was perilous. The opening was over a meter wide, certainly large enough to fall into. And while any unfortunate soul tumbling down that black chute wouldn't fall straight down, the angle of the shaft was steep enough to not only ensure injury, but also to utterly prevent escape.

The thought made her step back. As she did so, Harlowe pushed his way past some of the workers to join her. A moment later the men parted behind him, and Mohammed Rashwan followed him up to the shaft.

"Damn," Harlowe muttered, staring down into the darkness. "That's no well."

Miles nodded slowly. "It's cold, but there's no sound of water. The sides are dry, too. No moisture damage."

Rashwan peered into the shaft for a few seconds, and then stepped back. "We will need ladders."

"The longest we've got are three meters," Miles replied. "Can we bolt four of them together?"

He nodded. "I will instruct the carpenters. We will support the joints with slats, use the long nails and tie with rope."

"How long?"

"Thirty minutes."

Harlowe looked uncomfortable. "You're sure? I mean, a ladder made out of bits and pieces... Will it hold?"

Miles gnawed her lip. "It had better."

"I will anchor the top of the ladder here." Rashwan pointed at one side of the opening. "So it will not slide at the base. Lying against the slope will give it greater strength."

"Jeez." Harlowe crouched, taking the flashlight from Kemp and aiming it down into the shadows. "Maybe we should wait until we can get some specialized equipment in."

Miles and Rashwan exchanged a look. "Not a good idea," the Egyptian smiled.

"No?"

"No. Anna saw the truck leave just after this opening was exposed. She says that several of my men were on it."

Harlowe made an exasperated sound. "So what?"

"So," said Kemp, getting up, "I reckon they'll be back in Cairo within a couple of hours. Maybe three. Which gives us..." He paused, pulling back one sleeve to check his watch. "Oh, about six hours before you've got a hundred people on this site, all wanting a piece of whatever's down there."

Rashwan's extended ladder looked terrifying, but it got Kemp to the base of the shaft without incident. Andersson had wanted to be first, and Miles had been sure that Kemp would let her, if only to get back in her good books. But apparently the young Scot's concern for her went deeper than Miles had expected, and he'd brooked no argument.

Rashwan had made sure Andersson hadn't set foot on the ladder until Kemp reported that he was down safely. He trusted the carpenters with one person's weight, but no more.

Harlowe stood with Miles, watching the young woman disappearing into the darkness. "Envious?"

"You ask bloody stupid questions, sometimes."

"Professor, this is just a quick look-see. When it comes to the real stuff we'll lower you down, I promise. But there's no way you could make that climb."

"I know," she said simply. There was nothing more to be said on the matter — he was right, and she hated it, and there wasn't a damn thing she could do about it except watch Andersson's blonde head vanish into the shadows and wonder what awaited her down there in the dark.

She keyed the walkie-talkie Harlowe had given her. "Kemp? Can you hear me?"

For a moment, her only answer was the fizzing of static. Then: *"Yeah, I hear you."*

"What are you seeing, for God's sake?"

"It's dark…"

"That's why you've got a torch." She gave Harlowe an exasperated look. He grinned at her, then started down the ladder himself.

"I know, give me a second. It's really cold down here… I can see my breath."

Miles still couldn't understand that. She couldn't imagine anything that could suck the heat out of a structure like that.

"There's a doorway here, open, more of a square arch at the base of the shaft. Behind it… My God, Laura, it's huge!"

"How huge?" she snapped. "What do you mean?"

Voices echoed indistinctly from within the shaft. There was another burst of static from the radio, then Andersson's voice issued from it: *"It opens out a long way. I can't quite make out the layout yet — everything's made of that same black stone, and our light just sort of skates off it…"* A few seconds passed, then Andersson spoke again.

"There's something underfoot, like a fine grit or dust. Um…Hold on, Kemp's —"

There was a shout from Kemp. Miles felt her heart jerk in her chest.

"Greg? What's wrong?" Andersson's voice bounced. She was running. *"Are you okay?"*

Miles dropped to her knees, ignoring the spike of pain from her hip, and stared down into the shaft. She could hear voices down there, echoing and impossible to discern, and every now and then the beam of a flashlight would scan past the bottom of the ladder.

Kemp's voice floated up to her through the echoes. He was laughing.

"Am I dreaming? Are you guys seeing this?"

Miles leaned as far in as she could, straining her ears. She heard Harlowe and Andersson, their voices attenuated by the stone as they too broke into delighted cries.

Kemp was saying something about gold.

The voices had dropped to murmurs. Miles tried to make out what they were saying, but the words weren't reaching her. She keyed the radio frantically, but whatever her colleagues had seen down there had taken the memory of her from them.

"Sod this." She got up, the shouted into the shaft. "I'm coming down!"

"Professor," said Rashwan, his face creased with concern. "Please, just wait."

"I can't."

"I will arrange something. A hoist. Laura, you will fall…"

She reached out to him, touched his hand. "I've got see this. I'm sorry, Mohammed, but I've just got to."

Miles stepped down onto the ladder, her fingers shaking with the effort of holding on, and began to lower herself into the shaft. The first few rungs weren't too bad. It was only when she had climbed down about a quarter of the way that the pain in her hip began to flare, and the weakness in her left leg became apparent.

She stopped, breathing hard, trying to will the ache away. She had made a mistake, she knew, a stupid, prideful, impatient mistake, and now she was going to be stuck partway down the ladder and look like a bloody fool when somebody finally pulled her up again.

Miles opened her mouth to call Rashwan, but before she could speak she heard a scream.

It came from below her — a short, startled shriek of alarm. Miles froze, listening hard. She held her breath, said nothing, not wanting to miss whatever happened next.

She didn't have to wait long. Before she needed to take in

more air there was another scream, longer and more terrified. It was Andersson. Miles heard Harlowe shout, echoes robbing the words of meaning, and then there was a flicker of light and the flat, nasty sound of a gunshot.

Miles gasped, stunned at the sound of it. She could understand the screaming, awful as it was. There were any number of reasons why people would cry out in such a place — a rockfall, or gas, or a sudden inrush of water. She herself had screamed, when that pillar in the Samanud dig had come down and shattered her hip.

But there was nothing she could imagine that would make someone fire a pistol in a tomb.

As Miles hung there, pinned to the ladder by shock and fear, Andersson screamed again. This time, the scream went on for a long time. Then it wavered, changed to a choking rasp, to a dry, echoing series of sobs.

To silence.

Miles hooked an arm around the nearest rung, used the other to key the radio. "Anna?"

There was nothing, just the faint hiss of background static. Then even that cut off.

"Anna? Greg, are you there?"

Only the dying echoes of her own words answered her. Miles glanced up, to see Rashwan's head punctuating the square of light above her. Then there was a scraping sound from below, and Lucas Harlowe stumbled into view at the base of the shaft.

He had no torch, but just enough light filtered down past Miles to see him turn, gun still in his hand, and fire twice into the shadows. Then he simply dropped the weapon and went for the ladder.

Miles realized that she was blocking his way. She dropped the radio, saw it tumble past him, then used both hands to haul herself up a rung. The pain in her arms and shoulders was astounding, just from this brief effort, and her left leg was about to give way. If she was on the ladder for much longer, she knew, she would fall and take Harlowe with her.

She heard his voice, thin and dry: "Please," he croaked. "No."

Almost as if they had heard his plea, the shadows at the base of the shaft moved, gathered, and rose up in pursuit of him.

The sight defeated Miles' perceptions. Her first thought was that black wires were following him up the shaft, then that oily spiderwebs fluttered in his wake, then that he was about to be swamped by noisome threads of gas. It was smoke down there, it was shadow, it was an amorphous cloud of pure frozen darkness that was reaching out for him, touching, brushing at his skin and his hair and the whites of his eyes.

It was none of these things. It was simply *death*, and at its touch, Lucas Harlowe withered away.

In his last moments he reached out, his arm stretched imploringly towards her, or perhaps the light behind her, but the hand was already nothing more than paper and twigs. His arm contracted around its own corroding bone, his shoulder collapsed, his torso twisted and crumbled.

He tried to speak, or to scream, but all that issued from the lipless hole that had once been a mouth was dust, and a sound like sandpaper on stone. An instant later his ravaged frame lost its battle with gravity, and it fell away to crash down the shaft, nothing more than powder and ash and blackening, shattering bone. What had been Lucas Harlowe vanished into the writhing dark, piece by tumbling piece, and was gone.

It had taken a second to happen, maybe two. A few beats of the heart. And suddenly, Laura Miles was alone in the shaft with night-black threads spinning through the air towards her.

The air around her grew suddenly, brutally cold. A hair-fine tendril of shadow brushed her finger, and her left arm became *nothing*, a lifeless weight at her elbow.

There was no pain, just a wrenching absence. Miles could see the limb, but it was dead to her.

She moaned, swung herself around, back to the ladder. Raised a foot, her boot like a ton weight, dragged herself up half a meter. And another, expecting at any second for that freezing death to reach up and take her as she climbed.

Somehow she outran it.

She was no longer capable of wondering why: with the shaft around her she knew nothing except the climb. Even terror would have to wait until she was done.

Abruptly, there was light in her eyes, and a dark face before her. People in long robes and headscarves reaching out towards her. Someone had an open bottle of water, holding it close, urging her to drink.

Beneath her feet, the ground shivered. Every voice stilled. The desert became completely silent. Then sounds issued from the shaft; a scraping, thin and metallic, and the crunching splinter of wooden ladders being scissored apart.

All the strength went out of Miles, then. She slumped to her knees. She felt dry, like a statue, a column of wood and ash, a burned thing.

The bottle of water hovered before her. She reached out to it, with her dead hand.

Plastic touched her fingertips.

And Laura Miles, with no particular surprise, saw her withered hand crumble, the skin and tendons flutter apart from pitted bone and into fine ash that drifted away, a cloud of black dust borne on the warm Egyptian wind.

Chapter 2.

RIDERS ON THE STORM

IT WAS cold, up on the mountain. A frigid wind was whipping down off the high peaks, laden with powdered snow and sharp, stinging frost. As soon as Jack O'Neill stepped out onto the Stargate's dais the wind hit him in the face, making him duck away from it and shield his eyes. The transition from the flat, filtered air of the gate room to this painful scour — with only the subjective tumble through the Stargate itself between them — took the strength from him.

"Whoa," he gasped, blinking hard.

There was a sharp intake of breath next to him as Daniel Jackson left the gate and got a mouthful of the same jagged air that was battering O'Neill. "Okay, that's cold."

"Think it'll wake you up some?"

Daniel cupped his hands together and blew through them. "Nature's espresso."

O'Neill would have preferred the real thing. He was no stranger to early starts, but being rushed through the Stargate in the small hours of the morning wasn't really how he liked to begin his day. Not that he had any idea what kind of time he had just stepped into: no other world rotated at quite the same rate as Earth, or span at the same distance from its sun. All he could tell was he had left Stargate Command at three in the morning and had walked out of the gate into bright, if cloudy and bitterly cold, daylight.

There was another gasp behind him as Carter arrived on the dais, and then Teal'c followed her through, striding quickly across the platform and down the short set of steps to ground level. If he was surprised by the weather, he didn't show it, but O'Neill hadn't expected him to. "We should have sent a MALP," he griped, starting down the steps.

"There wasn't time," Daniel replied. "Anyway, Bra'tac said that the conditions were okay."

"I think he was lying."

"'Bracing'," said Carter. He saw her shrugging unconsciously deeper into her uniform, trying to let her tacvest take the brunt of the weather. "He said the climate would be 'bracing'."

"Gotta be a Jaffa thing," O'Neill felt the wind tug at his cap, and put a hand up to clamp it tighter onto his head. "Teal'c, this feel 'bracing' to you?"

"I had not noticed."

"Figures." Where the three humans were almost crouched against the wind, Teal'c was standing as upright and unconcerned as though he were indoors; his staff weapon held at vertical rest, his head tilted almost imperceptibly as he scanned the surrounding terrain.

O'Neill heard the grumble of the event horizon rise in pitch, and he glanced back in time to see the rippling mirror behind him fragment and spin away to nothing. The gate became an empty stone ring atop its dais, revealing nothing but gray rock and the pale, roiling sky.

In fact, apart from the sky and the mountain, there was almost nothing to see anywhere. To O'Neill's right the ground jutted into a cliff, ragged-edged and brutally steep. To the left it fell away into what looked like an uncomfortably sheer drop. The two cliffs joined somewhere behind the gate, and splayed away from each other ahead, forming a narrow, roughly triangular step that curled away out of sight. Broken stone littered the ground, parts of the upper cliff that had shattered away and fallen onto the step, and everything around the Stargate was rimed with slippery frost. It was a monochrome place, lifeless and desolate and utterly dangerous.

Which told O'Neill much about the people who would choose Sar'tua as a place of refuge.

He saw Teal'c lift his head slightly. "What?"

"We are being watched, O'Neill."

He had thought as much. "Up on the ridge?"

"And from the broken ground behind the Stargate."

O'Neill resisted the urge to check. "Nice job. Good lines of sight, no chance of crossfire." In such terms, the placement of the gate made a lot of sense. There wasn't enough room around it to form a staging area, no space to rank troops or set up equipment. Anyone emerging from it could go neither left, right or to the rear — an invader would always be funneled forwards, while anyone on the cliffs above could rain fire down on them with impunity.

The Stargate had been set up in a killing zone.

Realizing that made O'Neill even more anxious to get out of the cold. "Teal'c, can we hurry this up?"

"Our instructions were to wait and allow ourselves to be observed."

The wind gusted in a high whistle, spattering O'Neill with sleet. "If we wait much longer they're going to be observing four popsicles." He glanced up at the Jaffa's impassive face. "Three popsicles and, well, you…"

"Very well, O'Neill." Teal'c took a breath and shouted: the harsh, barking language of the Goa'uld.

An answering voice came from above, up on the cliff edge. O'Neill saw no-one. "What was that?"

"We are required to identify ourselves." Teal'c called back, a barrage of syllables.

As soon as he had finished, men appeared.

They were Jaffa, that much was obvious. O'Neill counted ten up on the clifftop, their heads and staff weapons suddenly outlined against the scudding clouds, and at the sound of scuffling behind him he turned to see another half-dozen taking up position behind the gate.

All the new arrivals were holding staff weapons. Like Teal'c, however, they were carrying them upright, which O'Neill took as a good sign, just like the fact that none of them were in any kind of uniform. Most were hooded against the cold, some wore long robes that fluttered madly in the wind. He did spot a few items of what he had come to know as typical Jaffa armor and equipment, but on the whole, the men approaching him looked like people who had picked up whatever they could and run for their lives.

The Jaffa on top of the cliff began to descend, running down a set of carved steps so narrow and fractured that O'Neill had thought them just another crack in the stone. Within a few seconds, they had reached level ground and spread out into ragged formation a few meters away. It was all O'Neill could do to keep his MP5 slung and his hands low.

Finally, one of the Jaffa stepped forwards. He shrugged back the hood he had been wearing and raised a hand. "Teal'c!"

In response, Teal'c tipped his head. "*Tek ma te.*"

The hooded man's dark skin was roughened by time, and a life in the service of terrible masters. He wore a skullcap, a neat white beard, and on his forehead the golden symbol of Apophis glittered in the meager light.

O'Neill let out a breath he didn't realize he'd been holding.

Bra'tac stepped forwards. "Greetings. You are here sooner than I had hoped."

"Couldn't keep away."

"Once we had your message, General Hammond wanted us here as soon as possible," Daniel explained.

"Yeah…" O'Neill suppressed a shiver. "He was eager. Nice place you've got here."

Bra'tac was perfectly capable of recognizing human sarcasm, although sometimes he chose to pretend he didn't. Today, it seemed, he had no time for such games. "It may be harsh, O'Neill, but for the moment it is safe."

"Perhaps no longer," Teal'c replied. "If you have indeed found what you describe."

"Which is why I contacted you as soon as I discovered the bodies."

That was news. "Bodies?"

"Of course. The significance of the ship was hidden until I saw who had been at the helm." Bra'tac turned away, into the wind. "Follow me."

He stalked away. The Jaffa he left in his wake shifted into a kind of expectant line, waiting for O'Neill and his companions to follow. None of them, O'Neill noticed, had acknowledged Teal'c in any way other than suspicious glares, and some looked as if they would have been happier with their staff weapons leveled and open.

Teal'c made no comment on this, and O'Neill decided it would be churlish to bring the subject up. *Maybe later*, he thought. *When things are a little warmer all round.*

He set off after Bra'tac, trotting to keep up with the man's long strides, Carter and Daniel falling in alongside him and Teal'c a few steps behind. A rearguard position. The fact that he thought this necessary made O'Neill feel even less comfortable than before, if that were possible.

Bra'tac reached the bottom of the stone steps and launched himself up them. Watching him, O'Neill winced slightly. "Okay, people. Don't try this at home."

"No intention, sir," muttered Carter.

O'Neill reached the bottom step, hesitated, then planted his boot on it. Immediately he felt it slide fractionally, frost and loose grit on its surface forming a treacherous coating. He sighed, then saw Bra'tac frowning back down at him. "Hurry," the Jaffa snapped.

"Fine…" O'Neill steadied himself against the rock on either side of the steps, and began to climb.

The ascent was frightening, but not impossible. O'Neill got to the top after only slipping off three steps, but he had done so slowly, one stair at a time. How Bra'tac had scooted up so quickly he could only guess. A combination of Jaffa physiology and alien boots, probably.

When he got to the top, he peered back over the edge. The drop was only about fifteen meters, but it made the Stargate looked small and lonely, like an abandoned toy.

Up on top of the cliff the wind was, if anything, more cutting than before, but there was shelter in sight. A ring of buildings, low and cut from the same drab stone as the cliff, huddled around a domed and circular structure, surprisingly close to the edge.

Beyond them the mountain leveled into a jagged, boulder-strewn plateau, and past that, softened into planes of silver by the wintery air, higher peaks rose up and out of sight.

"Is that the temple?" Daniel was asking. "It's bigger than I thought it would be."

O'Neill studied the sad cluster of buildings, with their empty windows and cracked walls. "Bigger?"

"It's in pretty poor repair, sir," Carter offered. "Looks like it's been abandoned for a long time."

"Many decades," Teal'c replied. "The temple used to be a place of pilgrimage for many Jaffa — to test themselves against the mountain and receive guidance from the clerics."

"'Used to be'?" Carter repeated. "What made them stop?"

"It was discovered what the clerics were truly worshipping."

O'Neill opened his mouth to speak, saw the expression on Teal'c's face, and decided not to. A moment later Bra'tac reappeared, his hood drawn up.

He didn't look happy. "Tau'ri! Why are you dawdling here?"

Daniel raised his hand. "Bra'tac, what were —"

"You know, Daniel, I think Bra'tac's right," O'Neill cut in. The situation was tense enough, without Daniel's curiosity putting the Jaffa any more on edge. "We should really get going."

"But —"

O'Neill glared. Daniel's mouth closed with an audible snap. Carter looked quickly between them, but thankfully said nothing.

"This way," Bra'tac muttered, and headed off towards the buildings. O'Neill could have sworn that he was shaking his head in quiet disbelief as he walked.

He caught up. "So Bra'tac..."

"O'Neill."

"Ah, how long have you guys been camping out here?"

The hood turned fractionally towards him, and O'Neill caught a flash of raised eyebrow. "Teal'c did not inform you?"

"Not really. He told us that you were here with some Jaffa refugees who wouldn't be hostile if we followed your instructions.

That was pretty much it."

The man snorted in amusement. "I see."

"See what?"

"It is of no importance. And to answer your question, O'Neill, these Jaffa fled here five months ago, after Apophis attacked Chulak."

O'Neill nodded. That explained a lot. "And you?"

"There are many such groups, scattered between the stars. I visit them as I can, to offer assistance. To make sure they know they have not been abandoned." The man raised his head, his hood tilted to the writhing clouds. "One day, perhaps, they will join one another as a united force against the Goa'uld. But until then, they are better apart. Their suspicions weaken them."

Which explained the Jaffa's reaction to SG-1, and Bra'tac's elaborate display of observing the team when they arrived. He needed to reassure the refugees that they weren't being attacked again. No wonder they had chosen such a malevolent place to hide.

"They almost fled when the ship crashed," Bra'tac was saying, "but I was fortunate to have arrived soon after. I was able to calm them."

O'Neill thought about a group of armed, displaced and nervous Jaffa, convinced that their tyrannical god had returned to finish what had driven them from their homes, and what it must have taken to talk them back down. It wouldn't have been a task he'd have relished.

"Teal'c's right, though. They can't stay."

"Of course." Bra'tac stopped, in the lee of one of the structures. O'Neill hadn't realized they would be at the temple complex so soon, and after Teal'c's admission about the place, wasn't all that sure he wanted to stay. Still, he was out of the worst of the wind here.

A few seconds later Carter, Daniel and Teal'c joined them. Daniel was paper-pale, his hands held tightly under his arms, and he was bouncing on his toes to try and keep warm. Carter seemed to have retreated even further into her uniform, until very little of her was visible at all.

"The bodies are here?" Teal'c asked. In answer, Bra'tac leaned down to a frost-covered piece of ground, found an edge, and pulled.

Something came up, a piece of board, or maybe fabric frozen solid. Beneath it was a shallow pit, just large enough for the two corpses it held to lay side by side.

They were Jaffa, as O'Neill had expected. One wore the elaborate armor of the serpent guard, while the other was wrapped in a long, decorated cloak. O'Neill could see that the clothes beneath were more ceremonial than armored, although they still had the familiar style and cut favored by the Jaffa of Apophis.

The robed man had a slack, vaguely surprised expression on his frozen face. The other no longer had a face.

"The vessel's damping fields must have shut down before the crash," Bra'tac said quietly. "These Jaffa were subject to the full force of impact."

Daniel had gone ever so slightly whiter, and was studying the horizon intently. O'Neill pointed at the robed man. "And you know this guy?"

"His name was Sephotep. He was one of Apophis' most trusted and revered scientists."

"Which is why you took a closer look at the ship," Carter ventured.

"Indeed."

"Well," said O'Neill. "I guess it's time we had a look at it too."

The ship had come down on the other side of the complex. As he got closer to it O'Neill could see the great gouge it had taken out of the plateau; a straight furrow ploughed out of the rock and ice, stretching far behind the vessel. It said a lot about the structure of the ship itself that it hadn't ripped itself to tinfoil on its journey across the mountain.

That was, presumably, small comfort to its occupants.

Even when O'Neill was within fifty meters of the thing, it was still quite hard to make out its shape. The crash had thrown up a large amount of debris, shattered stone and gravel, most of which had come back down on the ship's forward end. The rear of it was hunched up above the level of the plateau, but it was so frosted and scattered with rock dust that it was difficult to see where the ship ended and the mountain began.

It was Teal'c who identified it first, and did so with no small measure of disappointment.

"Master Bra'tac. This vessel is of no interest to us."

"You think so?" The old Jaffa sounded faintly amused.

"I do." Teal'c gestured at the vessel with his staff. "This is merely a Tel'tak. We have seen its like before."

O'Neill scowled. "Oh, *great.*"

While still hugely advanced in relation to Earth technology, Tel'taks were less than special compared to most Goa'uld craft. They were essentially cargo ships — unarmed, unwieldy and looking like some unholy fusion of a pyramid and a turtle. As far as anyone knew, Tel'taks were best suited for ferrying personnel and cargo between locations in the same solar system; perhaps from inhabited worlds to the mighty Goa'uld motherships and back again.

There were technicians on Earth who could spend their whole careers reverse-engineering the thing, but O'Neill couldn't work out how they might get the chance. Even if the Tel'tak was working, it would take decades to pilot the vessel back to Earth, and sending people through the gate to do the job was no option either. Apophis would want to know where his scientist had ended up. It was only a matter of time before he sent more ships.

The trip was a bust. The best option now would probably be to strip the Tel'tak of whatever they could prize free in the next few minutes, then blow it up and get the refugees through the gate before the flying pyramids arrived. "Okay, what now?"

"Colonel?" Carter was a narrow strip of face between tugged-down cap and pulled-up collar. "This doesn't make sense."

"You think?"

"No sir, I mean... Well, why would a top Goa'uld scientist be in flying cargo ship? And why here?"

"And why alone?" said Daniel. "You've got to admit, something doesn't add up."

"Tau'ri!" Bra'tac snapped. "And Teal'c, have you spent too long among humans? Why would I bring you here for a *hasshaki* cargo scow?"

"That was going to be my next question," O'Neill felt slightly embarrassed. "So…"

"Most Goa'uld starships are based on the designs of Ptah." Teal'c's voice was thoughtful. "Perhaps Sephotep was trying to improve on his works."

"A test flight?"

"The fact that this vessel crashed so far from assistance would suggest that its range has been increased."

It was a possibility. If true, it made the downed vessel considerably more valuable, and not just to Earth. "Carter, how much do you know about Tel'taks?"

"Enough to know if it's been modified."

"Great. Let's go have a look-see." He began trudging towards the ship, head low against the wind, trying not to imagine vast machines drifting down towards him through the icy sky.

As it turned out, O'Neill didn't need Carter's expertise to tell him that the Tel'tak had been altered. The outside of the vessel was very much like those he had seen before, although in somewhat poorer repair, but the interior structure had been heavily and obviously modified. The cockpit's central instrumentation block had been fitted with a large, intricate control board that overlooked the two original consoles, and further inspection revealed that almost a quarter of the vessel's cargo space was taken up by two massive equipment modules.

The changes seemed very much a work in progress, with open panels and patched cables everywhere. Had the ship possessed any power at all, its interior would have been a riot of exposed and glowing systemry. At present, however, it was utterly inert, and with the forward viewports covered with rock and ice, Carter had to begin working by flashlight.

With Daniel helping her, she quickly started pulling panels up and tugging at crystals. O'Neill watched the pair of them for a few minutes, trying not to waste too much time asking questions about what they were doing. After the initial search of the ship Teal'c had gone outside to talk privately to Bra'tac; although they could easily have slipped into pure Goa'uld, the two men must have decided that would be disrespectful to the Tau'ri, and just stepped back into the icy wind.

O'Neill wondered if they really were immune to the freezing temperatures, or just much better at hiding its effects.

After a while, he started to feel uncomfortably superfluous. He was no fool when it came to machinery: had the Tel'tak been an Earth machine, he could probably have stripped its engines down and rebuilt them in an afternoon. But Goa'uld technology was a very different matter, based around a system of crystalline control elements that looked, to O'Neill, like so much colored glass. Sam Carter was picking crystals out of their sockets, turning them, studying them, checking with Daniel on the exact translations of warning cartouches or identifying hieroglyphs, and gradually sorting out the Tel'tak's wiring in her head. O'Neill might as well have been watching her sort Christmas baubles.

He went outside, ducking through the ship's open hatch and back out onto the plateau. Brat'tac had gone. Only Teal'c remained, standing like a dark statue against the pale, skittering sky.

"Hey Teal'c."

"O'Neill."

"Where's Bra'tac?"

"He has returned to the refugees, to prepare them for the coming journey."

"I guess they're not going to be too happy about having to pack up and leave again, huh."

"They will have expected it. Even before this vessel fell. A Jaffa who rebels against his gods is never at rest."

There wasn't much O'Neill could say to that.

A silence fell across the two men. Past the whine and whoop of the wind, O'Neill heard small stones rattling across the surface the plateau, the hiss of grit and frost blown by the gale. Far away, along the next range of mountains, he saw a fine blue spark connect the clouds and the tallest peak. A moment later, another.

Thunder crackled, muted almost to nothing by the distance. "Storm's coming."

Teal'c said nothing.

Another silence. He tried again. "So how many are there?"

"Eighteen Jaffa warriors, along with their women and children."

O'Neill blinked at him. "There are children here?"

"Would you have expected them to be left behind?"

"No, I just… I didn't hear them."

"Silence in the presence of danger is one of the first skills a Jaffa child learns."

He thought about children being in this blighted place, frozen, hungry, made mute by what they had seen happen on Chulak, what they might see again. The thought lodged in his throat like a fishbone.

"Son of a bitch," he muttered.

Thunder pealed again, closer this time. It sounded like cloth ripping.

After a time, Teal'c said: "The position of this vessel troubles me."

"How so?"

"The scar it created during the crash leads directly away from the temple complex."

O'Neill frowned, checked quickly left and right to confirm his friend's words. The plateau was far from level, and with so many rock formations and jagged boulders littering the area it was hard to see exactly where anything lay in relation to anything else. But now that he knew what to look for, he realized that Teal'c was right: the grim, huddled wheel of buildings making the up the temple complex was right in front of the Tel'tak's buried nose. If the ship hadn't crashed, it would have flown directly over the central dome.

Or into it. "What was he trying to do, ram the place?"

"Perhaps he was trying to land close by."

"Nah, he was coming in fast. How do these things handle in atmosphere, anyway?"

"Badly."

"Sir?" Carter was standing in the hatch, hanging onto the side frame with one hand to avoid being dragged out by the wind.

"Find something?" O'Neill asked.

"I think so."

He followed her in, Teal'c close behind. At first he could see nothing different to when he had left, until Carter walked over to where Daniel was crouching. "Here, sir."

A small panel had been removed from the floor, and beneath it, a fist-sized cluster of crystals was pulsing a soft, amber glow.

"Sam thinks it's a phase relay," said Daniel, looking up. "Kind of like a circuit breaker."

O'Neill raised an eyebrow. "Circuit breaker?"

"Yeah, you know. Or a fuse. To protect the power in your house if there's a surge, or-"

"Daniel, I know what a circuit breaker is."

The man nodded, his glasses reflecting the golden light. "Yeah, sorry. Anyway, I think Sephotep managed to trip this one."

"He blew the fuse? Come on…"

Carter knelt down next to the open panel. "Colonel, this relay is at a critical junction between the ship's power plant and the rest of the systems. I missed it at first because there are so many new elements tapped into it, but I think this is a fail-safe. When it cut out it deactivated the whole ship, but the naquadah generator is still intact."

"Can you fix it?"

"If I'm right, it's just a matter of resetting it and restarting the plant."

That seemed too easy. Jack O'Neill knew better than to trust the offer of a free lunch. "So why didn't Sephotep do that?"

"He did not have time," said Teal'c quietly. "The vessel was already close to the plateau. The crash must have occurred almost instantly."

"They probably never knew what hit them," Carter added.

O'Neill made a face. He understood exactly what Carter was proposing, but it still left too many unanswered questions for his liking. He couldn't explain why a Goa'uld scientist was flying a customized cargo ship directly at a temple full of refugees, for a start. Or how he'd managed to blow the ship's main fuse at the last moment.

Still, there was no telling how long any of them had before Apophis came looking for his missing technician. And reactivating the ship might be the only way of answering those questions in time.

He sighed. "Okay, plug it in."

"You're sure?"

"Yeah. Just try not to blow us up, okay?"

"I'll do my best," Carter said absently. She was already reaching down into the relay, twisting two of the crystals, pressing a third back down into its socket…

There was a jolt, and a soft whine that faded away to nothing. The light from the relay changed from pulsing amber to a calm, steady green.

O'Neill looked around. The rest of the ship was still dark. "That was… Unsatisfying."

"Hm," said Carter, and twisted another crystal.

The cockpit lit up.

The change was enough to make O'Neill start, but almost instantly he saw that the vessel was far from repaired. The light that had appeared when Carter had triggered that final crystal wasn't coming from the ceiling, but instead was a dim, ruddy glow issuing from small panels near the floor. Several of the exposed sets of crystals were blinking fitfully, though, and smaller lights were winking on the three control boards. Something had worked, if only partially.

Daniel was standing up, peering about. "What is this, emergency power?"

"Maybe there's another relay," said Carter. She got up and went over to the centre board. O'Neill watched her press several controls in sequence.

A wide panel in the centre of the console changed from being golden metal into a slab of what looked like illuminated glass.

"Whoah," said O'Neill. "Carter, what did you just do?"

"I think this board is Sephotep's test panel. Patch feeds come off a lot of the new systems and filter through data crystals to here, so I'm guessing…" She trailed off, then grinned. "Got it!"

He joined her at the console. The panel was alive with graphics; animated diagrams and graphs in sharp blue-white vector, streams of Goa'uld hieroglyphs rolling down like tickertape. "Can you read this?"

"I'm just looking at the pictures. Teal'c?"

O'Neill stepped aside to let the Jaffa get close to the panel. He kept his silence as the big man studied the graphics for several seconds.

"You are correct, Major Carter," Teal'c said finally. "The panel monitors the systems data for this entire vessel. I believe Sephotep was recording this information continually before the power failed."

"Does it say *why* the power failed?"

"The error was Sephotep's. This vessel has many extra systems — an enhanced hyperdrive, sensors, weapons. Sephotep was attempting to activate too many at once."

"Guys?" said Daniel.

"Wait." Teal'c was scowling down at the panel, tracing a line of moving hieroglyphs with a fingertip. "Sephotep was readying the weapons to fire."

"Holy…" O'Neill glanced reflexively towards the front of the ship, to where the temple would be if he'd been able to see though half a ton of loose rock. "He was lining up to fire on the refugees!"

"A strafing run," Teal'c agreed. He straightened. "However, he could not have relayed that information back to Apophis."

"Yeah, he'd be here already."

"Ah, guys?" said Daniel again. He was near one of the forward boards, pointing down at the metal panels there. "I think this might be important…"

Teal'c darted forwards, startlingly fast. "A locator beacon."

Carter ran over to join him. "Daniel? How long was this—"

"I noticed it blinking as soon as I looked over here."

"Well switch it the hell off!" O'Neill poked his head through hatchway. The clouds above him were heavy, sluggish, and bluish sparks flickered from one to another. Lightning, he hoped.

"I cannot," Teal'c replied. "Major Carter, disengage the phase relay."

"Already trying…" There was a tight note to her voice that O'Neill didn't like at all.

He ducked back in. "What?"

"No go, sir. It's not built to be tripped manually."

"Can't you just pull some of those crystals out?"

She shook her head. "They lock when there's power going through them."

"Well, smash them or something!"

Carter stared at him. "I think that would be a really good way to detonate the generator."

"O'Neill," said Teal'c. "We must warn the refugees."

"Next on my list." He went for the hatch, stopped momentarily on the threshold. "Teal'c, you're with me. Carter, find a way to kill the signal. If you have to, drop a grenade into that relay and run."

"Understood, sir."

He jumped out of the hatch, his boots crunching onto the plateau's frosty surface. The wind had picked up, whipping at his uniform and stinging his face with sleet. "Next time, arctic gear," he growled to himself. "Regardless."

The temple was several hundred meters away, almost hidden behind boulders and jagged, broken ground. The clearest route to it was close to the edge of the cliff, which O'Neill didn't like at all, not with the storm almost on top of him. Probably better than clambering through the boulders, though. "What do you think, Teal'c? This way?"

The man didn't answer, just set off past O'Neill at a fast jog.

"I'll take that as a 'yes'." O'Neill took a second to tighten the sling on his MP5, then began to follow the Jaffa.

It wasn't easy. Teal'c didn't seem to notice the weather at all, but O'Neill was being buffeted by the wind with every step. Having to squint against the sleet made things even more difficult. It was all he could do to keep up the pace.

There wasn't any other option, though. The refugees needed to get through the gate *now*.

O'Neill forced his attention down to the stone beneath his boots, jogging forwards as fast as he could, only raising his head every few meters to gauge his progress. Teal'c was still ahead of him, already out of shouting distance. If that wasn't bad enough, the gale must have been whistling through some rock formation close by, giving forth a rising whine that O'Neill was finding quite painful.

There was another sound, more familiar: the crackle of his radio demanding attention. He lowered his head to it. "Carter?"

Static hissed out at him for a moment, before wind-noise he had been hearing rose suddenly into a rippling shriek.

He'd heard that sound before.

There wasn't even time to spin and face what was coming. O'Neill hurled himself forwards as the ground where he had been standing turned into a cloud of fire and shattered stone, a brutal explosion that sent him whirling through the air and straight towards the edge of the cliff.

Chapter 3.

GOODNIGHT, TRAVEL WELL

IF JACK O'Neill hadn't have jumped when he did, the shockwave from that blast would have pulverized him, shattered his insides. But in doing so he had given his body enough lift to be spun, by the blast and the freezing wind, to the cliff-edge and its frightening drop onto the killing ground below.

For one dreadful, airborne moment, all he could see in his future was a long dive and a messy impact, but then the hard edge of the cliff whirled up towards him and smashed heavily into his face and chest. The breath went out of him in a guttural whoop as his ribs compressed, then he was sliding wildly, grabbing at the rocks around him, feeling them slice his skin even through the deadening cold.

He managed to stop himself just before he ran out of plateau.

A second went past while he tried to remember how to breathe, how to think. He had fetched up on his belly, head and shoulders in mid air, and spent a short time staring down at the Stargate while pieces of cliff rained down past him. Then, when he had regained control of his lungs, he scrambled back a short distance and flipped himself over.

His gun had gone flying in the blast. He reached over to grab it, but then noticed that the magazine was gone, ejected or broken off. He threw the useless thing aside.

Teal'c appeared above him, reaching down to haul him upright. "Are you harmed?"

"I'm fine," he croaked. "What the hell hit us?"

The Jaffa pointed, towards the temple. O'Neill saw a tiny sliver of dark metal in the sky, turning, executing a tight curve under the cloud layer. The screaming sound had faded, but he knew that respite was only temporary.

He keyed his radio. "Carter?"

"*— on out there? Colonel O'Neill, where —*"

"Calm down, Major. I'm right here."

"*Where's 'here', sir?*"

"Out in the damned open, that's where." He and Teal'c had made it almost all the way to the buildings before the attack came; when he glanced back to the Tel'tak, it seemed very far away. The ship that had attacked him was already several kilometers beyond the temple, but racing closer with every second. Neither direction seemed a good choice.

Then he remembered who was in the buildings between him and the onrushing fighter, and started running again, Teal'c in close pursuit.

"*What's out there?*" That was Daniel. There was a staccato timbre to his voice that spoke of furious activity. "*We just heard shots, we didn't —*"

"Death glider." It was close enough now to be unmistakable; a glossy crescent howling down out of the sky towards him. As soon as he had spoken the machine unleashed its energies a second time; O'Neill saw gouts of fire spitting from its cannons.

He dived for cover, throwing himself behind a boulder.

There was a whiplash impact as a shot hit the rock, an ear-splitting din of frozen stone superheating and exploding away in lethal shards, and bolts of fire were ripping past as the glider fired over and over into the plateau. O'Neill felt the punch of each blast through his boots, through his bleeding hands as he crouched.

A shadow crossed him, viciously quick, as the glider hammered through the air over his head, and he heard the electric whoop of a staff weapon as Teal'c sent darts of energy lashing up into the sky. A shot connected, spattered uselessly off a wing.

The glider flew level for a second or two, then rose into a smooth, almost vertical climb, accelerated into a blur. In a heartbeat it was lost to the clouds.

"Damn," muttered O'Neill, getting up. He was starting to hurt all over. "That turned up fast."

Teal'c had been down on one knee, trying to get a better aim at the fighter. He rose, slowly, eyes on the churning whorl of cloud the machine had left in its wake. "If the glider arrived in response to the distress beacon, it must have already been close to this world. It is likely that a mothership is in this system, searching for the Tel'tak."

"And now they've found it. Thanks to us."

"Gliders may have been searching every nearby world. O'Neill, we do not have much time."

"No kidding." He turned away, towards the temple, and saw greasy smoke twisting into the air. "*Dammit!* Teal'c!"

He could hear voices, now that the death glider and its banshee screeching was gone from the sky. Even through the biting wind, shouts drifted across the plateau. He couldn't make out words; the gale was robbing the sounds of all but raw emotion. But that was enough. There was suffering in those voices. There was anger, and distress, and pain.

There was screaming. High, thin shrieks of agony came to him through the storm.

O'Neill and Teal'c were inside the complex within half a minute, and when they ran past the outer ring of buildings the source of the voices became instantly plain. As soon as O'Neill saw the tableau, his heart shrank in his chest.

No matter how much tragedy he had seen in his life, the universe always seemed intent on furnishing him with more.

One of the structures, a small two-story building just outside the temple dome, had been blasted apart by the death glider. Every remaining opening vomited thick smoke, and Jaffa were desperately trying to extinguish the fire with great urns and jugs of water. A couple were trying to fight their way in through the debris, but the flames were too intense, the smoke too dark and choking. There was no hope, O'Neill could see that before he even reached the place, but the cries from within the structure were pitiful.

Several other Jaffa were clustered around a figure that twisted on the hard ground.

He skated to a halt next to them, while Teal'c ran to the burning house. Bra'tac was there, along with some of the Jaffa he had seen earlier, their hands on the figure that shuddered on the cold stone. They looked as if they were trying to hold the man down, to restrict his writhing, but their efforts were becoming more redundant with every second. The Jaffa's strength was ebbing away into the air.

If O'Neill had seen this stricken warrior before, he couldn't have recognized him now. Fire, and the electric energies of the death glider's weapons had seen to that.

"What can I do?" he asked dully, his stomach a knot. "Morphine?"

Bra'tac shook his head. "His symbiote would have suppressed the pain," he said quietly. "Had it lived."

He spoke to the men with him, gesturing into the temple. Between them, they lifted the dying Jaffa and carried him into the darkness. O'Neill watched them go, then stumbled back towards the smaller building.

The screaming had ceased. The fires inside the structure were lessening, but wet smoke was still pouring from the openings. There was a vile reek to it. The Jaffa who had been throwing water were standing at the windows, looking in, silent and still. Teal'c was with them, as unmoving as the rest.

"Nothing could be done for them," he said, as O'Neill approached.

"Them?"

"The woman and the child."

O'Neill closed his eyes for second. "God," he breathed, in spite of himself.

He felt Teal'c move past him. "There are no gods here."

Not yet, O'Neill thought.

He followed Teal'c into the temple. As he went in he could see that the outer walls of the place were massively thick, which would have given him some hope if he'd thought for a second that death gliders were the only things on their way. The staff cannons carried by the Goa'uld fighters would be hard pressed to penetrate that weight of solid stone, it was true, but one good run by an

Al'kesh bomber and the temple would simply fly to dust, along with all who sheltered there.

Which, judging by the number of people crowding within, must have been almost everyone on Sar'tua.

The interior of the temple was dark, the shadows broken only by a few flickering lanterns. O'Neill glanced quickly about as he walked inside, trying to gauge his surroundings, but most of the space was lost to him. There were a lot of pillars, he could see that, and a circular dais at the centre, but most of what he saw were people; ragged, nervous Jaffa warriors, a few women, some stoic, hard-eyed kids. Many of them carried pathetic bundles of possessions, wrapped and bound remnants of whatever lives they had left behind on Chulak.

O'Neill wondered how long he'd last in this unforgiving place, with just a ragged cloak to keep out the cold and whatever he might have grabbed while fleeing a burning city. Not long, he decided. In fact, what were these people eating? He'd not seen a scrap of plant or animal life since he'd got here.

The burned Jaffa had been set down on a rough table. Bra'tac had taken up position at one end of it, and had the man's scorched head in his hands. If the feeling of carbonized tissue and bone under his fingertips caused him any distress he didn't show it. Instead he was soothing the stricken Jaffa with soft words and reassuring, if upside-down, smiles.

It looked like it was working, although O'Neill had an ugly feeling that the injured man's calm was more likely due to the loss of most of his nerve endings and lung tissue. He'd be unable to feel much pain by now, and the lack of oxygen in his blood would be causing him to slip into a coma. The death of his symbiote, at this stage, could only have been a blessing.

As O'Neill watched, the man spoke a few words, haltingly, his voice a dry rasp. Bra'tac answered, and with that the man nodded, very slightly, and did something with his mouth that might once have been a smile.

"What was that?" O'Neill whispered. Teal'c brought his head

a little closer.

"He asked if his wife and son were safe."

"I guess Bra'tac lied."

"He did not. He told him that they would be reunited soon."

O'Neill's knotted stomach twisted just a little tighter. "We can't stay," he said.

"I am aware of that, O'Neill." Bra'tac hadn't looked up. He was still holding the man's head. "We all are."

"So…"

"A moment."

The man on the table opened one eye. It was all he had left. *"Fre'tauc,"* he breathed — a name, O'Neill could tell — but the breath didn't reverse, just kept coming out, a thin, pale vapor in the cold, out, and out, until there was nothing more to come.

The eye didn't close, and there was no other change in the man. He simply became fractionally more still.

Bra'tac bowed his head lower, just for a moment, then took his hands away and stood straight. *"Jaffa!"* he snapped. *"Ya'isid ma'gue!"*

O'Neill didn't need a translation of that. "About time," he muttered, and turned for the door. As he did so, he caught a glimpse of the sky outside.

"Aw, crap," he sighed.

Dark scythes of metal, three of them, small but growing with horrible speed, were diving down out of the clouds to swoop in low over the plateau. O'Neill saw them race over the humped shape of the downed Tel'tak.

Sparks of fire appeared under their wings.

"Incoming!" he yelled. "Get down!"

As soon as he had shouted he knew he'd wasted his breath. The people around him were warriors, almost from birth, and had probably forgotten more about death gliders and their ways than he would ever know. They scattered, those with staff weapons forming up at the doorway and the temple's open windows, while the unarmed clustered low around the walls, children hustled instantly into the centre of each protective group. O'Neill heard the sizzle and click of weapons being readied, Teal'c's among them, and then the gliders were over his head, their shrieks battering his ears.

Outside, buildings were flashing apart in deafening, sledgehammer detonations, their walls hammered into gravel and burning shards.

Bra'tac was at one of the windows. He'd picked up a staff weapon from somewhere, and its business end was smoking hot. The man must have loosed as many blasts at the gliders as the staff was capable of firing, and then a few.

A puzzled frown was creasing his dark face. "O'Neill, where is the Tel'tak?"

"Say what?" O'Neill joined him at the window, staring out over the plateau. The window wasn't all that far away from the door he'd been looking out of. He should have been able to see Sephotep's doomed experiment from here.

The Tel'tak was gone. The plateau was empty.

"The hell? It was there a second ago!"

"Was it destroyed?"

He might have missed the sound of the ship exploding in the attack, but there was no wreckage, no fire. The cargo ship was simply *gone*.

"The gliders are on their return pass," growled Teal'c.

"Should we get to the other side?"

"No," Bra'tac replied, holding his aim. "We must weather the storm and wait for them to pass — it is sometimes possible to bring down a glider with a shot to the stern."

The rising scream of glider engines was making it difficult to think — the temple was ringed with glassless windows, and it echoed. "How possible?"

"Not very."

O'Neill grimaced in frustration, wishing there was a spare staff weapon, or that his MP5 had proved more resilient, but there was nothing for him to fire. All he had was his radio. He keyed it on, dipped his head to it, and then energy bolts burst out across the plateau.

The shots lashed out from nowhere, from empty sky, so fast and so bright that they were almost a solid line of ravening power, ripping the air above the temple with a series of high-pitched, reverberating whines.

The high sound of them was answered with bass, thumping impacts as they struck their targets.

O'Neill saw a death glider whirl into view from over the temple roof, two scythed wings and a ball of white flame where the body of the fighter should have been. The second glider shot over his head in a cloud of fragments. The last ship must have dodged the initial barrage, but as it accelerated the invisible weapon spoke again, and sheared one of the fighter's wings away. The rest of it spun upwards, flipped over and drove itself solidly into the plateau.

The first glider, a winged comet of fire, was still flying, arcing towards the distant mountains. O'Neill watched it go for a while, before realizing that his mouth was open. He closed it.

Above the plateau, an irregular patch of smoky air wavered, solidified, and became a rather battered Tel'tak cargo ship.

O'Neill's radio hissed into life. *"Colonel? What's your status?"*

"Status is cold, banged-up and really, *really* peed off. Major?"

"Sir?"

"I thought I ordered you to shut that ship down."

There was a slight pause. *"We had some technical issues. Thought we'd take a different tack."*

"Technical issues," repeated O'Neill, dully. He switched the radio off. "They had technical issues."

Outside, amid the smoke and the flame, Sephotep's grand experiment dropped hesitantly through the air, slowed, then fell the last couple of meters to crunch unceremoniously onto the cold flat stone of the plateau.

The Jaffa took their fallen with them, even those who had been inside the burned house. O'Neill watched the procession of the living and the dead move quickly up the short ramp and through the Stargate, each man and woman and silent child striding without hesitation into the rippling mirror of the event horizon, its liquid surface closing behind them as if they had never been.

The bodies were draped in robes and blankets. "We leave nothing for Apophis," explained Bra'tac. "Rites will be said for them on the other side, when there is time."

"This planet they're going to," said Daniel. "Is it, you know…" He gestured at the monochrome landscape around them. "Better?"

"It is called Tryea," Bra'tac replied. "And yes, Doctor Jackson, it is better. There are more Jaffa there."

"From Chulak?"

"Indeed."

Almost all the Jaffa were through. The last man through was the only one to pause. He stopped at the top of the ramp, and turned. When his eyes found Teal'c's, he nodded curtly.

Teal'c dipped his head, and kept it lowered until the man was gone.

O'Neill watched the gate's mirror break into a whorl of foam and spin to nothing. "Bra'tac, are you sure about this?"

"I am." The old man smiled. "Sephotep's creation may be flawed, but it should not fall back into the hands of Apophis."

"Flawed?" O'Neill's eyebrows went up. "Kind of an understatement. It doesn't *work*."

"Sir, it'll work fine as long as Bra'tac doesn't try to use more than two upgrades at a time." That was Carter, or at least what little of her that O'Neill could see. She had only been out of the Tel'tak for a few minutes, enough time for the Jaffa to get organized and dial the gate to Tryea, but she was already looking frozen. "Just don't use the weapons and the main drive if you have the cloak up, or —"

"Thank you, Major Carter," Bra'tac cut in. "I believe I can count to two."

O'Neill rubbed his hands together. "Okay, time to go. Daniel?"

"Sure." Daniel stepped up to the DHD and began to press its panels. The weird mechanical clank each icon made as it registered was oddly comforting, especially with the prospect of more Goa'uld ships on the way.

"I will fly the Tel'tak to Riyagan," Bra'tac told them. "It is a safe place. The Goa'uld abandoned its people many decades ago."

"We've been there," O'Neill said, keeping his voice low. "Haven't we been there?"

Daniel leaned sideways to whisper. "P4H-W29. Rainforest. Early Mesoamerican culture. They threw a feast in our honor."

"They did? I don't —"

"There were bugs in it," said Carter, in a small voice.

"Oh, right. *Them*. Gotcha."

"If the cloak is effective," Bra'tac continued, giving O'Neill a rather sour eye, "I will not be followed."

"Pretty big 'if'," O'Neill muttered. He would much rather the old Jaffa return with them to SGC and go on from there. So far the modified Tel'tak had cost five lives, and he couldn't bring himself to believe that its advances were worth the price.

If Bra'tac had heard O'Neill's comment, he ignored it. "Teal'c, I will send word once I arrive."

"Travel well," Teal'c replied. And with that, Bra'tac ran to the steps and began striding up them, two or three at a time, to the plateau.

Carter shivered. "How does he *do* that?"

The gate roared, billowed. O'Neill watched Daniel talking into his radio and started to really look forward to some of Stargate Command's famously bad coffee. Maybe a shower. *Definitely* a shower. Something to take the sting from his cut hands and bruised ribs and frost-blasted face.

He wondered, then, if he was filling his mind with such things to avoid thinking about burning children, and a name, whispered up into the still cold air of the temple on a dying man's last breath.

The Stargate's surface was stable, now. Daniel was still talking into the radio. "Say again? SGC, can you repeat that, please?"

O'Neill trotted over to him. "Problem?"

Daniel nodded. "I'm getting a lot of interference. I'm not sure, but I think they're saying they're not going to open the iris."

"What? Give me that!" O'Neill took the radio from Daniel's hands, a little too quickly. "SCG, come in."

Hissing answered him, and then a few guttural sounds that might have been words. He took the radio from his ear, shook it hard, and then tried again. "SGC, respond. It's cold out here."

Carter and Teal'c had moved closer, obviously expecting to be through the gate and away. "Sir?" said Carter, holding out her handset. "Try this."

O'Neill gave her a look. "I've got my own radio."

"Didn't you fall on yours?"

"O'Neill," said Teal'c, suddenly. "We are no longer alone."

He was looking up into the sky. O'Neill followed his gaze, and saw that the clouds above him had darkened, as though a great shadow moved above them.

The radio hissed and spat again. "*Ess gee*," it said, between bursts of static. "*Firm... Dentit...*"

O'Neill couldn't take his eyes off the shadow. He felt as though he were in a small boat on a great ocean, watching something vast and terrible slide past him, slow and ageless and unconcerned. "Stargate Command," he said flatly. "I confirm my identity as Colonel Jack O'Neill of SG-1, service number six-nine, four, one-four-one, freezing my ass off and about to be vaporized by a Goa'uld mothership, and will you *please* open the goddamned iris and let us come home!"

The radio issued a series of squawks and whines, and the words: "*Firmed, Colonel. Iris ope.*"

"Go," said O'Neill, still staring at the darkening sky. "Everybody through."

Daniel was closest to the event horizon, and was gone before the first cannon blasts ripped downwards into the temple. Carter ducked through as the entire building erupted upwards into a vast geyser of burning stone. Teal'c was just behind her, the liquid mirror closing around him as a humped shape lifted from the plateau, accelerated cleanly past the rising fountain of debris and vanished in a shimmer like heat-haze. O'Neill saw the clouds part as the cloaked ship made its escape, and then he too stepped through the gate, backwards, the radio still in his hand.

Just as the event horizon closed over his eyes, he saw that awful shadow break through the white sky, all edges and angles. And then he was gone.

A tumbling, whirling fall through a space that could not exist, a speed where there could be no motion, light where there could be no vision, time where none existed...

He stepped backwards onto the ramp, into the flat, warm air of Stargate Command. "Okay," he snapped, turning around. "What the hell's wrong with the..."

There was a small army of marines at the base of the access ramp, weapons leveled.

"Radio," he finished.

From behind him came a grinding, metallic squeal, like the closing of a giant's rusty shears. Someone was shutting the iris.

Daniel, Carter and Teal'c were still on the ramp, looking down at the armed men surrounding them. Daniel had his arms half-raised, as though he were considering surrender. "Ah, Jack? Any idea what's going on here?"

"Not much." O'Neill picked a marine at random, fixed him with the kind of quiet, frozen look his drill sergeants used to use on him, back in the day. "Aren't you guys supposed to be here for *un*scheduled activations?"

The man swallowed. "Sorry, sir."

There was an echoing click as the gate room's internal address system came on. "*Security teams stand down,*" it bellowed. "*Repeat, stand down.*"

At that, the entire gate room seemed to fall still. The crimson beacons above the big security doors stopped rotating and switched off, the sirens wailing into silence. The doors unlocked and slid aside. And then even the Stargate shut down, the rippling blue light of it fading as the event horizon lost cohesion.

There was the welcome sound of two dozen automatic weapons being switched to safety.

"Is it just me," O'Neill sighed, as the marines shouldered arms and filed away from the ramp, "or has today really not gone according to plan?"

"Internal security alert," said Carter, glancing around. "Level two?"

"Level three, Major."

The voice was deep, with an edge of Texan twang, and O'Neill was very glad indeed to hear it. "General," he smiled as Hammond stepped into the gate room. "Was it something I said?"

"Sorry about that, Colonel." Hammond didn't look at all happy. "Things have been a little on edge around here for the past couple of hours."

"What happened?"

"We got a message. From an old friend of yours."

O'Neill's chest tightened a little. "Apophis?"

"If only," said Hammond. "It was Ra."

Chapter 4.

BEDSHAPED

THE Stargate had begun to dial itself at three thirty-seven AM, not long after SG-1 had left for Sar'tua. Since it had been entirely possible that the team had run into trouble and needed to return ahead of schedule, the technicians monitoring the gate had been expecting an Iris Deactivation Code. Instead, what came through the wormhole was a multi-frequency signal of terrifying power.

The communications system went into overload immediately. Most of the failsafe cut-outs — designed to protect the operations room's delicate equipment from just such an assault — activated as their creators intended, but at least one didn't shut off fast enough, leading to a feedback spike that blew out two servers and actually started a small fire. By the time the signal had finished transmitting some seventy seconds later, the gate room's comms were completely down, leaving SG teams One, Seven and Fifteen stranded offworld.

General George Hammond had ordered a level-three security lockdown as soon as he had been woken and appraised of the situation, by which time emergency repairs had already begun. And while most of the effort in the operations room had been devoted to getting the GDO reception array back online, there was also the question of the precise nature of the attack Stargate Command had been subjected to.

It hadn't taken all that long for the analysts to discover the truth. All they had needed to do was to lessen the signal's strength by a factor of a thousand, and its exact nature became clear.

The signal wasn't a weapon.

It was a voice.

The voice was not human: there was a bass echo to it, a sibilant reverberation that spoke of an alien parasite working human vocal chords as though they were the strings of a puppet. There was little emotion in the words, just a breathy monotone, but there was something sneering to the voice too, something superior and contemptuous and just a little seductive. It was horrible.

It was unmistakable. Hearing it made Daniel Jackson's stomach knot.

He looked warily around the briefing room as the recording played out. Samantha Carter was leaning slightly towards the tape deck, her head cocked slightly to one side as it often was when she was analyzing a new problem. Teal'c sat ramrod-straight, his hands clasped on the tabletop in front of him, face utterly impassive. At the end of the table, General Hammond was reading through one of the files stacked up in front of him. He had heard the recording before; its serpentine echoes held no surprises for him. And Jack…

Daniel settled his glasses more comfortably on the bridge of his nose, and peered across the top of the tape deck at Jack O'Neill. The man was settled back in his chair, arms folded, his expression unreadable, his gaze fixed on a point several centimeters above the table. To someone who didn't know him very well, he might have appeared to be listening.

It was obvious to Daniel, though, that Colonel O'Neill was still under another sun.

The voice silenced. Hammond reached out and switched the tape off. "That's it," he said. "Eighteen seconds of that, pause for three seconds, repeats twice. Nothing else." He raised an eyebrow at Daniel. "Any thoughts, Doctor?"

"Well, it's definitely Ra."

"You're sure?" Sam asked him.

"Yeah. Yeah, I'm sure."

"That confirms what we suspected." Hammond closed the file. "We managed to pick his name out of the message, but if you're certain that's him…"

Daniel frowned. "You know," he said. "This really doesn't make a lot of sense."

"No kidding," Jack cut in. "General, Ra's dead. I mean seriously, you couldn't *get* any more dead. Someone's working an angle."

"No..." Daniel pinched the bridge of his nose. The tape deck had come from the operations room, and he could still smell the smoke on it. His sinuses itched. "What I mean is, the message doesn't make sense. At all. Unless my translation's way off..."

"And what *is* your translation, Doctor?"

Daniel held his silence for a moment, thinking back to the alien words he had been listening to. All those years ago, when he had been face to face with Ra, when those awful syllables had been directed at him... There was a difference, he knew, something subtle that he couldn't quite put a name to. Was it skewing his understanding of the message now?

"Daniel?" prompted Sam.

"Mm? Oh, okay..." He took a deep breath. "Ah, he starts off with something about a deep hole, or a pit, weeping or lamenting... Then *Kt'uey*, I think that's 'breached', or maybe more like 'defiled'..." He paused, until he saw Teal'c nod, very slightly. "Then he mentions a sacred seal or wall being built. Uh, 'The sacred seals are in place and that which feeds is once again...' *Ana'chi kel may'ia va?* Yeah, that's weird."

"Please, Doctor," said Hammond. "Just what you hear."

"Sure, sorry." He spoke more quickly now, translating as directly as he could. "'That which feeds is once again held in sleep. Those who dare defy the will of Ra, supreme of Heaven, will find eternal torment in the house of the...'" He looked across the table at Teal'c once more. "Eater of ash?"

"It is as you say, Daniel Jackson. This message holds no meaning."

"Have you ever heard anything referred to as an 'eater of ash'?" Hammond asked him.

"Indeed. 'Ash Eater' is a common phrase among the Jaffa, especially children." The ghost of a smile played about the man's lips, as though he had remembered something amusing from long ago. "It means one who cannot stop eating — he will eat the meal, the cooking pot, the fire and the ash beneath."

Sam turned to Hammond. "General, I take it there are no clues as to where this message originated from?"

"Not a one, Major." He ran a hand back over his scalp. "And now that I've heard what it means, I'm beginning to think we've only heard part of it."

"It does sound like a fragment of something," Daniel agreed. "If I've learned anything about the Goa'uld, it's that they really like to let you know what they're going to do to you. This is too, I don't know… Ambiguous."

"System Lords do not usually repeat themselves," Teal'c added.

"Fine," said Hammond, sitting back. "People, I think we've gone about as far as we can with this right now. We could debate the meaning of it all morning, but until we can gain further intelligence on this attack, I'm going to keep the security lockdown in place and devote all available resources to bringing the comms system fully online."

"Sir," Sam began, "I'd like to analyze this further. There may be some kind of information in the carrier wave that can give us a point of origin."

"Major, what I need from you is to make sure another signal of this type can't shut us down again. I can wait a little while longer before finding out where it came from."

She nodded. "Of course."

"You'll liaise with the tech team down in Operations as soon as we're done here. Doctor Jackson, Teal'c, I want you to start running your translation through the databases. There's already a copy in the lab — see if it matches anything we've met before."

Teal'c tipped his head a fraction. "As you wish."

"Colonel O'Neill, I'll need your report on P2D-771 as soon as possible. I want to know more about this modified ship, and the speed of the Goa'uld response to that locator beacon."

For a few moments Jack said nothing at all. Then he started, appeared to realize suddenly where he was. "Absolutely, General. Anything else?"

"Not for now." He looked around, taking the four of them in. "I understand that things got a little rough back there, and I'm sorry you had to come home to all this. But until I'm sure we're not going to get any more calls from Ra, the pressure's got to stay high."

Jack stood up, his chair rolling back. "No problem. It's what we do."

Hammond looked at him a little oddly — it wasn't exactly procedure for a lower ranking officer to get up from the table before a General, but he seemed prepared to let it go. Maybe he could see the same thing in Jack's eyes as Daniel had noticed. "Glad to hear it, Colonel. That'll be all."

The team dispersed. Sam headed down the spiral stairway directly to the operations room, while Daniel and Teal'c followed Jack out through Hammond's office to the elevators.

Jack went straight to the right-hand elevator door without a word. Daniel found himself holding back for a moment, unwilling to break into the man's reverie, but then remembered the look on Jack's face when the Jaffa refugees had been taking their dead back through the Stargate. He stood next to him as the floor indicators counted down.

"Hey," he began.

"Daniel."

"Look, do you want to grab a coffee or something before we start on this?"

"Nah, I'm good."

Level 20. Daniel tried another tack. "How are the hands?"

Jack raised them, looked at them oddly. There were dressings on some of the deeper lacerations, and the smaller cuts still looked angry and painful.

"They're fine."

"Jack…"

The older man's eyes locked on his. "Don't."

"It wasn't —"

"Yeah, it was."

The elevator doors hissed apart. Jack stepped inside. "Happy translating," he said, his hand up in an ironic wave, and then the doors were together again and he was gone.

"Damn," breathed Daniel. And then became aware that Teal'c was watching him intently. "What?"

"You were attempting to lighten his mood?"

"No, not really… I just wanted to let him know he shouldn't blame himself."

"The blame lies with Apophis."

"Yeah, I know that."

"As does Colonel O'Neill. But blame and responsibility are easily confused. It is the task of a leader to know the difference."

There was a soft chime as the second elevator reached their level. The doors slid apart. Daniel followed Teal'c inside, stood beside him as they closed again.

"Should that make me feel better?" he asked.

Teal'c said nothing while the elevator climbed. Only when it had reached its destination and opened again did he speak.

"The blame does not lie with you either, Daniel Jackson."

Maybe, thought Daniel, as the two men left the elevator. *But am I responsible?*

The notion would not leave him, no matter how hard he tried to concentrate on his work. The task of refining his translation of the message wasn't quite difficult enough to drive it from his mind, especially with Teal'c there to fill in the gaps, and even re-writing it into Goa'uld hieroglyphs to send it worming back through the SGC databases couldn't entirely distract him from it.

At first, his feelings remained a mystery. Certainly, the deaths on Sar'tua had been tragic, but he had experienced worse. There had probably been occasions where he had been far more directly responsible for awful events — when he really looked back at those fateful hours on the plateau, the only thing that truly haunted him had been not speaking up about the locator beacon more quickly. But could anything have been done about it if he had? In all honesty, he doubted it. The device had been designed to attract help in all but the most dire circumstances. Sephotep wouldn't have built the device to be easily disabled. It was only a complete and unexpected shutdown of the Tel'tak's entire power system that had silenced it in the first place.

In which case, Daniel reasoned, letting a mug of coffee steam his glasses while the database threw up an endless ribbon of negative results, why couldn't he let this go?

Part of the answer was, of course, if not staring him in the face, then at least torturing his eardrums. It was the effect of having Ra's voice played back at him through that accursed, smoke-stinking tape deck.

After all, his wife had only been dead a year, and her loss still impaled him.

Ra had been the chief among the System Lords, in as much as that squabbling, fragmented, murderous clan of tyrants could ever have a leader. No human could have known it at the time, but Ra's influence over the other Goa'uld was keeping them partly in check. Apophis, his despotic son, had only come to power once Ra had died.

But whatever Ra's last moments had entailed, it was arguable that his absence caused more woe and destruction than his existence. His demolition had almost certainly led directly to the abduction and appropriation of Sha're. So if responsibility were the issue, or fault, or blame… Who but Daniel Jackson could truly bear it?

How many people would still be alive if he hadn't travelled to Abydos?

He was tired, that was the problem. His mind had a tendency to wander forbidden paths when he was fatigued. All he needed to do was rest, to gather his thoughts and find his centre once again, and then he could make the loss and the pain and the regret go away, at least for a while.

He set the coffee on his desk and got up. "I'm going to head back to my quarters for a while."

"I shall alert you once the search is complete," Teal'c told him.

"Thanks." He took his glasses off to rub his eyes on his way out, and as a result almost collided with Sam Carter as she barreled through the door. "Hey!"

"Sorry," she puffed. "Didn't you hear the phone?"

"No, why?"

"Damn." She walked quickly past him, picked up the internal line and listened closely to the handset. "Still dead."

"Were you trying to call us?"

"For the past ten minutes." She put the handset down and raised a crumpled sheet of printout. "Something just red-flagged down in operations."

There was a look on her face that Daniel didn't like at all. Something had unnerved her. "Sam, is something wrong?"

"I'm not sure. Look, have you heard of a Professor Laura Miles? She's an Egyptologist, retired about four years ago."

"Miles? Yeah, I know her. We worked together on a couple of digs, before…" He rubbed the back of his neck, suddenly feeling a little self-conscious. Flashbacks to certain seminars, he guessed. "We had a sort of falling-out. Some of my theories weren't to her taste."

"Daniel, I'm sorry — she was admitted to a hospital in Cairo about ten minutes ago."

Even before the disagreements, Daniel could never have counted Miles as a friend. But he respected the woman's work, and he hated to think of her in pain. "That's a damn shame. What happened?"

"The report said that there was some kind of fire or explosion at a dig site she was working on."

"So she was working again…" Something Sam had told him a few moments earlier suddenly connected in his head. "Hold on, why do we know about this?"

"Like I said, it red-flagged. According to the Egyptian police report, whatever happened to Miles happened between one-thirty and two PM local time. Given the time difference between here and there…"

He grimaced. "Three thirty-seven. Ra's message."

There was an encrypted fax receiver on the transport plane. Six hours into the journey it began to chirrup and spit out pages. Daniel, who had been holding very tightly onto his seat with his eyes closed for most of the flight so far, looked up to see Jack bringing a sheaf of paper back along the gangway. "I tell you," he said, voice raised over the noise of the engines. "These in-flight magazines are getting thinner."

"Cutbacks," replied Daniel, rather wanly.

Jack handed him the pages. "You okay?"

"Been better. I kind of like facing front on long flights, you know?"

He had certainly been on more comfortable journeys. The plane was old, a slightly battered C-130 Hercules kitted out almost entirely for cargo, and it was flying through air that felt, at least to Daniel, as if it were made of gravel. Most of the plane's internal space was filled with piles of crates and equipment cases, leaving just a few meters up by the cockpit for a seating area. Two benches had been fixed there, one on either side of the fuselage, leaving SG-1 sitting in facing pairs. It was a far from ideal arrangement, simply the quickest way of getting them into the air, and although Daniel had been forced onto flights like this before he loathed them with a queasy passion.

If the seating arrangements and the lurching of the plane under him wasn't bad enough, he wasn't entirely certain that the stacked crates were as secure as they could be. He was getting visions of them breaking free during one of the flight's many turbulent bounces and sliding back along the fuselage to scissor his legs off at the knees.

The unbidden thought made his stomach jolt a little, so he focused his attention on the fax pages. "Oh," he mumbled, after reading a few lines.

"Oh?"

"Looks like the Air Force subpoenaed PLH."

Jack narrowed his eyes. "Who?"

"Parker Lexington Holdings. They're the company Laura Miles was working for — they financed the dig she was at." He read further down the page. "Hold on… Oh, you have got to be kidding me…"

"What?"

"PLH are in big trouble. Looks like they illegally hacked a satellite feed."

Sam's eyes went wide. "Sorry? A holdings company hacked a satellite?"

"From what I've got here, it seems they're into a lot more than just property... You know, I was wondering why there was a dig going on in the middle of summer."

"Is that unusual?"

"Have you ever been to Egypt in summer?" He saw her shake her head slightly. "Well, it's way too hot in Egypt at this time of year to do any real work — most digs take place in winter, spring at the latest. But it looks like these PLH people have been trying to go under the radar. It says here they hacked a feed from the TIAMAT satellite."

"That's a UN bird," Jack cut in. "Ground mapping, right? Pollution, erosion, underground water, that kind of stuff..."

"Yeah," agreed Daniel, rather surprised. "Thermal Imaging, Atmospherics, Mapping and Terrain. Why do you know that?"

"Because the United States Air Force paid for about half the instruments on it. We get a direct feed."

"And PLH hacked it?" Sam gave a low whistle. "Talk about being really smart and really dumb at the same time."

"They can't have known who they were actually stealing from."

"So what did they find?"

"An anomaly, that's all it says here — evidence of something under the ground, I'd guess. They didn't want to go through the usual channels because they didn't want anyone to know how they'd found it. Seems they assembled a team on the quiet and shipped them out two weeks ago." He flipped the page, onto the first of series of brief personnel files. "They had a fixer, Lucas Harlowe. Hmm."

"Daniel, you know how nervous I get when you say *Hmm*."

"Huh? Oh, right. It's just that he's had a pretty interesting career, that's all. Afghanistan, Mozambique, Somalia... I wonder if Laura knew she was working with a mercenary?"

"Anything else?"

The plane slid sickeningly to one side. Daniel swallowed hard, then fixed his attention on the next sheet. A young woman stared out of the grainy photograph at its top left. "Anna Andersson. Twenty-nine, archaeology graduate from Stockholm. Don't know her…" On the sheet under that, a bespectacled man with short blonde hair, dressed in black. "Greg Kemp, geophysicist from Glasgow University. Not my field, really. Hey, they got Mohammed Rashwan, I worked with him on the Saqqara dig in '92."

"He got Laura Miles to hospital," said Sam. "The police report didn't mention the others, though."

"Is there a search out for them? They might know what happened."

Sam shrugged. "No mention of them in the police report."

"So," said Jack. "What do we think — they triggered that heads-up from Ra?"

"It's a theory. Some of the message could be taken to mention something buried — a pit, or a deep hole, sacred seals…"

"And the massive strength of the signal could be simply due to the source being so close," Sam agreed. "It makes sense to me, sir."

"Sense?" Jack gave them a slow shake of his head. "I wouldn't go that far."

"Still, we've got to at least check it out," Daniel said, trying to keep his voice steady as the plane lurched again. "If they uncovered a Goa'uld artifact…"

"I know, I know…" Jack tipped his cap down over his eyes and settled back. "Tell you what, Daniel. You keep reading and I'm gonna go to sleep. Wake me when we get there or when this really *does* start to make sense, whichever's the sooner. Okay?"

"Sure," Daniel muttered absently, already turning the page.

He wondered if he should pace himself, save some of the fax for later. After all, the flight to Cairo West airbase was going to take another twelve hours at least, and the chances of him imitating Jack and being able to sleep through any of it were slim in the extreme.

As the notion occurred to him, the plane tilted vehemently to port, the sound of its engines rising to a tortured howl before settling again. Daniel clenched his jaw tight for a moment as his stomach flipped, and put away all thoughts of stretching his reading tasks any further. The sooner he could go back to holding onto the aircraft and keeping his eyes shut the better.

The plane touched down at three in the afternoon, on tarmac that was already gluey with heat.

The airbase was vast, and impossibly flat. Daniel's first view of it was from the C-130's hatchway, only a couple of meters from the ground, and there still didn't seem to be a piece of it he couldn't see. It just stretched away forever, runways and access roads blurring into flat desert, blacks and grays fading out to an eternal, uniform beige that didn't stop until it met the sky.

Apart from a few boxlike buildings and some sporadic clusters of shade trees, all that rose above that unending level were the aircraft ranked up in lines to either side of him. It was a depressing sight, lifeless and beaten and rippling under the baleful summer sun.

After his less than edifying time on the aircraft, Daniel wondered how long he would now have to stay in this barren place. He need not have worried, because General Hammond had already contacted the base commander.

The workings of the US military still had the power to puzzle and surprise Daniel Jackson, even after so long under its wing. In an edifice as vast and complex as the USAF, he had long ago decided, inertia was a default state — even though the personnel might seem to be in a constant hurry, the organization itself did nothing at any pace other than glacial. In fact, Daniel could think of no better analogy; a billion tons of frozen military bureaucracy, grinding its slow, inexorable way across the boulder-fields of budget and meeting, committee and oversight.

That is, until a man with a certain type of badge on his collar picked up a telephone, and instantly the glacier became an avalanche.

As soon as Daniel's boots hit the tarmac, events accelerated to a hazy speed. A humvee arrived to pick the team up and transport them to one of the outlying office buildings, and soon after that to the offices of the airbase commander. With very little preamble they were given new equipment, civilian clothing and information packs, and then shipped out to a third building where they had just a few minutes to change into their new outfits and read their orders.

It was no shock to Daniel that he and the others were under instructions to remain in civilian clothing during their investigation. What did surprise him a little was finding out that he was now Laura Miles' nephew.

"It feels weird," he told Sam an hour after landing, as they drove to the hospital. "I don't like the idea of this at all."

"I understand that," she replied. "And I'm sorry. But you have to speak to her. We just don't have time to let hospital policy get in the way."

"What if we're wrong?"

"About the artifact?" She shrugged. "Then you're visiting a friend in hospital. There are worse things to be doing."

They were alone in the car. Jack and Teal'c had stayed at the airbase, to confirm the location of the dig site via another pass of the TIAMAT satellite, and to arrange transportation out to the desert.

He drove in silence for a while. The airbase had provided them a with a white Toyota pickup that looked in much worse shape than it actually was. Its aircon was functional rather than luxurious, though, and while Daniel was able to keep to the main roads and drive at a decent speed, he and Sam had both opted to simply keep the windows open.

Daniel had driven in Cairo before, many times, and he knew the best routes. It seemed that Sam was content to let him take over this part of the operation. For once, he realized with no small sense of satisfaction, *he* was the expert.

"How far now?" Sam asked, after a few more kilometers had rolled under the Toyota's wheels. Daniel slowed for an intersection, swerved the vehicle wildly between a Volkswagen Beetle and a camel cart, and swung left onto Youssif Abas.

"Not too far." Stark white tenements were scrolling past to his right, blindingly reflective in the harsh sunlight. To his left, the stadium reared like an alien monument. "They took her to one of the smaller hospitals in the west of the city first, but she was moved to the Cleopatra last night."

Sam glanced around at him, pale eyebrows rising above the dark lenses of her shades. "The Cleopatra hospital? Really?"

"Really."

"I thought that was just a placeholder on the orders."

"No, it's actually called that."

He went right again, onto Salah Salem, a main thoroughfare that would take him almost all the way to Heliopolis and the hospital. The traffic was still fairly light, due in part to the heat. Few would choose to be driving on a day that could turn vehicles to ovens. Still, even light traffic in Cairo was a test of both courage and concentration. Daniel saw the sprawl of taillights ahead of him, settled a little more comfortably in his seat, and took a deep breath.

"You might want to hold on to something," he told Sam. And put his foot down.

There was a golden quality to the observation ward. Daniel had expected it to be brighter, more stark and antiseptic, but there were fabric blinds at the windows that attenuated the sunlight into glowing shafts of amber. The walls were plain, a color he couldn't even identify, but the filtered light warmed them, and the linoleum floor between the beds was broken into a soft chequer of sun and shadow.

He paused at the threshold, looking in, but oddly unwilling to intrude further. The ward was very quiet. Somewhere a machine bleeped gently, and there was a snuffling, a rustle of clean cotton bedclothes as somebody turned over. Apart from that, and the faint, continual hum of the air conditioning, there was only silence.

Daniel found himself thinking more of a museum than a hospital ward.

"Daniel?" Sam was just behind him. Her voice was hushed, but he could hear the subtle edges of her impatience. He didn't answer her, just steeled himself and stepped inside, the tennis shoes he had been given at the airbase making no sound on the hard floor.

There was a nurse's station just inside the door. Daniel announced himself to the woman who sat there, and they spoke in Arabic for a few moments; he explaining who he was — or at least who he was pretending to be — and she warning him that his aunt's condition was severe, and that two visitors might be enough to impair her recovery. A compromise was quickly reached. Sam would stay and wait for a doctor to explain more about Laura Miles' injuries and how they were being treated, while Daniel would visit her alone.

Miles was in the bed at the far end of the ward, closest to the intensive care unit. In effect, she was hovering between the two wards, not well enough to have been discharged from the ICU but stable enough to no longer need machines assisting her lungs and heart. That situation, the nurse told Daniel, could change at any time, and he must be prepared for this.

The bed was surrounded by curtains, sealing it off entirely from the rest of the ward. Daniel walked hesitantly over to it, lifted an edge of white fabric.

It took him several seconds to recognize the woman who lay there. When he had last seen Laura Miles she had been in her mid-fifties, slender in a way that spoke of hard physical work in bad conditions, her hair, a peppery mix of jet-black and silver, always dragged back from her angular face and tied thoughtlessly with a rubber band. She was animated, angry, short-tempered, fiercely intelligent, prone to bouts of swearing so florid and inventive that on more than one occasion Daniel had been forced to hunt down a dictionary to find out exactly what she'd called him.

They had never been friends. But when his theories had led to the established archaeological community turning its collective back on him, Laura Miles was one of the people he'd missed most of all.

The bed before him cradled someone very different. This woman wasn't slender, she was *shrunken*, emaciated, her skin pale parchment over birdlike bones. A small reading lamp had been left on over the pillow and its light turned her face into a patchwork of white skin and black shadow. He couldn't see her eyes at all, just the deep pits of her sockets, as though he were looking at an x-ray, at the structures and failing mechanics lying just beneath the surface.

Her hair was almost completely white, and the way it was spread over the pillow was all wrong for Miles. Daniel found himself looking around for a rubber band.

There was a chair next to the bed, on her right side. He stepped through the curtains and sat down.

"Laura?" he said, very quietly.

On the other side of the bed a monitor made almost imperceptible sounds, and from outside the curtain came faint voices; Sam and a man that Daniel could only assume was the doctor.

Within the curtains, nothing moved. Miles hardly even seemed to be breathing.

"Laura," he said again, louder this time. "It's Daniel Jackson. Can you hear me?"

There was no response. Daniel grimaced. He'd come a long way for nothing if she was going to stay asleep.

He rose a little from the chair, looking across the woman's body. For the first time he saw that her left arm was gone, severed just above the elbow, and the stump heavily bandaged. There was something odd about the skin of her arm above the bandage, though. Daniel leaned over her, making very sure not to touch any part of her or the bed. He didn't want to think about what might happen if she suddenly awoke to find him looming over her.

There was a patch of bare skin between the bandage around Mile's upper arm and the white gown she wore. Daniel had been expecting to see evidence of burning there, or a crush injury — what little he had been able to learn from the police report into her injuries had made him envision some explosion or rockfall. But the skin was smooth, and unblemished apart from a strange mottling, like the spread of dark veins in white marble.

The left side of her face was marked in the same way, ashen and swirled with a sprawl of bluish tracks.

Daniel winced, and slowly sat back down. The voices outside the curtain had stopped. He leaned close to the sleeping woman and touched her arm.

He skin was cold. It was like touching a corpse. He jerked his hand back reflexively, and as he did so the curtains moved behind him.

It was Sam, peeking through. She said nothing, but moved her head to beckon him outside.

He followed her, moving a short distance away from the curtained bed. "Find out anything?"

"Not much." She had folded her arms tightly around herself, as though cold. "What about you? Has she said anything?"

He shook his head. "She's asleep. I can try waking her up, but I don't know how responsive she'll be."

"You've got to try."

"I know." He looked away. "So what did the doctor say?"

"Daniel, I don't think they know what's wrong with her." She glanced back along the ward, to make sure no-one was close, and even though they were alone she kept her voice to a murmur. "He says that her arm was gone when she arrived, and that the wound margins were completely dry and... *Crumbling*. He's thinking maybe a chemical burn, or maybe even radiation, because it looks like there are a bunch of secondary lesions in the lymph nodes and muscle tissue around the injury. So far she's being medicated for pain relief and to keep her this side of organ failure, but until they know what happened to her they can't really do all that much." She gave a small shrug, restricted by her folded arms. "They just don't have a diagnosis that fits the facts."

"That's no burn," muttered Daniel. "Whatever she found out there..." He trailed off, his thoughts too chaotic to go further. "I'll try to talk to her again."

"Sure. Take your time."

"Something tells me we don't have too much of that," he said softly, then walked back to re-enter Laura Miles' silent, bed-shaped world.

Nothing had changed since he was last here. He sat down again, willing himself to more positive action, but the idea of shaking this stricken soul back to wakefulness seemed brutal, alien. This might have been the first peace she'd been afforded since her injury. What right did he have to rob her of that?

He was on the verge of turning away when she stirred.

The movement was slight, but it spurred him. He put a hand to her shoulder, squeezed it gently, fearing that if he gripped too hard he would splinter those narrow bones. "Laura, it's Daniel Jackson. I know you're in there, come on, help me out here…" He shook her, just once. "Please?"

There was nothing. He sighed, and got to his feet. There was no knowledge to be had here, and no point to his presence. He could no more be a help to this woman than she could to him.

"Sleep well," he breathed, and turned off the reading lamp.

And Laura Miles shrieked, a deafening scream of pure, raw terror.

"Jesus!" gasped Daniel, stumbling backwards, his heart leaping and jittering behind his sternum. Miles was arching up from the bed, her remaining hand clawed, her jaw wide around that awful scream. Her eyes were round and white in the shadowed sockets of her skull: he could see them flicking desperately left and right, and finally he regained the wits that shock had momentarily stolen from him.

"Oh crap, the *light!* Hold on…"

He fumbled for the switch, snapped the reading lamp back on. Instantly the scream stopped, and Miles sagged back. She was looking right at him.

"What the hell?" Sam hissed, nearby.

He could hear footsteps, running. "Keep them out," he begged. "Please."

Miles sucked in a rasping breath. "Daniel?"

"Yeah, it's me."

"God, they got you here too?" Her voice was thready, rapid. "Please tell me they didn't hire you too!"

"Who?"

"Bastards," she shuddered, then gave a wracking sob. "Oh God, how many more?"

This wasn't going as he'd planned, and he knew he only had moments. Sam wouldn't be able to hold the medics off for long. She wouldn't want to. "Laura, what happened out there? Did something happen at the dig?"

She shook her head. "No. No no no."

"Please, what did this to you?"

"Daniel, don't. Please don't. You can't. Don't let them make you."

"Laura—"

"I saw them… They… They ate him…"

He gripped her shoulder, hard. "Laura, *what did you see?*"

Her mouth worked for a second, silently. Her eyes were fixed on his, a look more completely afraid than he had ever seen. "*Shadows…*"

The curtain whipped back, metal rings chiming. The nurse was there, a doctor, an orderly. Daniel stumbled up and away from the bed. "She woke up," he managed.

They ignored him, brushed past him as if he were an irrelevant piece of machinery. All their attention was focused on the patient. He heard words in a soothing tone, and caught the glint of a needle catching the ward's golden glow. The monitor was chirping fitfully, demanding, as if it had woken too. Sam was speaking to him, tugging at his arm, but her words were dull, without edges, and his brain refused to process them into language.

All he heard with any clarity was the terrified, desperate sobbing of Laura Miles.

Chapter 5.

HOLE TO FEED

AFTER Carter and Daniel had been ejected from the hospital, they returned to the pickup and waited there for O'Neill's call. The vehicle was in a corner of the Cleopatra's car park, shaded by palms, and they were not disturbed, even as the sun set and the sky grew dark above them. Carter was thankful for that. After the terrible sight of the crippled woman screaming and sobbing in the observation ward, she needed some time to calm herself.

In her time at Stargate Command, Samantha Carter had been witness to many strange things; mysteries and terrors and dangers that few could even comprehend. She had seen wonders that she thought might burst the heart in her chest, horrors she feared could rob her of sleep forever. She had known any number of men and women who could not adjust to such sights, and there was no shame in it. In fact, Carter often wondered if there was something abnormal about *her*, that she could step from world to world so easily and still close her eyes when the lights went out.

But something about the fate of Laura Miles filled her with a dread that she could neither ignore nor explain. She had been frightened before, genuinely terrified in some of the more extreme situations she had found herself, but Carter was a soldier, and fear would always be her companion. She could deal with that, move through it, make sure it never robbed her of thought or function when it mattered most.

No, this was a deeper feeling, more subtle, and much harder to pin down. And the elusive nature of it was what Carter found hardest to deal with.

There were elements that hit her on a visceral level, of course. Who could have seen the thrashing stump of the woman's left arm and not react in such a way? Or be quietly sickened by the doctor's description of the secondary damage, those internal lesions that he had, before his hasty self-correction, referred to as *corruptions*. Tiny, wet sacs of necrosis; not tumors, but bubbles of rot deep within the tissues… The thought made Carter's gut rebel.

Perhaps, she reflected, her problem was that she couldn't imagine what might have caused Laura Miles such ruin. Maybe the simple fact that she was faced with a puzzle she could not solve was putting her so much on edge.

If she was true to herself, she was certain that the reason lay elsewhere. But it would have to do for now, because the satellite phone was ringing.

They had been given the phone at the airbase. Daniel picked it up, and Carter put her head close to the handset so she could hear both sides of the conversation. After a short tone and a series of sharp clicks, she heard Jack O'Neill's voice.

"*Where are you?*" were his first words.

"Heliopolis," Daniel answered. "Eastern part of the city."

"*Well, get your asses over to the western part. We're going hunting.*"

Daniel threw Carter a nervous glance. There was little doubt that he was as shaken by his experience in the ward as she had been, probably more so. "Sir," she said, "are you sure that's wise?"

"*I don't know from wise. I just don't want to wait around until morning.*"

The sun was almost gone, just a liquid layer of ruddy light coating the edges of the skyline's more prominent towers. "Colonel, it's looking increasingly likely that four people went into that dig, and only one came out. Believe me, she's in a pretty bad way."

"*All the more reason to get this done, Major.*"

He was right, Carter knew. Day or night, the threat would still be the same — her initial reaction, after Miles had shown such a terror of being left in darkness, was to think of daylight as safer. But the woman had been attacked in the heat of the afternoon, so there probably was no reason to delay.

Besides, out there in the desert, searching for whatever had burned off a woman's arm and caused corruptions to sprout in her body, she would at least have her comrades at her side and a weapon in her hands.

Right now, that was a comfort she could understand. "Where shall we meet you?"

During their time at the airbase, O'Neill and Teal'c had successfully secured a feed from the TIAMAT satellite, and used its imaging facilities to not only pin down the exact location of the dig site, but also to take some surprisingly detailed photographs of it. Carter and Daniel studied the images while O'Neill drove the four of them into the desert.

The pickup was still in Cairo. The trip to the dig site needed something with more storage and more muscle, and the airbase had provided both in the form of a modified Jeep Wrangler that looked like a civilian vehicle until one noticed just how solidly it was built. The Wrangler was piled high with equipment in sealed cases and bundles, and Daniel, upon seeing it waiting for them, had wondered aloud if O'Neill was overcompensating at all for his lack of winter clothing of Sar'tua. The comment had earned him a sour look from the Colonel, but Carter had been forced to agree that it did look as if they were taking along everything they might possibly need for this trip, and far more besides. Then again, SG-1 usually went out on their missions with no more than they could carry on their backs. Having some machinery to help lighten the load was something of a novelty.

There were reading lamps over the back seats, which enabled Carter and Daniel to compare the images even though night had fallen over the desert.

After they had been driving for about thirty minutes, O'Neill looked over his shoulder. "You kids okay in the back?"

Daniel didn't lift his head. "Are we there yet, Mom?"

O'Neill returned his attention to the road. "See anything in those pictures?"

"Well," Carter said, "I think it's more about what we're not seeing."

"Like what?"

"There's a lot of camouflage netting up, for one thing. I guess PLH didn't want anyone checking up on them. Some of it looks as if it's come down, maybe knocked over, but I can't see anything that looks like the entrance to a pit."

Daniel pointed at a long ribbon of sand-colored netting. "I'd guess that's under here. Sam, do you see any people in these shots?"

"I was going to mention that. But it's summer, you said yourself no-one stays out in the sun for too long. Maybe they're under the netting."

"Maybe." Daniel didn't sound sure.

"O'Neill," Teal'c said suddenly. "It is time."

Carter wasn't sure she liked the sound of that. "Time for what?"

"Time for things to get a little bumpy," O'Neill muttered, and swung the wheel over.

After that, looking at the satellite images wasn't really an option. Carter had seen all she needed to see of the site anyway, so was happy enough to drop the photographs and switch off the reading light. She needed both hands to hang onto the seat and the grab-strap, anyway.

There had been something on one of the photos that stayed in her mind, however, although she chose not to mention it. The resolution of the satellite imagery wasn't quite high enough for her to be sure, and anyway, it might not mean anything at all. So she held her tongue, as the vehicle lurched and bounded its way across the dunes.

Once they were at the site, she could find out for certain if she really had seen a single, abandoned wheelbarrow, tipped over and left unheeded between two camouflage tents, as if someone had flung it aside in their mad scramble to escape.

O'Neill parked the Wrangler a kilometer west of the PLH site. SG-1 crossed most of the remaining distance on foot, splitting into two teams when they were within a hundred meters or so. Carter and Teal'c headed south, while O'Neill came in from due west with Daniel.

It was truly night, now, and the sky was a lake of stars. The temperature had begun to drop sharply at sunset, and Carter judged it to be dipping close to freezing as she picked her way towards the site. The civilian clothing they had been issued included heavy jackets, and Carter was glad of hers. The cotton shirt she had been wearing during the day would have done nothing to stop the chilly wind cutting right through her.

The conditions were really nothing like Sar'tua's bitter climate, but just close enough to throw up some unpleasant memories.

It felt odd to be wearing civilian clothing and carrying a weapon, and stranger still to be looking at the world through night-vision goggles as she walked. Carter had always found the devices to be fascinating, but wearing them was a surreal experience. She trudged through a world made entirely of green, under a soupy, verdigris sky, seething with the random sparks of stray photons, while the sand beneath her boots was a livid emerald. Teal'c, stalking ahead of her and to her right, was an animated statue of dark jade, the leather jacket he was wearing so dark in the goggle's view that it was almost part of the night itself.

There was no sound, save that of a gentle desert breeze shifting sand from the tops of dunes, and her own breathing as she walked.

Abruptly, Teal'c stopped and raised a hand. Carter moved up next to him and pressed a key on her radio handset twice, letting O'Neill know they were in position. Then she dropped to one knee, looking down over the dig site.

The place seemed very different from the clear, daylight images TIAMAT had provided them, but its layout was familiar to her now. The rocky overhang was under her feet, curving away to either side for hundreds of meters before fading back into level sand, and ahead were the pitiful collection of fabric tents and battered furniture that had made up the dig itself. Carter spent a few seconds scanning the site carefully for any signs of movement, but saw nothing but green-lit stillness.

"Looks clear," she said quietly. "Teal'c, do you see anything?"

"I do not. There are signs of damage, but none of life."

She keyed the radio. "Colonel O'Neill, this is Carter. We're overlooking the site now."

"Same here. I think we missed the party."

Carter wondered if he would have used that word had he seen what had become of Laura Miles, but she kept her silence on the matter. "Shall we move in?"

"Affirm —" he began, then stopped. *"Hold on. What?"* The final word was fainter, and Carter realized it was not aimed at her. O'Neill must have been talking to Daniel.

A moment later his voice returned. He sounded a little uncomfortable. *"Ah, Major? Daniel's just raised an interesting point."*

"Which is?"

"Whether we'd considered the possibility of disease."

Carter frowned. She had been working under the assumption that the damage to Miles' body had been the result of some trauma; a chemical or radiation burn, explosion or crush injury. But could a pathogen have torn into her so vilely? The secondary tissue damage, those internal pockets of decay seeding her muscles and lymph nodes, certainly spoke of disease.

Maybe Miles had seen the work of some alien plague working its way up her arm, and had self-amputated to stop the spread of it.

Or perhaps Mohammed Rashwan had done it for her.

Remembering the Conservation Director put the theory out of Carter's mind very quickly. "Sir, I don't think that's likely. Rashwan took Miles all the way back to Cairo, and there must have been a couple of dozen other workers here too. There's no report that Rashwan was ill, and no scare stories about plagues in Cairo."

"Rashwan's not been found yet, though."

"PLH probably had him under wraps. I'm sure he'll surface once the company folds up."

There was a pause. Then: *"I think you're right."*

"Tell Daniel that he was smart to bring it up, though. He had me going for a minute there."

"You and me both. Okay, you and Teal'c go in and conduct a ground search. We'll get the Wrangler and bring the gear up."

"Understood. Carter out." She got up. "Come on," she said, keeping her voice low. "Let's find a way down."

Teal'c gestured to the east side of the site. "I believe there is a scree slope in this direction, Major Carter."

She peered out into the green darkness, but saw nothing. "You saw that from the photos?"

"I did not."

"Okay..." Was he even wearing the goggles? She checked, and noticed that he was. How low he needed the gain set was anyone's guess, though. "Lead on, Macduff."

"I believe it is '*Lay* on', Major Carter."

The Jaffa began striding down a jumble of broken rock and shifting sand, part of the curving rock wall that had shattered away to reveal the TIAMAT anomaly months earlier. Carter, slightly less sure of her footing, eased her way down behind him. "Give me a break, Teal'c. Everyone gets that line wrong."

"That is what led me to remember it."

He stepped off a jagged slope of sandstone, instantly dropping into a combat stance, staff weapon held at the ready. Carter watched his great head swinging slowly left and right, scanning for threats, and for a moment needed no reminding that he had been born a very long way away indeed.

She jumped down to ground level, bringing her MP5 up to cover Teal'c's blind side. Her failure to spot any movement at the site was no indication that they could relax. Until she was completely sure she and Teal'c were alone here, she would stay combat-ready. To do otherwise was to invite the same fate as Laura Miles, and Carter had every intention of avoiding that.

They began to move slowly through the site, one scampering forwards a few meters while the other covered, then switching positions, gradually eliminating every possible place an enemy might hide. They found no threats, but everywhere there was evidence of a panicked and hasty retreat — upturned tables, dropped tools, discarded notebooks. Carter almost tripped over the abandoned wheelbarrow, now half-covered in the shifting sand, and seeing it gave her an ugly thrill of recognition.

Much of the debris was scattered around the edges of a deep pit near the overhang. Carter went back to it after the sweep was completed, and peered down into its shadows.

A slab of pure darkness leered at its centre, surrounded by discarded tools. "They left in a hurry, all right."

"And have not returned," Teal'c replied quietly.

Carter hadn't thought of that. Thirty hours had passed since Miles had been attacked, if her injuries had occurred at the same time that Ra's message came through the Stargate. Wouldn't somebody have come back to the dig site to investigate before now?

The thought was, if anything, more troubling than that of the dig's initial, hurried evacuation. It didn't take much to make the average person flee for his life, not in Carter's experience. But to make him run and keep on running, to not return at all...

There was a sound behind her, a distant, rattling growl. She spun around, bringing the MP5 up against her shoulder, and a few seconds later saw the Wrangler's angular prow emerge over the far dunes. It was a welcome sight, but she kept her weapon aimed until she could clearly see O'Neill's face through the windshield. Theirs could not be the only Jeep in Egypt.

"All clear, sir," she reported as he turned off the engine and got out. "You were right about missing the action."

"Great." He hauled the goggles of his face, took a moment to rub the bridge of his nose vigorously, then reached back into the Wrangler's tangled stacks of gear. "Damn things never fit me right," he muttered.

"Sir?"

"Aha!" He pulled out a big, army-issue flashlight and switched it on, scanning the beam around. "Better. Lots better."

The beam glared like a searchlight in Carter's goggles. She tugged them from her head, shaking her hair back into some kind of shape once they were off. Without them, the world seemed ferociously clear, its edges sharp and crystalline. She had forgotten how much detail the goggles had to trade in order to turn night to day. "Sir, we found this."

O'Neill frowned past her, at the pit and its forlorn collection of tools. "Daniel?"

"Right with you." Daniel was ridding himself of his own goggles, unlocking them carefully to avoid snagging his spectacles. "Oh, I see... Ah, Jack? Can you give me some light down there? No, at the hole, that's it."

In the beam of O'Neill's flash, the dark rectangle Carter had seen earlier suddenly flipped its perspective. Through the goggles, she hadn't been exactly sure what it was, but now she could see that it was a smooth-sided hole in the sand, lined with what looked like black stone.

"Is that the TIAMAT anomaly?" she asked.

"I think so." Daniel took a deep breath. "I guess this is where we start unloading the truck."

The shaft didn't go down as far as Carter feared it might. After a few meters it terminated in a sheet of dull, golden metal.

Daniel was kneeling next to her, at the edge of the hole. He had been running his hands over the smooth stone of its interior for the past minute or two, as if trying to gain some insight into its origins by touch alone.

"It's granite," he said finally. "Incredible workmanship, but it's human."

"How old?"

He shook his head. "Can't say. It doesn't look old at all, but appearances can be deceiving."

"They sure can..." Carter stood up. "What about that base plate? That doesn't look like granite."

"No, I'm going to have to get down there. We're going to need a ladder."

"Funny you should say that," said O'Neill, walking quickly up to join them. He was carrying a heavy cylinder of olive-colored fabric in one hand, which he set down next to the shaft. "Got one right here. But check this out."

They followed him to a pile of debris, near the edge of the pit. There was a ladder bolted to one of the wooden boards that lined the excavation, and Carter initially thought O'Neill was showing it to them, possibly as a quick way of getting down into the shaft. But he was pointing his flashlight at the jumble of discarded items at the ladder's foot, probably dumped there by people scrambling to get up and out of the pit.

Daniel reached down and hauled something free of the pile. "I'll be damned."

It was another ladder, and much like the first; solidly built from square-section wood, reinforced at one end with angled iron plates. But the other end was very different — the wood there had been splintered apart, the bottom rung compressed laterally until its centre was a forest of shards.

The ladder looked as though it had been snipped messily in half.

Daniel passed Carter his flashlight, and then took the ladder in both hands and carried it over to the shaft. She followed him, making sure his way was lit, and then watched him lower it, damaged end first, into the hole.

The angled plates at the top edge dug solidly into the sand. "Look at this. It just hits the baseplate."

Carter aimed one of the torches down. Sure enough, the broken end of the ladder was resting a fraction above the golden metal. And there was something else, something's she'd not noticed before. "Splinters," she told him, pointing. "There, in the middle. See?"

A few pale shards of wood littered the centre of the baseplate. One or two stood vertical, as though trapped there.

"I think that plate is at least two separate pieces. They must have come together and snipped the ladder in half."

"'The sacred seals are in place'," Teal'c quoted. He had appeared from nowhere, and was looming at the shaft's edge, aiming his own flashlight into the depths. "It would appear that this entrance is deeper than we had first assumed."

"Depends how long the ladder was originally, I guess…" Carter leaned further over the hole, steadying herself with one hand as she scanned around the interior of the shaft with the beam of her flashlight. The stonework seemed featureless, the joints between the granite blocks so fine they were barely visible. She tried to visualize how the shaft was put together: long slabs of smooth black stone, maybe a meter across, half that high, set atop one another in a series of open squares. The only vertical joints she could see were at the corners, and the entire shaft was tilted back by maybe thirty degrees.

No, she corrected herself: not tilted, as such. Carefully and deliberately crafted to rake back at that puzzling angle. The slabs on either side of the shaft were cut so that their upper and lower edges were perfectly horizontal. They exactly matched the level surface of the baseplate, the 'sacred seal' that had closed like a sliding door and snipped a sturdy wooden ladder like matchwood.

The inside of the shaft seemed impenetrable, which made no sense at all. Something had caused the baseplate to scissor closed over the ladder, and Carter couldn't believe that what had closed could not be opened again.

The solution, she was sure, simply lay in detailed investigation. "Teal'c, can you hold the top of this ladder for me?"

Daniel's flashlight beam shone into her face. "You're going in there?"

"Yeah. I'm sure there must be a mechanism for opening that metal plate, but I can't find it from up here."

"Shouldn't I go?"

"You don't know what to look for," she smiled, made sure her gun was securely swung around at her back, and threw a leg over the edge of the shaft. The sole of her boot met a ladder rung, and it seemed steady enough. When she got her other foot onto wood Teal'c knelt down and took the ladder's upper end in his hands. Carter felt it lock in place as he gripped it.

Their relative positions put their faces almost touching for a moment. She found herself looking into Teal'c's dark eyes.

"Take great care, Major Carter," he told her sternly.

"It's just a few feet."

"I was not referring to the distance."

She nodded to him, then climbed down the ladder.

The air in the shaft was oddly cool, even colder than that in the dunes, and there was a strange stillness to it. It reminded Carter of some laboratories, where both the climate and the movement of air was precisely controlled. It felt as though the space encompassed in those polished slabs was waiting, watching her, its breath held.

She descended gingerly, testing her weight on each rung. The last two seemed unsteady, so she bypassed them and stretched a leg down to plant a foot directly onto the golden baseplate. It felt solid under her boot, as strong and still as the stone walls. She eased herself down onto it, still holding tightly onto the ladder in case anything moved.

There was just enough room to turn around, although the shaft's tilt was disorientating. Without ground-level as a frame of reference, it felt to Carter as though the shaft should be vertical, and the baseplate was angled to tip her over.

"Okay down there?" O'Neill called, his voice echoing oddly.

"Fine. It's cold, though."

"It's cold up here too. I was going to start a campfire, get some marshmallows going..."

"Save some for me." The flashlight beam was reflecting off the polished stone, making it difficult to see the granite surface in any detail. Carter paused, took a deep breath, then switched the light off.

Instantly she heard O'Neill's voice. "Carter? Something wrong?"

"Just using the Force, sir." In reality, she was using her fingertips.

Without the flashlight's shimmering reflections to distract her, she put out a hand and began to feel the smooth stone panels around her. After a few seconds she even closed her eyes, letting herself focus entirely on the coolness beneath her fingers, the slight variances in the stone's texture, the seams and edges that she could not have seen by torchlight alone. And she had been wrong about the shaft, she knew that now. Its surface was not quite perfect.

Almost, but not quite.

About half a meter above the baseplate, on the side of the shaft that tilted back towards her, there were two seams that had no analogue either above or below. Carter opened her eyes, switched the flashlight back on and, after a few moments letting her sight readjust, saw that the slab there was split into three.

The middle part was as wide as her hand, perfectly regular and set so skillfully into the surrounding stone that it was difficult to see it at all, even from so close. There was no space around it to get even a fingernail into, much less a knife or any other tool, and Carter didn't try. Instead she tried to remember the other pieces of Goa'uld technology she had encountered, and how they had been concealed. Sometimes, she thought, all one needed to do was push.

The panel clicked under her palm, sank in a short way, then slid aside.

Glassy crystals glowed faintly in the cavity she had revealed. "Got something," she called up.

"Define 'something'."

"Some kind of control array." She studied the crystals closely, noting their position, the way their facets aligned, the hair-fine tracery of golden circuitry linking them together. "Looks like it's designed to accept an incoming signal, maybe a sequenced override."

"So someone could open the seals by remote control?"

"I think so." She frowned. "One, no, two of these crystals are damaged. The surfaces are crazed. I think this array has been on standby power for a really long time, and there's been some decay…" She reached out to one of the damaged elements, brushed it with a fingertip. It was warm, and rough to the touch.

"Carter, didn't Teal'c tell you to be careful?"

"I'm always careful." She twisted the crystal a quarter-turn, and heard a slight humming sound issue from within the cavity. "Yeah, I've got this. I can open the panel from here, sir. I just need to —"

The crystal popped between her fingertips.

The decay must have been far worse than she had thought — some internal corrosion had robbed the glassy shard of all its internal structure, leaving only a shell of material to conduct power and information. As soon as Carter had applied pressure to it the crystal had shattered like a light bulb. In one second it was there, and in the next it was dust and shards.

She gave an involuntary yelp and jerked back as crystal fragments flew up into her face. The flashlight beam dipped away from the cavity as she moved, so that she saw the crystals there glow suddenly, intolerably bright, and then, with an ugly snapping sound, go dark.

The whole array had burned out. Smoke curled up into the cold air.

"Damn," she muttered. "Colonel, I think I broke something."

The baseplate slid out from under her.

She grabbed wildly at the ladder, just managed to catch a rung and then there was nothing below her feet but empty air. The flashlight dropped from her other hand as she flailed at the walls, trying to get a better grip, and she saw it spiraling down and away.

Her own words rang in her ears: *It's just a few feet.*

The others were shouting down at her, hands reaching into the shaft, but she had no time to answer. The rung was cutting into her hand, its rough edges digging painfully into her fingers. She managed to bring one foot up and around, to plant her boot on the lowest whole rung, but as she did the wood cracked horribly under her. Her body fell, slammed into the sloping rear wall of the shaft, and then her agonized grip on the ladder gave way.

She fell.

Chapter 6.

INTO DUST

POLISHED stone slid up past Carter, sickeningly fast. She struck out with her hands, spread her feet, trying to get some purchase, but all she managed to do was draw rubbery squeals from her boot soles. And then, with a massive, jolting impact, the base of the shaft hammered up into her and set her sprawling.

She twisted in mid-air, hit something broken and clattering with one shoulder, and tumbled face-first onto a hard surface. The breath went out of her, and when she sucked air desperately back into her lungs it was full of dust and grit.

Carter coughed, spluttered around that crucifying first breath, and clamped her jaws shut over a cry of pain.

The shock of the impact faded after a few heartbeats, leaving her aching. She spat dust, took a tentative breath, and then another. Somewhere far above, voices echoed in the darkness, but she couldn't make out any words at all.

"Ow," she managed, finally.

It was bitterly cold, and very dark. There was a soft beam of light issuing from the floor close by, though, and when Carter reached out to it she found her flashlight, half-buried in dust. As she lifted it, more of the gritty stuff came up, dropping in streams from the flash's grip and lens.

The powder was sifted against the shaft walls in piles. Perhaps it had broken her fall somewhat.

There was a noise in the shaft, a harsh metal clatter. Carter swung her flashlight around in time see the end of a chain ladder tumble down against the black stone, the contents of O'Neill's olive-colored roll. It failed to reach the bottom by half a meter or so, which gave her a nasty realization of just how far she had fallen.

More lengths of wooden ladder lay tumbled at the bottom of

the shaft. She'd hit one as she fell.

The chain ladder began to twitch. Somebody was climbing down. Carter got to her feet, in stages, each stage just a little more painful than the last. "I'm okay," she managed to call up.

"Coming down anyway." That was O'Neill.

"Wouldn't it be better if I came up?" Carter wasn't sure if she could have made the climb, but the alternative was staying down in this freezing darkness. And, given that there was a good chance Laura Miles had lost an arm in this very place, risking the unstable chain ladder seemed like an attractive proposition.

"Just stay put, Major."

"If you insist, sir." Carter turned away from the ladder and brought her gun up, her flashlight held alongside the barrel. There was a doorway at the bottom of the shaft; she could see the edges of it picked out in the cone of light. It was big, its sides angled slightly inwards. Beyond it she could see nothing but darkness, so she resisted the urge to scan the beam around any further, just stood covering the doorway until O'Neill jumped off the last few rungs and landed in the dust as the base of the shaft.

He moved quickly up to stand alongside her, his own gun raised. "Major?"

"I'm fine. Left ankle's still a little weak, but apart from that I was lucky."

"So I guess the sacred seals aren't in place anymore, huh."

She winced. "Sorry about that, sir. I should have taken things more slowly."

"Don't sweat it, Carter. Wasn't your fault." He scanned his flashlight around. Behind him, the chain ladder began to jerk again. "So what do you think?"

"I don't know what to think. This isn't like any Goa'uld structure I've seen. Maybe Teal'c or Daniel will be able to throw some light on things."

"No pun intended."

"Ah, no sir."

He moved forwards a short distance, lowering his gun and

moving his flashlight around, following the edges of the doorway. "Teal'c's on his way down. I told Daniel to stay up top. If there's only one way into and out of this place I don't want us all here at once."

That was wise. Although Carter would have felt more comfortable with all four of the team together, she could see the wisdom of keeping at least one person up at ground level. Putting all your eggs in one basket was never a good idea. Especially when the basket had a habit of killing the eggs you put in it.

She moved past O'Neill, still not trusting the dark enough to lower her weapon. Instead she put her shoulder to the side of the doorway and peered around it. "Bet he didn't like that."

"Yeah, I kinda got that impression."

Carter scanned the flashlight around, trying to get her bearings. Past the doorway, the space opened out a lot further, its echoes and the unnatural coldness giving her the impression of cavernous space. Once again, she found herself very glad of the jacket. Her breath was a pale vapor in the air.

The beam of her flashlight was catching random edges as she scanned it around, but if she moved it too far up or to the sides it vanished, its glow fading into the solid black of deep shadow. The interior of the structure was complex, she could see that, but at the moment she couldn't grasp its layout, even its true dimensions.

She brought the beam up past the base of the ladder and up over the doorway, saw a glimpse of boots at the end of the ladder, and then she was looking up at a shallow angle of stone, sweeping over her head before reaching an edge and disappearing into the dark. "It slopes," she whispered, unwilling to speak loudly here. "It's wider at the base."

"Pyramid?"

"I think it flattens at the top, but yeah." She moved the beam again, towards what looked like a vast rectangular wall up ahead. The wall didn't seem to reach the ceiling or the walls on either side — her light found its edges, but nothing beyond. Maybe there was a smaller, box-shaped structure inside this larger one.

It didn't make sense, but nothing about this place did.

There was a soft sound behind her as Teal'c landed at the end of the ladder. She risked a glance back, and saw that he had somehow climbed down the unstable construction of links and rungs with his staff weapon still in his right hand.

He walked slowly past her, his gaze sweeping the shadows. Carter watched him pause, frown slightly, and then move to the wall. He spread a hand over it, let his fingers slide across, then down. He was feeling for imperfections just as she had in the shaft.

"There was once writing here," he said finally. "Carved into this wall. The coloration is gone, but I am able to identify the characters."

Carter aimed her flashlight at the wall, but saw nothing. "What does it say?"

"There are exhortations to Ra, and instructions for those who enter the Pit of Sorrows."

"Instructions for what?"

"Preparing oneself for death."

Carter thought back to Daniel's initial translation: *a deep hole, weeping or lamenting.* It wasn't a huge leap from that to an ominous title like Pit of Sorrows. Even translating from one human language was an imprecise business. Trying to convert Goa'uld to English must have been especially fraught, even if most of that species did appear to be completely bilingual.

I guess sometimes you just need to see something written down.

"At least we know we're in the right place," said O'Neill. He walked to the corner of the wall and peered around it, aiming the flashlight. "Whoa…"

"What do you see?" Carter asked him. She trotted across the gritty floor to cover him, wondering why the writing couldn't be more easily seen. As Daniel had said earlier, System Lords tended to like their statements to be obvious. It didn't make sense that they would be subtle, not with such a message.

Perhaps time had worn the coloration away, although that didn't seem very likely either. The System Lords, immensely long-lived, built to last.

She reached the corner, brought the gun and the light up again. Past the edge of the wall, the structure opened out in a strange way, and it took Carter a second or two to realize quite what she was seeing. But once she had the spatial relationships fixed in her mind, it became simple.

The inside of the structure was a flat-topped pyramid, maybe twenty meters across. There were four walls set around its centre, not meeting at the corners, but free-standing, so that she had a clear view from one corner of the pyramid to the other, or would have done had the darkness not been so intense.

Within the four walls, something tall glittered dully in the flashlight beams.

O'Neill was already moving forwards. Ahead of him was a squat dais, square and stepped, and vast shapes loomed out of the shadows to overhang it. Carter brought her light up and saw statues, hawk-headed and utterly black, their arms raised in supplication. Each of them was three or four times her own height.

Between them, at the top of the dais, was what looked like a waist-high column of shining gold.

The sight was mesmerizing. Carter could see that the column was ornate, ridged and fluted in a design she couldn't quite grasp at her distance. There was something about its shape that was half church font, half communion goblet, but the proportions of it were oddly disturbing. In the midst of this frightening darkness, surrounded by four granite titans, the golden thing sparked nothing within her but unease.

She moved the light around, unwilling to fixate on the column while the shadows could still conceal horrors. As she did so, the sound of dust shifting echoed back to her from the far corner.

She froze. "Colonel!" she hissed urgently.

He knew her well enough to recognize the tone of voice, as did Teal'c. The Jaffa dropped to one knee, his staff weapon snapping open with a whine of barely-restrained energy. O'Neill was off the steps in seconds, taking up position to cover Carter as she crept forwards. "What is it?"

"Possible movement, northwest corner." She paused halfway along the strange inner wall, and as she did the dust ahead of her moved again. There was another sound, too, very faint, like something trying to breathe.

She still couldn't see the source of the noises. Her flashlight beam tracked left and right along the floor, picking out random piles of dust, and clusters of what looked like burned sticks, pieces of curved pottery or stone. She felt one of the objects beneath her boot as she moved on, but it gave no resistance to her weight, merely crumbled to nothing beneath her.

Reflexively, she swallowed. Her mouth was still dry from the dust she'd breathed in, and it was hard not to cough.

At least it didn't taste bad. It didn't taste of anything.

She had reached the corner. The piles of powder were higher here, as if some breeze had caused the stuff to drift. Carter aimed her flash at the floor, completely baffled.

A human skull leered back up at her.

Carter suppressed a jolt of shock, swallowed hard, and then dropped slowly into a crouch, running her light up and down the length of the corpse. "I've got a body here," she called.

"One of Miles' people?"

"I don't think so. Looks like it's been here a long time."

"No real surprise there, Carter."

Something wasn't right. "Hold on..."

Despite her unease, she forced herself to look more closely at the body. At first she had thought it ancient, a tattered, mummified thing, little more than pale bone and papery, patchwork skin, half-buried in dust. But now she could see it more closely, there were details that didn't add up. The few scraps of fabric that still adhered to the corpse looked modern — there was a Levis label near the hip, a button half-sunk between two ribs. A sad little pile of fragments near one hand that might once have been a watch.

Strands of white-blonde hair around the skull.

Carter took her hand off the MP-5's grip, reached out, and tried to lift some of the hair, but it simply went to powder between her finger and thumb. She grimaced, tried to wipe the stain it had left against her jacket, but the movement caused her gun to swing free on its strap. The barrel tapped the corpse's shoulder.

There was a soft, soughing noise as the entire ribcage sank into itself, collapsing into a pile of gray ash and powdery, gritty dust. The same stuff, Carter noticed, that was all over the floor.

The same stuff that still clung to the inside of her mouth.

She jerked to her feet, gagging, running her sleeve hard along her open mouth, desperately trying to get the awful stuff out of her. She heard O'Neill running towards her, boots crunching over the remains of countless human beings, of limbs and skulls and hearts and minds all rotted to powder in this frigid darkness, and the realization of what she was surrounded by made her stomach flip. A wave of nausea washed up from her feet to her head, and she bent forwards to steady herself against the wall, using the feeling of cold, hard stone against her hand to steady herself.

That was where she was when a skeletal hand reached out of the shadows and grabbed hold of her ankle.

Greg Kemp had been a good-looking man, Carter remembered from the faxed file she had read on the C-130. Twenty-eight years old, pale sandy hair, a kind, pleasant face that suited spectacles. Almost handsome.

He wasn't handsome any more. Whatever had turned Laura Miles' left arm into dust had chewed this man up and spat him back out again.

The arm was the only limb he could move. One of his legs looked largely intact, but there was a portion of his hip that had probably taken some major nerves with it when it had crumbled. There was no way he could have moved out of the corner, not even by crawling. If he'd even tried to stand, Carter thought despairingly, he'd probably have crashed apart like an ill-made scarecrow.

What hadn't been turned to ash looked ancient, shriveled and dry, as if he had been buried in hot sand for a thousand years.

If there was any mercy to be found in this situation, Carter reflected, it was that Kemp didn't actually seem to be in any pain. Distress, certainly — after all, how many hours had he remained in this Pit of Sorrows, staring out at the ashy corpse of Anna Andersson? Thirty? More?

Even the thought of it made Carter want to close her eyes and run. Instead she focused her attentions on the stricken man sitting with his back against the black stone wall, and tried to make out what he was saying.

He had been trying to talk ever since he had grabbed at her, but none of the sounds he was making sounded like language. She wondered if he was irreparably brain-damaged by the assault, or if the mechanisms of speech had been lost to him physically. In either case, she decided, giving him a little water probably couldn't make things worse.

When she reached for her canteen, O'Neill put a hand out to stop her. "Are you sure that's a good idea?"

"No, I'm not."

"It might kill him. He doesn't look like he could handle a coughing fit right now."

"You're right, sir," she said. "But he's been down here a long time. I think I'd want something to drink, even if it did, you know..."

He took his hand away, and nodded. "Sure. Good call."

Kemp spilt most of the water she gave him; his mouth wasn't the right shape any more. But what little went down his throat didn't seem to cause him too much pain. He coughed at first, but thankfully Carter's worst fears were not realized. The man did not shiver apart in front of her.

Teal'c appeared around the corner. "There are no other survivors," he reported. "I have appraised Daniel Jackson of our situation. He has contacted the airbase for medical assistance."

O'Neill opened his mouth to speak, but Kemp got there first. "Arra," he said.

His voice sounded like two dry surfaces being scraped together. "Mr Kemp, don't try to talk."

"Arra," he said again, his withered hand coming up. "Deh."

"Yeah, buddy, she's dead," said O'Neill quietly. "I'm sorry."

Anna. Carter gave the man a few more rivulets of water from the canteen. He nodded his heavy head in thanks.

"Mr Kemp?" she began. "Did something attack you?"

Another nod. The hand came up again. "Tha."

Carter looked back. He was pointing, vaguely, at the golden column up on its dais. Somehow that only confirmed her suspicions about the thing. She hadn't liked the look of it since she had first laid eyes on it.

"What is it?"

"Doh no. Blac stah. Wanned ow hee."

She threw a glance at O'Neill, but he only shrugged. "I'm not sure I understand," she told Kemp. "Wanted your…?"

"Heat," said Teal'c.

Kemp nodded.

Carter got up, turned to look back at the column. It seemed innocent, inanimate, but if what Kemp was saying made any sense at all, the body heat of three people — Anna Andersson, the mercenary Lucas Harlowe, and himself — had been enough to activate it.

There were four people in the structure now. "Ah, Colonel?"

"Way ahead of you," O'Neill told her. He stood, and keyed his radio. "Daniel?"

"Right here."

"We're coming up. The survivor's in a bad way — we're going to need a rope sling."

"I'm on it."

He reached down to Kemp. "Okay, fella. Teal'c and I are going to lift you up and get you over to the door. Ready?"

Carter stepped back to give her companions enough room, and held her light steady on Kemp's ravaged body. They lifted him out of the dust with a horrible ease. He must have weighed little more than a child.

They carried him slowly, and with infinite care, across the dust towards the base of the shaft. Carter could have stepped in and freed O'Neill's hands, but he wore an expression that kept the suggestion from her lips. She wondered if, when Kemp was safely on a helicopter and away, Jack O'Neill would feel any better about the lives that had been lost on Sar'tua.

Then she felt guilty for even thinking it.

It didn't take long to reach the doorway. Carter couldn't help looking back towards the column every few moments, but it didn't seem to be doing anything. Maybe Kemp and the others had gotten closer, she thought.

O'Neill called Daniel again as they reached the shaft. "How's it going up there?"

"Give me a couple more minutes," he replied. His voice sounded a little odd, and Carter realized he must have been working with both hands while he was using the radio. She imagined him jamming the handset between his cheek and his shoulder as he put the sling together, and the mental image almost made her smile.

The sooner she was above ground, the better. She'd had enough of being in the dark and the cold for one night. She felt as though the heat was leeching out of her very bones. The longer she spent down in the structure the colder she seemed to be getting.

No, she realized, with a sudden, crawling unease. She was colder now than she had been a minute ago.

O'Neill and Teal'c still had Kemp between them. Carter moved away from them, warily, back towards the corner, and then aimed her flashlight towards the column.

Smoke was coming out of the top.

"Colonel," she yelled, bringing the gun up fast. "I think we've got a problem here!"

Dark vapor was spilling languidly from the column's upper edge, like dry ice in negative. But as it inched down the golden sides of the thing it was separating, splitting into myriad hairs and threads that writhed and coiled in the air.

Some of them looked as if they were reaching out towards the beam of her flashlight. *Black stuff,* she thought wildly. *Wanted our heat.*

They had all kept their distance from the golden pillar as much as possible, but the meager warmth of their bodies must have still been enough to arouse its dreadful appetite. Carter dropped to one knee, pulled out the stock of the MP-5 and pressed it back hard into her shoulder. Her finger touched the trigger, stayed there, just a little pressure on it as she squinted along the weapon's iron sights, the squirming tendrils of shadow spilling out ahead of her.

"Carter," called O'Neill. "What the hell's going on back there?"

From the doorway he wouldn't be able to see the column. "Just get him out," she called back.

A moment later Teal'c appeared next to her. He saw what was happening and snapped his staff into firing position, triggering the business end to spring open like a lethal flower. "O'Neill, we cannot remain here."

"Where's Kemp?" hissed Carter.

"Over O'Neill's shoulder."

The thought was awful. Carter was about to answer him when something appeared above the rim of the column.

She tightened her grip on the gun. A pale curve was rising, surrounded and half-obscured by the shadowy feelers, but before Carter could see what it was or squeeze off a shot, the column changed shape.

The upper part of it unfolded into glittering metal leaves, each leaf flipping up and around, interlocking with a complicated metal noise. Carter had heard that sound before, in the armor of the Jaffa and the mutable technologies of the Goa'uld, but she had never seen a machine quite like the one she was watching now. Within moments the entire top section of it had become a fluted, armored cone.

The smoky black wisps fell away as if severed, vanishing in the light of Carter's flash.

And then the Pit of Sorrows came to life.

A deafening, unearthly gonging echoed out from every wall, the chime of a cracked iron bell beaten with a giant's hammer, over and over. It made Carter drop the flashlight in an attempt to get a hand free and cover her ears, but the blindness that caused ceased to become a problem a moment later, when the structure lit up.

Angled blocks were hinging out of the walls at floor level, each one pouring a sickly golden light out into the structure.

Carter staggered up, disorientated.

"We must leave." Teal'c's voice carried somehow, even past the gonging.

They ran to the shaft together.

O'Neill, she was gratified to see, was most of the way up the chain ladder with Kemp. The ladder itself was swinging wildly around, so she darted forwards and grabbed at the lowest rung, hauling it taut. She saw him look back down.

"Get up here," he called.

"You first, sir. The ladder won't hold."

"Dammit Carter—"

"Colonel, I think that thing's contained, whatever it was. The column—"

Her next words were lost as an almighty noise issued from the shaft.

It sounded dreadful, the worst noise she could think of: it was the sound of stone splitting. Carter saw dark fragments dropping towards her, and she ducked away as pieces of granite thumped heavily into the dust at her feet.

There was a dry hissing, and a gentle rain of sand sprinkled into her hair.

"Oh no." She could feel the floor shaking.

A flashlight beam shone down into her eyes. It was Daniel. "Sam, come on! They're out!"

She got a foot onto the rung. "Teal'c, climb with me. I don't know how much time we've got..."

He didn't answer, but then he didn't have to. She found out, before she could even climb another rung that she didn't have nearly enough.

Looking up, she had a perfect view of the shaft, its surfaces illuminated in the harsh beam of Daniel's flashlight. She saw the structure of it *ripple*, a wave of motion travel down towards her like a whiplash, and then every panel exploded inwards in sequence. This was no mere structural failure, she realized in that last, terrified second. There were bombs around the shaft, buried in the sand, and something had set every damned one of them off.

Her reflexes kicked in. She jumped back, faster than she could have thought possible, and Teal'c caught her in mid air and swung her away as the shaft erupted down at her.

They hit the floor together, rolled apart, and both scrambled back through the doorway just before the first tons of stone and sand smashed into the base of the shaft.

And then there *was* no shaft. Carter saw, just for a second, a solid mass of rubble crashing down and compacting and filling the narrow space behind the doorframe before a panel of dark metal snapped up from the floor. She'd not even seen the slot it had been concealed in, but the force of its rise was stunning. A meter-long slab of black granite was in its path, and the panel sheared through it without trying.

The severed end of the panel slammed down into the floor next to Carter's foot.

She got up, put her hands to the panel, but it was massively solid, unmoving. She couldn't even hear the shaft coming apart behind it.

Makes sense, she thought darkly. No point having a doorway if you haven't got a door.

The shaking ceased, and then the gonging stopped, which Carter initially took to be a blessing. She was just going to say so when it was replaced by an even worse noise.

Ra's voice.

It echoed out around her, as loud as the gong, sneering and sibilant, the voice of a snake in the head of a man. It hissed and snarled for several seconds, then fell silent. Carter waited for it to repeat, but it didn't. In its wake, there was nothing but silence and her own panicky breathing.

"What did he say?" she gasped finally.

"We are congratulated," Teal'c replied, his gaze narrow. "On successfully defying the will of a god. Also, it is hoped that we travel with happiness as the Ash Eater returns."

Carter didn't like the sound of any of it. "Travel with happiness?"

"I believe a more suitable translation would be: *enjoy your trip.*"

Carter suddenly went very cold. "Returns where?" she said, her voice sounding very small.

Her only answer was a renewed shuddering from the floor. And this time it didn't stop.

Chapter 7.

LEARNING TO FLY

EVEN BEFORE the shaft had imploded, Daniel Jackson could see that something dreadful was happening below his feet. The entire floor of the excavation was vibrating, the sand bouncing like hard rain spitting back up from the sidewalk, waves of it crossing and intersecting in a vast interference pattern. The sight was terrible and fascinating and almost hypnotic. Jackson had never seen anything like it.

He had tried not to let it slow his efforts to put the rope sling together, but the dancing sands, together with the growing thunder from below ground, must have had an effect on his concentration. In any case, he had only just completed the sling and was rushing it over to the shaft when Jack, and the awful thing he had been carrying, scrambled out.

The man sprawled, momentarily letting the corpse-dry body of Greg Kemp fall away from him. "Teal'c and Carter," he gasped, struggling to his knees. "Gotta get them up."

Daniel threw the sling aside and skated the last few meters to the shaft. He aimed his flashlight downwards and saw Sam's small, white face looking back up at him. She seemed very far away.

"Sam, come on!" he yelled. "They're out!"

She said something to Teal'c, who must have been behind her, and then the shaft blasted itself apart.

The explosions were deafening, a cascade of hellish detonations that shattered every panel. Daniel saw them go — the entire sequence of blasts so fast that it was done, top to bottom, before he could even fall backwards — and then he was stumbling away, half-deaf, part blinded by the flash. He staggered a few steps in reverse, lost his balance, and thumped down heavily onto his backside.

His flashlight was gone. He'd probably dropped it into the shaft.

In which case, that was the end of it. There *was* no shaft now, just a rapidly expanding cloud of dust and smoke and raining sand. He could feel the solid grinding of massive stones beneath him as the shattered panels hammered down on top of each other, the sand around them collapsing inwards to add to the mess. Under the cloud, a crater was sprawling outwards.

The bass vibration from underground had stopped as suddenly as it had begun. The sand, other than that which was still pouring down into the crater, had ceased to move.

Jack was at his side, dragging him up. "Daniel, what the hell just happened?"

"The shaft… Must have been explosives in the walls."

"Was Carter in there?"

"No, she was still at the bottom. She'd have had time to get out of the way."

Jack hauled out his radio and keyed it. "Carter, respond."

There was only silence, not even static or the hint of a return. Daniel wasn't surprised by that at all, given just how much solid material must have been between the two handsets. "Try Teal'c," he said anyway.

The desert was suddenly very quiet. The crater had stopped growing. While Jack shouted at the radio again, Daniel went to see if he could help Kemp. He knelt, willing away his revulsion at the state of the young man's body. Kemp looked like a broken scarecrow, like something that had been lifted out of a sarcophagus. There seemed to be nothing living about him, until he moved slightly at Daniel's touch and dragged in a dry, agonized breath.

He did not wake, though. The shock of being moved so violently must have been too much for him, which could only have been a mercy.

There was a hot, sick horror in Daniel's core. "Jack, tell me Sam and Teal'c aren't trapped down there with whatever did this."

"She said something about it being contained," Jack replied, his voice tight with fury. "Why the hell didn't I see this coming?"

Daniel got up. "How could anyone have seen that?"

"I'm in charge, Daniel," snapped Jack. "It's my job to see *everything!*"

This was no time for an argument. Daniel forced himself calm. "Listen, we can beat ourselves up all we want once we've got Teal'c and Sam back, but right now we need some heavy equipment out here, and fast. There's got to be about a hundred tons of crap between us and them right now, and they're only gonna have so much air."

Jack screwed his face up. "Okay, that place was about twenty meters across, ten high, sloped. How much is so much?"

"A day, maybe. Depends."

"On what?"

Daniel didn't want to say it, but he did anyway. "Carbon dioxide build-up. Look, we won't leave them down there that long. Call the airbase, tell them to get a backhoe or something out here. They must have…"

He trailed off. The ground was beginning to shake again.

"Daniel, that doesn't feel the same as before."

"I think you're right." Daniel found himself backing away from the crater. The vibration was stronger this time, a deep, fast hammer below the sand, and getting worse. There was a clattering impact from the edge of the excavation, where some of the team's equipment had been stashed, and Daniel looked around to see the whole pile of it sag over into a heap.

Out above the pit, the camouflage tents were fluttering to pieces. "Jack, we need to get the hell out of here right now."

They hurried over to Kemp, still sprawled inert in the sand. Wincing slightly, Daniel reached down and put one arm under the man's knees, the other below his arms. He braced himself, stood, and came up far more easily than he was expecting. Kemp was sickeningly light, as though there was barely anything left of him at all. He felt desiccated.

"C'mon, will ya?" Jack was at the ladder out of the excavation, beckoning Daniel to move faster. "This whole place is coming apart."

"Just get up the ladder and take him."

Jack climbed quickly up and out of the pit. As Daniel reached the foot of the ladder he passed the stricken man to him, then followed as fast as he could. There was a noise coming from the excavation that he didn't like the sound of at all; a long, bass moan, as though something vast were being stressed along its whole length.

As he reached the top there was a hissing, bellowing roar from behind him. He glanced back in time to see an immense fountain of sand vomit upwards from the pit floor.

The sight drew a cry of shock from him — for a moment he thought that some other explosion must have gone off underground, one last, gigantic demolition charge to destroy the Pit of Sorrows and its lethal occupant once and for all. But this was no explosion. Very different forces were at work here.

Another stream of sand powered up, soaring above his head. He could see it clearly because of the light funneling up from below ground, a stark, blue-white glare, flickering in the turmoil and impossibly bright.

"Daniel?" Jack's voice was all wonder and horror. "What the hell?"

Daniel could only shake his head. The floor of the excavation, along with the crater that had been caused by the shaft's destruction, was bulging upwards.

Jets of sand hissed and leapt around the bulge as it grew, the light stuttered and flared. Daniel saw the dome of sand crack, slide apart as something dark and angular broke through it, heaving itself up in one vast, birthing surge. It caught the overhang of sandstone as it came up and the rock wall exploded, blasted into razored shards by the impact. Daniel felt a slap above his left eye that turned his head around. A fragment of rock had caught him there.

He staggered, but could not fall. There was still too much to see.

The object was rising. Tons of sand rained from it, slabs of shaft-stone battered down into the huge hole it was leaving as it lifted, embedding themselves in the cold sand, and the sound of it was a tooth-shaking, reverberating drone.

It hovered for a few seconds, shedding desert, rotating slowly above the giant, debris-strewn crater. It was a flattened pyramid of pitted black metal, bigger than a house, covered in panels and pipework and layers of complex systemry. Another pyramid, upturned, capped its base, and this was stretching, splitting into sections that slid and rotated against each other with smooth mechanical precision.

Between each of the sections, blue light flickered, pulsed, increased to an intolerable flare, and then the entire Pit of Sorrows leapt upwards, accelerating with brutal speed. In seconds it was a whirling black square, spilling lightning, then it was a mote, then a star, dimming in the sky until it was completely gone.

All the strength went out of Daniel, then. He fell to his knees, the side of his face soaking with a wet heat. He brought his hand to it, already knowing that it was blood, but the slippery feel of it on his fingers was too much. He sagged, rolled onto his back.

The sky above him was dark and cool, dotted with stars. He lay there, looking up at them, until the helicopter arrived to block them out.

There were medics in the helicopter. One of them cleaned Daniel's wound and closed it with surgical tape, while the other two strapped Greg Kemp to a pallet and tried to find a vein to connect their saline drips to.

The machine was a big, open-sided Pave Hawk, designed for medical extractions and rescue operations under extreme combat conditions. Daniel, strapped into a seat with his head pounding and mouth dry with sand, wondered if those conditions had ever included the aftermath of an Egyptian tomb leaping out of the ground and flying away.

One of the medics asked him what the glowing object was, that had soared up past the helicopter so quickly, but Daniel could not answer. Even if the Pave Hawk's crew were security-cleared for that kind of information, he simply didn't know.

All he did know was that Sam, Teal'c and the awful force that had reduced Anna Andersson to dust and Greg Kemp to a crippled, broken tatter of parchment flesh and corrupted bone were all three locked together within the Pit of Sorrows, whatever it was and wherever it was going.

He was starting to believe that a lack of air was the least of his friends' problems.

Jack had been at the front of the helicopter, using the radio. He clambered back to where Daniel was sitting and dropped down next to him, not bothering to strap in. The wind of the Pave Hawk's passage tugged at his clothes. "Can't reach SGC," he reported. "Could be their comms are down again."

"Another message?"

"Wouldn't be surprised. Daniel, have you ever seen anything like that?"

Daniel shook his head. "The way it changed shape was a lot like—" He stopped himself, glanced about to see if any of the Hawk's crew were close by. They weren't, but he decided to play it safe anyway. "It looked like the way our old friends from out of town do things."

"Yeah, I thought that. The shape's a giveaway, too."

"So what now?"

Jack ran a weary hand back through his hair. "I've been on to Colonel Parker at the airbase. She's fuelling up a ride home—it'll be a hell of a lot quicker than getting here, but I'll have to drive."

Daniel closed his eyes. He an idea of what that meant. "We need to track that thing, Jack."

"Already on it. As soon as SGC get back online Parker will appraise them and tell Hammond to try and contact the Tok'ra. If anyone can get Carter and Teal'c back, it's them."

"What if they don't play ball?"

Jack gave him a dark look, full of pain. "They'd better."

As Daniel had feared, their ride home was a fast jet, an F-14 Tomcat, sleek and vicious-looking as it squatted on the runway. According to Jack it was perfect for the trip because it had two seats and could do the entire journey in less than five hours, as long as they could refuel regularly on the way.

There was no answer to that. Daniel knew that there was no better way to get back to Stargate Command, even though the thought of being thrown around the sky in such a craft for five hours filled him with dread. But while the F-14 could achieve a speed of mach two, even that seemed slow to someone who was used to stepping between worlds in the blink of an eye.

Both men had to be in flight suits for the trip, so they changed out of the battered and soiled civilian outfits they had been wearing. And then, very carefully, they sealed them inside large Ziploc bags and carried them with them to the jet.

Of all the things that Daniel had not mentally prepared himself for, it was for exhaustion to catch up with him just as the return to Cheyenne Mountain got underway. But the demands that Egypt and Sar'tua had placed on his body required their due, and he could only put off paying that particular tribute for so long. A muzzy wave of fatigue started to wash down through him as he was climbing into the F-14's cockpit, so hard and heavy that he almost stumbled under its weight.

Thankfully, Jack was already in the pilot seat, and either didn't notice or chose not to mention it. Daniel was quite pleased about that, until he realized that the colonel had only gotten a couple of hours more sleep than he had, back on the C-130. And while Daniel Jackson's eyelids had suddenly become stone, Jack was getting ready to punch a fighter jet through the sound barrier. Twice.

He very nearly said as much while an airman was strapping him in, but then it occurred to him that Jack's system was probably fuelled entirely by a combination of anger, impatience and caffeine right now, and while that was a potent mix, it had its limits. Informing the man of that fact might have unwelcome consequences, Daniel decided — after all, did he really want to remind Jack that he should be exhausted, just as he was taking off?

So he held his tongue. And, as the engines thundered and

surged behind him, he also held onto the inside of the aircraft, very tightly indeed.

For all the flight's terrors, and all the distress and uncertainty and worry coursing around his brain, fatigue finally won the war. Ten kilometers above the curve of the Earth, locked into a fragile skin of aluminum and titanium and sitting just ahead of two engines that were turning air itself into fire, he slept.

It was not a restful sleep; that would have been too much to hope. His surroundings were not conducive to rest, even though Jack was holding the F-14 straight and true. And even if he had been in his own bed, the past few hours still had their hooks in him. Images of his friends, and of what Greg Kemp had been turned into, kept shouting him awake.

So he dozed, fitfully, the flight helmet heavy on his nodding head, while the world turned beneath him. Occasionally the voices in his dreams turned out to be his own, or issuing from the aircraft's radio. Jack spoke to him once or twice, and he was surprised to be able to answer quite coherently, although after the flight was done he had no recollection at all of what those answers might have been. There was a moment when he awoke to see something vast and dark looming over the plane, and Daniel seemed to remember later the process of having the F-14 refueled in mid-air, but he couldn't be entirely sure which parts of that event were real and which were conjured from his exhausted imagination. Dream or no dream, his chaotic mental state leant it an unpleasant, violatory quality: something about the questing, oozing tube, wavering back through the air towards him made him want to cover his face, to recoil in his seat. But when he opened his eyes again it was gone, if it had ever been there at all, and there was nothing in front of him but sky.

General Hammond had a lot of news for the two men when they finally got back to the briefing room, but little of it was good. He got the worst of it out of the way first. "We lost telemetry with the object about an hour after it took off. Looks like it went into hyperspace just outside lunar orbit."

Daniel had been afraid it would do that. "Any clues as to its course at all?"

"We're working on that. If it kept the same trajectory in hyperspace as it did when it was flying sub-light, it's probably heading out of the ecliptic plane."

"That's a big 'if'." Daniel knew little about the mechanics of superluminal travel, but he was at least aware that a straight line in realspace could be a corkscrew once a ship went FTL. There simply was no direct analogue between the two universes.

"Right now, that's the best we can do."

"So what did the Tok'ra say?"

Hammond's frown deepened. "The Tok'ra have turned us down," he said flatly.

"Just like that?"

"Pretty much."

"Did you get in touch with Jacob?" Jack asked him.

"Anise answered our call. She said that there were no resources available. And offered her condolences, of course."

"Figures."

The failure of the Tok'ra to come through was a desperate blow, but Daniel could not have said he was surprised. Jacob Carter had probably been kept entirely out of the loop, in fact — if anyone could have convinced the Tok'ra to help, it would have been him. Sam Carter's father was host to the benign Tok'ra symbiote Selmak: unlike the brain-rape that a Goa'uld perpetrated on its host body, the Tok'ra existed in a partnership that left both entities intact and benefitting from each other.

Selmak was a worthy ally, and Jacob Carter loved his daughter as much as any father, but there was only ever so far he could go. The Tok'ra had a habit of providing help only when it benefitted their own cause, and although they opposed the Goa'uld just as Stargate Command did, they preferred to do things their own way.

It was possible that they really didn't have the resources at hand. It was equally likely that they simply didn't believe rescuing a human and a Jaffa from a flying tomb to be an appropriate use of them.

"General," said Daniel. "This isn't really leaving us with a lot of options. Sam and Teal'c have been inside the Pit of Sorrows for…" He checked his watch. "Almost eight hours. Even if that Ash Eater, whatever it is, stays contained, they can't last more than a day or two without fresh air."

"I'm well aware of that, Doctor Jackson," Hammond said, rather curtly. And then, in a gentler tone: "Believe me, I'm going through every option I can to get them out of there."

"How many more do we have?"

"The Asgard, for one. Our comms took another hit from that second message, but we're almost back online, and we'll see what Thor has to say once we can get a hold of him. There's also the question of Bra'tac and that modified ship."

A look of something like hope passed briefly over Jack's face. "Has he been back in touch?"

"Not yet. We'll run a check for GDO codes once the communications are fired up again."

Daniel sat back. A feeling was nagging at him, tugging the edges of his mind, but he knew what it was, and refused to give in to it. There was no time for despair now.

Fighting was hard, though. There was every chance that none of SGC's tenuous alliances could be of use in time, and Bra'tac had given no indication of how long it would take him to reach Riyagan. It could have been anything from hours to weeks. And with no idea of where the Pit was going, not even a true direction to follow…

"So what are we supposed to do in the meantime?" said Jack.

"We keep the faith," Hammond told him firmly. "Gentlemen, I think you're forgetting who we're talking about here. Teal'c's a Jaffa — he knows Goa'uld machinery as well as you know your own car, and Major Carter is our leading expert in exotechnologies." He gave them a grim smile. "I wouldn't be surprised if they didn't have that thing down in our parking lot by tomorrow."

It was a comforting fiction, but that was all. Daniel found it hard to believe that the interior of the Pit of Sorrows, a black nightmare of a place that had endured almost unchanged beneath the desert for millennia, would be as easy to hotwire as Sephotep's experimental spaceship had been.

He went to the infirmary to find Janet Fraiser. She had collected the Ziploc bags containing the clothes he and Jack had brought with them from Egypt, hoping to gain more information about the Ash Eater by the dust it had left on them. A dust that was the remains of human beings, according to what Jack had told him about the interior of the Pit, and after seeing the extent of Kemp's injuries he could well believe it.

Fraiser was Stargate Command's chief medical officer. It made sense that he would find her in the base infirmary; in fact, he seldom saw her anywhere else. He had met few people who were as hardworking and as dedicated to their role as she, and had once, in a moment of some weakness, told her so. She had favored him a with a rare laugh, and told him that she had little choice. Those who passed through the Stargate on a regular basis had such a talent for getting themselves either injured in new and exciting ways, or infected with exotic alien pathogens, that she had no option to be otherwise.

Fraiser was in one of the small labs adjoining the infirmary, together with a pair of assistants, and looked to be in the middle of a complex sequence of chemical analyses when he arrived. She didn't appear to notice him as he came in, but he knew better than that.

"What's cooking?" he asked, trying to sound more frivolous than he felt.

"Hey…" She held a small vial up to the light, shook it. Daniel saw dust particles falling slowly through clear liquid. "Blast."

"What?"

She set the vial down. "Nothing," she replied. "And by that I don't mean nothing, I mean *nothing*. At all. I'm getting no results off this stuff."

He raised a hand. "Ah, you do know what this 'stuff' is made of, don't you?"

"Only because you told me. There is absolutely no chemical signature here, or at least not one that I can read so far."

That was odd. "I'm not sure I understand. Surely it must be the same basic compounds as a human body?"

"Yeah, you'd think..." She picked up another vial, looked at it helplessly, and set it back down. "Okay, pop quiz. What's the first test *you'd* do?"

Daniel was no chemist, and certainly no doctor. He tried desperately to think back to science class. "Um, that paper... Litmus test?"

Fraiser smiled. "Good answer. It's the first thing I did, although the equipment's a little more sophisticated. Thing is, this dust has a pH of zero. Sorry, zero point zero zero *zero*."

"That's weird."

"It's more than weird. I've been running every basic test I have on what you and Colonel O'Neill brought back on you. Radiation, zero. Reaction to acid, zero. Spectroscopics, flat nothing. It's completely inert. Nothing affects it. It's just..." She shrugged helplessly. "Dust."

Daniel felt at a loss. "I'm really sorry, I guess I must be missing something vital here. But what does that tell us?"

She spread her hands. "All I've got at the moment are theories, and until I've had time to get this stuff under the electron microscope that's all I'll have. But if I was forced to guess, I'd say that this substance has had all of its energy removed, very fast and very brutally. It's been robbed of its ability to react to anything, including itself. Ninety percent of its molecular cohesion has just gone."

"So if a person was subjected to that..." Daniel looked away. The thought was horrible. "Oh, man..."

Fraiser was silent for a few moments. Then she put a hand on his arm. "How are you holding up?" she asked, very quietly.

"Okay." It was a reflex, and a lie. "No, I'm not. I'm… They're trapped up there. We can't track it, we can't trace it, and every second that passes takes them further out of our reach…"

She nodded gently. "I know."

"And I don't know what to do."

"You will," she told him, and patted his arm. "You always think of something."

He was about to tell her that he wished he had her faith in him when he noticed Hammond standing at the lab door. "General?"

"Doctor Jackson, I think we need to talk."

Later, he found Jack outside the main entrance to the base. The man was standing, still and silent, near the perimeter fence, his arms folded, his head back. He was looking up at the sky.

It was dark again. The F-14 had taken them back through the time-zones, into the night they had just escaped from. There were fewer stars visible over Colorado than over the open desert, but Daniel had seen enough lights in the sky for one day.

He walked quickly over to where Jack stood. "Hey."

"Daniel."

"Hammond was, ah…" He jerked a thumb backwards, at the cavernous entranceway behind them. "We were looking for you."

"I was just taking a minute."

"Oh."

"Trying not to start smoking again."

Daniel raised an eyebrow. "Really?"

"No. What have we got?"

"Well, some good news. We managed to get in touch with the Asgard. They can't spare any ships, which is kind of a blow." Daniel resisted the urge to check his watch again. He'd found he was doing it far too often of late. "Even if they could, the closest ones are three, four days away."

"I guess that thing with the Replicators isn't going too well for them."

"Looks that way. But there's an upside — Thor said they have probes dotted all over hyperspace. Looks like the Pit almost clipped one on the way past. We've got a pretty solid idea of its course now."

"'Clipped'?" Jack enunciated the word very carefully, as if making sure he had it right. Daniel spread his hands.

"I know. But they've given us some good data. I wasn't going to throw it back in their faces just because it looked a little, you know…"

"Convenient."

"Not the word I was going for, but yeah." He'd been thinking of *suspicious*. The idea of one object passing accidentally close to another in open space was ludicrous; the scales were just too vast. In hyperspace the chances of such an occurrence were infinitely smaller. "Gift horse, Jack."

"I guess. In fact, that's the best news I've heard all damn day. Can we make any sense of it yet?"

"Hammond's got people working on it, looking to see if it's going to go past any planets with active gates, but it looks like we were right — it's heading up and out of the galactic plane."

"We still need a ride, Daniel."

"Yeah, that's the rest of the good news. It seems like a Tel'tak travelling way faster than it should do has a really distinctive engine note. The Asgard have been watching it for a few hours, wondering what the hell it was. They can send a message to Bra'tac and tell him to divert."

"Okay, I take it back. *That's* the best news I've heard all day."

"We'll meet him on a planet called Amethun. Hammond's already authorized it. I've asked astrogation to download the Asgard telemetry onto a laptop…" He took a deep breath. "Jack? There's something else."

Jack didn't move. "Go on."

"Kemp died. Multiple organ failure."

There was a long silence. Then Jack said: "Just a little too late on that one too, huh?"

"No, you weren't." Daniel turned to him. "Jack, they rigged up a phone line for him. He got to say goodbye to his wife. If you hadn't gone in there he would have died of thirst, alone in the dark and the cold and *no-one would have ever known about it.*"

Jack didn't speak for a while. Then he tipped his head back again. "I can't lose them, Daniel. Either of them."

"We won't. We've got a map and a ride. We're golden."

"Yeah… Daniel?"

"Hm?"

"You got a cigarette?"

He smiled, privately, in the dark. "I don't smoke, Jack."

"Good. Damn things'll kill ya."

Chapter 8.

WHITE QUEEN

LIKE THE CORE structure of a Ha'tak pyramid ship, the heart of the Hall of Negotiation was a tetrahedron. Its base was a large triangle of burnished gold, as were its walls, and the great table around which the three System Lords sat. It had been designed to offer as little distraction as possible, to concentrate the minds of those within on the task at hand.

Of the three, the Lady Hera knew this best of all. It was she who had designed it.

Over the past four days, she had come to regret some elements of this design. While the Hall was extremely portable — Hera had based many of its mechanisms on the mutable armor of the Jaffa, allowing it to be unfolded from a basic chassis into the network of structures she now occupied — it was also just slightly too small. If Anshar and Tsukiyomi had agreed to enter negotiations alone, there would have been no problem, but Tsukiyomi had insisted on four Jaffa warriors at his back throughout the whole process. Lord Anshar had, of course, followed suit, and so for the entire four days of negotiation a dozen people had occupied the core Hall, which was rather too many for Hera's liking.

She had herself only taken one Jaffa in with her, but he was a Minotaur, which more than made up for the disparity in numbers.

The Minotaur had stood behind her throne for the entire negotiation, helm continually raised, his vast arms folded, impassive and silent and still. Hera knew he made the others nervous, which was almost the entire point of him being here. If anything would hurry this tedious process along, other than the events she had already set into motion, it would be that.

A pity, then, that Anshar and Tsukiyomi were becoming oblivious to his presence. For the past day they had been engaged in an argument of epic proportions, and had barely paid any mind to Hera at all.

There was little to do but sit and watch them. Hera kept her poise, her composure, but it was far from easy.

Lord Tsukiyomi had reached the point where, unsurprisingly, he had accused Anshar of attacking a diplomatic convoy commanded by his beloved First Prime, Hashitara. As expected, Anshar was denying it vehemently, while still trying to present himself as the one among them in a position of strength.

"No ships of yours entered my territory, Tsukiyomi! Had they done, I would have destroyed them without a moment's thought!"

"So," Tsukiyomi snarled, "you admit your treachery!"

"Treachery? Is that what you call defending my domains from your incursions?" Anshar folded his great arms. "Perhaps we should call it war and be done with this charade!"

He was a bull of a man, thick-set and powerfully muscled, his face largely obscured by a long and elaborately plaited beard. It was said that he used his sarcophagus as rarely as possible, to spare his host body the worst of its ravages, and instead kept his shell healthy and strong by means of a strict and brutal regime of diet and physical exercise. It was also said that he imposed the same ruthless regimen on the Jaffa in his service, and as such they had gained a near-legendary reputation for their skill and stamina in all the physical arts.

Had Hera not been involved with such delicate negotiations, she might have found these rumors intriguing, but at present she could not allow herself to be distracted.

There was already enough playing on her mind.

"My Lords," she began, hands raised slightly in a conciliatory gesture. "Such accusations are not the way to —"

"I have made no incursions into your territory, fool!" Tsukiyomi was out of his throne, leaning across the table at Anshar. "All I have done has been to protect my domains from your piracy!"

Piracy was a new word, as yet unuttered during the four days of negotiations. Hera put a hand to her forehead, wondering if things were about to go spiraling out of her control. It wouldn't be the first time.

"No incursions?" Anshar barked a deep, mirthless laugh. "I beg to differ!"

"My First Prime entered your territory on a mission of diplomacy." Tsukiyomi was trying to regain his usual calm, easing back down into his throne. Where Anshar was solid with muscle, the other System Lord was almost ethereally slender and slight. He was taller than Anshar, and pale, with long, jet-black hair down to his waist. While Anshar was layered in laminate armor, Tsukiyomi was robed in the finest silks. They were both Goa'uld, both System Lords of comparable power, but physically they could not have been more different.

The juxtaposition of the two, and of herself among them, amused Hera somewhat. And there was little enough amusement to be had in this golden coffin, she thought, rather wistfully. Anshar was still blustering, Tsukiyomi still making his snide insinuations, and Hera was sitting at the third side of the table, despising both yet forcing herself to sit still and quiet and not take a sword to the sorry pair of them.

"Hashitara travelled to your throneworld at your invitation, Anshar."

"I offered no such invitation, you effete cretin!"

"I have it on record."

"A fabrication!" Anshar slammed his big fist down onto the tabletop. "As you well know. Your spies should have told you as much!"

Tsukiyomi spread his hands. "How many times must I repeat the facts to you? I have no spies in your household."

"Not any more, you don't," Anshar growled. "And I commend you on the quality of your employees, Tsukiyomi. They didn't betray you, even under the best my interrogators could offer."

Hera suppressed a reaction. Anshar was well known for his predilection for torture, and for the centuries of research he had devoted to studying the art. The spies must have suffered beyond imagining before they went past the point from which even a sarcophagus could return them.

"I would be flattered," Tsukiyomi replied calmly, "if I had the slightest idea of what you are talking about."

Anshar made a disgusted sound and sat back. Hera was just wondering if she should interject again at this point when she felt a buzzing at her temple. The jeweled diadem she wore at her brow was vibrating, softly enough that only she could sense it.

She stood. "My Lords, please excuse me. There is an urgent matter to which I must attend."

Tsukiyomi frowned. "Are we under attack?"

Hera gave him a small smile. "No, my Lord, nothing so dramatic. I shall return in a few moments."

"Perhaps it would be as well to pause," Anshar rumbled.

"As you wish. In the meantime, can I offer you some refreshment?"

Tsukiyomi bowed. "Thank you."

She turned to Anshar, one eyebrow raised. He grinned at her, teeth very white among the thicket of beard. "I'll accept whatever *refreshment* you offer me, Lady."

Hera tipped her head. "I shall direct slaves to attend you."

She left the table, and walked to the door, not too quickly. She didn't want to appear eager to leave, and she could feel the eyes of both men on her as she moved.

To say that was no surprise would have been an understatement of cosmic proportions.

As Hera reached the outer door of the Hall she paused, halted by the sudden transition from dim coolness to dry, white heat.

The Hall of Negotiation had been set up in the centre of a level field of brown, scorched grass. A few hundred meters away, a sparse line of gnarled shade trees stood in black puddles of shadow, and beyond that rose rocky hills, jagged against the open blue of the sky.

The sun must have been directly overhead, and it's light came down on the plain like a hammer. Hera stood for a moment, a hand cupped over her eyes to block out some of the glare, feeling the warmth of the air around her. Even the breeze that came to her across the plain was hot and dry.

Although the scene was harsh, Hera didn't find it unpleasant. It had triggered something within her, an old fragment of memory, and for a few seconds she allowed herself to take refuge in it. The memory was not her own, nor did it lie in the ceaseless, ageless genetic recall of the Goa'uld. No, this was an image from her host, from the young woman whose body she had taken as her own more than two and a half thousand years before.

She closed her eyes, took in a slow breath, feeling it fill the lungs of the host with dry heat. In the memory, the breeze was scented with olive and lemon tree and the faint, salt freshness of a distant sea. The grass had been soft and green beneath her bare feet, and gulls had wheeled and turned in the cloudless sky.

Hera felt struck by a sudden and unaccountable sense of loss. She opened her eyes and then, purely on a whim, slipped out of her sandals and began to walk barefoot across the dry plain towards her yacht. Other System Lords would probably have thought her actions strange, but Hera prided herself on being atypical among the Goa'uld, and whimsy had always pleased her.

Behind her, two of her Jaffa hoplites stepped out of the shade and began to follow at a discreet distance. Hera assumed one of them would have picked up her sandals, but she didn't look back to make sure. It was their place to do so. It was their pleasure.

Her yacht lay a hundred meters distant, its slender hull gleaming white in the blinding sun. Far to her right squatted the dark bulk of Anshar's royal barque, fashioned in the stylized shape of a winged bull with a human head, cast from what looked like black iron. To her left was the imperial barge of Lord Tsukiyomi, all green and gold and angles. The three vessels had set down equidistant from one another, and the Hall of Negotiation had been erected in a direct line with the primary weapons of all three.

When System Lords met on neutral ground, little would keep their excesses in check save the threat of mutually assured destruction.

Hera put a hand to her diadem, touched a control at her temple. "Eri?"

"My Lady. I'm sorry to interrupt you, but the Oracle asks for you."

"I thought as much. In which case, your presence will be required while I am gone. Have you been listening in?"

"Of course, just as you commanded. Shall I transport across now?"

"Let them wait a minute or two. Have some slaves bring them drink and sweetmeats, then go in and start where I left off." She thought of Ericaceae among the two System Lords and their Jaffa, and grimaced. "Disgusting, the pair of them, but don't let that affect your reactions."

"What path shall I take?"

"Only that which presents itself to you. Oh, one more thing, sister. It is time that Lord Anshar heard news from home."

"By your will. I shall lift the communications block immediately."

There was a faint chime as Ericaceae broke the connection. Already she would be hurrying from her hiding place to take Hera's seat at the table. The thought made her smile faintly.

The smile did not last long. The captain of her yacht was waiting for her at the embarkation ramp, head tipped forwards in defense.

She reached out to him, used a fingertip to lift his head. "The Oracle?"

"In the communications chamber."

That took the smile well and truly off Hera's lips. "I shall attend her. Thank you, Captain." She strode past him, quickly, so that he would not see the displeasure in her eyes.

Or the fear.

Hera made her way through the yacht to the communications vault, quickly and without acknowledging the hoplites who bowed as she passed them. Once she reached the heavy, armored hatch she pressed her open hand against the gold panel in its centre, and waited a moment for the ship's mechanisms to recognize her essence. It was a slightly infuriating pause, and Hera was not usually accustomed to waiting for anything, at least nothing so trivial as the opening of a door. But the vault was a secret place, tended only by her most trusted Jaffa, and she would rather force herself to wait like a common slave for the door to admit her than she would risk its security being compromised.

After a few seconds the door shivered, its powerful locking fields ebbing away, and it slid aside. Hera stepped through, into cool, softly chattering gloom.

The chamber was long, angular. The only light came from the instrumentation ranged around its walls; glowing icons and pulsing data panels, the constant scroll of hieroglyphs and the whirl of graphics. Along each of the two long walls sat several Jaffa operators, hunched over their control boards. They did not move as she entered, did not look up or pause in their work. Hera would have been extremely surprised if they had, given the amount of modification they had endured.

She padded past them, bare feet silent on the cold floor.

The Oracle stood at the far end of the chamber, outlined in the fluttering blue light of three huge data panels. She turned as Hera approached, and dropped to one knee, her head lowered, dark hair flowing down almost to the floor. "My Lady."

"Pythia." Hera stooped, took the woman's hand and raised her. The Oracle was taller than her, but she was used to that. Most people were. "You have been inhaling the vapors, I trust?"

"Of course, Lady." The Oracle smiled wryly. It was a private joke between them, playing on the superstition of the lesser slaves. In legend, oracles would enter a frenzy induced by *pneuma*, the foul miasmas from some mysterious seismic process, and in that state would utter prophesies. On occasion, it amused Hera to hint that such an act was still carried out, that on her throneworld there existed a chasm from which *pneuma* still issued. Only a fool would believe such a thing, she knew.

Hera was painfully aware that there was no shortage of fools among the Goa'uld.

Pythia's 'vapors' consisted of raw data, of tactical information gathered by the Jaffa in the communications chamber and others like it in starships and palaces across Hera's empire. The gift of prophesy stemmed from her phenomenal ability to collate and process that data, to compare it to past histories and present conditions, and from that sea of raw information draw forth prediction. Hera employed the services of many such Oracles throughout her empire, but Pythia was, and had been for a thousand years, the utmost among them. Her forecasts had a degree of accuracy that was unparalleled.

It was not her only valuable quality. Pythia was a superb tactician, a trusted advisor, a brutal warrior and a skilled lover. She was, perhaps, the closest thing Hera had to a friend. All the more amazing, then, that she carried no Goa'uld within her skull. The woman was entirely human, or at least whatever a human became after a thousand years fending off time in a healing sarcophagus.

Again, Hera knew that many Goa'uld would regard her as — at best — a fool for such an act, and at worst dangerously insane. It mattered not one iota to her what they thought. She had known true Goa'uld folly, more than once. Compared to that, her own habits warranted no mention at all.

"And so?"

Pythia held her gaze. "Ra's voice has been heard a second time."

"You have analyzed the message?"

"I have. The terminal failsafe has been activated."

Hera had expected nothing less. But still, the news hit her like a physical blow. "And the demon?"

"In flight, Lady."

"I see." Hera turned away. Her heart — the heart of her host — was pounding. "So we were right. Ra had that creature all along."

"It would appear so. Unless the messages have been part of an elaborate ruse. I am working to eliminate that possibility."

Hera nodded. "There is a chance. And I would welcome it, believe me. But Ra was as stupid as he was cruel — he could easily have kept that nightmare around for his own amusement. It would not surprise me in the least."

"If so, then the vessel would already have left Tau'ri. I have my sources looking out for hyperspace activity in that area."

"Assuming this is not a ruse, can the demon be tracked?"

"I believe so."

"Good. Pythia, if that thing is out there, I don't want you to take your eyes off it for a moment. Whatever resources you need, I will—" She stopped in mid-sentence. Her diadem had vibrated, silently.

"Eri? What news?"

"My Lady, there has been a development."

"Unexpected?"

"No."

So soon, Hera thought. "Very well. I shall return immediately. Keep Anshar in place until I signal."

She cut the connection. "Things are moving more quickly than I had anticipated, Oracle. I need to return to the discussions."

"Of course. In the meantime?"

"Order the third and seventh squadrons to rendezvous at Perleptis. The *Clythena* will join them as soon as we are done here. Squadrons four to six are to make their way to our border with Lord Anshar's domain, eight to eleven to the edge of Lord Tsukiyomi's. And Pythia?"

"Lady?"

"Contact the shipyard at Perleptis. Tell them to ready the Auger."

Pythia paled slightly. But she set her jaw, and nodded. "By your will."

"If there were any other way, sweet Pythia, I would not suggest it." Hera reached out, brushed a fingertip gently along the woman's jawline. "And if there is any possibility of ending this without its use, I will welcome it."

"You are wise, my Lady." The Oracle's voice was a whisper. "Wise and strong."

Hera forced a smile. "I know."

There was a transporter in the yacht, and another in the Hall of Negotiation. Hera could have used the device to sweep her instantly to her meeting with the Oracle, but that would have spoiled her walk. Besides, she had needed time to think.

There could be no delaying now. Hera retrieved her sandals from the hoplite who had been dutifully carrying them since she had left the Hall, transmitted a pre-arranged signal to Ericaceae, and then stepped into the transporter. A moment later, she was back in the Hall of Negotiation, and bronze rings were flying up from around her and into the ceiling.

Ericaceae was waiting for her in the transport chamber. "Lord Anshar has gathered his retinue. He says that he must return to his domains at once."

"I see. And there has been no mention of why."

"None."

"No surprise there. Well done, sister. Now go to the yacht and wait for me."

She paused at the door to the chamber, until Ericaceae had transported away, then stepped outside. There was a concealed route around to the Hall's main entrance, and by the time she had reached it, more of her hoplites had assembled there, under Pythia's orders. She motioned them to form up behind her, then hurried out after Anshar. "My Lord!"

He turned at her cry, the Jaffa flanking him dropping into a fluid combat stance. She saw their staff weapons snap open, but raised her hand to prevent her hoplites from activating their own.

Instead, she paced forwards until she was face to face with Anshar. Or face to chest, at any rate. "My Lord, please forgive this impertinence. I could not speak freely in front of Tsukiyomi."

"Neither could I." He smiled wanly, but past the beard his face was pale with fury and distress. "Lady Hera, I apologize again. There are… Matters I must attend to."

"Of course."

"Tsukiyomi's spies…" He turned his head and spat onto the dry ground. "Thank you for helping me root them out. Your insight into their identities was invaluable."

Hera spread her hands. "It was only right. Alliances should be built on trust, openness, not the foul treachery of fools like Tsukiyomi."

Anshar raised an eyebrow. "There will be an alliance, then?"

"When your duties at home are completed, we will conduct our own…" She tilted her head, just so, and looked up at him, the ghost of a smile at her lips. "Our own negotiations, my Lord."

His eyes glowed, subtly. "Hasten the day, Lady." He span on his heel. "*Jaffa! Kree!*"

She watched him stride away towards his barque. When he was within twenty paces of it, the great iron head at its prow began to fold downwards, as if the winged bull-centaur was bowing to him. Its mouth gaped, hinged apart, became a ramp up which Lord Anshar strode, his Jaffa marching alongside him in a glitter of scarlet and brass.

To her credit, Hera kept her face neutral and her words in check even while the barque was lifting off. Only when it was leaping away into the hot sky did she turn away and make her way back to the Hall of Negotiation.

Tsukiyomi was still seated, waiting for her. He stood as she opened the hatch and stepped through. "Lady Hera."

"My Lord." She tipped her head, the slightest bow of deference. "Please, allow me to apologize."

"For what?"

"Anshar's conduct."

Tsukiyomi dropped languidly back into his throne. "I expect nothing less from him. He is a brute and a boor."

"He is an idiot," Hera smiled.

"That too."

"How lucky that we are not." She leaned forwards, just a little, over the table. She had heard rumors of Tsukiyomi's preferences, but the involuntary dip of his eyes belied them. She pretended not to notice. "However, I also must apologize for my own conduct."

"I do not understand."

"Alliances should be based on trust and openness, do you not think?"

At the mention of the word, Tsukiyomi did a little leaning of his own. "I do, my Lady."

"I could not mention this in front of Anshar, you understand. He is still convinced your First Prime, Hashitara, was killed during the attack on his diplomatic convoy."

Tsukiyomi gaped. "I… He… Lady, he lives?"

"Barely. He was critically injured. His symbiote suffered great damage. We have been treating him as best we can, but even so he requires many more hours in a sarcophagus before he can be truly well."

"Where is he?" The words were a whisper.

"On my yacht. I will have his sarcophagus transported to your vessel immediately."

Tsukiyomi frowned. "Lady, the sarcophagus too? How shall I return it to you?"

"Consider it a gift. To cement our alliance. Our…" She held out her hand, palm up for him to kiss. "Our friendship."

When Tsukiyomi's ship was gone from the sky, Hera went to join Ericaceae at the yacht.

She walked, again. There would be a time for haste, when the Auger was ready and her flagship, the mighty *Clythena*, was ready to take her to it, and then on in search of the demon. But for now, it pleased her to take refuge in her host's memory again, in the feeling of dry grass under her bare feet.

"They are gone, then?" Ericaceae asked, as she approached. She was waiting at the base of the ramp.

Hera nodded. Behind her, mechanical clatters and whirrs echoed out across the plain, as the Hall of Negotiation began to fold itself away. "They are indeed."

"Do you think either will trouble you again?"

"I very much doubt it." In fact, Hera thought idly, Tsukiyomi probably wouldn't even make it home. While the sarcophagus he had taken so eagerly aboard his vessel did indeed house the broken body of Hashitara — broken by Hera's own Minotaurs, in fact — it also contained an extra addition of Pythia's devising. A pulse emitter, powerful enough to destabilize the frequency of his Ha'tak's hyperdrive. If he did not find it before trying to re-enter realspace, his entire vessel would detonate before it ever reached its window.

If he did find it, certain aspects of its design would leave him in no doubt that the device had been planted by Anshar.

And as for Lord Anshar himself, his chances of survival were slimmer than Tsukiyomi's. Hera had been most adept in helping the System Lord seek out the spies in his royal household, and little wonder — it was she who had put them there in the first place. Unfortunately for Anshar, they too carried a little something extra with them; a genetically-tailored disease, unrivalled in its virulence and the agonizing, incurable damage it would wreak on a Goa'uld symbiote. Of course, had Anshar not been so fond of inflicting pain himself, his household would have been spared the pestilence that was tearing it apart. The disease had been designed to remain inert and undetectable until such time that it was activated by extreme levels of stress hormone.

And Anshar's interrogators had caused the hapless spies a very great deal of stress indeed.

In the best case, both Anshar and Tsukiyomi would be dead very soon, and what was left of their clans and households would each blame the other. Even if both System Lords survived, they would still declare war on one another, a war which would leave both weakened and ripe for the harvest.

In either case — in every possible case — Hera would take their domains within the year.

Somehow, that should have made her feel better than it did. But right now, all she could think of was the demon, Ra's monstrous Ash Eater, loose among the stars.

Evidently, Ericaceae was thinking about the same thing. "Do you think he will be seeking it too?"

"Neheb-Kau? If he still lives, then yes. I cannot imagine that he would not."

"So you may be required to fight him."

Hera glanced sideways at her sister. As usual, it was like looking into a mirror. "Neheb-Kau is the least of our problems, Eri. You never saw the Ash Eater feeding. I did, and it haunts me to this day."

"I know."

Hera's eyes narrowed. "You do?"

"You talk in your sleep, remember?"

"Ah." She looked up, into the hot sky. The first shades of twilight were beginning to show at the far horizon. Days were long on this world, but they did not last forever. Nothing did. "Eri?"

"Yes, my Lady?"

"This is not going to have a happy ending, is it?"

There was as slight pause, and then: "The omens are against it."

The Hall of Negotiation had completed its collapse. It had been reduced from a sprawling complex of tents and pyramids into a flat slab of metal, waist-high, ready to be picked up by Hera's yacht and borne away. "Then we must face our destiny, sister. Unfettered, the Ash Eater could destroy everything we have worked for. I will not allow that."

"The fleet is ready, Lady Hera. They only await your will."

Hera turned to her sister, and smiled warmly. "Then let us go. Keeping them waiting would be terribly rude, don't you think?"

Chapter 9.

HIGH AND DRY

ONCE, *many years before the awakening of the Pit of Sorrows, when Samantha Carter was very small, she had travelled with her mother and father and brother Mark to the shores of a great lake.*

This was a rare treat, because Samantha's father was away so much, and because her mother was often busy. But some combination of circumstance had occurred which allowed the four of them to be together for several days, and so the decision was made that they should have a vacation.

The lake was beautiful. It was surrounded by trees, and beyond the trees were mountains, and beyond the mountains a very blue, very clear spring sky. There was a jetty stretching out over the lake's still surface from which Samantha's father hoped to fish, and on the shore was a little log cabin for the family to stay in.

Samantha had a room all to herself.

During the first night, while Samantha lay awake, looking up at the unfamiliar ceiling, the weather had turned bad. A thunderstorm had rolled down from the mountains, and begun battering the lake shore with driving rain and bright white flashes of lightning. The sound and the ferocity of it were terrifying, and Mark had run into their parents' room for comfort, but Samantha would not do that. Instead she huddled alone in her bed, shivering with fear, the quilt pulled up to block out the lightning and the deep angry bellows of thunder. To her small ears, it sounded as though the whole world were coming to pieces around her.

At some point the storm must have shouted her into submission, because she awoke to see light on her ceiling. And then her father had appeared next to her, one finger to his smiling lips.

Together, they had gone outside, Samantha's bare feet cold on wet ground, into a dream, a wonderland. Morning was bringing a mist up off the lake, lit gold by the low morning sun, so dense that she could not see the water's far side. The jetty stretched off into mystery, and the shore was utterly quiet. There wasn't a breath of wind, nor birdsong, nor even the lap of waves against the sand.

It was as if the world had been reborn during the night, torn apart in the storm's fury and remade into something new.

Something wonderful.

Carter sat up hard, out of the dark and into pale, golden light.

She was suffocating, her lungs burning from the inside, and there was something covering her mouth. She ripped it away and dragged in a breath, tasting a flat, powdery foulness in the air, and immediately found herself seized by a fit of ragged, agonized coughing. Carter doubled up, trying to control her breathing, but the itch and burning were too deep. All she could do, for a long time, was to sit and cough the pain from her lungs.

Eventually she managed to still the spasms, although there was an ugly warmth within her ribs that she could only hope would fade soon. She had a pounding headache, and her vision was blurry. When she wiped her eyes, her fingers came down streaked with pale gray.

There was a memory of darkness, of dreadful noises and brilliant flashes. She squinted around, trying to get her bearings, and as she did so a silent, pale figure appeared beside her.

She blinked tears away, and saw that it was Teal'c. He was covered in dust, and a piece of cloth covered the lower part of his face.

"Major Carter," he said. "You have been unconscious."

"How…" Speaking was like chewing glass. She took a steadying breath and tried again. "How long for?"

"Twenty-seven minutes."

"What? Oh, that's not good." She tried to get up, but the floor felt as though it were moving. That, along with the pain in her chest, was enough to keep her where she was. "Any longer than a few minutes probably means I've got a concussion."

"Then you should remain still."

"Yeah." For a moment, it sounded like a good idea. And then she looked around her, at a world remade.

She was still in the Pit of Sorrows, of course — that much had been obvious even through her soiled tears. The dark outer walls still tilted claustrophobically around her. Behind her, the doorway remained firmly sealed by its slab of golden metal, and the air was bitingly cold.

But there was a mist in the air, thick and choking, lit by the yellow glow from the wall panels.

No, she thought, memories falling away from her. This was no mist. The air was full of dust; the fine, ashy powder that was all that remained of human beings, once the black force from the pillar was done with them.

It was everywhere, clinging to the walls, drifting down from the shadowed ceiling. It was on her clothes, in her hair, coating her skin. It had been in her throat and her lungs.

Even Teal'c was painted with it. He had tied a strip of cloth tied over his nose and mouth to keep some of the stuff from his lungs; part of his jacket lining. He must have done the same to her, while she lay senseless.

Carter tried to get up again. The floor still tipped and shifted under her, making her fear, momentarily, for her senses. It didn't take long for her to realize that the feeling wasn't illusory. The Pit really *was* moving.

"Teal'c? What's happened?"

He took her arm and helped her upright. He had his staff weapon in his other hand and was steadying himself with it. "I believe the Pit of Sorrows is in flight," he said gravely. "There was a period of violent acceleration. It was during this time that you fell and lost consciousness."

"Flight?" Ra's second message came back to her in a rush. "Oh my God, he said 'Enjoy your trip.' That's what he meant… Teal'c, we've got to get out of here!"

"I agree. However, there appears to be no way to exit this structure. Even if there was, at the level of acceleration we experienced, we would have left the Earth's atmosphere many minutes ago."

It took a moment for the implication to sink in. When it did, Carter felt a cold swoop of terror surge up behind her ribs.

To be locked into the Pit of Sorrows while it lay beneath the desert was nightmare enough, but for the whole awful place to have dragged her and Teal'c up and into the icy vacuum of space… If the Jaffa was right, then the pair of them were entombed in the worst possible way.

And, she remembered, they were not alone.

"The pillar," she gasped. "Teal'c, is that thing still in there?"

"Our continued survival would suggest so," he replied. "I have also made regular checks on the pillar's integrity, and it appears to have survived the takeoff unscathed."

"I need to see it," she told him.

"I will assist you."

"No," she said, too quickly. Then she gave him a wan smile. "I've got it. I *think* I've got it…"

She paused before moving, though: the floor was slippery with powder, and her vision wasn't entirely clear. She took a few seconds to bat at her sleeve until most of the dust came up off it, and then used it to wipe her eyes. That helped a lot, bringing her cramped and frightening new world into a sharper focus. Perhaps a little too sharp, even. There was much around her that she would rather not have seen at all.

She pushed that thought away. Self-delusion was a luxury she could ill-afford — distressing though their predicament was, Carter knew that their only hope of escaping it was to face its horrors square-on.

Her gun was lying on the floor next to her. She crouched to pick it up, checked that its mechanisms had been undamaged by the acceleration and by the polluted air, then made her way carefully to the nearest corner. From there, through the drifting dust and between two inner walls, she could see the golden cylinder still squatting on its dais.

Her view of it was partly obscured by rubble. The giant statues had obviously not been built to withstand the Pit's acceleration, or the violent hammering and shaking that had preceded it. They stood now only as jagged, disembodied pairs of legs, and as a surreal jumble of broken body parts. Carter eased her way between a beaked head the size of her own torso and a huge, reaching arm, and then climbed up the littered steps towards the pillar.

Thankfully, it looked undamaged — either the tumbling pieces of the statues had all missed it, or it was built of very tough stuff indeed. The fluted cone at its top was still firmly locked together, reminding Carter subtly of the back of a classic Egyptian headdress, and below it three rings of translucent material set into the body of the cylinder glowed a steady, comforting blue.

Carter hadn't noticed those before. When she put her hand near them, she could feel warmth.

"That's weird," she muttered.

"You refer to the cylinder emitting heat?" Teal'c was standing at the base of the dais.

"Yeah. You know, I think it's taking heat from the inside and dumping it into the air. Like a refrigerator."

"Gregory Kemp claimed that the Ash Eater was attracted to heat."

She stepped back. Her proximity to the pillar was making her skin crawl. "Maybe freezing it keeps it quiet."

"Let us hope that it continues to do so."

"It'll be all over for us if it doesn't. Unless it's vulnerable to bullets, of course."

Teal'c looked momentarily uncomfortable. "I discovered the remnants of a firearm some distance from the doorway. It crumbled before I was able to ascertain if it had been fired."

Harlowe. "Given my luck today, I'm guessing yes." She climbed back down the dais steps, joining Teal'c at floor level. "But let's assume that the cylinder is going to keep the Ash Eater contained for the moment. That leaves our next problems as air supply, then water, then food."

"The air will become unbreathable in approximately twenty-five hours," Teal's replied. "Unless other factors are at work."

"So I guess that give us a day to get control of this thing and turn it around." She glanced about, trying to reacquaint herself with the Pit's strange layout. "Teal'c, this has to be a Goa'uld structure — do you have any idea what kind?"

"I do not." The Jaffa frowned. "There are similarities to a *teluy'iirac*, a structure for the storage of hazardous materials, but those similarities are…" He paused. "Tenuous."

"Still, it makes a kind of sense." She nodded at the cylinder. "That's pretty hazardous."

"Indeed. However, chemical storage facilities are not usually designed to fly."

"I think we can safely say that this place has gone through a serious refit." She moved past him, out between two of the inner walls, until she found herself at the far side of the Pit from the doorway.

Anna Andersson's remains were gone. Carter had expected as much, but the thought of the woman's remains still floating in the air around her was still upsetting in the extreme.

She had once heard that a cremated body weighed roughly as much as a new-born baby, a piece of cosmic symmetry that Carter had found quite pleasing at the time. It certainly wasn't as pleasing now, not with what it was suggesting to her about the number of people who might have slid down that terrifying shaft before her.

More than would have fallen in by accident, that was certain.

She forced herself to concentrate. "Okay. The writing on that wall near the door mentions Ra, and his voice is recorded here somewhere. So this whole structure must have been built before he lost control of Earth, yes?"

Teal'c nodded. "And has been abandoned since that time."

"Which was…" She shrugged. "Well, even Daniel's a little hazy on precisely when, but let's just say a really long time ago. So from that we can say pretty certainly that no-one's controlling the Pit's flight in real-time. It must be a pre-programmed course."

"Then we —" The Jaffa stopped speaking. He tilted his head upwards. "Major Carter, do you feel that?"

She was about to tell him no, she couldn't feel anything, when she became aware of what he had noticed before her. It was subtle at first, but rising rapidly: a thin, high-frequency vibration coming up through the soles of her boots.

"What is that?" she breathed. "Are we stopping?"

"No. We are not."

The Pit lurched, violently.

Carter's vision burred for a moment, and she almost fell. The lurch was awful; not a change in direction, but a motionless whirl, a surge of nausea and disorientation. She had felt it before, although filtered and dampened until it was barely noticeable.

This, though, was raw. And unmistakable.

The Pit of Sorrows had just jumped into hyperspace.

Over the next few hours, Carter became aware of two things. Firstly, the air around her was not becoming noticeably stale, which made her start to ration her water supply fiercely — if some mechanism within the Pit was refreshing the oxygen and keeping the carbon dioxide in check, then thirst was now her most immediate danger.

And secondly, the Pit of Sorrows was starting to get warm.

At first, she had thought that this was merely a product of the work she was doing. Teal'c had drawn on his memories of the storage facility he had called a *teluy'iirac*, and had located the position of a panel which should have allowed them access to some of the facility's primary systems. But just getting at the panel had been far from easy: the access cavity was concealed beneath a heavy slab of the Pit's dark stone cladding. And even when Teal'c had shattered that away with massive blows from the club-end of his staff, the panel itself was sealed down with a hard, resinous epoxy. It had taken her and Teal'c two hours of painful labor to get the thing up, chipping at the stuff with their combat knives until they had removed enough to get their fingers underneath a panel edge and drag it free.

Just as she had hoped, Carter found a bank of control crystals beneath the panel. She sat down to map out their functions while Teal'c went hunting for another panel to smash open. There should, according to his recollections, be several.

Carter had started to get warm then, or at least to realize that the heat she felt was not simply due to exertion. The air in the Pit was definitely less cold.

She hesitated, then stripped off her jacket and laid it on the floor next to her. It raised a small cloud of dust as she set it down, but that fell slowly to settle back onto the white fabric and the black stone. Most of the ash in the air had settled, now.

The access cavity was about a meter across, a strange six-sided shape, like a distorted coffin. Inside, a block of dark metal housed several control crystals, their sockets labeled with Goa'uld hieroglyphs, and alongside that was a bundle of thick conduits.

Below these was a floor of metal meshwork. Carter could just see a deep space beneath, and a distant flutter of blue-white light.

"The hyperdrive?" she wondered aloud.

Teal'c poked his head around a corner. "Major Carter, did you speak?"

"Just thinking out loud," she assured him. "There's something bright down here that might be the hyperdrive. We could try cutting its power, if we could isolate it from the rest of the systems."

"That might not be wise," Teal'c replied. "Cutting power to an active hyperdrive can have unforeseen effects, even in the most well-maintained of vessels."

"That's true." Carter admitted. She had already caused havoc by letting a decayed crystal break in her hand. There was no telling what might happen if the hyperdrive control suffered a similar malfunction. At best, the Pit of Sorrows could simply break into realspace in an unknown, and possibly interstellar, location. At worst, they could return to the universe as a swiftly moving cloud of high-energy particles.

Perhaps she should continue her hunt for the navigation system, and leave the drive running unhindered for now.

There was a solid impact from behind the wall, followed quickly by several more, and then the unmistakable cracking of stone.

Carter raised her head. "Have you found another panel?"

"I have." The Jaffa sounded almost disappointed. "It is sealed, much like the first. I shall attempt to free it."

"Hold on, I'll help you."

"It would be better if our efforts were divided, Major Carter."

"You're sure?"

There was a few moments of silence, and then her answer came; the sound of a knife-point chipping at thick, glassy resin.

Carter did not know how long it took Teal'c to free the second panel. She had been lost in the complexities of the system she was working on and, amazingly, lost all track of time.

It had been careful work. Several of the crystals displayed the same surface crazing as the one Carter had crushed in the shaft, so she made sure that she didn't so much as brush those. It was an effect she had not seen before, even in the most ancient of Goa'uld technologies, and she was beginning to wonder whether some other corruption had been at work on the Pit's interior systems. In fact, some of the crystals looked so decayed that Carter was amazed they worked at all. Presumably there was a lot of redundancy built into the structure.

The systems she was able to access proved to be of little use. Had Carter wished to switch off the life support, compromise power to the pillar or turn the lights off, there was no doubt she could have done it from where she was sitting. But apart from that, there was nothing. The navigational systems she needed must have been located elsewhere.

She arrived at that depressing conclusion not long before Teal'c got the second panel up. She had been sitting back and trying to stretch the ache from her shoulders when there was a high metallic noise from behind the wall, a squeal of overstressed paneling that ended in a violent impact. Carter scrambled up, and scampered around the corner. Teal'c? Are you okay?"

"I am uninjured." He was standing with a distorted hexagon of sheet metal still in one hand. He hurled it aside. "The panel proved less resilient than the resin."

"I can see that…" Carter could see a ragged strip of gleaming silver along one edge of the cavity Teal'c had exposed — he had literally ripped a chunk of the panel off. But a moment later all her attention was on the cavity itself.

She dropped to her haunches in front of what he had found. "My God," she whispered.

Where the previous cavity had been a shallow depression, this was a cylindrical hole in the Pit's structure, long and wide enough to accommodate a large man. It was angled downwards and towards the centre of the structure, and set down the length of it were a series of metal rings, each a fat, complicated torus of gold and wound cable and solid-looking blocks of silvery mineral. Long probes speared from the inner edges of the rings, while arm-thick conduits circled the outer wall, dividing and dividing again to fill the cavity with a sprawl of wiring and control crystals.

The crystals were all unlit, quiescent, but small tubes in the walls of the cavity emitted a pulsing golden glow, and Carter could feel a dry heat coming off it, a flat electrical warmth that spoke of a recent and massive release of energy.

It was an unearthly contraption, complex and unfathomable and oddly disturbing.

"Teal'c, have you seen anything like this before?"

"I have not." The Jaffa leaned past her to study it. "Could it be part of the hyperdrive?"

"I don't think so." Goa'uld propulsion technology had been one of Carter's research projects for a while now, and this tube full of glass and metal looked nothing like the devices she had so far been able to study.

Still, even though the cavity's contents were puzzling, there was something about its layout that she almost recognized. Carter looked again, trying to see past the complexity of the thing, to ignore the exposed conduits and overlaid paneling, the jagged, fang-like crystals arranged in their rings like some kind of arcane instrument of torture…

"Hold on," she said suddenly, and not entirely to Teal'c. "Those rings... They've each got seven segments."

"They are reminiscent of the Chappa'ai."

"Seven probes on each ring, seven functional chevrons around the Stargate... Teal'c, I think this is where Ra's message came from."

"This is like no communications device I have seen."

"I know, but the message came through the gate. I thought that another gate must have been used to dial through to us, but what if this did it?" She pointed into the cavity. "What if one end of the wormhole is formed here?"

Teal'c shook his head. "I cannot see how a device this small could create a functional wormhole."

"Oh, I know the rings aren't nearly big enough to form a proper event horizon, and the probes inside them would be destroyed if they did. But I've been working on a theory that it might be possible to create a one-dimensional wormhole with far less energy than it takes to power a Stargate."

He frowned. "I do not understand."

"Well, the Stargate creates a wormhole that is effectively two-dimensional — it has height and width, so we can walk through it, but no measurable length. It's like a flat sheet, although each side of the sheet can be separated by light-years."

Teal'c tipped his head slightly. "Of course."

Carter got to her feet. "But a one-dimension wormhole would have... Well, looking at this set-up, I'd say just *length*. It would be like a hair running down the centre of the cavity."

"Nothing could pass into such a wormhole." The Jaffa narrowed his eyes, deep in thought. "Except energy."

"That's right — there would be no mechanism for translating objects into the high-energy signature that traverses our gates. But you *could* send a signal through it." She ran a hand back through her hair, trying not to notice how dusty her fingers were when she brought them down. "Like I said, it's only a theory, and working out how the wormhole can be one-dimension here and still cause a gate to form a two-dimensional event horizon at the other end makes my head hurt."

Teal'c leaned back down to the cavity. "Major Carter," he said quietly, not taking his eyes from the softly glowing machinery within. "If this device was used to send the voice of Ra to Stargate Command, could we not send our own message?"

"If we could isolate the control matrix, I don't see why not. It must already be tuned to our gate… But wait, that's the Antarctica gate. Why would it send to that?"

"Perhaps we must also consider the number of rings in this cavity."

She looked up at him. "How so?"

"If the wormhole extends through all rings at once, the messages might have been sent to multiple Stargates."

She stared. "Is that even possible?"

"I do not know. But we must take great care, Major Carter. The voice of Ra might have been heard on more worlds than Earth."

There were no other panels.

Teal'c searched for a long time, while Carter lay with her head and shoulders inside the cylindrical cavity, trying to find the part of the communications system that contained Ra's recorded voice. She could hear him battering at the stone flooring with his staff, shattering the floor wherever his memory of the storage facility's design told him he should find access, but each time he broke through the cladding, only bare, seamless metal was revealed.

Eventually, he gave up and went back to help Carter.

As he approached, she extricated herself and sat up, her back against the wall next to the opening. Her head was pounding, worse than ever, and her throat was parched, her lips cracked and caked with dust. She was exhausted, aching all over. She refused to look at her watch, but she knew the pair of them must have been in the Pit of Sorrows for many hours.

Her water was gone. The last drops had dribbled from her canteen long before.

"I can't find it," she said eventually. The sound of her own voice frightened her. It sounded whispery and fragile, as though she were already becoming dust, like the Ash Eater's victims. "There's a recording matrix in here somewhere, but I can't isolate it."

"I too can only report failure." Teal'c sat down in front of her, cross-legged. He looked quite calm, but the dust on his skin made him seem ghostly. He took the canteen from his belt and offered it to Carter. She shook her head at first, but his hand didn't move. She knew it wouldn't until she drank, so she took it from him.

Half full. She sipped, just a little, and handed it back. "Even if we could send a message, they wouldn't know where it was coming from."

"Perhaps it would be heard by our allies."

"Perhaps." Carter knew the chances of that were microscopic. "I was hoping we could get to the navigation system, but I think that's down in the drive itself. We can't reach it."

"This structure was not designed to be easily compromised."

She nodded. "We just triggered a five-thousand year old failsafe. No-one else heard that message, Teal'c. Nobody knows where we are or where we're going. Everyone that did is dead."

He must have heard the ragged edges of despair in her voice. "Major Carter, you are exhausted."

She couldn't help but smile. "You think?"

"Perhaps you should sleep."

Carter blinked at him. "You're kidding."

"I am not." He smiled back at her, gently, his dust-pale lips curved almost imperceptibly. "I can survive on very little water. You will require less while asleep. Once you are rested, we can continue searching for a solution to our predicament."

"Sleep," she breathed. She shut her eyes.

It was tempting, to give herself over to oblivion. She was ferociously tired, her body quaking with fatigue, and the thirst was awful. Had she not taken in so much of the dust she would not be so dehydrated, she was sure, but everything about the Pit was conspiring to make her feel as bad as possible. Teal'c too, she guessed, although he would never show it.

If she rested for an hour, maybe two, perhaps she would wake feeling better. More alert. The correct combination of crystals would become clear to her, once she had slept.

She was fooling herself, of course.

If she slept now, she would never wake.

Carter opened her eyes. "I can't. I'm sorry, Teal'c, but I can't stop. Not now."

"I do not believe you will be able to remain functional for long."

"Yeah?" It sounded like a challenge. She grinned, even though it hurt her lips to do so. "Bet you twenty I last longer than you do."

"Fifty would be a greater incentive."

At the words, her heart surged within her. She knew that he had been doing what was needed to spur her on. He had shown her the alternative, the easy way, knowing she would never take it.

Only someone who knew her as well, as deeply as he did would have ever taken such a risk.

"You're on," Carter smiled. And she clambered back into the cavity again, disgusted with herself for even considering giving up. *You can sleep when you're dead, Sam.*

She would go on, and work on getting them both home, until there was not a breath left in her.

Finally, after she and Teal'c had been inside the Pit of Sorrows for almost twenty hours, Carter found the voice of Ra.

She lifted it carefully from its socket, mindful of the breakage that had dropped her into the Pit in the first place, and held it up. It was a faceted, yellow-green crystal no bigger than her index finger. "What do you think?"

Teal'c leaned close to study what she had found. "That is a data storage crystal," he agreed. "Vocal recordings are commonly held in such devices."

"That's what I was hoping." She set the crystal down, very carefully, onto her jacket, and settled back onto her heels. She had been kneeling next to the cavity for so long her legs felt like lead pipes, heavy and utterly without feeling. "It was in one of the conduit junctions. I'm guessing Ra would have used a separate device to record his messages — somehow I can't see him with his head inside here."

"It does not seem likely. Can you modify what we have to record a transmission of our own?"

"I think so. It looks like there's a simple loop-store function in the other cavity, for recording power spikes. I should be able to modify that. At the very least, we can get Morse code out of it."

Teal'c handed her the canteen. She sipped a little of the flat, warm water in celebration, feeling her throat cracking as she swallowed. She ignored it.

"We should begin," he said, taking the canteen back. "I grow weary of this structure."

"Oh, I don't know. I was just starting to find myself." She started to rise, putting a hand flat on the floor to push herself up. She didn't trust her numb legs to provide much support.

As she touched the cold floor, the hyperdrive shut down.

There was no warning. The vibration of the drive simply faded, died. Carter felt it through the bones of her wrist, her knees and her backside, and a moment later there was an awful, sickening twist of sensation that almost made her cry out. She clenched her teeth over a sudden rush of nausea.

They were back in realspace.

Carter hauled herself upright. Whatever had been simulating gravity during the journey was still functioning, but there was no other sensation of movement. "Floor's steady," she gasped. "We're not altering vector."

"The Pit is coasting in space," Teal'c replied.

"This could either be very good, or very bad." The cold numbness in her legs was turning into a buzzing sting as the circulation returned. "If we stay in open space, it could make us easier to find. But if there's a gravity well out there…"

"Then our wager could be void."

"You don't get out of paying that easily." She picked up the crystal, and started to walk towards the first access cavity.

Something brushed the outside of the Pit.

Carter felt the impact of it, and then a subtle change of direction. She froze. An object had struck the Pit's exterior, hard enough to feel through all the metal and the stone, hard enough to set the place rotating slowly.

Teal'c was on his feet too. He reached down and retrieved his staff weapon. Carter slipped the crystal into her pocket and staggered over to the communications cavity, where she had left her MP-5. She picked it up. It felt very heavy.

"What do you think?" she hissed.

"Perhaps nothing. Some piece of debris. A small asteroid."

"Then why are we holding guns?"

"In case I am wrong."

There was another impact, solid this time. The Pit shivered. There was a scraping sound, a series of clatters. Carter looked up as the sounds seemed to move above her, across the ceiling. "That's no asteroid," she breathed.

More sounds, then a heavy jolting that almost had Carter off her feet. She steadied herself against the wall, grabbing at the corner as an even more violent jolt shook the Pit.

There were a few seconds when the floor seemed to see-saw under her, then a final, massive impact, followed by a stillness so complete and so sudden that Carter could only think of it as being *grabbed*, and held still.

All the lights went out.

She gasped. The Pit had become completely dark in an instant. "Teal'c?"

"I am here, Major Carter."

"Something's caught us. A ship, or something... We're being held, aren't we?"

"Indeed."

A rush of unreasoning relief went through her. She knew, on a purely intellectual level, that it was a foolish thing to feel, that the chances of the Pit encountering a friendly starship were vanishingly small. But on a far baser level, she needed to be free of the place.

One way or another, Carter knew she was going to leave the Pit of Sorrows soon. And she could not view that prospect with anything but joy.

There was a grinding noise, heavy and metallic, and a sliver of light knifed towards her. The door was opening.

As soon as Carter saw it start to move she turned and stumbled away, around the nearest inner wall. Teal'c darted past, taking up position just behind her.

She raised the gun, blinking away the blurriness in her vision as she aimed down the barrel, hunching around the corner to watch the doorway with one eye. The slab was coming back down, quite quickly, and letting in a swiftly expanding band of light. To Carter's eyes, adapted to the dim golden glow of the Pit's internal lighting, it seemed intolerably bright.

The door slid entirely away, and a figure stepped from the light.

Glare distorted it, robbed it of mass and outline. For a second it seemed impossibly thin, skeletal, and Carter wondered unbelievingly if they had been discovered by the Asgard. But the hope was short-lived — as the figure moved into the Pit, it bulked out, became tall and strong and solid.

It was holding a staff weapon. Carter realized she was aiming her gun at a fully armored Jaffa.

The man walked carefully into the Pit of Sorrows, his staff held at high port. The mechanical head atop his shoulder armor swiveled left and right: it was strange, oddly bifurcated, two narrow serpent heads fixed side by side. Four eyes glowed a dull red into the Pit's gloom.

"Neheb-Kau," Teal'c breathed. "It cannot be…"

The serpent-headed Jaffa halted, and then barked a command. Behind him, two more warriors entered to join him, their double-helms turning warily.

Then more men came. These were not warriors — they wore robes, not armor, and their shaved heads were bare. Each carried a device, a strange block of golden metal the length of a man's arm, and studded with pipes and handles.

Technicians, thought Carter, as the men stopped in a ragged huddle, looking cowed and nervous. As she waited, the lead Jaffa pointed towards the centre of the Pit, and snarled out another order. The technicians started to move forwards.

Three of them went straight for the nearest corner. The last of them must have decided to take a different route, around the far side of the wall, because he almost walked right into Carter before he saw her.

Their eyes met. "Hi," she said, helplessly.

The man shrieked, a thin, high scream of pure terror.

She watched as he scrambled back, the golden machine tumbling heavily from his hands, and then the interior of the Pit erupted into a cacophony of yells and bellows. The technicians were scattering, the warriors barking out panicked commands. Carter ducked slightly out from the wall to see what was happening and a staff-blast ripped past her, scaldingly close. The lead Jaffa had fired, brutally fast — if his aim had been better in the darkness the plasma bolt would have carbonized her skull.

Instead it detonated against the wall behind her, throwing her forwards. Teal'c stepped out over her, firing his own staff, and Carter got the MP-5 up one-handed and loosed off a clattering stream of bullets. She wasn't exactly aiming, but the bullets ripped into the wall next to the lead warrior, peppering him with jagged shards of stone, and his next shot went wildly into the ceiling.

Molten stone rained down, hissing in the dust.

All three warriors were firing now, their blasts howling out into the Pit. Teal'c fired again, striking one of the snake-headed men full in the chest, the blast tearing through his armor. He fired as he fell, and the staff loosed its energies at a wild angle.

The bolt sizzled through the Pit and screamed off the golden cylinder.

Carter saw the impact, the sudden ripple of energy that coursed over its surface, and then, in utter horror, watched the illuminated strips start to flicker. If the container failed…

She threw her gun down and dropped to her knees. "We surrender!" she yelled.

Teal'c was staring at her. "Major Carter!"

"The cylinder," she hissed. "If it gets hit again we're all dust!"

He looked back at the pillar, his jaw set hard, then back at the Jaffa ahead of him. He lowered his staff. "*Hol mel!*"

The firing stopped.

Carter looked up, towards the doorway. The lead Jaffa was stalking towards her, raising a hand to his neck armor as he did so. She saw the double snake head split, split again, separate into a jigsaw of metal leaves that folded and compacted and slotted away into nothing.

Beneath them, the man's face was dark and lined. A golden symbol gleamed at his forehead, a curling Y. His staff weapon, open and livid with golden energy, was held steadily at her face. "*Aray kree,*" he snarled.

"We are required to remain still," Teal'c translated. Carter didn't tell him that she had worked that part out for herself.

"Be silent!" The other Jaffa snapped, switching to English. "Identify yourselves."

"I will speak only to your master," Teal'c replied.

"You will speak to me or die!"

"You are the First Prime of Neheb-Kau." Teal'c's voice was utterly calm "I also am First Prime. I will speak to your master, or not at all."

The other man glared, then barked out a command. The other warrior, the one still on his feet, ran forwards. He snatched up Carter's MP-5 and Teal'c's staff, while holding his own weapon to cover them. "Up," he growled.

Carter got to her feet. The Jaffa moved to one side, motioning her past him. She took a breath, looked out into the light, and saw more snake-headed warriors peering in at her. "We've drawn a crowd," she said quietly.

The warrior prodded her, not as hard as he probably could have done. Carter sighed and started walking.

As she reached the door, she glanced back. The four technicians were at the cylinder, surrounding it, plugging their golden machines into its base, and just as she was shoved out of the Pit by the warrior behind her, she saw them lift it free of the dais.

The machines had been built to fit the cylinder, she realized. They had been made for it.

Whoever Neheb-Kau might be, he already knew about the Ash Eater.

Chapter 10.

BLACK BURNING HEART

AFTER HIS ENCOUNTER in the Pit of Sorrows, Kafra needed time to think.

His orders had been to report back to his master as soon as the Casket had been secured. Kafra was First Prime to Neheb-Kau, his most trusted Jaffa and second in command only to the God himself, and as such he would not even consider actually disobeying the order. He had been loyal to Neheb-Kau for seventy years, through the worst of times.

He would not, *could* not fail his God.

After all, if he did not have his loyalty, what else was there left to him?

But the thought of facing Neheb-Kau now, so soon after the firefight, was like a shard of ice in his heart. And so, instead of going directly to the royal decks as he had planned, he walked out into the glider bay to watch the removal of the Casket, telling himself that it was necessary and right to make sure such a dangerous artifact did not suffer any accident on its way to the vaults. When that job was done, he would make his way to a transporter on one of the garrison levels, and centre himself as he walked. To be at his best for his master.

It was a lie, and he knew it. A procrastination of the worst order. But it was also a vital survival tactic, and one that had already served him well, on the days when Neheb-Kau's rages became too much to bear, when the God's internal darkness had spread to consume those around him.

There had been many of those, in the past seven decades. Too many to count.

Besides, the God was in his coffin. Kafra had a little time yet.

The glider bay had been modified to accommodate the Pit of Sorrows. It was far from the only change Neheb-Kau had made to his throneship over the centuries. In fact, Kafra wondered at times if there was anything left of the original vessel at all.

A great claw had been installed, fixed to the end of a thick, hinged arm that had reached obscenely out of the Ha'tak's belly to snatch the Pit from space. Kafra had overseen the operation himself, following Neheb-Kau's instructions to the letter. As usual in these things, the God's calculations were flawless, and the Pit had emerged from hyperspace exactly when and where he had said it would. Kafra had been able to use the arm to reach out and grab it from the blackness as easily as taking fruit from a tree.

It hung, now, in the golden grip of the metal claw: less like a fruit and more like an angular black tumor, dangling high in the open air between the glider racks. A narrow, railed bridge stretched out to it, over which the prisoners had been marched several minutes before. Now, Kafra stood on one of the surrounding gantries, death gliders hunched over his head like roosting birds, and watched as the Casket of the Ash Eater was carried, with infinite and terrified care, by the four *ch'epta*, the lower technicians.

The prisoners would be in a ring dungeon by now, if they were still alive. Kafra had left them in the care of Shenet, one of the warriors who had accompanied him into the pit with the ch'epta. The man who had been shot was Arekhat, a close friend of Shenet. Kafra knew that the two were in fact lovers, which had not concerned him in the past: however, if Shenet was stricken with grief over Arekhat, he might disobey his orders to keep the intruders alive.

Kafra rubbed his lacerated right arm thoughtfully, and wondered how concerned he should be about that. The thought of losing Arekhat, though, was of note. The man was not expected to survive his injuries, and there were few Jaffa aboard the throneship that were as skilled and reliable. Neheb-Kau's domains were small, and far from those of the other System Lords. There had been no fresh blood in his armies for centuries.

If Arekhat died, his loss would be felt by more than just Shenet.

Once the Casket was safely off the bridge, Kafra waited where he was for a time, watching technicians swarming over the Pit. It was said that most System Lords kept far fewer ch'epta in their retinues: maybe a handful of *ka'epta*, the senior engineers, each with their own small staff. But Neheb-Kau was not like most System Lords. His priorities, Kafra had learned, were very different to others of his kind.

Eventually, he knew he could delay no longer, and began to make his way out of the glider bay. Explaining the presence of the two prisoners to Neheb-Kau was going to make for an interesting discourse, he thought sourly, as he walked the long gantries. And more to the point, who were they?

The human woman was a small, pale thing, of little consequence. Or would have been, had she not been wielding some kind of primitive projectile thrower. Primitive, he thought ruefully, but potentially lethal: it had shattered the wall next to him with quite astounding force, each of the dozen or so impacts sending glassy shrapnel into his arm and shoulder. His armor had stopped most of it, but the suit was not in the best of repair, and some pieces of stone had made it through. He had heard Neheb-Kau talk of rogue human worlds, technologically advanced planets that could possibly even pose a threat to the rule of the Goa'uld, but he had passed them off as more of the God's ranting fantasies. Could the woman have been from such a place?

And of the Jaffa, Kafra could fathom even less. He wore the mark of the First Prime of Apophis, but what could that mean? Apophis and Neheb-Kau had never fought directly, it was true, but the God had been outside the territory of any other Goa'uld for so long that it was impossible to know what Apophis might be planning.

Most disturbing of all, though, was how the Jaffa and the Tau'ri seemed to know each other, and well. Was she a plaything of his, maybe? Some kind of concubine?

Kafra doubted it, but he had heard of stranger things.

Still, what concerned him most greatly was the Ash Eater. If everything he had heard about the monster was true, Neheb-Kau had brought a force of untold destructive power onto the throne-ship. Obviously, he thought he could control it, but Kafra doubted that very much indeed.

There were times when Neheb-Kau couldn't even control himself.

Once Kafra found the nearest transporter platform, he keyed in the location cartouche for Neheb-Kau's chambers with his wrist console, and stepped into the circle.

He felt a moment's concern as the stone rings hovered down around him. A transporter had malfunctioned only a few weeks before, one of the continuous series of system errors that plagued the throneship, and had explosively dismembered one of his Jaffa when he had tried to use it. Much of the man had since been located, although there were some parts that Kafra believed would never be found. After all, the throneship was a big vessel. They could have ended up anywhere.

There was always the possibility that the malfunction could occur again, although Kafra couldn't bring himself to exactly fear such a demise. After so long in the service of Neheb-Kau, self-preservation was no longer his primary instinct.

No such event occurred. The rings functioned perfectly, sweeping him from the lower levels of the ship to the God's most secure deck.

As the light of reintegration faded, Kafra stepped off the platform and into the Colonnade, the long, pillared hallway that lead to Neheb-Kau's throne room. He began to make his way along it, his pace measured. The Colonnade was lined with Royal Guard, and each dropped to one knee as Kafra passed them, in perfect sequence, helmed heads lowered in supplication. Only when he reached the great doors at the end did he hear them start to rise again.

He swept his hand across a control, and waited while the doors swung inwards. He had been half-expecting the God to be there already, waiting for him, but he saw no-one. Kafra closed the doors behind him, then marched quickly across the throne room towards the revival chamber. Thankfully, the great viewport that backed the room was sealed, protecting him from the desolate sight that lay beyond. It would do nothing for his state of mind, and he needed his focus.

Now, perhaps, more than ever.

Two more gold-clad Jaffa were at the door to the revival chamber, and they too dropped at Kafra's approach. He acknowledged them with a nod, then paused, and went in.

The chamber was long, but narrow. The only light came from burning lanterns set into the walls, so that the corners of the place were lost to fluttering shadow. Kafra slowed his pace, letting his eyes adjust to the gloom.

When he neared the chamber's far end he could see that the golden bulk of the sarcophagus was closed. Neheb-Kau was still within, dreaming his strange and terrible dreams.

There were two other occupants in the chamber: human slaves, robed in gold and silk, their heads shaved but for a single long trail of hair down their backs. They stood side by side, behind an ornate throne, the only other object in the chamber. Neither of them acknowledged Kafra as he walked in, but he hadn't expected them to. It was entirely possible they didn't even know he was there, since their eyes had been put out long ago. It was a requirement of their profession.

Kafra had never heard them speak. He wasn't sure he wanted to know why not.

At least Djetec, the God's hawk-faced *Tjaty*, was not in evidence. Kafra had lost count of the times he had been summoned to the revival chamber, only to find Djetec whispering some poison into the Neheb-Kau's ear. It was a matter of debate which of the two was the most actively dangerous — Neheb-Kau, with his rages and his black despair and his terrible thirst for knowledge, or his vizier, whose ambitions could only be guessed at. Kafra had his own theories on the matter, although to voice them, even in private, was to invite death. Through Djetec, the God heard all.

Kafra walked up to his position in front of the sarcophagus, rested the club end of his staff on the smooth dark floor, and waited.

Long minutes passed. Kafra did not move.

Finally, the sarcophagus began to open. Its cover hinged upwards, split, spread slowly like great wings. The flanks moved apart, and light spilled from within.

Something rose from the light, fumbled for the edge of the sarcophagus, and gripped it hesitantly. Something which, once, had been a hand.

Kafra dropped to one knee and bowed his head while Neheb-Kau rose from his healing rest.

He didn't look up as the God clambered out, but he caught a glimpse of the hem of his robes trail past him. Still, he waited.

After a time, his God spoke.

His voice was thin, breathy, like an excited child. "Ah, Kafra. My beloved First Prime. I was hoping you would be here when I awoke."

"As you commanded me."

"Indeed. And what news do you bring me?"

Kafra kept his head down. Neheb-Kau was not masked. "My Lord, the Pit of Sorrows was as you foresaw. The Casket is intact, and has been taken to its place in the Vault."

For a time, silence. Then a long, satisfied sigh.

"It begins," whispered Neheb-Kau, his high voice echoing around the chamber. "Oh, Kafra, do you know how long I have waited for this day?"

"I do not," Kafra lied.

"Many lifetimes, my friend. Many, many lifetimes."

There was a dry rustle of robes as the God sat down on his throne. Behind him, the blind slaves moved. Kafra could hear the chime of their jewelry; the bands at their wrists and necks, the rings through their empty eyelids. They were lifting Neheb-Kau's golden pectoral onto his chest, the holy armor onto his shoulders, placing his scepter in what was left of his hands.

Better they were blind, Kafra thought. He could not pity them. The thought betrayed his body. Despite himself he looked up, and saw the face of his God. He dropped his gaze, quickly, but not quickly enough. Neheb-Kau had seen the reaction.

He had torn the eyes from Jaffa who had done the same in the past, but his mood seemed too good for such excesses today. Instead, he gave a dry chuckle. "Is my appearance really so upsetting, old friend?"

"I… I fear for your wellbeing, my Lord." Kafra forced his gaze up again. "Your host is failing again. The sarcophagus no longer helps. Please, choose another, and swiftly."

"Kafra, my loyal First Prime, I have had host after host fall away from me. It is the natural order of things." Neheb-Kau touched a control on his pectoral. His helm rose like a swarm of blades from the armor at his back, folding to enclose his peeling head in strips of gold and bright lapis lazuli. His mask, glittering and bearded, came up in segments, joining seamlessly to complete his encasement.

The eyes glowed white-gold, just for a moment, as the God tested his power. "I know I must choose a new host soon, but not today. We have a guest, one who demands obeisance."

Kafra cleared his throat. "On that matter, my Lord…"

The mask tilted towards him. "Yes?"

The word was a warning.

"When we opened the Pit of Sorrows, there were others within."

"Others."

"Yes, my lord."

"Do you mock me, Kafra?"

He was close to death. He could feel it in the air between them. It was like seeing water, cold clear water, and suddenly finding himself desperately thirsty.

No. He could not drink, no matter how much he craved. He had a holy duty.

"Never, my Lord. But I speak the truth — there were two survivors within the Pit. They must have been trapped there when the terminal failsafe was activated."

"Survivors!" Neheb-Kau rose from the throne, his voice liquid with excitement. "These others were *alive?*"

"Alive, and armed. They attacked as we entered. My Jaffa subdued them."

"Who? Who were these survivors? Tell me quickly!"

"One is a Jaffa — he bears the symbol of the First Prime of Apophis. The other is a human woman. She bore a strange weapon."

"Apophis, you say? *Really?*" The God raised a ravaged hand to stroke the metal beard of his mask, an affectation that spoke of intense thought. "Now why would that cretin send me his First Prime, hm? As an assassin? A gift? An emissary, perhaps…"

"Give me the order, and I shall cut the answers from him."

"Perhaps later. For now, we must consider the fact that this First Prime survived many hours in the Pit, apparently unharmed. I believe a proper study of him could be enlightening." The mask tilted upwards slightly, as though the God were listening to something only he could hear. "Inform Pa'Nakht that his services will be required."

A cold weight grew inside Kafra. Pa'Nakht was the ka'epta of surgeries, chief of medics aboard the throneship; a technician of prodigious skill and vast experience in the workings of the living body. A pity, then, that the man seemed to possess no moral sense whatsoever. He was just as likely to be found taking a slave apart to see how it worked as he was to be healing its wounds.

If the First Prime of Apophis was fated to be turned over to Pa'Nakht, it would have been better for him had Shenet had been unable to control his grief, and murdered him on their way to the ring dungeon. "I will see to it, my Lord. You will have your answers."

"I desire many. We have been away for too long, Kafra, and there is much we do not know. This is a most delicate time. We must be open to all things."

"I understand."

"And besides…" Neheb-Kau stalked closer, the mask's gleaming gaze fixed implacably on him. "Oh, to be in such a place, with such a thing… And to have lived… Kafra, can you *imagine?*"

"I cannot, my Lord." It was another lie. He had imagined worse.

"And what of the woman?"

"Bring her to me. And the weapon you took from her. Once she is bathed, of course."

"My Lord?" Kafra stared. "*Bathed?*"

"Of course. She will have been in the Pit for hours. Days. I have no wish to be near such a foulness. That awful dust… Give her to the slaves. Have her bathed if she is dirty. If she is hungry, feed her…" He waved a hand, dismissively. "Have her prepared for my audience."

"As you command, my Lord." Kafra stood up, bowed, and turned.

When he reached the door, he heard an odd sound. He paused, and risked a glance back over his shoulder.

Neheb-Kau was standing by the sarcophagus, watching it fold itself shut again. And he was humming, softly, to himself. An old song.

A lullaby.

Kafra sighed, and headed back to the transporter. Perhaps, this time, it would show mercy and rip him limb from limb.

Chapter 11.

OVERDRIVE

DANIEL and Jack had spent an hour on Amethun, waiting for Bra'tac to arrive. It was an hour too long, and not only because Amethun wasn't a very nice place to be. According to the Asgard data, for every minute Daniel Jackson had spent pacing anxiously around the Stargate, the Pit of Sorrows had flown almost five hundred billion kilometers further from Earth.

The figure had astounded him. He had made himself read it again and again, and finally had to bring up a calculator on the laptop and check the figures. But the answer he got matched that measured by the Asgard hyperspace probe. The Pit of Sorrows, a black metal and stone pyramid not much bigger than a large house, was powering through hyperspace at almost thirty thousand times the velocity of light.

The revelation was disheartening. Daniel was no technician, but he knew of little that could match such a speed. A Goa'uld Ha'tak pyramid ship, at the peak of its powers, could outrun the Pit of Sorrows. The modified Tel'tak, even with Sephotep's upgrades, couldn't even get close. And by the time Bra'tac arrived to pick Daniel and Jack up from Amethun's swampy surface, Sam and Teal'c had already been in flight for thirteen hours.

Once the Tel'tak was underway, Bra'tac helped Daniel interface the laptop to Sephotep's command board. This was only possible because the laptop was a Stargate Command special issue device, and had been modified by Samantha Carter herself to include a crystal interface. Within half an hour, the glassy panels in the command board were displaying the Asgard telemetry, and Daniel was able to shut the laptop down and put it away.

The Pit's course was plotted on the display as a thin cone. Earth was at the tip, and the cone angled sharply upwards and out of the galactic plane. The graphic defeated Daniel for a while — astrophysics was Sam's field of expertise — but a few minutes scrolling around the data eventually told him what he was looking at.

When he was certain, he called Jack and Bra'tac over to join him. The Tel'tak could fly itself for a while.

"Okay," he began, pointing at the cone. "This is where the Pit's going, according to what the Asgard are telling us. You can see that the cone widens the further they go: the further they are from Earth, the less certain we are of where they'll be."

"Makes sense," said Jack. "The little dots are stars, right?"

"Yeah." Daniel traced a line along the cone with his fingertip. The panel, sensing his touch, joined the stars he brushed into a thin silver chain. "The closest to Earth is this one here, Ross 248. We'll stop there, run a sensor sweep, and then move on to the next one if we don't find them. Rinse and repeat."

Bra'tac surveyed the slowly turning graphic thoughtfully, stroking his beard. "What evidence do you have that the Pit of Sorrows will end its journey close to a star?"

"It's more hope than evidence. But Ra's second message did talk about the Ash Eater 'returning', so we have to assume it's actually going somewhere. Back to where it came from, maybe. I'm sure he wouldn't have said that if it was just going to fly through space forever."

"You're assuming he was telling the truth, too," said Jack.

Bra'tac gave a mirthless chuckle. "The threats of the System Lords are most often true. Bargain with them at your peril, but when they boast about their plans for you, do not doubt them."

"That's what I'm counting on." Daniel pushed his glasses up and rubbed the bridge of his nose. Working on the data was making his head ache. "On the downside, every time we drop out of hyperspace and run a sweep, the Pit of Sorrows will be moving even further away. It's travelling nearly twice as fast as we are."

Jack squinted at the cone. "How many stars have you got?"

"Nine plotted. There's more…" He sighed. "But if we don't find them in the ninth system, the cone gets so wide we'll have to start moving across it. Doubling back on ourselves, even."

"So we'll be out of time."

"We won't. Teal'c and Sam will be."

"Then we must find them before the ninth system," Bra'tac said. "I shall increase power to the naquadah turbines, and we must be ready to reconfigure the Tel'tak's systems for a sensor sweep as soon as we leave hyperspace."

Daniel nodded silently. The two giant modules taking up most of the Tel'tak's cargo space were powerful generators, stores of superdense high-grade naquadah feeding a rotary energy-transfer system. According to what Bra'tac had learned from flying the vessel so far, Sephotep had not simply enhanced the ship's drive system; he had basically stripped it out entirely and replaced it with something very different.

But how long the turbines could keep running at such a high rate was worrying everyone. Daniel hadn't been in the Tel'tak for an hour and he was already feeling uncomfortably warm. The units were pumping dry heat into the cargo bay at such a rate that the life support system was having trouble dumping it all. Hot, dry air, thick with static electricity, was wafting forwards through the big open hatch.

He watched Bra'tac and Jack go back to the forward control boards, rather envying them their tasks. Flying the ship or reconfiguring its systems might have taken his mind away from the fact that Teal'c and Samantha Carter could already be dead, or lost, or simply unreachable.

They were soaring through hyperspace in a flying tomb with a monstrous, lethal alien force. He was trying to catch up with them in the galaxy's fastest cargo scow.

Five hours later, close to the ruddy orb of Ross 248, the picture looked even more bleak. Because by that time, Daniel Jackson was certain something was wrong with the ship.

Ross 248 was a red dwarf star just over ten light-years from

Earth. According to the Asgard data — and the best guesses of human astronomers — the little sun had no attendant planets. As a prospect for finding the Pit of Sorrows intact and containing two living members of SG-1, then, it was poor indeed. But it had to be searched, which mean the Tel'tak was forced to put off its headlong chase and return to the universe of men and matter.

Daniel had returned to the command console for the breakout. The Tel'tak, for all its improvements, still possessed only two seats, with the additional board being positioned for Sephotep to use while standing. It gave a clear view through the forward ports, but that paled quickly in the face of severe discomfort, so Daniel had taken to sitting back in the cargo bay with the laptop, idly searching through the Asgard telemetry in an attempt to stop himself thinking about how far ahead of him Teal'c and Sam had to be.

He had been in ships leaving hyperspace before, and was prepared for a slight jolt upon re-entry. Goa'uld damping systems were not quite perfect, and even in the vast bulk of a Ha'tak he had felt the deck tip under him under vector change. He held onto the sides of the board, planted his feet a little more widely on the floor, and waited for the ship to decelerate.

There was a graphical representation of the approaching breakout point on the command board's display: two rings of light, moving towards each other, intersecting. When the two rings became one, the ship would drop back into normal space.

He resisted the urge to count downwards out loud. Neither Jack nor Bra'tac would have appreciated it, he was sure.

The rings passed over each other and locked into place. Daniel glanced up to see the silver-blue whorl ahead of the viewports part onto darkness. Then the ship bounced under him so hard that he almost bit his tongue in two.

He grabbed wildly at the console to avoid being flung off his feet. There was an awful noise coming from the cargo bay, a stuttering electrical whine, and the heat in the ship had increased dramatically. Daniel half expected to see fires engulfing the turbines, but when he looked back through the hatchway they were as he had last seen them.

A faint ripple showed in the air above the port module, though.

The bouncing slowed, starting to fade out along with the sound. Daniel let go of the console, warily. "What the hell was that?"

The others had felt it too. Jack was on his feet, holding onto the back of the control throne as the vessel trembled back to stillness, but Bra'tac was still busy with the controls. "I am detecting no malfunctions," the Jaffa called back. "Is there any visible damage?"

"Not from here," Jack replied. "Daniel?"

"Don't think so." The shuddering was gone, now. "I could see a heat haze on one of the modules. We're pushing them too hard."

"Perhaps we will reduce power on the next leg of the journey," said Bra'tac, his seamed face grim. "Maintaining this speed means running the turbines at maximum output. They may be starting to fail."

"Whoah," said Jack, putting his hands up. "C'mon, guys. My old Pinto used to sound worse than that, and I kept her running all the way through Basic."

"At eighteen-thousand Cee?"

"I used to push her, yeah."

"We have no time for this," Bra'tac muttered, hands working the controls. "I engaged the stealth cloak shortly before leaving hyperspace, but in order to effect a sensor sweep I must reconfigure the power system."

"How long will that take?" said Jack.

"Several minutes."

"So just run the sweep."

"We'd blow the phase relay," Daniel cut in. "Resetting the whole system would take a lot longer, believe me. Even if we could. I only saw Sam do it once."

"Right, I remember." Jack stretched. Rubbed the small of his back. "Damn, they don't build these things for comfort, do they?"

"No," replied Bra'tac, curtly. "They do not."

When Bra'tac ran the sweep, it did throw up one surprise. The astronomers had been wrong — Ross 248 did have two tiny worlds, little more than scorched rocks tumbling around in orbital periods of six weeks and nine years respectively. Other than that, the Tel'tak's sensors gave exactly the results everyone had been expecting, which was nothing. There was no residual hyperdrive signature, no vented particles of spent naquadah, none of the subtle, but detectable, gravitic disturbances that proved the recent activation of a Goa'uld reactionless drive, other than those caused by the Tel'tak itself. And so, after thirty minutes of searching, Bra'tac disengaged the cloak and the long-range sensors and engaged the hyperdrive once more.

Daniel took the laptop back into the cargo compartment. The sight of hyperspace racing past the viewports was making him feel a little queasy, and he no longer wanted to be reminded of motion. He felt as though he had not been still for days. He wanted, suddenly, to lie down and stop, to let the universe rush on without him for a while.

Immediately the desire entered his head, he forced it angrily away. Sam and Teal'c probably wished they could stop moving too, and Daniel's perpetual motion might be their only hope. He couldn't afford to be still for a minute, for a second. Every delay extended their nightmare.

He found a place on the cargo bay floor that was free from trailing cables, and which wasn't too close to the heat of the turbines, and sat there, his back against the golden wall and the laptop propped against his knees.

Around him, the ship murmured and clicked. He could feel the faint vibration of it through his back, could feel the subtle rocking as it powered through hyperspace. The air smelled of hot metal and machine oil and something like spices.

The heat coming off the turbines was really starting to prey on his mind.

They were pushing the ship far too hard, he knew. It had never been built for prolonged use — it was a prototype, a test-bed. There was no way it could last.

There was a footfall beside him, and he looked up to see Jack there. "Something wrong?"

"Nah. Bra'tac says the next system is about two hours away. I thought I'd, you know, mingle…"

"Kruger 60," Daniel replied, absently. "Jack, I've got to ask you —"

"Don't."

"But —"

"Daniel, we've been over it. I *know*, okay? Chances are slim. But you know damn well they'd never give up on us if we were in the same situation." He leaned against the wall and folded his arms. "Just let's do this for now. Once we get past nine systems we'll maybe start thinking about the alternatives."

There was a rather awkward silence. Then Daniel said: "I, ah, wasn't actually gonna ask that."

"You weren't?"

"No. I was going to ask if you've worked out what we'll do when we actually catch up with them?"

"Get 'em out and head for the nearest gate."

"Yeah, it's the *getting them out* part I'm still a little hazy on. If the Pit's still in space, we'll need some way of docking with it. And there's the door to get through."

"That part's easy," said Jack. "I've brought enough C4 for everybody. As for docking, let's cross that one when we get to it." He got up, patting Daniel on the shoulder as he did so. "This is a cargo ship. There's got to be ways of getting awkward stuff onto it."

"What's it worth not to tell Sam you called her awkward?"

"Not as much as you think." Jack stood up. "I'll go talk to Bra'tac about docking."

"Have fun." Daniel watched him go, then returned his attention the laptop.

Two hours, he thought. Almost seven light years.

Ross 248 was a red dwarf star. Kruger 60 was *two* red dwarf stars, a binary system, each sun about a quarter the mass of Sol and orbiting one another at a distance of nine AUs. Kruger 60 B was a flare star, a variable entity that randomly flashed out lethal solar storms. Once again, a less than likely destination for the Pit of Sorrows.

By the time Bra'tac started to engage the stealth cloak, the port turbine had been whistling steadily for almost an hour, and it was getting louder. Daniel no longer trusted it. He had taken to standing alongside the command board rather than behind it, to keep his back out of line with the hatchway. It made reading the display more difficult, since the strings of Goa'uld hieroglyphs on it scrolled rapidly upwards as data came through to the board. Daniel had started to notice that many of the symbols were now in red, rather than their usual yellow-gold.

He couldn't take that as a good sign. "Bra'tac? How are things looking up there?"

"As they should be, Doctor Jackson."

"Oh good." Daniel swallowed. The air was getting very dry, and he was getting static shocks whenever he touched metal. "Just checking."

The two rings shivered towards each other. Their outlines wavered, writhing like the waveform of a plucked string.

"How long?" called Jack. Was he having to shout over the whistling?

"About twenty seconds." He reached up, slowly so as not to draw attention to the act, and gripped the edges of the console very hard.

"Fifteen."

"Daniel, don't do that."

"Sorry." *Twelve*, he thought.

The rings lurched together.

The deck jerked, shivered, and then began to hammer hard up into the soles of his boots. From the corner of his eye he saw a dot of blackness appear in the racing azure nothingness of hyperspace, expand, surge towards the ship and swallow it whole. As the ports went dark, the whistling rose to a painful shriek.

"Shut it down!" yelled Jack. "It's gonna rip itself apart!"

"I cannot!" snapped Bra'tac. "To do so would leave us powerless!"

"We'll be worse than powerless when the ship blows up!"

Whatever Bra'tac was doing, it was starting to work. Daniel

could already feel the vibration lessening, and the screaming from the turbine was becoming less piercing. "I think we're going to be okay," he called, trying to release his grip on the command board. His fingers were locked more tightly around it than he had thought, and it took an effort to let go.

He pulled himself free and stepped back. Outside the ship, velvet blackness had replaced sliver-blue light. There were stars everywhere, large and bright and crystalline. Oddly, they were moving sideways across the viewports, slow but steady. The ship had come out of hyperspace turning on its axis.

The naquadah turbines throttled back to a low growl and fell silent.

Daniel puffed out a breath. "I think this prototype needs work," he croaked.

"Jesus…" Jack got up from the control throne and walked around to where Daniel was standing. "Another one of those and we'll be in pieces. We'll be lucky if this rustbucket even gets out of the system."

"Maybe it's something we can fix."

"Fix? Us?"

"Yeah…" He found himself looking away from Jack and back out of the viewports. Bra'tac was doing the same, half out of his seat to stare and the inky night outside. "Oil, or something…"

"Doctor Jackson," said Bra'tac. "Why are the stars golden?"

"Because they aren't stars," Jack breathed. "Oh crap. What the hell have just walked into?"

What Daniel had first thought were the crystal points of distant suns were nothing of the sort. They were too big, too close. They were the wrong color.

Space around Kruger 60 A was full of Goa'uld craft.

Most of the stars Daniel had spotted earlier were small ships, far off — death gliders and Tel'taks, Al'kesh bombers and a swarm of other vessels he could not immediately identify. But as the ship turned slowly around, he saw vaster forms slide into view. A Ha'tak pyramid ship loomed out of the night, surrounded by smaller craft like a hive by bees. Behind it, another. And yet another.

When he had counted six of them, Daniel gave up keeping track.

"It's a fleet." Jack's voice was dull, subdued. It was one shock too many. "Goddamn snakehead battlefleet."

There was an odd quality to the vessels. All the pyramid ships Daniel had seen before tended towards the same color and design; a golden tetrahedron at the core, surrounded by a dark, complex outer disc containing the primary power and weapons systems. It was said that the core pyramid could operate free of the disc, but he had never seen the two apart. Only Ra's ship, back on Abydos, had been a lone pyramid, and that had been unlike any other. It was probably a personal vessel for the supreme System Lord alone.

These ships, however, did not follow precisely the same pattern. The shape was similar, although the outer discs were sleeker, and set around their edges with tall, curving projections that reminded him of something he couldn't quite remember. Their coloration, too, was different. The pyramids gleamed white in the raw sunlight, and their discs were gold and bronze and bright blood red.

One of the Ha'taks moved, turned to change vector, and Daniel saw that the curved projections arcing up from its disc had vast eyes painted onto either side of its root. "*Opthalmoi*," he gasped.

"Op-what-oy?"

"Eyes painted on the bows of ships — pretty standard practice in Classical Greece. They called them *Opthalmoi*." The huge curving spine was looking more and more like the raised prow of a trireme. "What, you never saw *Jason and the Argonauts*?"

"Thought the skeletons were cool."

"Everyone does."

"So, a Greek Goa'uld, huh… Cronus?"

"Maybe. In any case, we've got to get out of here."

"We are still cloaked," said Bra'tac. "At present, we have not been detected. Our hyperspace deceleration must have gone unnoticed among such a large number of vessels. However, if we engage the drives, we will be spotted."

"Can we use maneuvering thrusters? Just edge ourselves away?"

"I am endeavoring to do that," the Jaffa replied. "We shall drift out of the fleet, and jump back into hyperspace when we are a safe distance."

"I'm starting to think that might be quite a long way."

Something else had moved into view. At first Daniel thought that it was simply closer than the rest of the ships, that perhaps the Tel'tak was in danger of colliding with a Ha'tak, but then one of the pyramid ships passed *in front* of the new sight, and he realized that he was looking at a mountain.

It was vast, kilometers from end to end; a great stepped pyramid gleaming like white marble, tier upon tier soaring upwards towards a golden Parthenon at its tip. The tiers were set with columns, thousands of them, and it wasn't until an Al'kesh raced along one of the colonnades that Daniel saw that it was flying past ranks of slender pillars the size of skyscrapers.

"It's Mount Olympus," he muttered, shaking his head slightly. "Somebody's flying Mount Olympus through space…"

"Probably powered by raw ego," said Jack. "Bra'tac? How long before we can get away?"

"Many minutes, Colonel O'Neill. We must be patient if we are to…"

He stopped mid-sentence, frowning down at his control board. "That must be an error," he growled.

"What are you seeing?"

"An imbalance, between the two turbines."

Daniel glanced back into the cargo bay. "I thought you'd shut them down."

"I had."

"I'll go check." He trotted back towards the hatch and stepped through. Sure enough, the port turbine was whirring softly, too faintly to hear from the cockpit, and the air around it rippled with heat. "Yeah, we've got a problem all right."

Jack appeared next to him. "What do you think? Switch it off and on again?"

"Works with everything else." He turned back to the cockpit.

"Hey Bra'tac? Can you try—"

The turbine blew up.

Daniel didn't see it go, because he was looking the wrong way. All he heard was one single, brutal, hellish sound, a scream and an impact and a howl of tearing metal all in one, and then he was off his feet, skating forwards across the Tel'tak's deck in utter darkness.

The sound died into a shuddering, stuttering clatter.

Daniel rolled over, groaning. He couldn't see anything, and his ears were ringing from the sound of the explosion. He could just about hear Jack asking if he was okay.

He sat up, slowly. "I'm blind."

"You're not blind. It's dark. The relay tripped."

"This vessel is without power," said Bra'tac quickly. "If we do not restore it, we will be destroyed."

A hand came down on Daniel's shoulder, and there was a sudden light. Jack's face appeared in front of him, lit by the beam from a tactical flashlight. Then the beam swung aft, across the sloping, golden bulkhead separating the command section from the cargo bay, and through the hatch.

Jack whistled softly. "Well, that's the end of that."

The port module's casing had burst, blown itself open along its entire length. Smoking debris littered the cargo bay, some of it still glowing a dull red, and the interior of the casing was a tangle of shafts and cable and fragments of shattered crystal.

The beam moved, and stopped again at the edge of the hatchway. A serrated metal disc was imbedded horizontally in the frame, roughly at neck height.

"Looks like you're up, Daniel."

"What?"

"You saw Sam reset the relay. We've lost the drives, but if we can't get the cloak back up we're sitting ducks."

"No pressure, then." Daniel staggered to his feet. He'd been dreading this moment.

"The panel is here," Bra'tac said. He was crouching in the dark, close to a patch of floor that was pulsing a soft amber, the miniscule primer feed tapped directly from the naquadah generators in the stern.

"I only saw her do this once, okay?" He knelt down next to the panel. Inside it, below floor level, a cylindrical complex of gold filigree and multicolored control crystals glowed softly, lit from beneath. The crystals themselves were dull and lifeless without power. In his memory, they had been alight. And there had been less of them.

He sighed. Closed his eyes, tried to think back to Sar'tua. The cold wind, biting into his skin. The dull thump of death glider weapons fire, blasting at the plateau. A dead Jaffa, frozen, the front of his skull a mass of frosted meat...

Daniel winced, and opened his eyes. He reached down, twisted a crystal around in its socket, counted four anticlockwise, and twisted a second.

"Nothing's happening," said Jack, his voice soft but his tone a warning.

Daniel didn't answer. His memory was phenomenal, but not eidetic. He was a good study, he knew that: he'd had to be. But this was different, there had been no time, and there hadn't been a fleet of Goa'uld vessels turning their myriad electronic eyes to seek him out.

His fingers darted to a third crystal and pushed at it. He felt it resist, then slide downwards and lock.

The light from the relay went green, and there was a faint electrical whine.

"One more," he said. The red, two clockwise on the centre ring. He moved it around in its socket, and the cockpit lit up with a dull crimson glow. "Yes!"

"Nice work." Jack switched off the taclight. "Can we get the cloak up now?"

"Not yet. This is only stage one, emergency power. Now we've got to —"

Alien words, harsh and imperious, echoed through the Tel'tak.

Daniel stared at Jack, then at Bra'tac. Neither of them had spoken. "What was that?"

"The communications system has restarted." Bra'tac got to his feet. "I do not believe visual transfer will be possible, but to be safe, remain here and keep silent."

He crossed the deck and sat down at the controls. Daniel saw him touch several icons, then lean closer to the board. As he did so, the message sounded again.

The dialect was different from what Daniel knew of the Goa'uld language, and the first time he had heard the words their meaning had escaped him. He picked it up on the second time around: "*Unidentified cargo vessel, speak or be destroyed!*"

"*Jaffa, hold your fire,*" said Bra'tac, in much the same inflection. He was mimicking the accent of the caller.

"*Identify yourself, fool!*"

"*There is no time for your petty bureaucracy! We have suffered a major power failure. All our primary systems are down, and we require assistance immediately!*"

Jack gave Daniel an exaggeratedly bemused expression: *What?*

"They're asking who we are. Bra'tac's told them we need help."

"That's crazy!"

Daniel hushed him. The Jaffa was speaking again.

In fact, he had laughed; a mirthless bark. "*You are not the first this day, pilot. Nor will you be the last. Our Goddess demands much.*"

"*We live to serve her.*"

"*Indeed. Sit tight, my friend. I have you guidance-locked. You will be taken aboard the* Clythena *and reassigned.*"

There was a click and crackle as the communications system shut off, and then the ship lurched.

Daniel got up. Outside the viewports, the sideways motion of the fleet was slowing. He felt the vessel accelerate, although not quickly: if the main drive system was damaged, all the ship would have to move itself would be its maneuvering thrusters.

"They've taken control of the ship," he told Jack, as the man rose and paced back to the cockpit. "They're going to take us on board a ship called the *Clythena*—I think that's our flying mountain."

"Great. The bigger the better."

"You're being sarcastic, right? Because you know, sometimes I still can't tell…"

"I do not believe so," Bra'tac smiled. "The larger the vessel, the greater our chances of losing ourselves within it."

"And of picking up a new ride." Jack reached under the control throne; he had stashed his daypack there. "Come on, we'll need to rig the other turbine with C4. Whoever this new guy is —"

"It's a woman."

"Whatever. I don't want her getting anything useful out of this prototype. And the more havoc we can cause when we're on board, the better."

When Daniel and Jack had finished placing charges around the Tel'tak, they headed back to the cockpit in time to see the *Clythena* looming above them.

It was an awesome sight. Unlike the tetrahedral cores of the Ha'taks, the flying mountain had a square base. It was a true pyramid, but scaled up to insane levels: the vessel could have landed atop a small town, and covered it entirely.

While the ship's flanks gleamed like smooth white marble, the underside of it was less prepossessing, a maze of thruster bells, docking ports, kilometers of exposed pipework. It reminded Daniel of a gigantic foundry, hundreds of pits of glowing metal connected by vast tubes and gantries and factory buildings, turned upside-down and moving slowly over his head.

"There have got to be tens of thousands of Jaffa in there," he breathed.

"Maybe less than you think." Jack was sitting on the deck, checking his weapons and equipment — an MP5 with multiple spare magazines, a sidearm, a zat gun, grenades and more C4. "Every time we've been inside one of those pyramids we've see a lot of empty space."

"It is true," Bra'tac agreed. "Goa'uld vessels are vast in order to terrify those who might oppose them. Within, there will be many unused areas, unless an army is being transported. This ship, for all its size, will be crewed by a few thousand, no more."

"That's still not very comforting."

"Daniel, we can do this." Jack got up, his MP5 slung, the rest of his gear stashed efficiently in his tactical vest and daypack. "They don't know anything's wrong, so they won't be on alert. Bra'tac can find us something sporty, while we go hunt down the navigation system and cripple it. We'll fly out and be in hyperspace before they even know why they can't steer."

Daniel just looked at him. There were so many things he could have said, so many flaws in the plan, so many dangers and logical gaps and leaps of faith. The idea of sauntering into the vastness of that spaceborne Everest as if it were a local shopping mall was simply insane. It was true that the ship was not on alert now, but they only needed to be spotted once, and all hands would be against them. The fleet might enter hyperspace while they were still inside, dragging them untold light-years off course. It was a terrible plan. It was suicide. Madness.

It was as likely to work as any other option, frankly. And in the face of such nightmarish odds, perhaps audacity was the thing that would see them through.

"Let's do it," he replied.

"Humans," said Bra'tac. "Observe."

He was standing at the viewports, looking up at the endless base of the *Clythena*. Past him, Daniel could see a huge shape gliding upwards, glittering white and silver. Another starship, as long as a Ha'tak was tall, was docking vertically with the mountain's underside.

It was only when he got closer to the ports that he realized his mistake. The object was not a ship. It was being towed into place by dozens of smaller vessels; stubby tenders with spidery manipulator arms, Tel'taks with crane-like winch gear bolted to their flanks. The object itself was a series of flattened saucers, joined by a complicated series of radial tubes set around a vast central barrel. It was rising, with infinite care, into a huge central shaft drilled into *Clythena*'s base; an obscene mechanical mating.

"It looks like a gun," he said, wonder turning his words to a whisper. "Bra'tac, is that a weapon?"

The Jaffa shook his head slowly. "I have not seen its like before. But I can only assume its purpose is destruction."

"Wouldn't want to be on the receiving end," agreed Jack.

Above the Tel'tak, a great disc of metal split into teeth, gaped like the maw of some fanged worm, vomiting light. Daniel felt the ship jerk to a halt, then begin to rise.

They were going in.

Chapter 12.

BLACK AND GOLD

ALMOST as soon as Teal'c had been marched out into the high cool air of the Ha'tak's glider bay, he had begun formulating his escape plan.

There was a very slight delay, however: he had allowed himself a moment of relief upon leaving the Pit. It was a weakness, of that he was well aware, and under normal circumstances he would have denied himself such feelings. But his time in the structure had been difficult, not least because of the suffering the place had inflicted on Major Carter. Teal'c hadn't enjoyed watching that at all.

The feeling had been his celebration, and it had only lasted a second or two. Anything beyond that was a self-indulgence, a luxury he could ill afford, so he stored it away. When he and Carter were on safer ground, he would, perhaps, allow himself to revisit it.

But not now. Not until he was very far from the Pit of Sorrows and its mysterious occupant.

A bridge had been extended to the Pit's doorway. It was narrow, only just wide enough to allow two men to walk side by side, but it spread slightly where it touched the pit. Four Jaffa, clad in the armor of Neheb-Kau, stood there, two at either side, covering him with staff weapons as he and Carter were ushered outside. He half expected one or more of them to speak as he passed, to spit an insult or a curse, to call him *shol'va*, traitor against the Gods. But none of the Jaffa uttered a sound — if anything, their attitude spoke of silent respect. As soon as he and the surviving snake-guard from the Pit went past them they simply fell into formation behind him.

The First Prime of Neheb-Kau stayed behind.

Carter walked in front, coated with the Pit's foul dust. The stuff was in her hair and on her skin, aging her. Perhaps that was why the Jaffa had not cursed him, Teal'c surmised. He was disguised by dust. That could work to his advantage.

On the other hand, the reason might lie in the fact that to his knowledge no Jaffa had seen nor heard from Neheb-Kau in hundreds of years. And if the Goa'uld had been cut off from the other System Lords, either by accident or design, it was entirely possible that no-one here knew that Teal'c was anyone other than the First Prime of Apophis. This, too, could work in his favor.

Gather your advantages like seeds, Master Bra'tac had once told him. *Tend them well, and when the time is right they will flower into victory.*

There could be no wiser teacher. The lesson had been learned, and learned well: Teal'c never let such a seed fall from his grasp.

The bridge clattered and moved beneath his feet as he walked. It was not well-made; he could see fractures in its flooring panels, spots of corrosion on the handrails. The supports that suspended it from the ceiling were ill-matched, as though built from scavenged materials. That was unexpected, and Teal'c thought for a moment about the possibility of using the structure's poor state of repair to his advantage. He quickly dismissed the notion, however. It was already obvious to him that there could be no escape from the bridge itself.

He calculated his chances of overpowering the Jaffa around him without significant injury to himself or Carter, and decided that those chances were, at present, so small as to be effectively dismissed. Instead Teal'c eyed the far edge of the bridge, where it met an access platform and joined the vast triangle of gantry that edged the bay. There were two more Jaffa there, weapons trained on him. And even from this distance he could see that their armor was stained and patched, hastily repaired.

Teal'c decided that his next action would depend on how well-trained these two were. If their tactics were as poor as their equipment, and they remained still as he and Carter approached, then their line of fire would cross the Jaffa behind him. If they moved…

When he was still ten meters away, the two guards spread out, triangulating their aim with that of the five at his back. It seemed that, at least, their First Prime had trained them well.

It was of no consequence. His opportunity would come. All that was required of him was to watch for its approach, and be ready to act when it arrived.

As First Prime of Apophis, Teal'c had probably spent more time with his feet on the decks of Ha'tak pyramid ships than he had with them on solid ground.

The throneship of Neheb-Kau should have been no surprise to him. To begin with, it had not been: as soon as he had been released from the Pit of Sorrows and stepped out into the glider bay, he had felt a surge of recognition. He could tell at a glance that he was on one of the older models of Ha'tak, very much like that he had served aboard during the subjugation of the Ylantrii, and again at the scourging of Korapsis. He knew almost without thinking that the ship would have certain weak points — the shielding around the pel'tak could be breached by a well-targeted fusillade of staff-cannon bolts, for example, and the atmospheric containment fields in the glider bays could, in the heat of battle, leak enough air to impair the performance of the Jaffa within. He knew that the refectories would be too far from the dormitories, that the transporters would be too widely spaced, and that the frequency of the hyperdrive would start to make his teeth ache after about a week.

He knew the best way to destroy such a vessel from without and from within.

Or at least, he thought he did. It was only when he and Carter had been taken out of the bay that he realized the Ha'tak was not precisely as it should be.

Instead of a narrow accessway from the glider bay to the staging areas, the gantry instead opened into a broad, high chamber, roughly hexagonal in shape. A balcony around it looked as though it could be reconfigured to accommodate either cargo manipulators or an effective guard duty, and it was at present sporting the latter. Teal'c looked up to see at least twenty Jaffa glaring back down at him, and each of the balcony's three long sides was fitted with a remote staff-cannon aiming into the chamber.

The attention was almost flattering until he remembered the Ash Eater. The guards were not here for him and Carter at all.

The hatchway he had just passed through was replicated twice more in the chamber, leading him to think that he was probably in a central area between three glider bays, spaced equally around the triangular layout of the Ha'tak core. Teal'c felt one of his advantages wither and die. The vessel must have been extensively modified, and so it was unlikely that he could rely on his knowledge of its layout. Not until he had seen more of it, in any case.

How much of the ship he would get a chance to see, he knew, depended very much on what happened in the next few moments.

He had reached the centre of the chamber. There was a broad disc of pale stone set into the flooring there, and as he walked onto it there was a sudden hiss and click of staff weapons. He glanced back, over his shoulder, and saw the five Jaffa guarding him had spread out. All were aiming their weapons at him and Carter. Above them, the blunt snouts of the three staff cannon snapped open, too.

He stopped, in the centre of the circle. Carter had already paused there, at the sound of the guns.

"Teal'c?" Her voice was still weak and dry.

"Remain calm," he told her. "And ready."

Behind him, there was a series of whisper-faint clicks and whirrs as the leader of the five retracted his helm. Teal'c turned to watch the mechanism slide back into his collar, and was interested to note that the process was not smooth. Several of the leaves seemed to snag on each other, briefly.

That was telling. A Jaffa's armor was not only his protection in battle, but a mark of pride. To see it maintained so badly spoke of a significant lack of resources.

For a System Lord's throneship, the Ha'tak and its occupants seemed to be in puzzlingly poor repair.

The lead Jaffa stepped forwards. His face, exposed, was fine-featured and dark with rage.

"What is your intention?" Teal'c asked him, in English. At the sound of the words, the other man's lip curled, and he took a step forwards.

"My intention is to gut you like a fish, First Prime," he spat. "You killed the best of us today."

Teal'c raised an eyebrow. "If he was the best, it does not speak highly of those he leaves behind."

He was trying to goad the man into coming forwards again, to draw close enough for Teal'c to grab his weapon. It almost worked — he saw the man tense forwards, as if to attack. But then the Jaffa took a breath, visibly centered himself.

"My intentions take second place to those of the God," the man growled. "So I spare you. For now."

"Your God is false."

The Jaffa's reaction was surprising. He shrugged.

"False, true… It is of no importance." The Jaffa lowered his staff, and instead pressed a jeweled control on his right wrist. "All I know is this: in the hours to come, you will wish I had not followed his orders so well."

I already do, thought Teal'c, but light was spilling down from above. A transporter aperture was grinding open, the fangs of its cover sliding quickly away and allowing a series of rings to drop around him and Carter.

The light grew blinding, all-encompassing. When it faded, he was elsewhere.

He heard Carter stumble slightly. The transporter was fractionally out of phase, and had imparted a very slight torque to the pair of them upon reintegration. More evidence that the Ha'tak was not only heavily modified, but also in need of mechanical attention.

When the rings darted up and into their ceiling cavity, they left Teal'c and Carter standing in a tall, cylindrical shaft.

"What is this?" Carter asked, looking wildly about. "Teal'c, where have they put us?"

"A dungeon."

"Oh my God."

"One of most effective design. The only entrance is via the transporter. Unless that is activated, there is no way to escape."

"Great." Carter sat down heavily, and folded her arms. She raised a small cloud of dust as she did so. "Out of a tomb and into a prison cell."

"Do not despair, Major Carter."

"I'm not despairing. I'm thinking."

"What are your thoughts?"

She coughed weakly. "That I'm glad we're not still in the Pit of Sorrows."

Teal'c smiled slightly. "As am I."

He took a moment to study the place more closely. It was, as he had told Carter, a very well-designed prison. The curving metal wall sloped slightly inwards, making it impossible to climb. There was just enough light to be demoralizing, and the only concession to a prisoner's physical needs was a bare hole in the centre of the floor. Somewhere above there would be a means of surveillance, but Teal'c could not see it from where he stood.

There were normally holding cells in a Ha'tak — there would always be prisoners to interrogate, after all — but Teal'c had never seen one built in quite such a way before. It told him much about Neheb-Kau, that he would require such facilities.

Teal'c sat down, slowly, in the lotus position.

"So," Carter asked him. "This Neheb-Kau. Do you know him?"

"I do not. His name has been no more than legend for as long as I have been alive. I believed him long dead."

"Can you tell me anything about him?"

"There is little to tell. Rumors of a terrible crime committed against the other System Lords, perhaps even against Ra himself. Nothing more."

"That's not very helpful," Carter sighed. "Still, if he's no friend of the other Goa'uld, maybe he won't be immediately hostile to us."

"We may be of no interest to him at all." Teal'c regarded her, across the dungeon floor. She was a pale form in the gloom, like a ghost. "Neheb-Kau's primary concern will be the Ash Eater."

"So that grab in the glider bay isn't standard issue."

"It is not. In fact, nothing I have seen of this vessel so far has conformed to accepted design."

Carter smiled. "So we know one more thing about this guy. He tinkers."

"Indeed."

A silence fell between them.

In a way, the utterly sealed nature of the dungeon was a blessing: the Pit of Sorrows, for all its horrors, had at least offered a chance of escape, if one could overcome its defenses. Here, there was not even that slim hope. Which made it easier for Teal'c to accept that he should not try.

After a while, in fact, Teal'c heard a soft, rhythmic sound. It was snoring. Carter had fallen asleep.

Teal'c allowed himself a small, fond smile, and closed his own eyes. Sleep, in the human sense, was beyond him, and in this situation he could not even allow himself to enter *kel'no'reem* and renew his connection with the symbiote. There were, however, shallower levels of meditation that would serve him as well as Carter's slumber served her, and from which he could rouse himself instantly should the need arise.

He straightened his spine, took a long, slow breath, and retreated within himself.

Teal'c's eyes snapped open.

There had been a sound, faint, at the edges of his perception. Something metallic, as though a mechanism in the dungeon's structure had been activated. After close to two hours in dark iron space, it had roused him instantly.

Carter was still asleep. She had slumped forwards, her head resting on her knees. Teal'c reached out to her. "Major Carter."

"Mhwphmr," she said.

"Major Carter, you must wake."

Her head came up, her eyes blinking rapidly. "Are we there yet?"

There was no time. He took her arm and pulled her up with him as he stood.

She shook her head vigorously, as if trying to clear the fuzziness from her mind. The grogginess humans experienced upon waking was something Teal'c wanted no part of. There had been times when his survival had depended on becoming very quickly alert.

He hoped this was not one of them.

There was a faint click to his right, and a squeal of rusted machinery. He saw a small panel unfold at chest height, hinging sideways to reveal the opening of a dark metal tube.

It was a weapon. He darted sideways, shoved Carter hard out of the tube's line of fire.

The tube shook, rattled, and then began to spit an arcing stream of clear liquid into the central drain. Carter stared at it for a few moments, then reached out to it.

"Major Carter," Teal'c warned, but she already had some in her cupped hand. She brought it to her face, sniffed it.

"It's water." She took a sip.

Under normal circumstances she would have been more wary. But the thirst and the weakness had robbed her of care — before he could stop her, she was under the stream, letting it fall directly into her mouth, swallowing gulp after gulp.

A few seconds later she must have realized what she was doing, and stepped aside with a rather guilty look on her face. "It's fine," she told him. "You should drink too."

Now that the water was there, he realized how dry he was. Despite himself, he reached out to the stream.

The water stopped, and the panel began to close.

"Hey. *Hey!*" Carter leaned back to glare up at the ceiling. "We're not finished!"

"I do not require it," he told her, but she ignored him.

"Come on," she called. "I know you're listening up there! Please, we need more water!"

There was a mechanical clatter far above them. Teal'c saw

Carter frown in puzzlement.

And the water she had asked for crashed down onto her face.

Freezing jets blasted down at them from above, a hundred powerful sprays that pounded down onto the dungeon floor. Teal'c heard Carter give out a startled yelp, and then all he could hear was the thunder of the jets. It was like being under a waterfall.

It had to be some kind of cleaning mechanism — Teal'c could see how the jets were designed to arc slightly outwards so that every part of the structure was sluiced — but its operators obviously did not consider heating the water to be an effective use of energy. Instead, it was icy. Carter had folded herself under its pressure, and it was battering at her so hard Teal'c could barely see her outline. He stepped towards her, hoping to shelter her somehow, but she was staggering away towards the wall. There was no escaping the deluge, though. The cleaning system had been designed too well. Every part of the dungeon was a cascade.

It went on until it had beaten Carter to her knees, then stopped.

Teal'c waited, feeling the last fine spray of it coming down to spatter him. He was ankle-deep, but the water was already spiraling away into the central drain.

Carter started to rise, and Teal'c reached down to help her. She was utterly saturated, shivering with cold and shock. Her sandy hair was plastered to her scalp, and she was blinking furiously, wiping her hands down over her face to try and get the water out of her eyes.

"What," she muttered, her voice tight with fury, "the *hell* was that for?"

"I believe we have been cleansed," Teal'c replied.

"Cleansed?"

"It is possible we are being made ready to face Neheb-Kau. His Jaffa might have considered us unclean, since we still bore traces of the Pit of Sorrows."

"Are you saying they just gave us a *bath?*"

He did not answer. Above his head, the dungeon ceiling clattered, then began to split into a narrow star of white light. The transporter was being activated. Teal'c waited, looking up into the cavity as the cover retracted in eight triangular sections, and then the rings were dropping down around them.

There was a rushing, an instant of blinding glare, and then the transporter was lifting away from them once again, ring after ring vanishing up into the ceiling maw.

Thankfully, the gloom of the dungeon was gone. He and Carter had reintegrated in a very different space.

They stood at one end of a long, wide hallway. The floor beneath their feet was of smooth, black marble, inlaid with strange designs, while the two long walls were lined with pillars of bright gold. The ceiling, claustrophobically low above his head, was set with illuminated panels that gave the hallway an opulent glow, and lanterns stood on tall metal stands, their open flames setting the hall's shadows jumping weirdly.

Between each of the pillars stood a Jaffa guard, heads obscured by the sinister double-serpent helm of Neheb-Kau. Their armor was golden, and in far better repair than that of the other warriors he had seen. The God's personal guard, Teal'c guessed. In fact, this entire chamber was as polished and well-maintained as Teal'c would have expected a System Lord's property to be. He and Carter must be close to Neheb-Kau.

It told him much about the Goa'uld that he apparently chose to decorate the interior of his vessel as one might design a tomb.

The golden warriors remained motionless, but Teal'c was certain that if he so much as moved, their weapons would be on him. So he stood, mirroring their stillness, while water dripped from his skin and his ragged civilian clothes and pattered onto the gleaming floor.

Beside him, Carter shivered uncomfortably.

A hatch opened somewhere behind them. Teal'c listened, counted five Jaffa approaching him. One of them had a stride he recognized, a weight to his footfalls that he remembered from the Pit of Sorrows. Four of the warriors took up guard positions at his back, but the First Prime of Neheb-Kau continued walking, slow and unconcerned, until he was facing Teal'c and Carter.

His lined face creased in a grim smile. "Better," he said in Goa'uld. "At least now, the slaves will not fear that specters walk amongst them."

"Your hospitality is most…" Teal'c searched for the best word. "*Refreshing.*"

The Jaffa's lip curled. "The least I could do."

"Now that we are bathed, are we to meet Neheb-Kau?"

"The woman will. You cannot share her honor."

"I see no honor in bowing to a false God."

"And I see no intellect in insulting those who hold your life in their hands. I suppose that makes us even." The Jaffa raised a hand, gestured to the guards behind Teal'c. "Take her."

He heard the men move forwards. Perhaps these were different warriors than those he had encountered on the bridge, and not so well-trained, or maybe their closeness to Neheb-Kau was making them nervous. Whatever the reason, one of them stepped just a little too close to Teal'c as he moved towards Carter.

Teal'c whirled. He snapped his right arm back, his elbow hitting the First Prime hard in the chest, and then hammered his first forwards into the other man's neck armor. The control for his helm was there: not only did the blow stagger the warrior, but it also set his serpent-head retracting.

The First Prime snarled in anger, recovering instantly from the blow Teal'c had given him and whirling his staff weapon around in a hissing arc at head-height. Teal'c ducked under the weapon, using his momentum to kick out and sweep another Jaffa's legs from under him, then launched himself up again and barreled into a third.

Behind him, the man whose helm he had caused to retract stepped away, completely disregarding Carter. Teal'c heard a brutal impact of bone on bone — her elbow, he guessed, slamming with stunning force into the man's temple. As he swung around to dodge another staff blow he saw the Jaffa she had struck stumble, clutching the side of his skull.

He kicked out again, into the man's thigh, and as the Jaffa howled and fell Teal'c snatched the staff weapon from him. He whipped it about towards the First Prime, thumbing the activation stud, and caught a zat beam clean in the chest.

In an instant, the world was a coruscating storm of lightning and pain. Dimly, he felt the black marble floor hit him in the knees, but sensation was already fleeing him. He reached out, clawing at the air, pure anger keeping him conscious long seconds after his wits should have fled him, but holding on to them took more strength than he possessed.

The last thing he heard, before he tumbled headlong into darkness, was Carter shouting his name.

Chapter 13.

A DUSTLAND FAIRYTALE

THE OUTPUT of the Goa'uld zat'nik'tel pistol was not wholly electrical. Samantha Carter had subjected several captured weapons to rigorous experimentation months before, and had determined that the energy pulse they fired was more akin to a tuned resonance of the central nervous system than it was to raw voltage. Nevertheless, once the pulse had struck a target, it did tend to propagate very much as lightning would.

The clothes Carter was wearing when Teal'c had been shot were still saturated with water from the dungeon, and she was standing close by him. When the beam struck him, it had her off her feet too.

It was only a fraction of the zat's full power, but it still paralyzed her for a second. As soon as she saw Teal'c hit the energy of the shot flooded through her, jerking her hard backwards as her muscles spasmed, filling her vision with light, her ears with a stuttering whine. She staggered, tried for a moment to regain her balance, but the strength had gone out of her. She sagged to the floor.

As she collapsed, Teal'c was already on his knees. She saw him fighting the effects of the beam, but there was never any hope of overcoming it. He reached out, skin still crawling with brilliant serpents of light, and then topped face-down.

"Teal'c!" she shouted, uselessly.

"Silence!" Carter looked up to see the zat's head flick in her direction. "On your feet."

Behind the weapon, the First Prime's face was set hard. Carter tried to raise herself, gingerly, but her first attempt failed. Her muscles were still weakened by the residual energy. As she tried a second time, the man made an exasperated sound, put his gun away and reached down to take her arm.

He hauled her upright as his companions gathered around Teal'c.

Carter watched them lift him. "Is he all right?"

"He lives, for now." The man released her, watching her carefully. To make sure she didn't fall again, Carter guessed. His master had probably demanded she be delivered intact.

"What do you mean, for now? What's going to happen to him?"

"That does not concern you."

"Of course it concerns me!"

The First Prime raised an eyebrow. "Perhaps I should have made myself clear. His fate is utterly beyond your control, and yours hangs in the balance. Therefore, you would do better to focus on what is about to happen to you."

The four Jaffa were standing around Teal'c, holding him upright. One of them pressed a control on his wrist armor, activating the transporter. As Carter watched, the rings dropped down around the little group, surrounding them in a cage of stone for a moment before light flooded down.

"No," she breathed.

When the rings rose again, they were empty.

Carter found herself staring at the place Teal'c had been. For a moment, the suddenness with which he had been taken almost felled her, as brutal as the zat's stray charge. She had been in the Jaffa's company so long, since the Pit of Sorrows had swallowed them both and flung itself up towards the stars, that for a second or two she had to fight back a wave of panic.

The hallway around her felt very large, and very quiet.

She took a breath, straightened her back, and forced herself calm. The panic retreated. In a way, its threat had been a positive thing — the spark of adrenaline it had brought served to sharpen Carter's senses. It was a lesson she had learned long ago; fear was not always the enemy, as long as it was kept on a tight enough leash.

And standing in the depths of a Goa'uld starship, an unknown distance from Earth, unarmed and alone and with no immediate prospects for escape, Carter knew she had to keep the leash very tight indeed.

"All right," she said coldly. "What happens now?"

"You are to be presented to my master," the First Prime replied. "The God, Neheb-Kau."

Carter lifted her arms a little way from her body and looked pointedly down at herself, at her sodden jeans and stained cotton shirt. "Like this?"

"Better that, than with a hundred of Ra's victims on your skin."

The dust, she thought. And the expression on the man's face told her that he took no pleasure in the notion. She stored that knowledge away, along with the tiny measure of hope it brought her.

This Jaffa, this First Prime, seemed as repulsed by the Ash Eater's works as she was.

"Since you put it like that…" She ran a hand back through her hair. Drying in the hall's cool air, it was starting to stick uncomfortably to her scalp. "So. When does he want to see me?"

"He commanded that you be brought to him as soon as you were cleansed." The Jaffa glanced warily up the hallway, towards the big golden doors at the far end. "Against my counsel."

"Really?"

He nodded. "His curiosity is mighty. Now, walk with me. And do not try to escape again."

"You don't need to worry about that," she said grimly. The gold-clad guards lining the walls were just as motionless as when she had arrived, but Carter knew just how fast their staff weapons could be brought to bear if she was foolish enough to try anything. If she was honest with herself, even Teal'c's attack on the Jaffa was probably ill-judged. She had little doubt that these men would have cut down their own First Prime, without hesitation, if it meant protecting their God from danger.

Instead, Carter had decided to follow the basic military doctrine that, when faced with overwhelming odds, a soldier should retreat and gather as much intelligence as possible. Her life, and Teal'c's, might depend on her discovering everything she could about their situation. Now looked very much like the time to start getting some answers.

The Jaffa was nodding her forwards. Carter set off, keeping

her pace measured, as regular and unthreatening as possible, as she began to walk up to the golden doors.

It took longer to get there than Carter had estimated. The hallway was very long indeed. The First Prime's footfalls matched hers the whole way. And as they passed each set of guards, the golden men dropped to one knee in perfect and practiced sequence.

Unusually, the doors did not slide apart when she reached them. Instead, they swung inwards, silent and heavy. Carter stepped through, into flickering gloom and hazy air.

The ceiling of this new chamber was somewhat higher than that of the hallway, but it still felt oppressive. It was a wide, square room, lit only by burning lanterns set into alcoves. The rear wall sloped oddly, and the centre of the floor was dominated by a low, stepped platform, topped with a golden throne. There was a door to either side of the chamber, each guarded by two more of the Jaffa Carter had seen in the hallway.

The air smelled of lantern-smoke and spices.

Behind her, the doors swung closed; Carter felt a slight brush of the air they displaced as they moved. A moment later the First Prime appeared next to her. "Human," he said quietly.

"Yes?"

"I say this not for your well-being, but for my own. Should the God choose to remove his mask, you may find the sight unsettling." His voice lowered further. "You will keep your eyes longer if you do not react."

"Unsettling?" There was something in the way he had spoken that Carter didn't like at all. "What do you mean?"

"Pray you do not find out."

Carter hated it when people made cryptic statements at her, then refused to follow them up. She was about to say so when a sound rang out through the room; a soft, metallic chiming. It rang three times, then silenced.

A door to Carter's right, behind the throne, slid aside.

Through it stepped two more Jaffa guards. Then a pair of human slaves, one male, one female, naked but for loincloths and thick chains of gold at their wrists and throats. Their scalps were shaved, their eyes were ringed with kohl. They looked utterly terrified.

Behind these two walked the God, Neheb-Kau.

As his First Prime had hinted, the Goa'uld's head was enclosed in glittering mechanized armor, gold and gleaming like the death-mask of a pharaoh. His shoulders were similarly adorned, and he wore a jeweled pectoral across his chest. The rest of him was concealed in long robes of silk, utterly black.

Next to her, the First Prime dropped to one knee.

The procession continued walking behind the throne. Behind Neheb-Kau paced a tall, robed man, his face gaunt and frowning, and behind him two more Jaffa. As Carter watched the guards spread out, taking position on either side of the platform. Neheb-Kau made his way to the throne and sat, carefully, while the slaves stepped behind him. The robed man stood to the God's left, beside the throne.

Once everyone was still, Neheb-Kau raised a hand. "Kafra, rise. Introduce our guest."

His voice was high, a thin rushing behind his mask, yet backed with the unmistakable echo of a Goa'uld parasite tugging at human vocal chords. There was a strangeness to it, a liquid, pestilent quality, and the hand he had raised was withered and skeletal, the flesh of it blackened like rotted fruit.

No wonder his First Prime — Kafra — had warned her about what lay behind that metal face.

"My Lord." The Jaffa got up. "This is the human we discovered within the Pit of Sorrows. We found her with the First Prime of Apophis."

Neheb-Kau's mask tilted a fraction. "You are a long way from home, human."

Carter had seldom felt further. "I know."

"I wonder if you do." The God leaned forwards, the silk of his robes whispering. "Perhaps I should explain your situation. You were discovered, armed, aboard my personal property, in the company of the First Prime of a rival System Lord. You attacked my Jaffa, killing one of them. My technicians tell me that you had attempted to access the control systems of the Pit of Sorrows during its journey, no doubt to prevent it reaching me." He settled back again, and spread his ruined hands. "And now you stand before me, aboard my throneship, and do not even afford me the proper respect. Tell me, why should you not die now?"

"Because I'm not your enemy," said Carter. She hoped it was true. "Neither is Teal'c — he doesn't even serve Apophis anymore."

"He does not? How can this be?"

Carter wondered how far she should go with her explanation. *Not very far at all,* she decided. "He chose to work with us… With me, instead. Against Apophis." She shrugged. "It's kind of a long story…"

Silence descended upon the chamber, broken only by the faint clatter of golden chain links. The slaves were shivering.

And then Neheb-Kau chuckled. It was a dry sound, like leaves rustling at the base of a dead tree. "So, the First Prime of Apophis has defied his God, and now serves the Tau'ri. What do you think of that, Djetec?"

The robed man's voice was a hiss of rage. "It is a blasphemy, my Lord."

"Manners, Djetec. Apophis is no concern of ours. I would rather a renegade Jaffa on my ship than a loyal envoy of that tedious little insect." The mask turned to Kafra. "Where is this Teal'c?"

"With your ka'epta of surgeries."

The word was like ice in Carter's chest. "Surgeries?"

"He is merely undergoing medical tests. As a Jaffa, his physiology is known to us — the tests will provide baseline data on the state of the Ash Eater."

"So he won't be harmed?"

Djetec glared down at her. "He is responsible for the death of one of our Jaffa. Should he not be punished?"

Carter glanced across at Kafra. To relate what had happened in the Pit of Sorrows, at least as she saw it, would place the blame firmly on him — it had been he who had fired first, in the fear and confusion and the dust-laden darkness. She didn't know how much trouble that would get him into, but she suspected it would be a lot, and not the kind she would wish on anyone.

And he had, in the past little while, started to show her at least a kind of respect.

"That was a…" She searched for the best word. "A misunderstanding. I don't think your men expected to find us in there, and we just wanted to get out."

Neheb-Kau's eyes glowed, subtly. "Kafra?"

"It is possible, my Lord. The ch'epta who entered with us were afraid. One cried out… Perhaps the situation was not as clear-cut as I had thought."

At that, the robed advisor leaned down towards Neheb-Kau's mask. There was a brief, whispered exchange. Carter tried to listen in, but the chamber was too full of echoes.

Then Djetec straightened, and Neheb-Kau spoke aloud. "Human, you tried to steal the Ash Eater from me. Attempted to access the Pit's control matrix."

Carter shook her head. "That's not true."

"The damage you caused has been catalogued," said Djetec.

"I'm not denying that we tried to access the control system, but we weren't trying to steal anything. We were just trying to get home, that's all. When the Pit took off we were trapped."

"I am told you very nearly succeeded," replied Neheb-Kau.

"We did?"

"Indeed. Given more time, you would either have taken control of the Pit's primary systems, or caused the hyperdrive to explode."

"Oh." Suddenly, the throne room seemed rather cold. "Okay."

"Which implies considerable knowledge of our technologies," Neheb-Kau went on. "You say you have worked against Apophis, alongside your traitorous companion. In so doing, have you learned of our machines?"

"I know something about them."

The mask tipped, quizzically. "Impressive. You are a scientist among your people?"

There was little point denying it. "I am, yes."

"As am I." There was something in the Goa'uld's awful voice that might even been a smile. "I too study technologies alien to my race. And have been persecuted. Human, we have much in common."

That drew a swift, sideways glare from the thin-faced advisor. Carter could see that the man had not approved at all of the comparison, but if Neheb-Kau had noticed, he didn't show it. In fact, he seemed almost eager to engage with Carter.

"You have questions," he was saying. "We scientists always do. Let me answer them for you." He reached to his pectoral and pressed a gem.

The room shivered. There was a grating, a deep, sonorous grinding, continuous and powerful and frightening, like vast blocks of stone sliding one against the other. For a moment Carter couldn't determine what the sound was or where it was coming from, until she realized that the sloping rear wall of the chamber was moving.

The entire wall was sliding downwards, and at its upper edge, the glossy black of its facing gave way to an even deeper darkness.

It was a window, she realized. The wall was a viewport, a section of the ship's angled outer hull that was as transparent as air. Outside, she saw space, a velvet night spattered with diamond pinpricks. Entranced, she stepped forwards, hardly even seeing the gold-clad guards bringing their staff-weapons to bear on her, or the naked slaves cowering behind the throne. She was looking at the stars.

Samantha Carter had seen the depths of space before, untold times. But not like this. The stars were wrong. Their profusion was impaired, misshapen. At the top of the viewport she could see hardly any, but as the sliding wall dropped entirely away she saw that there were far more below her.

And along the right-hand side of the viewport, there were none at all.

It took Carter several seconds to work out that there was a planet there, a dark crescent, almost featureless against the night. Its surface was black, with just a faint, ruddy glow of reflected sunlight giving it any solidity at all. If Carter concentrated on it, she could just make out a texture, a slow roil of cloud, but as soon as her eyes moved it was gone again. Black on black, impenetrable.

It was an oddly disturbing sight. Carter had never seen a world that looked so utterly dead.

The ship was above the ecliptic plane. If the whirling disc of the galaxy could be thought of as horizontal, her voyage aboard the Pit of Sorrows had taken her up, either directly or at a steep angle. The ship was still aligned in the same plane, so there seemed to be more stars beneath Carter's feet than above her head. It was a strange feeling, vertiginous and dizzying.

The grinding of the viewport shield had ceased, replaced by a softer noise. Behind her, the platform was rotating.

"It has a certain beauty, does it not?" Neheb-Kau's voice was hushed, even the Goa'uld vibration behind it suppressed. "From the surface, even more so… A magnificent desolation, an endless sea of ash beneath a leaden sky…"

Carter couldn't think of anything less attractive than the corpse-world beyond the window, but she refrained from saying so.

"My Lord," said Kafra, his voice strangely subdued. "If I may leave your presence briefly?"

"The sight too much for you, old friend?"

"There is a matter I must attend to. A minor thing. I shall be but moments."

"Very well." The Goa'uld waved him away, as one might shoo away a fly. "Human, forgive my First Prime. He finds this world disturbing. You and I are of sterner stuff."

Carter watched Kafra walking out, the golden doors swinging open at his approach. "It sounds like you've been down to the surface."

"Long ago. But I never forgot it. Human, I have seen wonders beyond your comprehension, worlds of ice and fire." He was almost whispering now. "But nothing I have experienced matches this nameless world. *Nothing.* It affected me greatly."

Carter looked back at him, and past him. At the black chamber, lit with small fires, the low ceiling, the silent and terrified slaves… "I can see that."

A thunderous expression had appeared on Djetec's face. Carter spoke quickly. "But what brought you all the way out here?"

"Legends," replied Neheb-Kau. "Rumors. Scraps of data collected over a thousand years. The lost history of the race which ruled the galaxy long before the Goa'uld."

"The Ancients."

He laughed. "Those sickly fools? Before even them… Long before, when the stars were young, they left this world and built an empire to which even the Goa'uld cannot aspire. Human, as we are Gods to you, we would be worms before them."

No wonder Neheb-Kau had sought the place out, Carter thought. The promise of any technological advantage would draw such a creature like blood draws a shark. Not, judging by the state of his vessel, that it had done him much good. "But they must have died out too, surely?"

"Ah, that is the one true answer, human." Neheb-Kau gestured at the black planet, his rotted hand sliding horribly from his robe. "They are indeed gone, dead and vanished as though they never existed. Their hunger was too great."

"Hunger?"

"For energy. At the start, to power their machines, their starships, their civilization. But over time, they adapted themselves to feed on pure energy itself. And as they became more powerful, they in turn required more power."

It was an equation that had troubled Carter herself, on more than one occasion.

"They were voracious," continued Neheb-Kau, obviously enthused by the subject. "They became creatures of pure appetite, nothing more; able to strip all energy from a sun in weeks, from a world in mere hours." His voice was louder, now, filled with a breathy passion. "*All* energy, even from solid matter. Where they trod, only dust remained."

Dust. "Oh my God," Carter breathed. "You mean —"

The Goa'uld was on his feet. "Yes… You see? Do you see? When their hunger for energy outstripped their means to acquire it, their civilization fell. Imploded!"

"My Lord," hissed the advisor. "Your host!"

"They retreated, devouring their own empire as they went. Back here, to their homeworld, where the last of them fed on the only source of energy available to them."

"They ate their own sun?"

"That first. Then each other. Until only one remained."

Carter turned back to the window, stared out over that blighted, lifeless planet. *He eats the meal, the pot, the fire and the ash beneath…* It was a child's phrase now, robbed of all fear, all meaning. Too old to remember. Nothing except scraps of rumor, fragments of legend, unimaginably old and corroded and terrible. Shards of story that should have been left to decay, to vanish, not pieced back together and brought into the light. Not followed, across gulfs of space, to reveal the dead homeworld of a carnivorous nightmare.

Laura Miles, she thought, sickened. Greg Kemp, dried and withered in the ruins of the Ash Eater's victims. Lucas Harlowe. Anna Andersson — when the creature stripped all the energy from her, even from the very cells of her body, she became dust, inert powder.

"How can it be alive?" she whispered. "After all this time?"

"Life and death are distinctions that no longer apply. It exists, and it feeds. That is all. It has no mind. Unchecked, it absorbs all energy within reach. Nothing remains but ash." Neheb-Kau slumped back down into his throne. The mask tipped forwards. "The last survivor of the most powerful race in all history, and that arrogant cretin Ra kept it as a pet. Threw victims to it whenever the whim took him…"

There was a breeze behind her, a subtle shift of the chamber's spiced air. Carter looked back over her shoulder and saw Kafra hurry in. He paced quickly up to the throne, then dropped to one knee before it, staff held vertical . "My Lord, I bring news."

"Speak."

"Our long-range sensors have detected a fleet in hyperspace, heading towards us."

The mask tipped towards Djetec. "They seek the prize?"

"It seems likely. Ra possessed many chappa'ai."

"Then it is time to leave this beautiful world." Neheb-Kau straightened in his throne. "Djetec, have the pel'tak made ready for my presence. I shall guide us back to our own domains."

"You're leaving?" Carter gasped.

The words left her lips before she could stop them. If there was a chance, however small, that the approaching fleet was somehow allied to Stargate Command, then she needed the throneship to stay right where it was. But now it seemed that Neheb-Kau was ready to take his new toy and go home with it.

"For now," the Goa'uld replied "The time for confrontation with our enemies is not yet at hand."

Kafra was getting up. "We are but one vessel, human. Would you have us challenge a fleet?"

Neheb-Kau barked a dry, thin laugh. "You forget, Kafra. When the Ash Eater is fully in my thrall, one vessel is all we will need. And then, our rise to power will be inexorable!"

Beside him, Djetec nodded sagely. "Until that day, we must retire. There is much to prepare."

"And what of you, human?" Neheb-Kau's mask turned towards Carter. "Whatever shall I do with you?"

Djetec leaned down to his master's hidden head. "Be wary, my Lord. There is still much we do not know about this slave." His eyes flicked to Carter. They were cold, like little chips of black ice, and somehow greedy. "Do not forget the weapon she carried. Does a scientist go armed?"

"I suppose that depends where she goes," replied the Goa'uld. He sat back, his withered hands clasping the arms of his throne. "But still, she intrigues me. There is much we could learn from each other…"

"The God is most wise. Yet perhaps I might prepare her, personally. To make sure she presents no threat to your plans."

Carter stepped forwards, her hands spread. "I'm no threat to you. And neither is Teal'c… And sir, I'm sorry, but I don't see how we can be of any use to you, either." She gestured at the black world outside the viewport. "You have the Ash Eater now, you don't need us. All we want is to be allowed off this ship."

Djetec's expression had been getting increasingly furious as Carter spoke. "Silence, slave!" he snapped. "You dare speak to your betters in such a manner?"

"Betters?"

He turned to Neheb-Kau once more. "Please, my Lord, let me prepare her. She must be schooled in the proper manner by which to converse with a God."

"My Lord Neheb-Kau," said Kafra suddenly. "I respectfully disagree with your *Tjaty*."

"What a surprise," the Goa'uld replied.

"Determining whether the human is a benefit or a hazard is a matter for warriors, my Lord. For your First Prime. Is it not my duty to stand between you and all who would threaten you?"

"It is."

"I will take charge of the slave, and her *shol'va*. When I see fit to pronounce them safe, I shall have them delivered to you." He turned his dark gaze on the advisor. "After all, *Tjaty* Djetec, are you not required to prepare the pel'tak?"

Neheb-Kau's mask bobbed. "Your counsel is wise, old friend. The human is in your charge. Have her delivered to my chambers, when you are sure she is suitable for my company."

"And the traitor?

"Once Pa'Nakht is done with him, take him to the generator core. A year or two tending the converters might teach him some humility."

"As you command." He glared at Carter, then whirled and strode away towards the golden doors. "Human, with me!"

Carter took one last look at Neheb-Kau, his metal face impassive atop the black silk morass of his robes, and then walked quickly back to where Kafra stood waiting for her by the doors.

"Don't do this," she breathed.

His answer surprised her. He kept his voice low, and without looking at her leaned slightly to put his head closer to hers. "Human, your life hangs by a thread. Snap it if you will, but do not drag me down with you."

"Drag you?" Carter stared at him. "Is your position here really that precarious?"

"You have no idea. Now, if you wish to see tomorrow, follow me. *Quickly.*"

Chapter 14.

CANNED HEAT

IN ANCIENT Athenian legend, the *Clythena* was a trireme, an oared warship of polished gold, so perfect and so reflective that enemy crews would be blinded by its radiance. Stories of the vessel told how it once evaded a Persian attack by entering a bank of fog before them, only to emerge an instant later *behind*, as though it had travelled, unharmed and unaffected, beneath the surface of the sea.

Daniel Jackson wondered how the tellers of those stories would react to the *Clythena* he was seeing now.

The Tel'tak, stuttering the last of its energies through its maneuvering thrusters, had been remotely guided into a launch rack in the Goa'uld vessel's flight bay. Looking out through the forward viewports, Daniel had given up trying to count how many other racks the bay held before he had even started; there must have been hundreds, a sea of curved claws reaching down from the girdered roof, an insane maze of walkways and platforms below. He had seen the glider bays of Ha'tak pyramid ships before, and they had seemed cavernous enough at the time, but they were tiny compared to this.

And, given what he had seen of the *Clythena*'s structure on the way in, this was not the only flight bay the ship possessed. Possibly not even the primary one.

Some of the racks were occupied, but at least three quarters were not — most of the bay's complement must have been still in space, darting between the fleet's vessels or guiding that obscene weapon into the flagship's underbelly. This gave him some hope, at least, of being able to get out of the Tel'tak without being immediately apprehended. "Okay guys, hatch or transport rings?"

Jack was checking his gear again, making sure that the remote detonator for the charges he had set was active. "Is there enough power for the transporter?"

"There will be some stored for that purpose, in case of emergency," Bra'tac told him. "However, the hatch is less likely to draw attention."

"Hatch it is." Jack crossed the deck to the hatchway and keyed it open. He peered outside. "Looks clear."

Daniel watched him step through. He found himself trying to think of something pithy to say, but the scale of the task ahead of him had robbed him of wit. All he could do was to take a couple of deep breaths, and follow Jack out into the heart of the flying mountain.

There were mesh steps leading down to a metal walkway. Daniel climbed down them, keeping as quiet as he could, trying not to look through the open mesh at the hundred-meter drop beneath his feet. From what he could see, the ships racked up around him could be launched by simply dropping them from the rack into the space below, and letting them power out through vast horizontal slots in the ship's hull. The open space was needed for maneuvering. It all made perfect, logical sense, like a kind of three-dimensional truck stop, but the scale of it was awful.

The cold winds rushing through the bay weren't helping him, either. He guessed they were necessary just to keep air moving through the vast space, but they still made him feel as though he were on the edge of a cliff.

Once on the walkway he moved next to Jack, and watched Bra'tac jump down the last few steps to join them. "So far, I do not believe we have been spotted," the Jaffa said. "But we should act quickly. Surveillance in the flagship of a System Lord will be more intense than in other vessels."

"We'll keep that in mind," Jack replied. "What about the radios?"

"Use them only when necessary. I shall contact you when I have access to a suitable vessel."

Daniel looked around. "You should have plenty to choose from."

"Indeed. But none will be of use while this ship functions unimpaired."

"You worry about getting us a ride," Jack said. "We'll worry about the impairing part."

Bra'tac grinned, and slapped his shoulder. Then he turned and sprinted away along the walkway, his staff weapon held low.

"Fast, for an old guy."

"He's fast for a young guy," said Daniel. "Come on, let's find a transporter."

It took several minutes to even find their way to the bay's nearest edge. By the time they had done so, Daniel was almost starting to become used to the frightening drop beneath his feet. Actually stepping off the mesh and into a corridor with a solid floor felt slightly strange, and somewhat claustrophobic.

The feeling didn't last. As soon the two men found themselves in what was obviously one of the vessel's main access ways, all thoughts of being enclosed vanished.

It was more of a street than a corridor, paneled in gleaming white marble and trimmed with gold. The floor was a checkerboard of stone inlay, and the ceiling curved high above their heads, glowing a pale, open blue. Doric columns lined the walls, and the hatches Daniel could see were tall and rectangular, an elegant contrast to the trapezoid openings normally favored by the Goa'uld.

Daniel had no doubt that the *Clythena* operated on exactly the same stolen technologies as any other Goa'uld vessel, but cosmetically there was very little he recognized.

"This is different," Jack muttered, as they leaned gingerly around the hatch frame to check for danger.

"No kidding," Daniel whispered. "Looks like this Hera's really run with the whole Athenian look."

"See anyone behind us?"

Daniel checked. "No, we're clear."

They padded out into the corridor, keeping as close to the pillared walls as they could. So far, the vessel seemed remarkably unpopulated, but that was no surprise. Goa'uld capital ships could be operated by a very small number of people; one skilled pilot could fly an entire Ha'tak. Many of the larger ships were more like mobile garrisons than attack vessels, and if the warriors they carried were in their barracks entire decks could remain empty.

It would be too much to hope that Hera's flagship would remain so quiet, Daniel decided. But while the fleet was still massing, it was very possible that everyone aboard had more important things to do than wander the corridors admiring the décor.

Of course, just as he had started to allow himself a measure of hope, he heard footsteps.

Lots of them.

Jack had heard them too. He glanced quickly about, then pointed to a junction just a few meters ahead. Together, they ran around the corner and then split up, each finding a column to hide behind.

Daniel pressed himself behind the pillar, feeling the smooth coolness of it against his skin. It might have looked like stone, he realized, but it wasn't. Some kind of solid, resinous plastic, which made more sense than actually using marble on a starship. No doubt Hera could have afforded to do so if she had wanted to, but in a battle, impact-shattered stone would become lethal shrapnel.

The footfalls, the unmistakable sound of a column of armored men marching in unison, reached the corner. Daniel hugged the wall, trying to think small, unassuming thoughts.

The march continued past for thirty, forty seconds, until Daniel heard the last men go past. At that point, he couldn't resist poking his head out, just enough to see them.

As he had expected, their uniforms did not conform to the usual norms of Jaffa armor design. He could see the similarities — the Goa'uld had never been fantastic innovators, but there were enough differences to mark these men out as serving a very different God to those SG-1 had encountered so far. Their armor was formed from smooth, bronze-colored plates, and their heads were covered in helms that were more like Corinthian helmets than the animal-Gods of Egypt. They wore short, scarlet cloaks, and their staff weapons were slender, lacking the clubbed end but tipped with wicked blades at the other.

"Daniel? Why am I getting a serious *Clash of the Titans* vibe off of these guys?"

"Well, we've seen different kinds of Jaffa armor before. The only reason most of them tend to follow the same pattern is just inertia on behalf of the Goa'uld. Maybe Hera likes to do things her own way."

"Or she's got a thing for gladiators."

"They were Roman."

Jack gave him a look. "I know that."

"Whatever she's into, I don't like the look of those spears. Maybe we should head down this corridor instead."

"Suits me."

They moved on in silence for a short while, then Daniel had a thought. "Hey, should we blow the Tel'tak yet?"

Jack shook his head. "When we've blown the hyperdrive on this thing, then we'll do it."

"What if they find the charges before we find the navigation system?"

"That would be bad."

"For who?"

"For the poor son of a bitch who's got a hold of them when I press the button." They had reached another junction. "Okay, where now?"

Daniel looked around, spotted a small cartouche at the corner. The text was strange, a bizarre fusion of Goa'uld hieroglyphs and classical Greek characters, but he was already beginning to make sense of it. "From what I'm seeing here, this whole level is mainly equipment and consumables storage, warehouses ranged around the systems core. Probably accessed directly from the flight bays."

"That makes sense. You'd want to be able to ferry materiel directly from the Tel'taks into the stores."

"So if we take the wrong turning, we're going to be walking around between warehouses forever... Ah, hold on. This word here, *metagoi*. Means to convey from one place to another."

"That's good, right?"

"Yeah, that's good. It doesn't mention a specific room or chamber in relation to the *metagoi* — I'd guess we'll see one if we find a primary intersection. We need to keep heading towards the outer hull, away from the flight bay." He glanced back over his shoulder, suddenly unsure of which way he was facing. "Ah, Jack? I think I've gotten myself turned around…"

"It's this way," said Jack, with a note of exasperation.

"You're sure?"

"Reasonably."

"Fine. But you know what? I'd give anything for a map with an arrow and 'You Are Here' on it."

They set off, walking in silence, their boots making little sound on the solid flooring. Daniel breathed shallowly, straining to listen for the sound of marching footsteps. More than once he stopped, convinced he had heard the approach of more Jaffa, only to discover that the beat he heard was that of his own heart.

When they found the intersection, it looked worryingly exposed. Jack used a tiny mirror to check around the corner. "It's clear."

"You're kidding."

"Don't knock it." He darted around. Daniel followed him, into a corridor twice as wide and high as the first they had entered. It was so tall that it had a second story, a railed balcony projecting from the outer wall.

There was a golden ring set into the flooring at the intersection, and a control cartouche on a raised pedestal. Daniel studied it for a few moments, then saw the combination of icons he was looking for. "Location, system, unrestricted, *Kubernhosis*."

"Goober-what?"

"*Kubernhosis*. Steering or piloting."

"So why the hell didn't you just say 'Navigation?' Why do you always have to leave one word untranslated to make me look like an idiot?"

"Because I've got to justify my paycheck somehow." Daniel pressed the icons, and looked up to see the ceiling iris open. Slender rings dropped down around them, gleaming like brass, and an instant later he was surrounded by light. He fancied that he felt an electric shiver race through him as the transport rings took him apart on the molecular level, but the process was too swift, too complex to really perceive. One moment he was staring through the cage of rings at the open, columned corridor, and the next he was in near darkness, surrounded by machinery.

And people were looking at him.

If there was a disadvantage to the Goa'uld ring transporter, it was that the system lacked any element of surprise. The occupants of the navigation control room knew that someone was beaming in as soon as the rings had begun to hover down from the ceiling iris at their end. It wasn't like kicking in a door: Daniel was on full view of three white-robed technicians and two Jaffa guards for several seconds before he could even move.

Jack was faster. Even as the rings had started to lift he had ducked between two of them, leaping between one as it rose and over the one below, rolling out of the way before the shouting even started. Daniel saw him use the zat gun to blast one of the guards. The bronze-clad man gave a guttural cry and slumped, his body wreathed in lightning.

One of the technicians ran at Daniel. He ducked aside, grabbed the man as he went past and slammed him into the wall behind the transporter. As the tech bounced away, Daniel heard the zat snarl twice more.

He glanced up to see the remaining Jaffa raise his left arm, fist clenched, armored forearm horizontal to the floor as if he was holding a shield. A moment later, he *was* — a raised boss on his armor had fanned out, impossibly fast, snapping out a ring of gleaming metal and then another to encircle the first, and the Jaffa was raising his staff weapon behind a round shield, like that of a Greek hoplite.

The next zat blast caromed off the shield and spattered into the ceiling.

The Jaffa's staff weapon opened, the cruel spear-end snapping into two halves to unleash a sizzling bolt of white-hot plasma. Daniel was already hurling himself floorwards, and he felt the heat of the blast across his shoulders. He dragged his MP-5 up, thumbed off the safety and tugged the trigger, felt the gun hammer back into his hand as a burst of armor-piercing bullets crashed deafeningly into the shield. They didn't get through, simply whirled away in a lethal storm of ricochets, but the Jaffa had not been expecting the force behind them. He stumbled, the shield coming up on reflex, and Jack shot him in the knees.

A zat gun's stunning discharge is effective no matter where it hits. The Jaffa collapsed, latent voltage curling across his armor and snaking away into the floor.

Daniel scrambled up. "Are you okay?"

"I'm fine." Jack was blinking down at the unconscious Jaffa. He made a vague circular mime around his own forearm. "Neat trick."

"Think we can get some of those?"

"If you meet this Hera, maybe you can ask."

Daniel glanced quickly around. "Jack, get the door. I'll see what's best to break." He went for the centre consoles, shoved an unconscious technician out of his seat and then pressed a series of icons, activating a display panel. "And here we go."

"What are you doing?" hissed Jack. He pointed at a bank of control crystals. "All the fragile stuff's over there!"

"Just give me two minutes."

"Carter and Teal'c might not have two minutes."

"And if I blow all these systems without knowing what they do, I could lock down this entire section, or cause the hyperdrive to overload and blow up, or —"

"Okay, I get it. Just…" Jack turned back to the hatch. "You know."

The screen was filling with data. Daniel stared at the pages of meaningless hieroglyphs for a few moments, then found his way back to a core menu. "Here we go. They were running course calculations before they went into hyperspace, coordinating the fleet. Looks like they were going to send all this data up to the pel'tak in a few minutes. I think we found this place just in time."

Jack didn't answer. Daniel tapped at the screen, watching as the menu shrank to a new series of options. He didn't want to interrupt the course calculations before he had to. That would alert the pel'tak — the ship's control deck — too early. Instead, he navigated around the course data, idly watching the program running as a systems diagram came up over it.

And then he froze, his finger halfway to the screen. "What the hell?"

"Ah, Daniel?"

"Two minutes."

"You said that two minutes ago!"

He wiped his finger across the screen, shrinking the system diagram. He no longer had any interest in it. Instead, all his attention was on the course calculations. "Jack?"

"Don't tell me we can't blow up the navigation system."

"Ah, sorry."

Jack left the hatch and ran over to him. "What have you found?" he asked, with the weary tone of a mother indulging a curious child: *and whatever it is, no, you can't keep it as a pet.*

"Hera's orders to the fleet, the core seed for the course calculations." He pointed to a block of golden text on the screen. "Jack, she's after the same thing we are."

There was a moment of silence. Then: "Say again?"

"Hera is amassing this fleet with the express purpose of capturing the Pit of Sorrows."

Jack stepped back. "How the hell did she... Daniel, who else got that message from Ra?"

"Obviously it wasn't sent just to our gate. If Ra was really serious about knowing when the Pit had been compromised, maybe it dialled *all* his gates."

"How many did he have?"

"A lot."

"Look, don't think I'm not impressed, okay?" Jack gestured at the screen. "Really, I am. But how does this change what we need to do here?"

"Because we can use this! Jack, you know how far behind the Pit we were in the Tel'tak, and there isn't a small ship in this fleet that could even match that performance. Hyperdrive speed is all about how much power you can throw around—I'm guessing the only reason the Pit itself is so damn fast is because it's a one-shot engine. I'd lay money down that it makes one trip and burns out for good."

"Oh, *right...*" Jack nodded, suddenly understanding. "So if we stay right here..."

"...And let Hera go exactly where she wants to go, we'll get to the Pit of Sorrows faster than we ever could on our own." Daniel pushed the seat back and got up. "Plus, she knows where it is."

"Where is it?"

Daniel pointed vaguely at the screen. "There. I don't know, Sam's the astrophysicist."

"She's gonna be so disappointed in you when I tell her about this."

"You called her awkward, remember? Come on, let's get out of here before somebody finds these guys and sounds an alarm."

They ran back to the transporter. Jack readied the zat gun again, while Daniel found the controls to return them to their original destination. He pressed the sequence, and waited.

Nothing happened.

"Okay, that's not so good." He keyed the icons again, with the same effect.

"Daniel?"

"It's not working."

"Yeah, I can see that. *Make* it work."

"That's kind of what I'm trying to do..."

"Did I mention that I could hear marching out there?"

Daniel gave him the sour eye. "Making up stuff like that isn't the best way to motivate me, you know."

"Who said I was making it up?"

"Maybe there's a reset button somewhere." It was a slim chance, probably no chance at all. He had used ring transporters before, and none of them had ever needed a reset before they would work twice in a row.

Still, the alternative explanations — that he had been actively locked out of the system, or that weapons fire had damaged the machinery — were considerably less palatable, especially if Jack really had heard an approaching patrol. He searched rapidly through the available icons, but none looked immediately like a reset key. In desperation, and certain that the yammer of his own pulse masked the stamp of approaching hoplites, he pressed the original combination again.

There was a grinding from above, and the ceiling began to dilate. "Oh thank God," he breathed.

"Hm?"

"Nothing." The rings were dropping down around them. "Had it all under control."

"Glad to hear it," Jack replied. "So, where would be the best place to hole up?"

There was a blast of white light, a singing along Daniel's nerves. The light obscured all sight, all sound, and then it raced up away from him. "One of the storage areas. It'll be close to the flight bay and there should be plenty of —" He stopped, abruptly. "Where are we?"

They were not back at the intersection. The corridors around them were narrower, the floor darker, the ceiling solid and devoid of illumination. The only light came from burning lamps set into alcoves in the walls, and the glow of the transporter aperture above his head.

When that closed, there was only the flickering glow of the flames.

Daniel suppressed a curse, and began to study the control pedestal. "I must have hit the wrong icons."

"Daniel..."

"Working on it."

Jack grabbed his arm and dragged him sideways, hard. "We've got company!"

Daniel heard it a moment later: the rhythmic stamp of marching feet, and close. He tugged free of Jack's grip, and together they darted to the nearest corner. "This is getting to be a habit."

"Shh." The first Jaffa were already striding past the corner.

Daniel crouched, shrank into the wall. There was a pillar, but it was set into the corner, and provided little cover. If any of those marching men so much as glanced in his direction, he would be facing a forest of spears in an instant.

The patrol was larger than the one they had seen on the storage level — these Jaffa marched four abreast. That was, until a gap appeared in their formation, a gap two men wide, ten men deep, and occupied by a lone figure in white.

Daniel frowned, and looked closer.

It was a woman. She was compact, a head smaller than the Jaffa surrounding her, and dressed in a flowing white *chiton* that only hinted at what curved beneath. Her skin was pale gold, her hair had the metal iridescence of wet sand under shifting sunlight. A jeweled headdress glittered at her crown, matched by rings in her ears and bands at wrists and ankles.

She walked with a mix of unconscious grace and restrained, nervous fury. "Hera," breathed Daniel.

"Looks like trouble," whispered Jack.

"Capital Tee." The last men in the patrol had gone past. "C'mon, let's get out of here."

He stood, turned, and saw what was rounding the far corner. "Holy—"

Two more Jaffa were walking towards him, but unlike any he had seen before. They were vast, their heads almost scraping the ceiling, their shoulders broad, their limbs thick and powerfully muscled. They wore little armor, save for a mail kilt and a great curved disc over their shoulders, but their heads were covered by huge helms. Bulls' heads in bronze and dark iron and gold, their horns long and wickedly pointed.

The eyes of the Minotaurs glowed red in the fluttering gloom.

Daniel shrank back around the corner, knowing he was directly behind Hera's procession, but the Minotaurs were almost around the corner, and the thought of being charged by the monsters was terrifying. Somehow he knew that a zat gun wasn't even going to slow them down. He ducked back around, out of their sight, and noticed Jack had done the same.

More marching sounded from the opposite direction. Suddenly Daniel realized that they had, by some horrible accident, found their way onto the decks favored by the Goddess Hera herself.

There was no way he could get back to the transporter.

Jack held up a hand, gestured for him to move forwards. Daniel nodded, and began to pace as silently as he was able along the corridor. If he kept at just the right speed, he might be able to stay between the two patrols until he reached an unoccupied intersection.

Again, a slim hope, but better than no hope at all.

Jack was just behind him. He could hear the second patrol, seemingly on his heels, and beyond that the heavy, measured tread of the two Minotaurs.

And then, from ahead of him, the sounds of the first patrol stamping to a perfectly-executed mass halt.

Crap, thought Daniel. He slowed.

"*Lokhagos*, take your men and return to the pel'tak. I shall call you when you are needed."

The voice must have been Hera's. It was deeper than Daniel would have guessed from the woman's stature, and backed with the unmistakable snarl of a Goa'uld, but there was a honey to it, too. A seductive lilt that, coming from a System Lord, spoke to Daniel Jackson of pure danger.

He had been right in his initial assessment. Hera was trouble, and far more.

The patrol began to march again, and Daniel almost sighed with relief when he heard their footfalls moving away. If the pel'tak had been back in this direction, he and Jack would have been sandwiched between two platoons of Jaffa and the monstrous Minotaurs. As it was, only Hera remained ahead.

He moved on. Sure enough, the woman stood alone. She glanced back, almost in his direction, and he saw that her features were narrow, delicate, almost childlike. Until he saw the intensity of her gaze, and the subtle flare of golden light from her eyes.

She was beside a tall hatchway. At a wave of her hand, it slid aside, and she stepped through.

Jack was at Daniel's side. "How much further to the next intersection?"

"Can't be too far. We'll carry on, see if we can't get to a corner and then double back."

"And don't screw the address up this time."

"Picky." They moved on.

There was a corner just ahead, twenty paces past the hatch, maybe less. Daniel increased his pace, almost involuntarily, and headed right for it. He wanted to be as far from Hera and her oversized warriors as possible — there was something dreadful about the Minotaurs that went far beyond their mere size. Had he been asked to explain it, he would have faltered, but the reaction of his skin and his gut was enough. They were *wrong*, somehow, and he needed to be away.

Fate, however, had other ideas. As he neared the corner another brass-headed monster peered out from around it.

Daniel cursed, realizing with a horrible swoop of despair that he and Jack were trapped. He slowed, turned as fast as he could without sliding on the smooth floor, and bolted back towards the hatch.

There was no other way. It was after Hera, or into the hands of her Jaffa.

Jack passed his hand over the control. There was a second's nerve-jangling delay, and then the hatch slid open. Daniel waited until Jack was through, then ducked in and waited until the hatch closed behind him.

He looked back. They were in a wide, open chamber, dotted with furniture, with a kind of railed gallery along one wall and a series of viewports against the other. Outside the ports, splinters of light moved between the stars. In the centre of the room stood Hera and another woman, a slave with dark hair. Both were looking right at them.

Jack was already striding forwards. He raised the Zat, snapped off a shot at Hera, but the slave was hurling herself into his path. The beam caught her in the throat, span her around. She collapsed in a storm of voltage.

"Wait!" Daniel ran towards Jack. He had seen what Hera wore on her right hand.

It was a spiral of bright gold, wound between her fingers and curling fluidly down her wrist. Daniel saw the gem in Hera's palm glow, and flash out a pulse of distortion at Jack.

She was too slow. Jack snapped sideways, caught the woman's arm and dragged her off-balance. She gave a scream of rage, cut instantly short as she found the emitter of the zat gun pushed hard into her throat.

"You know," Jack said, his voice very low and very flat. "When people try to ribbon me I get really twitchy. Sometimes I try to press a button once and I end up pressing it over and over again…" He stepped partway behind her, twisting her arm up and ripping the device free from her hand. "Kind of a nervous thing."

Daniel was staring at Hera. She was breathing hard, her eyes wide. Her head was twisted back away from the zat emitter, neck muscles tight under golden skin. Her forehead shone.

Something cold and heavy formed behind Daniel's ribs. "Jack."

"I got this."

"I don't think you do." Daniel was watching a single bead of sweat on the woman's skin. It had started at her temple, and was tracking a glistening path down her jawline. "She's afraid of you."

Jack threw an accusing glance at him. "That's kind of the point."

"When was the last time you saw a System Lord afraid?"

"Oh, for crying out loud…" Jack jerked away from her, stepped back, the zat still aimed unerringly at her face. "Who is it?"

"I don't know. Not Hera."

"Okay, how much trouble are we in here?"

"More than you can possibly imagine," said Hera, stepping out from the shadows under the gallery.

Behind her, a dozen Jaffa hoplites raised their arms in perfect unison, shields whirling out of nothing, spears snapping apart to crackle with deadly energy. More appeared on the gallery, and from hatchways on either side of the chamber came the huge Minotaurs, stooping to get their horned helms under the doorframes. In moments, the room was full of Jaffa.

Daniel turned slowly, watching Hera walk out into the room. She was dressed in the same flowing white garment as the first woman, was jeweled in the same way, had her hair set in the same style. Her face was the same, her compact stature the same. Even her voice had sounded entirely as the woman in the corridor had sounded.

As far as he could see there was not a single difference between them. They were utterly alike.

No, he realized, not quite. The woman Jack had threatened was clearly shaken, her hand to her throat, eyes still on the zat. She was shaking, very slightly. Hera, the new arrival, was striding forward as calmly and confidently as she might walk alone, under a summer sky.

"Do not be afraid, Ericaceae," she smiled at her duplicate. "You have made me proud, as always."

"We were being herded," Daniel said, despairingly. "Jack, she's known all along."

"Of course I did," she told him, raising one eyebrow very slightly.

Her eyes were gray, like frost on steel.

"I am not sure which I find the most insulting," she continued. "That I should find assassins on my ship, or that it should be a pair of ridiculous dullards like you."

"Hey!" Jack looked hurt. "That was uncalled for!"

"Be silent," she snapped. "And stop aiming that weapon at my sister."

Daniel saw him hesitate. It was the wrong thing to do: in a heartbeat one of the Minotaurs was on him. It's head-sized fist closed around his forearm, wrenched him back, lifted. The zat tumbled from his grasp as he was dragged into the air.

Hera caught it. She turned it over, studied it for a moment or two. "Crude."

Daniel stepped towards her. Instantly every weapon in the room was aimed at his face. He stopped, raised his hands. "I promise you," he said, trying to keep his voice level. "We are not assassins."

"Daniel," grated Jack. His boots were a half-meter from the floor. "Don't tell her a damn thing!"

"*Daniel*," she repeated. Her lips curled in a smile. "Here are your choices, *Daniel*. You may ignore your… Well, whatever he is, and tell me which of my enemies sent you, or you may heed his words and watch my Minotaur pulls his arms out of his sockets." Her head tilted, quizzically. "I wonder what you will do?"

"No-one sent us," said Daniel desperately. "I swear to you, we aren't assassins."

"Given the evidence before us all, I find that unlikely." She drew closer to him, looking up at him with those frost-gray eyes. "So was it Lord Anshar or that effete fool Tsukiyomi? One last chance to make your choice, Daniel — delay me further, and the next choice you make will be which of his arms comes away first."

"I don't know either of them."

She smiled again. "I can *make* you choose, you know. I can make you do *all kinds* of things."

He looked up at Jack. The man's face was white with pain.

"Don't," he gasped.

There was no choice to be made, despite Hera's words. No choice at all.

"We seek the Ash Eater," Daniel said quickly.

The smile fell from Hera's lips. She opened her mouth, closed it again, then span on her heel. "Clear the chamber!"

One of the hoplites stiffened. "My Lady?"

"Has my voice suddenly become unclear? Leave the chamber!" She pointed at the nearest man. "Not you. Disarm them first, thoroughly. Then take the slave with you. Only the Minotaurs are to stay."

Daniel stood, perfectly still, while the Jaffa took his weapons. He was watching Hera. She was with her duplicate, her sister, and was whispering to her. He saw Hera stroke the other woman's face, a gesture of incredible gentleness and affection, and then the sister bowed, and hurried away.

"Let him down," Hera said finally, when all the hoplites had gone. "Slowly."

The Minotaur lowered Jack to the floor, then moved back from him, the bronze head dipping in reverence towards his Goddess. O'Neil sagged, almost fell, but then straightened, stood with his right arm dangling by his side, rubbing his shoulder with the hand that still worked.

"You okay?" Daniel asked him.

"I'll live."

"Such optimism," Hera growled. "Now, what do you know of Neheb-Kau's demon? Quickly, and do not try to deceive me."

"Neheb-Kau?" Daniel had heard the name, but not in relation to any Goa'uld. Neheb-Kau was said to guard the entrance to the *Duat*, the underworld, to have power over snake-bites and venomous stings, to be two-headed and uncontrollable. Binder of *ba* and *ka* after death, and protector of Ra as he travelled under the Earth. "I don't know him, I'm sorry."

"The blame for that abomination lies with him. He sought it out, and saw fit to loose it upon his betters." She lifted her head, narrowed her eyes piercingly. "Now, if you do not know of Neheb-Kau, what *do* you know?"

"The Ash Eater resides in a structure called the Pit of Sorrows."

"A crude translation." She shrugged a little. "But adequate. Continue."

"The Pit was opened on our world, by some scientists… They didn't know what they had found, and the Ash Eater killed them." Daniel wondered how much he should tell the Goa'uld, and how much he should conceal. He decided to keep things simple. "We were investigating their disappearance. I think we tripped some kind of failsafe device, because the Pit of Sorrows… It took off and flew into the sky."

"And you chose to follow it. Why?"

"Two of our friends are still in there," said Jack.

"Ah… And to save your friends, you stole that wreck of a ship from Apophis?"

She'd found it, of course. Daniel could only hope that she hadn't found Bra'tac too, although that was looking less likely by the second. Hera still displayed the classic Goa'uld need to self-aggrandize. If the old warrior was in her custody, he was sure they would have heard about it by now. "In a manner of speaking. It, ah, kind of broke down."

"Indeed. I'm surprised it even got you this far. In one way, Daniel, you are extraordinarily lucky."

"Only one?"

"Oh yes. Your luck has truly deserted you now. You have trespassed on my flagship. Do you really think I can let that go unpunished?"

"You could give it a try," Jack nodded.

"No. I cannot."

"But we seek what you seek," said Daniel. "Look, we're not your enemies."

Jack was rolling his right shoulder around. It looked like the feeling was coming back. "Just got off on the wrong foot, is all."

Hera grimaced. "In many ways, human, you owe your language to us. To hear it so abused is painful." She turned away, fixed her gaze on the viewports. The space beyond them was almost free from ships now. "In a very short time," she said quietly, "this fleet will enter hyperspace and travel to a planet that has no name. That is where I shall find the Pit of Sorrows. And once I do, I will use the Auger to drill a thousand kilometers into the crust of that world, and then I shall drop the Pit of Sorrows into the borehole and blast the surrounding surface with staff-cannons until Neheb-Kau's abomination is buried, utterly and forever."

Daniel stared. "Why? Why would you do that?"

"Because I have seen what the Ash Eater can do. I watched it devour a *world*, human. I was on Setraxis… I saw every living thing on a thriving planet reduced to oceans of dust, mountains of ash. A storm of black fire, roaming, unstoppable…"

"Are we talking about the same demon here?" Jack asked. "Because the one that I saw could barely eat three people. It lost interest halfway through the last guy."

"You doubt me, human? You doubt what I have seen?"

"No," said Daniel, hurriedly. "But the Ash Eater is contained. There is a pillar, a golden cylinder at the heart of the Pit of Sorrows. It's locked up in there. It's safe."

"Safe." Hera snorted a laugh. "*Contained.* Is that what you have been telling yourself, while you chased the memory of your friends? That the Ash Eater is locked away in Ra's little tomb, and can do no-one any harm?" She shook her head. "No. The Pit cannot be opened. The risk is too great — I will not unleash that horror on the galaxy. Not again."

"But —"

"*No*, human. Accept this as truth, and say your farewells. Perhaps it will make your captivity easier to bear."

"Ah," Said Jack. "So we're not going to go with the whole 'letting us go unpunished' thing."

"We are not." She raised a hand, still without turning from the viewport. "Minotaurs? Take them into the dark."

"I don't like the sound of that," said Daniel, as the massive figures turned towards him. Behind them, Hera turned her head, looking back over her shoulder at him.

"There are worse places to be, human. There truly are."

Chapter 15.

FROZEN

THERE WERE four Jaffa guards outside Neheb-Kau's throne room, in addition to the rows of gold-clad warriors lining the walls like malevolent, serpent-headed statues. Kafra nodded to the new arrivals as the doors to the throne room closed behind him, and walked past them. They fell into precise formation behind him, in two rows. Before she knew it, Carter found herself surrounded by warriors.

"Kafra," she began.

"Be silent."

"You think I'm a threat?"

"I do not."

"Then what's going on?"

He snarled, and stopped dead, spinning around on his heel to face her. The four guards clattered to a halt also.

"Human," he hissed, his face very close to hers. "You owe me your life. Hear this: your words about what happened in the Pit saved me from humiliation before the God, perhaps worse, but that debt has been *paid*. Do not presume upon my good nature further!"

"What are you talking about?" she snapped. "Saved my life? You just threw me to Neheb-Kau!"

"Better him than Djetec" He glanced warily past her, back to the doors. "He had no intention of schooling you in anything. You would have died at his hand, after he had stripped all the knowledge from your mind."

"He didn't seem to think much of me."

"Do not be fooled. The man is a trickster. I have known him too long. He has the ear of the God, and whispers poison… Trust me in this, human. In thwarting him, I have bought you time. How you choose to spend it is up to you."

Carter put a hand to her head. There was a dull pain behind her eyes, and a weakness in her legs and shoulders. It had been bothering her for a while now, but it was starting to get worse. Dehydration, probably. "Kafra, I have to get off this ship. Teal'c, too."

"That is impossible. Even if your presence here were not willed by my master, where would you go? The planet below us?"

"I was thinking more along the lines of taking a ship."

"With the fleet of a rival System Lord heading directly towards us?" He shook his head. "Human, accept your fate. You will accompany my master on the journey back to his domains."

"I don't even know what he wants from me!"

One of the guards chuckled, and odd, metal sound from within his helm. "Perhaps he intends taking you as his queen."

"Silence!" bellowed Kafra. "How *dare* you presume to know the mind of your God? Any of you?" He snorted, and turned away, resumed his pace along the hall. "Although, in defense of this fool, you would make a fine host."

She glared at the back of his neck. "I'd rather die."

"I have heard those words many times," he told her, wearily. "It is surprising how difficult they are to put into practice."

Past the transporter platform the hallway sprawled out into separate corridors. As Carter and her unwelcome guardians neared the platform a Jaffa hurried out from one of these, dropped to one knee in front of Kafra and uttered a short series of Goa'uld words.

"Rise," said Kafra. "Speak the slave-tongue."

"Forgive me, master." The man got to his feet, but kept his head lowered. He looked very young.

Slave-tongue? wondered Carter. She never heard her own language referred to as that. Then again, the use of Earth languages among the Goa'uld had been a matter of fierce scholarly debate in Stargate Command for some time. Carter stored the fragment of knowledge away. She would torment Daniel with it later, she decided.

Should she ever see him again.

"Is your mission complete?" Kafra was asking the man. In response, the Jaffa shook his head, eyes still fixed on the floor.

"My lord Kafra, I have failed you."

"Explain."

"The sensors in the Vault still do not respond, and the ch'epta who entered have not returned."

"Hm." Kafra clapped his hand down on the man's shoulder. "The inefficiency of the ch'epta is no reflection on you, Jaffa. When I have secured this prisoner, I shall give them cause to hurry."

The man raised his head. "The God will fear for his prize."

Prize? Carter felt a jolt. That was the word Neheb-Kau had used, when he had heard of the approaching fleet.

"The God knows no fear," Kafra was telling the young Jaffa. "Return to the Vault, and I shall meet you there."

Carter stepped forwards. "Wait."

"Behold, the God's new plaything," Kafra muttered, with exaggerated weariness. "What is it now, human?"

She ignored the insult, and spoke directly to the younger man. "The Casket… Look, when the sensors failed, did they register a drop in temperature before they went dead?"

He blinked at her. "They did!"

"Human," Kafra grated, his eyes narrow. "What do you know of this?"

Carter returned his gaze. "Your master's prize is loose in the Vault."

"Impossible!" There was a shifting around her, a click and clatter of armor. The Jaffa surrounding her had reacted to her words, stepping slightly back, as if the very mention of such an event could cause them harm.

"Kafra, I was in there with it, before the Casket was sealed. The Pit of Sorrows was buried under hot sand for five thousand years, and we only found it because it was freezing cold. The Ash Eater feeds on energy, remember? Including heat from the air…"

The young Jaffa swallowed hard, and reached up to his neck

armor. There was a series of sliding clicks as his helm rose to cover how pale his face had become.

"Listen to me, all of you." Kafra was leaning in slightly, drawing the warriors closer. "Our lives are forfeit if Djetec learns of this. We will deal with it ourselves, quietly. Do you understand?"

"But the God—"

"Is concerned with other matters. And once we are successful, he will be doubly forgiving." Kafra smiled. "Now we will go to the Vault, recapture the creature before it can do any harm, and be at our barracks before the throneship enters hyperspace. Agreed?"

"As you command," the young man breathed, his voice unsteady behind the impassive serpent faces of his helm.

"I'm coming too," said Carter.

Kafra tilted his head. "For what reason?"

"Because I can help. I know your technologies, remember. And you don't want to have to waste a man guarding me while you could have us all down there."

"I will stay," said the man who had joked at her expense earlier. "It is my honor."

"You have none," growled Kafra. "Human, so be it. *Jaffa, kree!*"

The Vault was only four decks down from the throne room, no more than a few hundred meters by corridor. The Jaffa ran all the way, their pace unhindered by the weight of their armor and the ungainly length of their staff weapons. It was a testament to their strength and stamina that they were not even out of breath by the time they reached their destination.

After her recent ordeals, Carter was in far poorer shape. When she got to the Vault's hatchway the sprint, and the thought of what she might be heading into, almost took the strength from her.

She wasn't even entirely sure why she had demanded to accompany the Jaffa. The idea of facing the Ash Eater a second time was, quite frankly, terrifying. The image of Anna Andersson's body sliding into dust under her hands would not leave her, nor that of Greg Kemp's wrecked face or Laura Miles' vanished, crumbled arm. Oddly, though, it was the fate of Lucas Harlowe that disturbed her even more than the others, in that no trace of him had been found at all. Teal'c had found the powdered remnants of his gun at the foot of the ladder, but the man himself no longer existed, even as a shape. He was a couple of kilos of dust, nothing more.

And there was every possibility, given where she had fallen, that Carter had brought a sizeable component of him out of the Pit with her.

That thought caused her empty stomach to clench painfully. She winced, suddenly weak, and a wave of giddiness swayed her. She stumbled away from the Vault's massive, armored hatch to steady herself against the nearest wall.

A shadow loomed next to her. It was Kafra. "I'm fine," she told him.

"You are a danger to us."

"I told you, I'm okay." She fought the weakness down, and straightened up. He was peering at her carefully.

"When did you last consume food?"

"What? You think I'm *hungry*?"

"I think your species is weak, and must be replenished often." He took something from his belt, and held it out to her. It was a small bar of yellowish matter, like modeling clay. "Eat."

"Thanks," she said, waving the bar away. "I'll get drive-through."

"Human, you will eat this and be sustained. Otherwise you endanger me and my Jaffa."

She no longer had the strength to argue. She took the bar from him, nibbled off a corner. "There. I'm eating, okay?"

The stuff was sugary, with a slightly spicy tang. Not unpleasant. As Kafra turned away, Carter took a bigger bite, and then put the rest of the bar into her pocket as she chewed.

She watched him open a panel by the side of the hatch. Behind it, a slab of smooth, matt glass glowed softly. The Jaffa placed his palm flat against it, until it pulsed and gave a single, harsh chime.

The door slid aside, slowly, as if it was immensely heavy. Beyond it was more darkness. Carter sighed to herself, and rubbed the bridge of her nose absently. Neheb-Kau's funereal choice of décor wasn't improving her headache at all.

Lights flickered on behind the door. Carter walked over to get a better view, and saw a chamber being gradually revealed as a series of illuminated panels switched on in sequence. "At least there's still power," she said.

"These lights should have been on." Kafra lowered his staff weapon from the vertical and stepped into the chamber. "The Vault's sensors keep them lit, as long as there is life within."

Carter went through just after him. The First Prime glanced back, and raised an eyebrow. He'd not been expecting her to be so eager, she thought. But then he didn't know her very well.

With the others behind her, she followed Kafra into the Vault.

There was little to see. The Vault was roughly the size of the throne room, and its décor was not much different from the other chambers Neheb-Kau frequented, with dark, inward-sloping walls and a floor of glossy black marble. Armored hatches ranged along each side wall, and at the end of the chamber, raised on a stepped dais and lit by a ring of powerful beams, stood a squat golden pillar,

"The Casket," she said. "He must have had a place set up for it, way before he got here."

"My master has sought the Ash Eater for many lifetimes, human." Kafra was pacing carefully forwards, his staff at the ready. "The empty space he kept for it reminded him of its loss."

"Many lifetimes," Carter repeated, under her breath. It was a vast understatement. Neheb-Kau had mentioned Ra keeping the Ash Eater as a pet, and Ra had been driven off Earth five thousand years earlier. Which meant that Neheb-Kau had been pining for his lost monster all that time, at least.

She could easily believe it. The Goa'uld were often single-minded to the point of mania, and with their host bodies continually maintained by their sarcophagi, or simply discarded in favor of new and prettier models, time didn't have the same meaning for them as it did for humans. They simply continued, as they had always done; ageless and unchanging and utterly obsessive.

From what Carter could gather Neheb-Kau had found the Ash Eater on its lifeless homeworld, lost it to Ra somehow, and then spent five thousand years plotting to recover it. And now, thanks to a stray staff-blast, there was every chance he had just lost it again.

No wonder Kafra didn't want him to find out.

The Casket was open; the cup at its top exposed, the cover retracted. "It's gone."

"Human…" Kafra was aiming his staff weapon at one of the side hatches, the last door on the left.

It was open.

Carter swallowed, and edged forwards. She reached out, put her hand into the open door, and spread her fingers.

"The air's not cold. It's not here."

"You would feel it?"

"Oh yeah." She remembered the chill of the Pit, suppressed a shudder, and then leaned into the doorway. As soon as she did so, she saw what lay on the chamber floor, and froze. "Kafra?"

"What do you see?"

"Could you come in here?" She glanced back outside, at the Jaffa waiting, staffs aimed, behind their First Prime. "Just you."

As he entered, she stepped aside to let him see what she had spotted. On the floor, partially concealed around a corner, lay the withered, desiccated corpse of a man.

She stood for a few seconds, looking silently down at the body, then dropped slowly to crouch next to it. The man had been curled up when he had died, hands over his head. He lay on his left side. His back was against the wall.

The Ash Eater had reduced him to a papery, withered tatter, a stick-figure of powder and crumbling bone.

"One of the ch'epta," said Kafra. He tapped the exposed skull with the toe of one boot, and the part he had touched sloughed and collapsed, a small cloud of dust rising from it. Carter got up, stepping back to avoid having the stuff on her skin again. She had borne too many dead already.

"How many were there?"

"Three." Kafra was examining the door frame. "This mechanism has been destroyed. The ch'epta must have tried to seek refuge here."

"So if it came through here after them, where did it go?" Carter moved past the corpse, around the corner and into the chamber beyond.

"Oh no," she breathed. "Oh God, no…"

The chamber must have been a store for Neheb-Kau's other treasures. Square columns of smooth black stone stood against the walls, waist-high, some bearing gleaming objects inside transparent cases. Several columns had been pulled to the floor, their contents dashed apart. Carter's boots crunched on broken glass as she made her way forwards.

The other two ch'epta must have pulled everything they could down in front of the Ash Eater. It hadn't done them any good. They were sprawled at the far end of the chamber, dark twists of sticks and powder and gaping, collapsing skulls.

Past them, light was spilling in from a hole in the thick metal wall, ragged and powdery and dripping dust and fragments. It looked like the Ash Eater had chewed its way clear through to the mechanical crawlspace, filled with ducts and crystalline conduits and the sickly blue glow of safety lighting.

"It must have stripped the energy from the molecules of the wall," Carter whispered. "That's incredible. I didn't know it could do that."

"There are lights in the crawlspace. Why are they not destroyed, as the door and the sensors were stripped of their power?"

"That's what scares me. Kafra, these mechanical spaces — are all the decks connected by them?"

"Indeed."

"Then we're in really serious trouble. Neheb-Kau said that the Ash Eater is mindless, it's a corpse. The only reason it wouldn't take power from the lights here is if it sensed a bigger meal elsewhere. How far from here to the reactors?"

"Not far enough." Kafra turned away from the light. "What can we do?"

"The Casket," she replied. "Somehow, we've got to get it back in there."

"The Casket no longer functions."

"I know." She moved past him, and out through the open hatch. "But maybe we can fix it."

She headed back towards the dais. Behind her, Kafra emerged from the chamber. "Jaffa!" he called.

Carter crouched down next to the pillar's base. There was a dark patch on its gleaming flank, rough and carbonized. The impact of the staff-blast. She ran her hands over it, felt a slight imperfection in the metal, and pressed. A panel slid aside, revealing a bank of glowing crystals.

Several of them were darkened, their surfaces crazed.

The other Jaffa had gathered around their First Prime. "You two," he said, "will remain here. The rest will make their way to the reactor chamber, and watch for the demon's arrival."

"My Lord Kafra?" Carter recognized the voice of the youngest Jaffa. "What does the creature look like?"

"Like a black cloud," she called back, over her shoulder. "When I saw it, that's what it was like. And if you see it, don't get anywhere near it. I think it's got a long reach."

She heard the man hurrying away, two of his fellows in tow. The other two must have been looking rather too nervous for Kafra's liking. "Lower your helms, fools," he snapped. The demon is far from here."

"Then why do we remain?"

"You will bear the Casket, of course." She heard his footsteps, and then he was at her side. "Well?"

She pointed at the darkened crystals. "I saw this in the Pit. Some of the control crystals there exhibited the same damage. The staff blast must have been the last straw. Kafra, this was always going to break down. Shooting at it just accelerated the process."

"Forgive me if I find that small comfort. Can you repair this damage?"

"No." There was no way she could replace the crystals, not

quickly. But behind them, flexible crystalline waveguides bunched like glowing wire. Several were dark and fractured. Carter began to tug at them, freeing them from their sockets at one end. "But what I can do is run a bypass."

"Explain."

She pointed at the three rings of radiant material beneath the cup. "When the Ash Eater was contained, these glowed. I thought they must have been taking heat from the inside and dumping it into the air, but I think it must have been every kind of energy. Starving the Ash Eater to keep it quiet."

Carter swapped out one of the broken waveguides with an intact one from another part of the Casket. "When I'm done, only two of the emitters will work, so it's a temporary fix, but at least we'll be able to trap the Ash Eater in here for a while."

"Succeed, and the God will look kindly on you."

"I'll bear that in mind." She swapped the last waveguide, stripped out the damaged ones and dropped them onto the dais. "What I don't understand is, if the Ash Eater can just eat its way through solid metal, why did it stay in the Pit of Sorrows all that time? It was only covered by stone and sand."

"The Lure," said Kafra.

"The what?"

"A poison, of the vilest kind. To the Ash Eater it is irresistible. To all other life..." He shook his head. "My master encountered it when he first located the Ash Eater, on the dead world below us. He tells me that he was exposed to its effects for a few seconds, at most. Now he spends twenty hours of every day in his sarcophagus, and hosts still drip off him like spoiled fruit."

Carter froze. "Sorry, are you saying there's some of that in here?"

"Very little. Enough to induce it to return, should no greater source of energy be present."

"That's not going to help us much. Not if there's a naquadah buffet on offer instead."

"Indeed."

He left her to make his way down the steps, to an open area in front of the dais. Carter watched him for a moment, then returned her attention to the Casket, trying not to think about the hideous toxicity it might contain. Or about what the sarcophagus was doing to Neheb-Kau. Continued use of the healing devices was addictive, corrosive. It was even surmised that the reason most of that species were megalomaniac sociopaths was due entirely to their use of sarcophagi.

If Neheb-Kau was spending all his time in one, Carter thought, no wonder he was unstable.

There was a trigger crystal inside the panel, and as she twisted it the containment cover unfolded from around the cup, enclosing empty air.

Beneath it, two of the emitter rings fluttered into fitful, glowing life.

Carter reset the crystal, and left the panel open. She might need to reach it again in a hurry. She got up, in time to see him touch a control gem on his wrist armor, one of several adorning its surface. The gem glowed softly, and a part of the floor began to lift.

Carter watched as a square column rose, soundlessly, from the marble. The first part of it was featureless, polished to a fine gloss, and she was disconcerted to see her own reflection skating over its surface. Then, when a meter of mirrored black stone was exposed to the air, an opening appeared. A cylinder had been cut through the column, and floating unsupported in the space it made hovered a gleaming silver sphere.

The column came up another meter or so, and then stopped.

Carter drew closer. From a depression in the column's side Kafra took a long metal cylinder. He held it up, and then twisted a section of it. A needle as long as Carter's hand whispered out of the far end.

Very carefully, he brought the needle to the side of the sphere, found a specific point, and eased it all the way in.

"That's the Lure," said Carter. She forced herself not to move away from it.

"Your perception does you credit." He touched a control on the cylinder. Carter heard a soft whine, and lights began to expand along the side. "I will insert a sizeable amount into the Casket. Is the containment system repaired?"

"Yeah…"

"Do not fear, human. My master has informed me as to the function of the Casket." He drew the needle out, and held the cylinder upright. It looked heavy now, as if it contained something incredibly dense. "It is shielded. But do not be tempted to look into its open end, unless you wish to spend the rest of your days masked."

Chapter 16.

THE BAD TOUCH

WHEN HERA had ordered Daniel and Jack into the dark, she was not speaking figuratively. The holding cell was utterly lightless.

It was also cold, and rather damp. Daniel could feel the solid chill of the wall behind him, the greasy wetness of it against his skin. It was starting to drag the heat inexorably out of his body. Had he been able, he would have dearly liked to move away from the wall, to sit down, to rest the throbbing muscles of his shoulders. But the manacles around his wrists and ankles had been drawn tightly back to the wall, by some magnetic force or gravitational manipulation, and he could barely move at all. He could only stand, arms stretched out horizontal at shoulder height, with his back to the cold wall, and wait.

He had been waiting for quite some time. He had no idea at all how much. Nor did he know how long he had been unconscious before that: after Hera had ordered his detention, one of her hoplites had shot him with something that looked like a sculpted bone, but had turned out to be a zat gun in disguise. When he had awoken, he was against the wall.

There had been an awkward silence between him and Jack for a while, now. The colonel had spent his time in the darkness going through a range of emotions; defiance, at first, then rage, and now he was sliding dangerously close to despondency. It was not a pattern that would do either of them any good. Daniel couldn't be certain, but he had a strange feeling that Hera was not going to leave the pair of them locked away in the dark forever. And when they finally emerged into the light, he needed Jack to be at his best.

Daniel could not simply wait and let the man brood.

"You know," he said, after a time. "In a way this is kind of encouraging."

For a few moments there was no answer. Then Jack's voice echoed from the far side of the cell. "Ah, Daniel?"

"Hm?"

"I appreciate the positive attitude and all. I really do. But you want to try and explain to me just which part of being glued to a wall in a Goa'uld's flying mountain is 'encouraging'?"

"I didn't mean for us. I meant for Sam and Teal'c."

"Right. So being dropped down a shaft and buried is a good thing, now."

Daniel sighed into the darkness. "Jack, think about it. We heard Ra's message through our Stargate. Hera must have heard it through one of hers. There's no telling how many other gates that message came through."

"All at once?"

"Maybe. I've not heard of it before, but I guess it could be possible. Or maybe there was some mechanism to dial one after another. It doesn't really matter." He tipped his head back until it touched the wall. With his arms pulled back so tight, it was hard to keep his head up, and his neck felt terrible. "The thing is, if Hera knew that the Pit was just going to crash on some nameless planet and be forgotten, she wouldn't have gone to all this trouble to bury it."

"Got to admit, that was a big drill."

"I think it's safe to say she really doesn't want anyone else getting their hands on it."

"So if the Ash Eater's still a hot property, then any number of Goa'uld could be on their way to pick it up." Daniel heard him shift against the wall, trying to loosen his own stiffening muscles. "Still not sure if that really counts as 'encouraging'."

"They've got to open the Pit first. That's got to be good for Sam and Teal'c hasn't it?"

"Better than being trapped inside it, I'll give you that." A slight pause, then: "So now all we've got to do is stop Hera getting there first."

"Yeah..."

A faint rattling as Jack tested his bonds. "I think we can both see the flaw in that plan."

"Oh, we've still got an ace or two up our sleeve." Daniel cleared his throat. "Figuratively speaking."

"I have no idea what you're talking about, Daniel," said Jack pointedly.

Daniel grinned. He was certain that they were being monitored, and so there was no way he was going to even mention Bra'tac. Their ship was gone, and the remote detonator for the explosives they had set up had been taken with the rest of their equipment. But as far as Daniel could tell, Bra'tac was still free, and roaming the interior of the *Clythena*.

Hera might have liked to boast of her infallibility, he had decided, but in the most part it was typical Goa'uld braggadocio. There was no way she would have let them board the flagship had she known their ship was not of her fleet, and doubtless the Jaffa who had let them aboard without security checks was, at the very least, experiencing his own period of darkness right now. Neither would Hera have let them go into the navigation room, and risked them doing catastrophic damage to the flagship's systems.

She had herded them into her clutches after that point, but before then she had been as ignorant of their presence as she was about Bra'tac's.

"Just trying to make Hera paranoid," he replied.

"You're too late. She's a Goa'uld. She's about as paranoid as it's possible to get." Jack's voice sounded light, but Daniel knew him well enough to hear the edge it had, when he said that. "And what's with the double, anyway?"

"It's not unheard of for rulers to have body-doubles." Daniel shrugged, although the gesture didn't get far. "Political decoys go way back... Hitler, Stalin; hell, even Henry Kissinger had a double in China."

"What, all the time?"

"Probably not. But who'd know? Anyway, I guess she's just taken the practice to extremes."

"Some kind of clone?"

"Not sure. What did she call her sister, back up there?"

"Erica something."

Daniel frowned. "That doesn't make a lot of sense. Hera's sisters were Demeter and Hestia. She was Zeus' sister, too. Then she married him, which makes things a little complicated, but still."

"Married her brother," said Jack, flatly.

"Yeah… You know, those wacky Greek gods… But I don't know where Erica-something came from."

"It was Chalcis."

Daniel froze. The voice was female; deep-toned and precise, with a honeyed lilt. It was Hera.

"Hey," said Jack. "Kinda hoping you'd stop by."

"Hmmm…" Soft footfalls moved through the darkness. "I was curious. A failing of mine, I know, but I do like to satisfy my urges whenever I can."

"Let me guess," said Daniel, warily. "You can see in the dark?"

"Oh, *extremely* well."

"Ho boy," breathed Jack.

"Okay," Daniel said hurriedly, to cover Jack's discomfort. "Erica, er…"

"Ericaceae. It was the name of the host-sister. We decided to keep it, since all who saw us would know us both as Hera, and the sound of it pleased us." There was a smile in her voice, soft and sly. "We keep things that please us, Daniel. There is so little pleasure in the galaxy. It must be sought out, and treasured."

Twins, thought Daniel. *Of course.*

And then something touched his hair. He flinched.

"So which are you?" asked Jack. "Hera, or the other one?"

"Does it matter?"

"Well, one of you had your big bull-guys try to deprive me of my arms."

"The Minotaurs like to destroy pretty things," she said nonchalantly. "They are bred to be… *Dissatisfied.*"

Daniel heard Jack give a started yelp. Hera, or Ericaceae, had moved across to him. In the dark, she could do as she wished.

It was not a comforting thought. "So you took twin sisters as hosts, back in Classical Greece, what, two thousand years ago?"

"You are perceptive, Daniel." She pronounced his name slightly wrong, as Hera had done. *Dan-ee-yel.* "It was a new start for us. And now we have favored these hosts for, oh two and a half millennia. There were others, before, but in these we have found most worthy vessels. Do you not agree?"

Jack made a noncommittal sound. "I'd have gone with something, I dunno, taller…"

Twin lights flared in the darkness. Her eyes, glowing with a sudden rage. To Daniel's dark-adapted gaze they seemed intolerably bright.

In a moment, though, the Goa'uld had regained control of her emotions, and he was blind once more.

"Forgive me," she purred. "I should not become angry at such *small* things… It is the host, you see. Her emotions ran deep. Some rise to the surface even now, on occasion."

Her footfalls went quickly across the cell, and when she next spoke she was very close to Daniel's ear. "Even now, after two and a half thousand of your years, these bodies are still a mystery to us. Still a constant surprise. Others will tell you that we choose humans as our vessels because they are so easily repaired, but do you know the other reason? The *real* reason we inhabit you thus?"

"I think I'm about to."

"Because they are fun."

Daniel stared, at where he thought she was. "Fun?"

"Indeed." She chuckled, a dark, liquid sound. "No other species we have encountered has given us the sensations that humans can. No other race is built so well, *responds* so well… Oh Daniel, if only you knew what these bodies are capable of…"

"Lady," hissed Jack. "That's not your car you're driving."

"I sense disapproval. How disappointing…" She sounded as if she was pouting, and even closer now. "And what of you, Daniel? Do *you* have a twin?"

"No, no I don't…"

"A pity. It would be pleasing, if there were two of you." She drew closer. He felt a tickle. Her lashes, spun gold and impossibly fine, were at his cheek. "For so many, many reasons…"

He closed his eyes. "I really need to get out of here."

"When I have a use for you." She drew away. "Farewell, Daniel. It has been a pleasure, *seeing* you…"

He heard her walk away. For a while it was rather difficult to gather his thoughts, so he didn't say anything at all.

Eventually Jack spoke, his voice wary. "What was that all about?"

"I, ah…" Daniel swallowed. "I have no idea. Maybe she's after a new host or something."

"Seems to kind of like the one she's got."

"Yeah."

There was another silence, longer. And then: "Daniel?"

"Hmm?"

"When are we going to get our clothes back?"

Chapter 17.

LITTLE BLACK CLOUD

COMPARED to the dark, enclosed spaces of Neheb-Kau's upper decks, the throneship's conversion hall was dizzying. Had Carter not already eaten most of the yellow food block Kafra had given her, she wondered if she would have been able to keep upright when she stepped out of the access arch and into the open, beating heart of the vessel.

She was in a chasm, a faceted valley of burnished gold and black glass, standing on a narrow railed bridge above a distant floor. Above her, power converters jutted down from the high ceiling, a row of vertical cylinders the size of railway carriages, and past them, in the hazy distance, something huge turned slowly and inexorably, emitting a searing blue-white glare.

Pipes from the cylinders above her speared down through the bridge to join a sprawl of ducting below, each one surrounded by sturdy consoles and safety railings. The nearest converter was meters away, yet Carter could feel the heat of it from where she stood, the vibration of it, could smell the stink of oil and ozone. The constant thrumming thunder of the reactor beat at her ears, came up through her boots and made her bones ache.

It was a hellish place. The few Jaffa and ch'epta technicians she could see working in the conversion hall must have made themselves desperately unpopular at some point, to have earned such a fate. Little wonder, then, that Neheb-Kau wanted to see Teal'c condemned in the same way.

After he'd been worked over by the ka'epta of surgeries, whoever that might be. Despite Neheb-Kau's assurances, the thought of Teal'c being in the hands of someone who bore that title was a knot in her gut. "Kafra?"

He tipped his head, to hear her above the noise of the machines. "Speak."

"Has there been any word on Teal'c?"

"Your shol'va?" His face twisted. "Put such trivialities aside, human. His fate lies elsewhere. Look to your own."

"But—"

"Speak of this no more," he hissed. "And make haste. The reactor is still some distance away."

Carter shook her head. "I don't think it'll go there. The reactor's too well-shielded. It won't be able to sense the power."

"You think it will be drawn to the converters?"

"I'm kind of banking on it." She began to walk along the bridge, peering up between the towering cylinders. Although she hated the idea, in a way Kafra was right. She had to keep a focus — she'd be no help to Teal'c or anyone else if she blundered into the Ash Eater.

Behind her, the two Jaffa who had stayed were carrying the Casket. The devices she had seen used to unlock the device back in the Pit had been stored with it in the Vault, and the men now held the golden cylinder upright using these as handles. Despite its load of superdense Lure, they didn't seem overly bothered by its mass. Their only concession to the Casket's bulk was that Kafra was carrying their staff weapons as well as his own, and that was simply because they had no free hands to wield them.

Carter had offered to carry the staffs, but no-one else had thought that was a very good idea.

Together, the group moved warily on. The three Jaffa that had gone on ahead were monitoring the other two canyons — there were three conversion halls, spreading equilaterally from the reactor core — but this one was the closest to the Vault. If Neheb-Kau had been right about the Ash Eater, it was more automaton than living creature, with all the guile and intelligence of an iron filing seeking out a magnet. If it was going to head for a power converter at all, Carter reasoned, it would be here.

The bridge was not crowded. Like many of the ship's systems, the conversion hall was mainly automated, and the few Jaffa and technicians she encountered paid her no mind as long as she stayed conspicuously close to their First Prime. They seemed too busy dropping to one knee in salute as he passed.

When they were roughly halfway across the bridge, Kafra raised a hand in a signal for them to stop. Carter heard the Casket set heavily down onto the metal flooring behind her. "What's wrong?" she asked. "Shouldn't we keep going?"

"This tactic is ill-advised," he growled. "The creature could be emerging behind us. If, indeed, it is not already here. We have no idea how fast it moves."

"Or even *how* it moves," Carter agreed. She looked along the bridge, suddenly aware that Kafra was right. There was no way that the four of them could cover the whole conversion hall between them.

And then the space between two converters flickered and went dark.

Carter swallowed hard. The first of the stricken converters was a dozen meters ahead, towards the reactor. She tipped her head back, and saw that there was an array of illuminated panels set between each cylinder. Those ahead of her had failed.

"Kafra, did you see that?"

He turned to the men behind him. "Make ready. The beast could be near."

"*Could* be?"

"The lights might have suffered a technical fault. It is not unknown."

She moved forwards, gaze fixed upwards. "I don't think so."

Far above her, in the gloom between the two converters, a patch of ceiling was changing color.

A pale spot had appeared, oddly luminescent in the gloom. *Frost*, thought Carter, her heart hammering. The metal up there was cold enough to freeze water in the air.

Fragments of powdered gold began to sift down.

"The Casket," grated Kafra. Then he raised his staff weapon high in the air. "Jaffa! Ch'epta! Leave the bridge! We do the God's work!"

There was a murmur of confusion. Carter could see maybe half a dozen people close by, ch'epta and the odd Jaffa guard or two. She saw the nearest of them hesitate, then turn and run. In moments, the rest had followed, beginning a minor exodus from the bridge.

She felt relieved. In other circumstances those Jaffa and their human slaves might be doing their best to kill her, to threaten Earth or carry out some scheme of their Goa'uld masters that would necessitate her taking up arms against them. Today, however, they were no risk to her or her world. They certainly didn't deserve the Ash Eater's attentions.

Besides, they would have gotten in the way.

Kafra was guiding his Jaffa to set the Casket down as close to the frosted patch as they dared. As they released it, he threw their staff weapons to them. "Human, are you ready?"

"Sure." She crouched next to it, sliding open the access panel. The control crystal was still in place, glowing brightly. As soon as she twisted it askew, it would shut down the containment system, opening the top of the Casket and exposing the dreadful Lure.

If Kafra was right about its properties, it would draw the Ash Eater back into the Casket.

She got up. As she did so, a distant glitter caught her attention. She looked down the length of the bridge, cupping a hand over her eyes to shield them from the glare of the reactor.

"Uh-oh," she said under her breath.

Past the converters, marching in perfect formation, a column of Neheb-Kau's gold-armored guard was coming right at her.

"Kafra? I think we've got company."

"I see them." He moved forwards, between the approaching men and the Casket.

They stopped a short distance away. The man at the column's head took a pace forward, lowering his helm as he did so. He tipped his head in a perfunctory bow. "First Prime."

"Captain, your men must leave."

"I am here on direct orders from the *Tjaty*, Djetec."

"You take your orders from the God, Neheb-Kau." Kafra narrowed his eyes. "And then from me."

"Djetec speaks the work of the God."

Kafra barked a laugh. "You believe that?"

"Of course. Are you not here, with the God's possessions, as he predicted?"

Carter shook her head in exasperation. "Sorry, but could you two *please* compare the size of your helmets some other time?"

The captain glared at her. "Hold your tongue, slave!"

"Human," Kafra growled. "Leave this to me."

Carter could hear ugly cracking sounds from above. "We don't have time for this!"

"I see," said the captain. He stepped back, lowering his staff to aim it at Kafra. "This human has poisoned your mind, worked her magic upon you as she did on the First Prime of Apophis!"

"There is no magic here, fool! Only death!" Kafra pointed desperately upwards, between the converters. "Do you not see? The demon is loose!"

"I see only one demon here," the captain snarled. His weapon swung around towards Carter.

His men followed suit. Kafra's men responded, and for a few seconds the sound of opening staff weapons was loud enough to drown out even the thrum of the reactor.

Above their heads, a meter-wide patch of ceiling simply fell to pieces.

The metal tumbled, disintegrating as it fell. A section of it held cohesion long enough to hit the bridge not a meter away from the guard captain, shattering into dust and splinters.

The man whirled, his staff weapon snapping open. Energy sizzled between its emitters.

"Don't!" Carter yelled. "If you shoot at it, you'll just—"

"Silence," he snarled, half-turning to backhand her viciously. She tried to step away from the blow, but she wasn't fast enough. His armored hand cracked hard across her face.

She cried out, stumbled, hands clamped over the pain. She saw Kafra raise his own weapon, face a mask of fury, but then all her attention was on the ceiling.

A cloud of living shadow was drooling down from the frost-rimed hole.

It was as she remembered it, from the glimpse she had seen in the Pit. A swarm of pure-black threads, falling slowly through the air like blood through water, constantly moving and writhing. The threads snapped and shifted in the way that sustained arcs of electricity do, but each of these arcs was curved, fluid, not jagged and forking. It was as if a million hair-fine snakes, each an eye-aching black, were continuously biting and striking at the metal shell of the converter.

Carter could feel the chill of it, cold air falling from it down to the bridge. It was utterly silent.

The Royal Guard stared at it, transfixed. "By the Gods," he breathed.

The cloud was hugging the converter shell. It dropped vertically along its height, leaving a trail of white frost. Carter heard crackling sounds from the metal, a rising electrical whine. The converter was being strained by the Ash Eater's presence.

She edged backwards, towards the Casket.

The guard captain shouted abruptly, in his own language. He raised his staff weapon to fire. Carter saw his thumb on the trigger, and past him, his men swinging their own weapons up to track the cloud. She opened her mouth to shout again, but it was far too late. The first bolt hammered into the Ash Eater before she could even take a breath.

The effect was immediate and ghastly. The bolt vanished into the swarm of threads, and in response the cloud spurted back down the path of the shot. Black filaments raced to the bridge, lashing at the guard captain. He screamed, a raw howl of pain.

Above him, the Ash Eater emerged from its cloud.

She had seen it before, she remembered, back in the Pit of Sorrows, a pale dome emerging from the rim of the Casket. Mercifully, the creature had been contained before she could see more, but now it was completely exposed, sliding out from its swarm of freezing darkness.

It was small, maybe as tall as Carter's forearm, curled over on itself. It was a withered thing, dry and papery, gray as dust, hovering down through the air towards the bridge; vestigial limbs twisted at its belly, its great swollen head bent and misshapen. There was a hint of a face there, of closed slits where eyes might once have been, of a ragged mouth, frozen open and lined with black, broken needles.

Once, thought Carter wildly, the Ash Eater might even have looked human. Now it was a floating, mummified fetus, a sickening pallid larva sucked dry of all but hunger and set hovering in the midst of its foul, swarming shroud of blackness.

More staff blasts came up at it, but they never reached it. They struck the cloud and were gone, instantly, scraps of food lost to the Ash Eater's voracious appetite. Half the cloud was stretched back towards the converter, whipping filaments licking its surface to powder, but the rest was spreading into the crowd of Jaffa.

The guard captain was on his knees. Carter saw what was happening to him and tried to look away, but it was too late. The sight of his face, a mask of ash crumbling off his skull, was in her mind for good. She moaned in horror.

The bridge was in chaos, a cacophony of screams and the snarling roar of staff-blasts. Each man that fired was followed by black threads, each man that was touched shrieked and fell and crumbled. Five were already down, the guard captain and four of his men, their bodies already collapsing into each other as the Ash Eater tore the energy from their cells. It was not a quick death, not a painless end. The men who died did so screaming, emitting dusty howls of lament as they saw their own bodies withering to powder on their bones.

"Cease firing, you fools!" Kafra had launched himself into the midst of the Royal Guard, was tearing the weapons from their hands and flinging them away. "Human, the Casket! Hurry!"

Carter ran towards the golden pillar. Before she reached it a guard stumbled into her path, wreathed in black threads. He sagged, his cries drying in his throat, and crashed heavily backwards into the Casket.

The Pillar teetered, despite its weight.

Carter skated to a halt, and came face to face with the corroding scarecrow that had been a man seconds before. He grabbed at her. His last breath, thick with powdered lung, hissed into her face.

Nauseated, she pushed him aside

He swiveled, falling apart in mid-air, and struck the Casket with all that was left of his weight. The golden pillar, already tilted wildly over, tipped.

It smashed solidly into the metal surface of the bridge, and the control crystal span out of its socket.

Carter saw the containment system fail, the emitter rings grow dark as the angular cover separated into a hundred metal blades and retracted back into the rolling column. She heard Kafra shout a warning and ducked back away from it, saw a sickly, reddish radiance spilling from its open end.

Threads of shadow lashed down to it.

The Ash Eater was hovering mid-way between the ravaged converter and the bridge, its cloud stretched from one to the other. As Carter watched, more and more of the filaments snapped back from their victims to connect to the open end of the Casket, the Lure enticing the monster inwards with its promise of unspeakable energies.

But it wasn't enough. The mummified horror still hung, motionless, in the air.

Carter began to edge towards the fallen pillar. She saw Kafra move towards her. "Human, are you insane?"

"We've got to get it upright!" she hissed. "Something's wrong, the Lure's slopped out of place, maybe."

"You do not have the strength." He ran to her, keeping low, and from behind her one of his Jaffa scuttled forwards to help. Carter glanced back, to see if the third was on the way, and saw that he was sprawled on his back, his chest opened by a staff-blast.

The Jaffa gripped the Casket, and began to tilt it up. "Beware, human," he growled, his voice strained. "Its weight is shifting."

As she had surmised, the dense, semi-liquid Lure was moving within the Casket.

She backed away, picking up the control crystal. Kafra moved in past her, wrapping his arms around the pillar and tilting it back towards the vertical. "Be ready," he told her.

"I will."

There was a sudden, deafening screech from the converter. Carter ducked at the sound of it, turned back to see livid tongues of voltage darting out from a rent in its flank.

The Ash Eater began to rise.

Kafra snarled, hauled at the Casket. It slipped suddenly from his grasp, tilted back the other way, dragging black threads with it. The other Jaffa grabbed wildly at it, lost his grip, and half fell into the ruddy glow of the Lure.

He gave a choked scream, and staggered back, clutching at himself. Kafra suddenly found himself trying to steady the pillar on his own. Carter ran towards him, put her shoulder to the golden cylinder and shoved hard, trying not to think about the red radiation flowing out over her head, the Ash Eater's lethal feeding cloud whipping a meter from her back.

The Casket thumped heavily upright. The Ash Eater's cloud came with it. Kafra jerked back from the threads, and for an awful instant the red light of the Lure surged up into his face.

He twisted away, supernaturally fast. Carter looked up, saw the Ash Eater flowing down towards her, and jammed the control crystal back into its socket. The emitter rings stuttered into life.

Metal leaves whirled up from nowhere, wrapped themselves around the dry fetal bulk of the Ash Eater, and drew it down.

Carter sagged back, shivering from shock and the hammering cold. "Kafra?"

"I am here." He half-rose, slumped back down again. Carter wrenched herself towards him, trying to help him up, but he was too heavy, too weak.

One side of his face was a mass of blisters.

"It's over," Carter told him, kneeling beside him. "We did it."

"No," he mumbled. He shook his head. "Not over."

And light, ice-white and intolerably harsh, seared out from above her.

The power converter was vomiting energy. Its shell had ruptured, peeled back as the banks of storage capacitors inside vented their power in vast, gouting arcs. As Carter watched a huge tongue of lightning arced brutally out to the side of the canyon, sending up sheets of sparks, then snapped upwards and hit the next converter in line.

The cylinder resisted the attack for a second or two, blue serpents of voltage slithering over its surface, then it too erupted.

The bridge shook. Carter scrambled up, hauling Kafra with her, allowing fear to lend her strength.

"You two," she called, shouting over the noise of the disintegrating machines. She pointed at the nearest surviving guards. "You need to take the Casket."

"That?" The man took a step away from it. "You are insane, human!"

"If it's in here when the rest of the these converters go up, the Ash Eater will get free again! Do you really want that?"

Perhaps, if the next cylinder in line had not blasted itself into shrapnel and billowing flame in that very instant, the guard might not have obeyed her, but the sound and the raw heat of the explosion was all the argument she needed.

Kafra took some of own weight from her. He was horribly injured, she could tell, but he was forcing himself upright.

Partway along the bridge, the Jaffa who had taken the full brunt of the Lure was completely still. Carter tried not to look too closely at what was happening to his body, but what she did see gave her some very unpleasant notions about what Neheb-Kau might look like under his mask.

"We must leave," Kafra snarled, as if enraged by his own pain. "Now."

"I hear you." She began to stagger forwards, still bearing him up, trying to be as gentle as she could.

"Faster, human!"

"You're not well enough —"

"A matter of little importance. If we are not gone from this place before the destruction reaches the reactor, all our lives are forfeit!"

"The reactor?" Carter twisted under his weight, looking back along the bridge

Lightning was connecting every converter in the chasm. It was a chain reaction, a cascade of destruction, a river of released energies, gathering pace and speed and power.

Death was leaping from cylinder to cylinder, racing like a flood towards the throneship's heart.

Chapter 18.

HURT

TEAL'C awoke to see a strange metal face looking right at him.

It was a Goa'uld armor-mask, he could see that at once, but he had not seen its like before. It was narrow, close-fitting to the head beneath, and formed from leaves of a dark, glossy bronze. There was very little decoration to it, and not even the suggestion of a mouth; the helm merely stretched and thinned into a featureless extension where the chin should be.

It was a haunting sight. Teal'c thought that it was probably meant to be.

He was restrained, of course. He could tell without looking that he was suspended above the floor at an angle, his head pulled up and back and his arms held out to either side. The bonds were well-designed, tight, and strong; self-adjusting electromagnetic bands of solid, unbreakable metal. Teal'c tested his strength against them for several seconds, but quickly realized that he couldn't move at all.

The mask watched him, impassively, as he did so.

When he stilled, it nodded, very slightly, and moved away. Teal'c's view was limited, but he could see that the man who wore it was dressed in simple attire of much the same dark bronze as his mask; a long sleeveless tunic over a jacket and robe. There was armor at his shoulders, to support the mask, and encasing both his forearms, but even that was functional and utilitarian.

The room around Teal'c, or what little of it he could see, was white, strongly-lit, and gleaming. Teal'c couldn't see any corners, and the wall ahead of him was slightly curved. He guessed that he was suspended from some kind of framework in the centre of a drum-shaped chamber, a situation he could find no comfort in.

"Release me," he said, largely as an experiment.

"No," the masked man replied, his voice utterly without malice. "Now that we have that out of the way, I am Pa'Nakht, ka'epta of surgeries. And you are Teal'c, First Prime of Apophis."

"I no longer serve Apophis."

"He cast you aside?"

"I cast *him* aside."

"Ah, I see." Pa'Nakht moved out of his field of view. "A First Prime who has deserted his God."

"The Goa'uld are not gods."

Teal'c heard faint clicks and chirrups, the sounds of machinery being operated. A few seconds later, Pa'Nakht returned. He was holding a small, shining instrument of glass and bright metal. "The depends entirely," he murmured, "on your definition of a god."

He held the device near to Teal'c's face. A section of it unfolded, and a long, silver needle slid from within.

Teal'c set his jaw, waiting for the inevitable pain. The needle was thick, wickedly sharp. Pa'Nakht moved the device out of his view, but he could feel the cold touch of the needle at his temple. There was a scratch at his skin, a pressure...

The device chimed softly. Pa'Nakht drew it away, and Teal'c could see that the glass section of it was glowing a faint blue.

He let out the breath he had been holding, slowly and silently, as the ka'epta of surgeries moved beyond his sight once more. He heard the device being set down on a hard surface, and then a rapid series of faint clicks. Pa'Nakht was entering data into some kind of recorder.

Teal'c felt as though he were suspended in a sea of mystery. The device that had been used on him was unlike any he had seen before, and it was strange indeed for the servants of a System Lord to indulge in radical innovation. The Goa'uld were, for the most part, a race that relied on familiar, proven technologies. Once they knew something worked, they tended to use it, almost without change, for hundreds, if not thousands of years.

Too much of what he had seen on the throneship was abnormal, unknown. He was lost here. Teal'c knew that he could not prevail if the ship and its occupants remained a mystery to him. He needed more information, if he were to learn Neheb-Kau's weaknesses.

Luckily for him, this oddly-masked technician seemed to be a talkative sort. "What purpose did that serve, torturer?"

"Torture? Hm." There were more machine noises. "If this is how you define torture, I would suggest you have lead rather a sheltered life." Pa'Nakht walked back in front of him, holding the device. "You spent many hours in proximity to the Ash Eater. I am attempting to catalogue the physical changes this will have caused you."

"The Ash Eater was contained."

"Obviously, in as much as the creature could ever be truly contained. However, even when entirely dormant it has a corrupting influence on physical matter. My master is intrigued by the strength of this effect." He lifted another device, a fist-sized sphere of dull iron, and raised it to Teal'c's forehead. "This may cause you some discomfort."

A moment later, raw agony coursed through Teal'c's frame. The shock of it, the scything pain that tore out of the iron sphere and into his bones, into his very core, ripped a cry from him. He clamped his jaw shut over any further exclamation, determined to give the masked man no further satisfaction, but the pain was getting worse, increasing with every second. His vision was a shuddering blur of blood and white light, his ears were filled with a screaming, sawing din that drove into every nerve in his body. His lungs were on fire. His heart was jolting in his chest, a leaping misfire that added a new flood of agony to the pain he already felt.

Abruptly, the torment ceased. Teal'c sagged in his bonds. Every muscle in his body had been tugged taut by the pain. Now, had he not been held aloft by Pa'Nakht's restraints, he would have collapsed into a heap.

"Neural response is within tolerance," the masked man said, seemingly without surprise.

"What," gasped Teal'c, "have you done? What are these devices?"

"The acquisitions of my master." Pa'Nakht held up the iron

sphere. "Interesting toys, are they not? Neheb-Kau discovered this in the Cineran Halo. It causes resonances with the central nervous system."

"For what purpose?"

"I cannot surmise as to its original purpose, First Prime. The species that developed it were unlike you and I in every way, or so their remains would suggest. Their civilization was dust long before the first Goa'uld."

He set the sphere down, out of sight, and lifted another object into Teal'c's view. It was a sculpture of greenish, iridescent stone, a half-melted hourglass pierced by a jagged blade. "This was buried under a city of crystal spires, on a world orbiting a neutron star. It causes dreams."

"That is no great feat."

"These dreams are… *Different*."

Teal'c's gazed warily at the device. "They are terrible?"

"They are beautiful. So beautiful that those who experience them cannot face life without them, even for a moment. I watched the System Lord Lei Gong tear out his own eyes and tongue, so that his senses would not besmirch the memory of them."

So the awful legends of Lei Gong's final madness were true. "Your master has many such acquisitions?"

"Indeed. It is his obsession. Over the centuries he has travelled to hundreds of worlds, tracking down the most strange and wonderful devices. It is how he first gained his place among the System Lords."

"I see." At last, Teal'c felt that at least a part of the mystery of this ship and its master was close to being solved. Neheb-Kau was a collector of alien technologies, the products of long-dead civilizations. He roamed the galaxy in search of these forbidden trinkets, and when he had acquired them he used them to his advantage in any way he could. Such a practice would have been viewed with suspicion, even fear, by many of the Goa'uld, but Neheb-Kau would not have let the disapproval of his peers stall his rise to power. He had even modified his ship to better store and use his devices.

Who knew what alien horrors had been fitted to this vessel?

"And the Ash Eater is his newest toy."

"Newest? Oh no… You have merely returned to him what was lost."

"Lost or stolen?"

"Ah, First Prime. You are an inquisitive soul. I feel that you and I would get on well, under different conditions." Pa'Nakht must have operated a control, because a moment later Teal'c felt the frame that held him aloft shiver a fraction, then begin to turn. "But we can no longer be distracted by such talk."

The rotation was not fast. It took several seconds for him to turn ninety degrees, away from where Pa'Nakht was keeping his devices. The ka'epta of surgeries walked with him, slowly pacing back into his field of view just as the frame swiveled him around to face what could only have been the pride of Pa'Nakht's collection.

As soon as Teal'c saw it, he knew that things had taken a turn for the worse. The devices Pa'Nakht had shown him, had used on him, were disturbing enough, but this creation was more awful than anything he had yet seen on the throneship. It hung before him on a jointed gantry, an insane tangle of limbs, like a great insect or spider cast from chrome and gold and black glass.

Every one of its limbs was different in size and form, and each was tipped with some nightmarish cluster of needles or blades or gleaming probes. As Teal'c watched, horrified, the machine quivered slightly, as if waking.

Even that slight motion was livid with malign intent.

"I cannot tell you how my master acquired this device," Pa'Nakht told him. The masked man's voice, for the first time, had changed. It seemed a little somber, now, as if he were feeling just a hint of regret. "The circumstances are too disturbing. Even I have tried to forget them."

"What is it?"

"It has no name. As for its purpose…" The mask tilted a fraction, and the eyes in that blank metal face gleamed with strange desire. "Wait a while. You will see."

As he spoke, the jointed gantry began to unfold, hinging open in complex, inhuman geometries.

Teal'c tugged at his bonds, heaved desperately at the restraints holding his arms, his ankles. If there was any structural weakness there he had to find it, to bring his strength to bear on it in these final few seconds. To get even one limb free could be his salvation.

But there were no weaknesses. The frame held firm, as the machine spread its metal arms to welcome him, bright needles and mirrored blades sparking in the chamber's harsh light.

As the instruments came close, a scalpel passed close enough to Teal'c for him to see his reflection in it, his own dark eye staring back at him. A second later, the razors touched him. He could feel how cold they were. How sharp.

"Do not struggle," Pa'Nakht told him, his voice strangely gentle. "The machine will compensate, and move with you. This, in turn, will cause you more pain."

"Your concern is touching."

"Hush, First Prime, and be still. It begins."

The chamber shivered.

At first, Teal'c thought that the machine had touched the frame he hung on, that some part of its mechanics had struck the restraint gantry hard enough to shake him. But then he heard a faint rattle from behind. The vibration had caused some of Pa'Nakht's devices to move against one another.

The machine must have felt it too. It retracted its arms a fraction and held itself motionless, as if waiting to see what was going to happen. Teal'c felt the blades and the needles leave his skin.

It was true, then. The ship had shaken.

The force required to move several thousand tons of starship was not inconsiderable, and Teal'c knew the gut-deep lurch of an entry into hyperspace too well to mistake the shiver for that. No, the ship had been moved by some external force. An attack, or a collision.

As the thought struck him, another shudder coursed through the frame, and the chamber lights flickered. Teal'c felt the slightest shift in the position of his bonds, and readied himself.

The machine shrank away from him. Its motions were so fluid, so lifelike that he found himself wondering if there were some sort of mind within its metal shell. Then he realized that, if there were, he had no desire to know anything about it.

Behind him, he heard Pa'Nakht cross the chamber. There was the sound of a door sliding open. "Jaffa," the ka'epta said urgently. "To me, quickly."

Teal'c tensed his right arm, exerted leverage in a very specific manner. The restraint around his wrist, its electrical connection to the frame reset during the power fluctuation, shifted.

He pulled, then put all his strength into his right shoulder. There was a soft cracking of fractured metal, and the restraint came away.

A tiny fragment of systemry fell, and rattled against the hard floor.

The restraint was heavy, a thick band of gold around his forearm. Teal'c lifted it back into position, holding the arm where it had been as more footfalls sounded.

He listened closely. From the weight and speed of the steps he knew that two Jaffa warriors had entered the chamber. Both carried staff weapons. Neither had his helm raised. Both of them had been surprised by the shaking of the deck, and neither had quite recovered.

"Guard this man," said Pa'Nakht. "I will discover the cause of this disturbance."

"By your will."

One of them men came around in front of Teal'c, his staff weapon open and aimed. The other was behind him. Teal'c watched the man in front for a few moments, knowing he didn't have long, but needing to prepare. He closed his eyes, formed a mental map of the chamber; himself at the centre, the two Jaffa in their positions ahead and behind. Pa'Nakht outside, unaware of the partial failure of his restraint system.

Teal'c opened his eyes, and let his gaze flick to the piece of metal that had fallen from the frame.

The Jaffa in front of him followed his eyes, saw the fragment, and stooped to pick it up. "What is this?"

Teal'c slammed his arm down, the edge of the restraint band crashing with shattering force into the back of the warrior's skull.

The man jerked horribly, a massive neural shock straightening his muscles at the instant of death. Teal'c's hand, still on its pulverizing downward arc, closed around the staff weapon as it fell from the warrior's grip. He jabbed it backwards, letting it slide between his fingers for an instant before catching it again around the control stud.

The weapon went off, the recoil almost taking it back out of Teal'c's grip. There was an explosive, meaty impact from behind him, and the crashing of an armored body being blasted back against a wall.

The warrior in front of him hadn't even hit the floor yet. As Teal'c raised the staff, the man who had once held it slumped, the last scraps of life shivering out of him.

Teal'c raised the staff, still held the wrong way round, and tilted it at the frame behind him. He hesitated, adjusted his aim a fraction, and fired.

The plasma bolt detonated at the point where the frame met the floor. Teal'c had judged that the power feed for the restraints would emerge there, and his guess was rewarded a second later when the metal bands dropped instantly away from him. He almost fell, the shift in weight and position stumbling him, then regained his balance and moved away.

The base of the frame was on fire, black smoke stinking up into the air.

The blast had scalded his back and legs, but the injuries could be easily endured. He flipped the staff around and caught it in firing position, just as Pa'Nakht stepped back through the door.

Teal'c fired. The ka'epta ducked aside, surprisingly nimble, the bolt shearing through his shoulder armor but not slowing him down. His slender, gloved hand darted out to his collection of devices, ranged along a curved metal table.

He snatched up the green stone artifact, swung it around under Teal'c's arc of fire and towards his head. "Dream," he said.

Teal'c felt something slide past his mind — an instant of unutterable beauty — but his reactions were already in control. He ripped the device from Pa'Nakht's grip with his free hand and then swung the staff around in a blurring arc. The emitter slammed into the ka'epta's mask, spinning him about.

The blade of the dream-maker was not sharp, but Teal'c was very strong. When he hammered it into the back of Pa'Nakht's neck, between the back of his mask and the top of his shoulder armor, it went clean through him.

Pa'Nakht gave a choked sigh, and folded up. Teal'c let him fall. Perhaps, in his final moments, the man had experienced one of his own terrible, beautiful dreams, his life fluttering out in the face of some unimaginable ecstasy.

Or maybe he had just died. The result was the same.

Teal'c went to the door, and peered out into a black corridor. He heard running footsteps, but they were distant and going away from him. There was no-one in sight. He stepped out of the chamber and reached for the door control.

Then he paused, and found himself looking back into the circular room. The three bodies were quite still, and there was a small fire guttering at the base of the restraint frame. The glittering torture machine, with its insane array of limbs, was hunched against the curving wall.

Teal'c lifted the staff weapon, aimed it carefully, and began to fire into the chamber.

The plasma bolts it emitted were constrained in such a way that most of their power was released in violent, armor-shattering explosions. But they were also searingly hot. In Teal'c's expert hands, the staff turned the interior of the chamber to an inferno in moments.

When he was sure everything within would be destroyed by

the fire, Teal'c closed and locked the door. Pa'Nakht and his collection of dreadful artifacts would do no more harm.

Now that he was free, his first priority was to locate Major Carter. When he had last seen her, she was in the columned hall, on one of Neheb-Kau's personal decks. He would have to begin searching for her there.

First, of course, he would have to determine both where the hall was, and in fact where *he* was. Amidst the throneship's maze of oppressive, tomb-like corridors and chambers, it was difficult to get his bearings.

Teal'c began to make his way along the corridor, pacing carefully at first and then, when he realized that there was no-one in his immediate vicinity, at a steady trot.

He reached a junction, and paused. The three other corridors leading away looked almost identical, although one was shorter than the others. Teal'c chose that way, and had just started down the passageway when the deck jolted hard under him.

This was no mere shiver. Something had exerted a very sizeable force on the ship.

It felt as though the jolt had originated from within the vessel.

He set off again, noting the way that the lights were starting to flicker and dim around him. This confirmed his intuitions somewhat, and also caused his pace to increase. Internal damage to a starship was never good news for those within. When that damage was enough to cause the power to fluctuate, and set off measureable vibrations in the decks, then the situation was truly one to be feared.

He rounded another corner, and almost ran into a group of slaves.

They were just emerging from a doorway. Teal'c counted six of them, four men and two women, their heads shaved and their bodies almost naked. It seemed that Neheb-Kau enjoyed not just the worship of his subjugates, but also their degradation.

The sight of them tore at him. For their part, the fact that he was still dressed in his battered civilian outfit seemed to offer them no comfort. It was not a surprise. No matter how he was dressed, he was an armed Jaffa, and to be feared.

And feared he was. The group dropped, as one, to their knees.

"Rise," he told them. "And quickly. You are in great danger."

"My Lord," a woman whispered, not looking up. "What is your will?"

"I am no-one's Lord," he replied. "This vessel has suffered great damage. It would be wise to seek a place of safety."

The slaves looked at each other nervously. "I… I do not understand," the woman said.

"Listen to me. If you wish to live, go to the glider bays. Find a ship and leave this vessel."

The woman glanced nervously back at her companions. "My Lord, none of us can fly."

"Then find someone who can." He stepped past her, then paused. "What deck number is this?"

"Forty-two, my Lord."

"Thank you. Now go, and heed no-one else." He tipped his head to her, in deference. "Follow your own will."

Once he knew what deck he was on, finding his way to the columned hall was not hard. For all its funereal décor, like most Goa'uld technology the throneship was basically a standard design, handed down and copied over hundreds of generations. It had been heavily modified, but even that could not alter its basic layout.

Before long, Teal'c had climbed up through the decks to the hall. He could have used a ring transporter and been whisked there in an instant, but the power fluctuations had been getting steadily worse over the past few minutes, and he no longer trusted the system to take him apart and put him back together in precisely the right order.

The gold-clad Royal Guards were gone when he got there. In fact, throughout his travels through the ship he had seen almost no-one, and been easily able to avoid any Jaffa he had encountered.

Perhaps most of the Jaffa on board had all been diverted to damage control duties. This was not a comforting thought.

He made his way into the hall, heading for the great golden doors at the end. The floor shook under him again when he was partway there, but this time the movement was followed by a distant, thunderous roar, and then a far stronger jolt than he had yet felt almost had him off his feet. The entire ship seemed to tilt. Several of the burning lanterns tipped from their stands, spilling their flames across the floor, and there was a hefty splitting noise from above Teal'c's head. He ducked to the side as a coffin-sized slab of ceiling hinged down and exploded against the marble.

The ship was coming apart.

From behind him, he heard voices. He ducked behind the nearest pillar and waited, as running footfalls drew closer.

He peered around the column, just enough to see a handful of Royal Guard emerge from a passage behind the transporter platform. Two of them were carrying the cylinder from the Pit of Sorrows. They were intent on their burden, and he was able to ease back out of sight without being noticed.

He readied himself. If he fired as soon as he emerged, he would be able to take, two, perhaps three before he had to seek cover from their retaliation.

"Set it down, quickly. There is little time."

That was the First Prime of Neheb-Kau. Teal'c recognized the voice, but the man sounded injured. His words were thick and strained. He had also spoken in English, which was puzzling. Unless...

Teal'c held his fire. A heartbeat later he head another, more familiar voice. "You don't have to do this."

It was Major Carter.

Teal'c felt a surge of relief, and of pride in his friend. She had not only survived the attentions of the Goa'uld, but had thrived.

"I have no choice," the First Prime replied. "My master commands it."

"Everyone has a choice, Kafra!" She sounded distraught.

"In your world, perhaps. Do not make the error of believing that everyone lives like you."

The hallway shook again. More of the ceiling cracked away, falling with shattering impacts against the floor. Teal'c stepped from his hiding place. "Major Carter!"

"Teal'c!" He saw her shock, then her smile. She was standing in the centre of the transporter platform, supporting the First Prime with her shoulder. Then his view was blocked as the Royal Guard closed around them, their staff weapons leveled.

The First Prime pushed through. "Hold your fire," he snapped. "Teal'c?"

"Correct. Release the woman."

"She goes where my master wills. You are not under the same restraint. Find a secure location, and remain there."

Light shone down around the group, and the transporter rings dropped to surround them in a cage of stone. Teal'c started towards them.

"Heed my words, Teal'c," the First Prime called. "To stay in the open is death!"

The light surged, flooded upwards, and was gone.

Teal'c ran to the transporter. The rings started to lift again, but before he could reach them another blast hammered through the ship. He felt it through the deck, the walls, heard it shatter the ceiling and fracture the golden pillars. The lights flickered, dimmed, and finally failed altogether.

The transporter rings tumbled, unsupported. Teal'c dived aside as they crashed down, the lowest shattering under the weight of the others, the ones above tilting, sliding, toppling into a messy, broken heap of stone hoops and rubble.

The topmost ring crunched onto its side, rolled forlornly halfway down the hall, and then fell over.

In the darkness of the corridors beyond the wreckage, Teal'c could see fires burning. He got up. Finding his means of following Major Carter cut off at such a moment was distressing, but given the nature of his day so far, he could not say that he was surprised.

He turned, and sprinted down the hall. The golden doors were unpowered now, but he was able to push his way between them, forcing their weight aside and squeezing into the chamber beyond.

It was a throne room, gloomy and tomb-like, typical of Neheb-Kau's morbid vanity. There was no-one in sight, just the empty throne on its stepped dais. And behind that, a vast viewport.

Teal'c ran to it, and saw in an instant how desperate his situation had become.

There was a world below him, a turgid black ball, featureless and forbidding. Its curve was huge in the viewport, a great slanted edge taking up three-quarters of the window. It was moving.

The throneship was no longer in a stable orbit.

Teal'c moved closer to the port and looked down. Below him, the outer structure of the Ha'tak stretched away, a sullen black in contrast to the core's bright golden hull. Its surface was pocked with bright spots of fire, jets of flaming atmosphere gouting into the vacuum, and the edges closest to the planet were starting to glow an ugly, dull red.

Which meant that the shields were down, and the vessel was falling into the planet's atmosphere.

As he watched, there was another jolt, but this was no explosion. The Ha'tak's core had separated from its outer structure: the dark curve of the surrounding hull began to rise, slowly, towards the viewport.

Teal'c stepped back. He had seen enough. The throneship was doomed, and there was no means by which he or Major Carter could escape.

All he could do was to ride the core down to the planet's surface, and hope that whoever had separated the two hulls still retained enough control to slow its descent. There were still explosions ripping through the golden tetrahedron's decks, but if the secondary engines and their control matrix could be preserved, it might be possible for the ship not to turn itself into a disintegrating fireball on its way down.

For those within, however, even the journey itself could prove fatal. Flesh would always be weaker than metal.

Teal'c knew he needed to find himself somewhere to shelter if he was to live through the next few minutes. He turned from the viewport and headed for one of the throne room's side doors.

There was a narrow, dark chamber behind it. Again, he was alone there, and nothing but a few scattered items of furniture inside offered any protection. If he stayed, he would probably be shaken to death as the ship came down.

Teal'c was about to leave again when he noticed what squatted in the gloom at the end of the chamber.

The sight of it filled him with loathing. For a long moment he actively considered simply leaving the place and taking his chances, and if Major Carter had not been aboard the throneship he might well have done. But he didn't just have himself to think about. Sometimes, he reflected, survival was more important than honor.

And so, with an expression of considerable disgust on his face, Teal'c ran to Neheb-Kau's open sarcophagus and climbed inside.

Chapter 19.

OLD FRIENDS

JACK O'Neill had no way of knowing for sure how much time had passed since he and Daniel had awoken in the utter darkness of Hera's holding cell. Even without his watch it would have been easier had there been light to see by, but the cell had been disorientating. He had lost track of his senses there, of his heartbeats. After Hera, or her identical twin sister, had ended her humiliating visit and left them in the dark, it was possible that he might even have dozed.

They must have been in the dark for quite a while, though. After it, the gleaming white corridors of the *Clythena* were painfully bright.

At least he was warmer now. His clothes, thoroughly emptied of any kind of equipment, had been piled next to him in the cell. Even so, he and Daniel found it a little difficult to meet each others' gaze when they first emerged.

Hera's Jaffa were waiting for them when they came out of the cell; two of the monstrous Minotaurs, along with a squad of bronze-armored hoplites. O'Neill squinted at them, his eyes watering from the light. "Hi guys. Long time no see."

"The Goddess requires your presence," one of the hoplites replied.

"Guess she found a use for us," Daniel said. O'Neill grinned.

"Once you've had Jack, you never go back."

The hoplite's eyes narrowed behind the slit of his helm. "You will accompany me to the pel'tak. In silence."

"Yeah, that might be a problem. I'm kind of a talkative guy."

The nearest Minotaur rumbled, and took a step forwards. O'Neill found his nose almost touching its naked chest. He tipped his head back, slowly.

"Okay, I get it. No talking, or it's the 'arms out of the sockets' thing again, right?"

"The Goddess was wrong. You are not completely without intellect." The hoplite gestured towards the far end of the corridor. "Walk."

O'Neill gave Daniel a sideways look, mimed drawing a zipper along his own lips, and set off into the light.

The control deck of Hera's flagship was, even O'Neill had to admit, impressive. It was a broad, sweeping place, tiered and ramped, with floors of dark stone and control consoles of brass and white marble. Huge doric columns supported the ceiling, trimmed in shining gold, while the ceiling glowed softly, like a summer sky. It was airy and calm and open, not very much like a Goa'uld structure at all.

"Looks like a health spa," said Daniel.

O'Neill looked around, at the tanned operators at their consoles, the muscular hoplites ranked at the walls and flanking every hatchway, at the silent, terrible Minotaurs. "Kinda. Maybe one of those orgy scenes in a bad gladiator movie."

"That was the Romans."

"I told you, I know that."

"And when you two have finished trying to raise your spirits with tired banter, we shall continue."

O'Neill glanced up. Hera was scowling back down at him from a wide throne, atop a high, stepped podium. She was much as when he had last seen her, although she had discarded her headdress to let her glossy golden hair flood down around her shoulders. Her expression, of haughty disdain, was quite identical.

Nevertheless, he had to ask. "So which one are you?"

A smile quirked at the corner of her lips. "Does it matter?"

"Nice of you to let us out," said Daniel. He rolled his shoulders. "I had this itch, you know, right down here…"

"Oh, I'm sure *someone* could have scratched it for you, Daniel. You only needed to ask…"

"You know," said O'Neill. "Where we come from, that's just… Well, it's inappropriate."

Something chimed softly. Hera reached to the arm of her throne and touched a control there. "Speak."

A barrage of alien syllables issued from it, the strange, fluid-sounding dialect of Goa'uld they had heard on the stricken Tel'tak. Daniel seemed to pick up on one word from it. "Pythia," he muttered.

"Pie-who?"

"The Pythia. They were oracles."

Hera finished her conversation, and sat back. "You are well informed, Daniel. The legend of the Pythia was one I personally helped perpetuate."

"You really had a high old time back in Greece, didn't you?"

"If only you knew."

There was a gonging from one side of the pel'tak, and then a thin scrape of metal on metal, like swords drawn across one another. O'Neill looked around to see part of the ceiling iris open, light spilling down to a circular design on the floor. A set of transport rings dropped, hovering into a stacked brass cage. He winced slightly as the transporter flared. His eyes were still a little sensitive, after the dark.

When the rings flew up again, a woman stood in the centre of the circle, clad in brilliant red.

She was tall, slender, with straight dark hair to the small of her back and an open, sorrowful face. She dropped to her knees. "My Lady."

"Pythia," said Hera. "What news?"

Pythia got up. "All scans have been completed, Lady. Data has been received and collated from all vessels in the fleet. There was no error."

"I see." Hera frowned, her ice-gray eyes narrowed. "Pilot, I would see this."

An operator nodded, and touched a control. In response, the entire forward wall of the pel'tak separated into sections and slid apart, leaves of white metal folding away to reveal a panorama of intense blackness.

The contrast between it and the whiteness of the pel'tak was almost painful.

"Widescreen," said O'Neill. "Very nice."

"Tell me, human." Hera pointed a small hand at the viewport. "What do you see?"

"Space, I think."

"Very good. And?"

"Looks like a planet." It was hard to see, but there was a curve of darkness between him and the stars, its surface showing a faint curve.

"And."

"Ah…" O'Neill was running out of things to say. "Ships?"

"My fleet, yes. Now tell me, human; do you see the Pit of Sorrows?"

He whirled, all humor gone from him. "What do you mean?"

"I mean, fool, that it is not there. We have arrived at the precise location programmed into it by Ra's technicians. We have activated every sensor array on every fleet, searching for the Pit or its locator beacon. And yet, there is no sign."

"Oh crap." He looked at Daniel. "Were we wrong?"

"I don't know. Maybe someone else got here first."

"Or maybe there is something about the Pit that you did not tell us," hissed Hera. "Some action you took against it that you failed to mention, while I was sparing your worthless lives."

"No, we didn't leave anything out," insisted Daniel.

Hera held up one hand, examining the brassy device that curled around her fingers. "I think," she said slowly, "that I will find out for myself. Hoplites?"

Four of the Jaffa strode forwards. O'Neill saw two coming for him, two breaking off towards Daniel. "Hey! Wait!"

"I think I have waited long enough."

A Jaffa's hand came down hard on his shoulder.

O'Neill grabbed it, pulled it past him and twisted around, slammed his elbow back into the man's face. The hoplite's helm was up, but the impact rocked him.

Pain flared up O'Neill's arm, but he ignored it, swinging the hoplite around and off balance. He grabbed at the man's staff weapon. His fingers brushed it, at the instant the other hoplite hammered his own staff into O'Neill's back.

The breath went out of him. He turned, tried to strike back, but the blow had been well-aimed, and his time in the cell had not been kind to his muscles. He took a second blow under the sternum, and sat down hard.

In moments, the two Hoplites had dragged him to his knees. He looked sideways, and through a haze of pain saw that Daniel had been beaten down just as brutally.

Hera was walking down the steps of her podium. She gestured at the hoplites. "Closer."

O'Neill felt himself shuffled along, until he was only a meter from where Daniel knelt, his arms dragged agonizingly behind his back.

"And we were getting on so well," he grated.

"Such spirit. So many little jokes." Hera raised her hand, and spread her fingers. The gem in her palm glowed. "I wonder how many more I will find inside that tiny brain of yours?"

"My Lady!"

It was Pythia. Hera rolled her eyes. "I am *busy!*"

"A communication."

"From where?"

"The planet's surface, Lady."

"The surface?" Hera stepped back, a look of utter confusion on her face. "How can that be?"

"We told you," O'Neill replied. "Someone beat you to it."

She gave him an odd look, frowning, her head slightly tilted. Appraising him. "Pythia?"

There was a flash of scarlet at the corner of O'Neill's eye. Pythia had swept up to Hera's side. "He speaks the truth," she replied. "In part. Wreckage of a Ha'tak class vessel lies under the cloud layer, scattered over a wide area."

"Wreckage?" O'Neill felt his heart shrink in his chest.

"The particulate nature of the atmosphere makes tracking imprecise. However, the communication is from an active source."

"So something survived…" Hera put a finger to her lips, thoughtfully. "It has to be Neheb-Kau. The fool regained his demon, yet in doing so flew his ship into the ground. Which surprises me not in the least… Give me a full sensor sweep of the surface. I want to know where the Ha'tak's core lies. It must be relatively intact for him to signal us."

"Shall I ready the weapons?"

"Yes, and alert the crew of the Auger. But hold your fire. I want to know exactly where that monster is before I risk an attack."

"By your will." Pythia moved away, the scarlet train of her gown fluttering across the stone floor.

Hera straightened, lifted her chin slightly. "Open a communications channel," she called. Then, briefly, glanced down at O'Neill and Daniel. "And get them out of my way."

O'Neill was hauled back to his feet, and dragged to the side. Daniel was moved with him. "Jack, what the hell?"

"Search me."

"Yeah, I think she was about to. The hard way."

The viewport rippled and changed, turning from a view of open space into a theater-sized picture.

As O'Neill saw it, he shouted.

The scene itself was not what drew the exclamation from him: it was a magnified image of another Goa'uld control deck, one that seemed to be decorated in little more than black with gold trim. The visual feed was fizzing with static, broken and jumping, and the pel'tak looked in even worse repair: O'Neill could see hanging cables, smoke, a length of bent girder crossing the whole screen at an angle.

There was a throne in front of the girder, occupied by a black-robed figure in a golden, pharaoh-style helm. To his left stood an old man, his scowling face narrow and creased by time, and to his right a Jaffa who wore a golden symbol at his forehead. O'Neill noticed, barely, that the man had suffered some kind of dreadful injury, an awful burn that looked as if it had turned half his head to blisters.

But what made O'Neill shout was the fact that Samantha Carter was in the picture too.

She was in the front of the shot, as if kneeling before the throne. She looked exhausted, battered, her civilian clothes torn and stained. Her hair was a random mess, some of it glued to her scalp, the rest sticking up wildly. Her eyes were hollow and dark, and there were bruises on her face.

"Carter!" O'Neill bellowed.

"Colonel?" She grinned tiredly. "Oh, thank god!"

"Sam, you're looking great! Where's Teal'c?"

"He's, ah, around, sir."

As she spoke, the System Lord raised a hand behind her head. The hand was blackened, withered, and wrapped round by the unmistakable gold banding of a ribbon device. The gem at his palm pulsed once.

Carter cried out, and sank out of shot.

"When spoken to," said the Goa'uld, quite calmly.

"Carter!" O'Neill called again. "You son of a bitch, what did you do?"

"Human," snarled Hera, "if you speak again I will have your lips sewn shut."

"But—"

"Do not test me!"

On the screen, Carter was slowly getting back up, wincing. O'Neill relaxed slightly. However, it was now very obvious that she was not among friends.

Still, she was alive, and free from the Pit of Sorrows. That alone was a relief almost too much to bear.

Hera had returned her attention to the screen. "My Lord Neheb-Kau," she smiled, tipping her head in a slight bow.

"The Lady Serqet."

Her smile lessened a fraction. "I have not used that name for a long time."

"Indeed." His voice was high and whispery, behind the mask. "I knew that you had taken a new identity. I simply had no idea that the change was so… Radical."

"I made a new start after Setraxis."

"I wish I had been afforded the same opportunities."

Hera's jaw set a little tighter. O'Neill could see that she was struggling for control. It looked to him as if it was something she had to do on a regular basis. "That was a great deal of time ago, my Lord. Ancient history."

"For you, perhaps."

"Your memory of that time is no doubt better than mine. We should meet, and combine our recollections."

O'Neill saw the older man at Neheb-Kau's side bend slightly to whisper something. As he did, there was a flicker to one side of the screen, and a strip of hieroglyphs appeared.

"Beware, my Lord," breathed Daniel, translating on the fly. "She seeks to… Um… A tongue of honey, of poison…"

"Lip-reading software?" said O'Neill. "Oh, she's good…"

The old man straightened. Neheb-Kau's golden helm tilted a fraction. "There will be no meeting between us, Lady. You divested yourself of the right to speak to me as an equal after Setraxis."

Hera stiffened. "I see. In which case, if we cannot be civil, at least let us be honest. You have the Ash Eater."

"And you fear it."

"Of course I do. Any sane creature fears it. It must be contained, forever. I have the means to do that."

"You would rob me of my prize, Hera?" The mask's eye pulsed a glow of white light. "Again?"

"Neheb-Kau, look around you. Your ship is destroyed. You are trapped on a lifeless world with no hope of escape. Hand over the Ash Eater to me, and I will see you and your crew returned safely to your domains."

Neheb-Kau hissed out a horrible, powdery laugh. "You would assist *me*?"

"Dude, it's a good offer," O'Neill called out. "Seriously, it's nice up here. They've got a pool."

Hera's shoulders dipped slightly. "As you can see, I have a slight infestation problem."

"I too. They get everywhere, do they not?"

"My Lord, abandon the Ash Eater. It will bring only suffering."

The mask turned, side to side. "No. I know you, Hera. I know your deceptions, your manipulations. I have known for a very long time. And you will not rob me of my prize, not again!"

At that, her control finally gave way. "Fool!" she snapped. "Do you not see you have no choice?"

"Choice? You speak to *me* of choice?" He touched a gem at his chest. His helm separated, became a swarm of leaves and blades that whirled apart, shrank away, settled one on another to stack and fold and collapse into his shoulder armor, leaving his head bare.

"You think I chose *this?*" he snarled.

At the sight, Hera recoiled.

O'Neill sucked in a breath. The man's face was a ruin; tatters of pulpy, oozing flesh layered haphazardly over pitted bone.

His cloudy, lidless eyes glared out from open sockets, and glowed in fury.

"A thousand hosts, Hera! A thousand, dripping off me, one after the other! Do you think I fear you, after such an existence?"

She pointed a shaking finger. "You condemned *yourself* to that life!"

"*It was your fault, you whore!*"

Hera screamed in rage, a deafening, inhuman screech. "Skull-faced lunatic! Give me the Casket!"

"If you want the Ash Eater, come and take it!"

The screen went blank. Hera balled her fists, her whole small body taut with fury. "Pythia!"

"My Lady?"

"I want ten wings of death gliders at the surface, and another ten on point-defense. Six wings of bombers to follow and vaporize anything other than the core. And mobilize the Spartan Guard for ground assault. No survivors!"

"By your will." The Oracle turned away.

"Hey!" O'Neill shook himself free of the Jaffa holding him. "Come on, you don't have to do that!"

"You think so? What choice do I have?"

"Plenty," said Daniel. "Please, Hera, we have friends on this ship. If you can get us in there…"

"You?" Her eyebrows went up somewhere into her hairline. "I should put the galaxy's fate in *your* hands?"

"Wouldn't be the first time," O'Neill muttered.

"We could get onto that ship, hook up with our people and get the Casket for you," Daniel insisted. "Look, we're good at this kind of thing. We made it halfway into the *Clythena* before you even noticed."

"A mistake I do not intend to repeat." She raised a hand. "Minotaur!"

"Ah, not those guys again…" O'Neill watched the nearest bull-headed Jaffa striding towards him, the horned head a solid half-meter above his own.

"Human, you test my patience. Repeatedly." She stepped aside to let the Minotaur past. "Luckily for you, I have an abundance of it. So go now, and quietly. This is out of your hands. And I need you out of my sight."

Had the Minotaur alone been taking O'Neill and Daniel off the pel'tak, he thought, they probably could have just run away. The modified Jaffa were phenomenally strong — O'Neill had a collection of throbbing shoulder muscles that could attest to that — but he doubted they were built for speed. Also, the Minotaur had to keep ducking to avoid catching its brass horns on the roof braces. In a sprint, O'Neill would lay serious money down that the Jaffa would eventually miss a brace and end up flat on its back.

Regrettably, Hera seemed to be of the same opinion. She sent four hoplites with them.

O'Neill had wondered if he was going to be zatted unconscious again, but that did not happen. Instead, he found himself and Daniel being marched swiftly along one of the ship's open thoroughfares, with the Minotaur at his back and four hoplites surrounding them. The glowing *faux* sky of the corridor ceiling had, he noticed, turned from its normal glowing blue to a sullen, stormy red, obviously to denote that the ship was at battle stations. "Neat. I think I saw them do that in Vegas."

Alongside him, Daniel was more jittery than he had seen him in a long time. "Jack, what the hell are we going to do?"

"I'm working on it."

"Well, can you work faster? I don't know who the Spartan Guard are, but I can kinda guess restraint isn't in their training."

"Look, Sam and Teal'c have made it this far."

"And I'm glad to know they're okay too. I mean seriously, you've no idea how relieved I am. But they're going to find themselves in the middle of a war really soon."

"You think I don't know that?" O'Neill gave Daniel a hard look, and lowered his voice to a hiss. "And as soon as we can, we'll get out of here and help them. Okay? I'm just waiting for the right moment."

There was a shout from behind him. "Jaffa!"

The whole group, Jaffa and humans alike, turned as one.

Bra'tac stood in the centre of the corridor, next to the last junction they had passed. His staff weapon was across his back on a makeshift sling, and he had a zat gun in each hand.

"Surrender!" he bellowed.

The hoplites dropped into a fighting stance, perfectly synchronized. Their left arms came up, shields whirling into being, their spears leveled and snapped open with an electric hiss. At their back, the Minotaur lowered its head, fists clenched and its great horns glinting.

It was an impressive display, O'Neill thought. It would have been even more impressive had he and Daniel not, in the heat of the moment, been completely forgotten.

Maybe Bra'tac was too honorable to attack a man whose back was turned. Jack O'Neill wasn't. As the old Jaffa fired, the two zat guns snarling out their blue beams in unison, he slammed the heavy sole of his boot into the back of a hoplite's knee.

The man stumbled. O'Neill grabbed him, threw his weight into him to push him even further off balance, and spun the man into the wall. Next to him, Daniel had his arms around a hoplite's neck, pulling him backwards.

One of the front two hoplites was already down; Bra'tac had aimed the beam perfectly over the top edge of his shield to catch him in the face. The second beam had caromed wildly off a shield and into the ceiling, but Bra'tac was already firing again, and the man O'Neill had attacked was struck as he staggered back across the corridor. He collapsed, covered in sparks, but his companions were already firing a stream of staff bolts up the corridor. Bra'tac dodged back around the junction, began to fire swiftly and accurately around the corner.

O'Neill put his shoulder down and body-slammed the hoplite Daniel was hanging onto, trying to get him off-balance too, but the man must have been either stronger or better prepared. He whipped around, shrugging Daniel off and slamming his shield into him, crushing him against the wall.

The staff whipped towards O'Neill, the wicked blades at its tip glinting. O'Neill dodged back to avoid being eviscerated, ducked under the next blow and came in past the staff to strike the man hard in the arm with the edge of his hand.

It wasn't the most effective place he could have struck the Jaffa, but there was a lot of armor to get past. It made the warrior recoil slightly, though, which was all Bra'tac needed to put a zat beam into him.

Daniel was slumping down the wall. O'Neill grabbed his arm and pulled him up. "You okay?"

"Couldn't be better…"

Massive footfalls were hammering away up the corridor. O'Neill looked up to see the Minotaur charging towards Bra'tac, head down, fists swinging. Watching it, he realized that he had been wrong to think he could have outrun the monster. It was a lot quicker than it looked.

Bra'tac had just found that out. He had tried to duck under the Minotaur's reach, but instead it had grabbed him and flung him bodily across the corridor.

The zat guns flew from his grip. O'Neill saw them skittering across the floor, and then the last hoplite was trying to take his head off. He dived to one side, the bladed end of the staff parting the air across his shoulders, and rolled.

The spear jammed hard down into the floor next to his head.

He scrambled up, ramming the hoplite with his shoulder. In a straight fight, he knew he was outclassed. Even though none of these warriors could match Teal'c's physical prowess, they were still far stronger and more resilient than O'Neill. He had to get another advantage.

In this case, it turned out to be Daniel Jackson. As the hoplite readied himself to strike, Daniel reached to his shoulder armor and triggered his helm control.

The man snapped around, fumbling at his neck armor as his helm split apart and retracted. O'Neill stooped, picked up the staff weapon of one of the fallen men and swung it as hard as he could into the back of the hoplite's skull.

There was a dull thud of alien metal on bone. The warrior sank to his knees, then toppled.

From the junction, there was the heavy, complicated sound of a fully armored Jaffa being flung into a corridor wall. O'Neill ran towards it, Daniel at his side, and as one they stooped to pick up the fallen zat guns.

"Hey!" O'Neill yelled. "Big feller!"

The Minotaur whirled, horribly fast for something so huge, and began racing towards him.

He fired, catching the Jaffa clean in the chest. The Minotaur thundered, a booming metallic moan, but didn't stop.

O'Neill fired again, another hit, and then a fist the size of his own head came out and slammed into his ribs.

The corridor whirled past him, spinning. The floor came up

and hit him in the back. He lay, his entire torso a cage of pain, trying to draw breath, while a shadow crossed him to block out the ruddy light from the ceiling. It was the Minotaur.

Voltage crawled over it. It was swaying, like a tree.

O'Neill rolled, as fast and hard as he could, and the Minotaur crashed down right next to him.

Hands gripped his arms and pulled him up. For a few seconds all he could do was to sag in their grip, then he got his lungs to work and sucked in a long, very painful breath.

"Ow," he managed.

"Jack?"

"I'm fine."

Daniel nodded. "Look, this 'right moment'? When it happens, you'll let me know, okay?"

"Humans, ready yourselves!" Bra'tac had recovered quickly from the Minotaur's attack, and was striding up the corridor towards them. "We must go to the glider bays."

"You found a ship?"

"I have found and lost several, while you were here consorting with the witch Hera!"

O'Neill frowned. "I didn't consort. Daniel, did you consort?"

"Well, there was that time in the holding cell. Does that count as consorting?"

"It was dark, I couldn't see if you consorted or not."

Bra'tac gave them both a very sour glare. "Are you done?"

"Yeah." O'Neill had enough breath to run, now. "Yeah, we're done."

Chapter 20.

VERTIGO

AS SOON as he had cut the communications to Hera's flagship, Neheb-Kau had risen from his throne. "It is time," he said. "We shall retire to the glider bays."

Carter got warily to her feet. Although she had been ordered to kneel during the communication, the Goa'uld made no move to keep her there. Even Djetec paid her no heed.

As she rose, Neheb-Kau moved into her line of sight, and her first sight of his face — coupled with the pounding headache she had gained from her brush with the ribbon device — almost had her back on her knees again. She swayed, closing her eyes so she didn't have to look at the Goa'uld's rotting, destroyed features any more.

Kafra must have seen her reaction, because he stepped quickly towards her and steadied her, at the same time putting himself between her and Neheb-Kau. "My Lord. I will go to the garrison levels."

"For what purpose?"

"To marshal our defenses."

"There are to be no defenses. Come, Kafra, your place is at my side." The Goa'uld moved closer, past him, and his lidless eyes rolled towards Carter. "You too, human."

"I don't understand," she replied weakly. "When Hera sends her forces —"

"We will be where she least expects us," Djetec cuts in. "Do you doubt the God's plan? His mastery of the situation?"

Neheb-Kau's face did something, a stretching of the exposed tendons to either side of his broken mouth. A smile, Carter realized. "I knew the Lady Hera when she was still Serqet, before she became the consort of Ra. She fancies herself a master manipulator, but in turn she is surprisingly easy to manipulate."

"You provoked her," said Carter, suddenly feeling rather stupid. Her exhaustion must have been affecting her more than she had thought. "To draw her attention here deliberately."

"Of course." Neheb-Kau raised a stick-like arm to one of the Royal Guard who had survived the crash. "You."

The man approached, limping. Although the pel'tak had been protected by damping fields, the repeated impacts of the crash had been catastrophic. No-one, save for Neheb-Kau and Djetec, had gone unscathed.

"What is your will, my Lord?"

"Use the transporter. Go to the secondary glider bay, and return to me with a report on its status."

The guard bowed, then headed for the transporter platform towards the rear of the pel'tak, ducking under the broken girder to get there. Neheb-Kau watched him go, his cloudy eyes following him like the glass orbs of a broken doll.

"Do you think he will return?"

Djetec made a noncommittal gesture. "The glider bay is intact. I have seen it on the remote monitors. As long as the transporter link still functions, he will return."

"The transporter is what I am testing, my friend." Neheb-Kau smiled again. "Perhaps I should have made myself clear. Do you think he will return *intact?*"

During the crash, which had lasted for quite a long time, Carter's worst fear had not been that the ship would explode. She did not find herself concerned that the pel'tak's forward viewport would shatter and expose them all to the lifeless, choking atmosphere beyond. She had not even worried overmuch about the damping fields failing, even though the memory of what had happened to Sephotep and his co-pilot in the absence of such a field was still far too fresh in her memory.

No, what had really caused her heart to hammer and her guts to roil was the thought of the Casket shutting down and releasing the Ash Eater again.

Thankfully, this hadn't happened, due in no small part to the two Royal Guard who had knelt on either side of the awful thing and wrapped their arms around it, holding it steady while the ship began its whirling descent to the planet's surface. The endless sledgehammer impacts as the ship battered down through the atmosphere had failed to dislodge them, and even the crash itself, when the vessel had slammed sideways into a black mountain of ash and skidded, shuddering and spinning and shedding great chunks of hull, for kilometer after kilometer across that blighted landscape, had somehow failed to break their hold.

Huddled on the pel'tak, watching through the open viewports, Carter had seen the whole crash happen, from the first cherry-red glows of atmospheric friction against the hull to the final rain of black dust over the core's broken body. She still couldn't quite believe she had survived it.

In fact, given the ruin which the Ash Eater's hunger had wrought on the ship's systems, it was something of a miracle that anyone aboard was alive at all. If the monstrous little fetus had found its way directly to the reactor, the whole power distribution network would have shut down at once. The backup systems would have been overloaded and failed, and there would not have been enough stored energy to sustain the damping fields.

As it was, the ship had died in stages, as the converters fell one by one.

Any joy she might have taken in her continued survival had vanished upon discovering that Neheb-Kau and Djetec were still alive as well. When Carter had reached the pel'tak neither had been in sight, and she had been fantasizing about the pair of them being trapped on some other, less well-protected area of the ship.

But, when the fires were out and the debris stopped falling, they had re-appeared, having ridden out the destruction in some kind of stasis antechamber.

If there was any hope for her to cling onto now, it was the fact that, somehow, Colonel O'Neill and Daniel Jackson had followed the Pit of Sorrows across space to find her. Although their own journey did not seem to have been without its trials — they had fallen into the power of a System Lord who was not only an old enemy of Neheb-Kau, but who also had once been consort to the supreme System Lord himself, Ra.

The very Ra that O'Neill and Daniel had destroyed with a tactical nuclear weapon over Abydos.

Carter resolved to stay quiet about that fact. Things were complicated enough as it was.

The glider bays were at the base of the throneship's core. As with almost all the ship's systems, the bays had been heavily modified, split into three identical hangars with flight tubes exiting all sides of the hull. As far as Carter could tell, looking around the chaotic ruin of the secondary bay, some of the tubes might still be useable as long as not too much of the planet's surface dust had piled against them, but it would be almost impossible for any ship to make the return journey. Access to the throneship was usually through shielded openings in its base.

The vessel was standing like a forgotten, tilted building on the surface of the Ash Eater's homeworld, and it would never fly again.

A small backup reactor and a few undamaged storage capacitors were all that provided its power now, and they wouldn't last more than a few hours. But if Neheb-Kau cared about that, he didn't show it. He had, it seemed, other fish to fry.

He stood on one of the intact gantries, immobile and impassive as Jaffa pilots hurried to ready their vessels. His helm was once again in place, sparing Carter the sight of his deathly face, but in a way that was worse. All she could think of, when she looked at that perfect golden mask, was the corruption beneath.

A corruption that went far beyond the physical.

She had been given no chance to make her escape, even in the chaos after the crash. Both Djetec and Neheb-Kau seemed to be keeping her very carefully in sight, and there were still enough of their fiercely loyal guard with them to make sure she was always in reach. Neheb-Kau, she had decided, had plans for her.

What they might entail, she hardly dared guess. Especially since he had ordered the Casket carried down to the glider bay as well.

Kafra had been assembling the pilots, and now he turned from the rail he had been leaning on to stand, twisted in pain, before his God. "My Lord, thirty death gliders are ready to fly, in this and the other bays. There are also two Khepesh scouts, four freighters and your personal craft."

So the Goa'uld had his own ship, Carter thought. Probably some kind of fast yacht. He was going to load the Casket onto it and take off, leaving his crew to die on this dust-choked nightmare of a world while Hera's fleet rained fire down on it from heaven.

That was when Carter realized her place in Neheb-Kau's design: she would be required to tend the casket aboard that yacht, all the way to wherever he was going. She was going to be trapped in a ship, for the length of an unknowable journey, with the two most loathsome creatures she had ever encountered.

The thought was horrifying. She edged slightly away from the group of Jaffa assembling on the gantry, wondering if she could somehow get them between her and the Royal Guard.

"What of the Al'kesh bombers?" Djetec was asking.

"They were stationed in the same bay as the Pit of Sorrows, *Tjaty*. It fell on them."

"A pity."

"It is of no consequence," declared Neheb-Kau. "What we have is more than sufficient." He gestured at the waiting fighters, hanging above on their curving launch racks. "Have the Casket loaded aboard one of the gliders, and slave its controls to that of the flight leader."

Carter stared. *A fighter?*

Kafra stepped towards him. "My Lord, slave controls are used only for training. The flight leader's vessel will be too slow to fight."

The mask's eye glowed. "Do you question me, Kafra?"

"I… I merely urge caution. Our situation is desperate."

One of the Jaffa pilots stepped forwards, and bowed. "First

Prime, it is my honor. I shall fly two ships into battle, and emerge victorious!"

"Victorious?" Carter blurted. "It's suicide! There are dozens of ships out there. You're going up against them with thirty fighters?"

"Human," Kafra warned. His voice was weak, but still had the edge of command to it. "It is my place to advise the God. It is yours to sustain the Casket until it is aboard the glider. Do not forget that."

"Oh dear God." Her eyes widened. "He wants this. He wants them to die up there."

"Their sacrifice will be a glorious one," Djetec replied. "They will lead our greatest weapon into battle, and when Hera's own weapons unleash the Ash Eater, it will destroy her."

"And then what? You'll have lost the Casket, remember?"

"I have other Caskets," said Neheb-Kau airily. "Once Hera is no more, I shall draw it back to them with the Lure."

"And all those who oppose us will fall," said Djetec. "One after another, until my master is revenged upon them."

At the other end of the gantry, five death gliders dropped from their racks, turned in the smoke-laden air, and accelerated smoothly away towards the launch tubes.

Carter gaped, her mind spinning with the full realization of just how deranged the Goa'uld in front of her truly was. She had known, for a long time, that he was obsessed to the point of monomania, but the sheer scale of his madness was overwhelming.

From what she had learned aboard the throneship, Neheb-Kau had gained his place in the hierarchy of the System Lords purely by his willingness to search the galaxy for terrible artifacts, to seek out their secrets and then to use them where he could to poison and destroy. It must have been a dreadful climb to power, slow and hateful, cumulating with his greatest discovery, here on this black, dust-choked planet. The Ash Eater had become his ultimate goal, his holy grail. He had even exposed himself to the Lure in order to take control of it.

Then, on a world called Setraxis, something had happened,

and he had lost the Ash Eater to Ra.

Neheb-Kau had no fleet, only this one battered ship. He spoke of his domains, but they were far away. He must have lost everything after what happened on Setraxis. Whether it was his obsession with the Ash Eater that had reduced him to an outcast, a hated, shunned wanderer, or something worse Carter did not know. Teal'c had mentioned rumors of a terrible crime committed against other System Lords. Had he set the Ash Eater among them?

Whatever had happened, Neheb-Kau had come out of it badly. And he had spent the next five thousand years doing little except modify his ship and mourn the loss of his pet monster. He flew a tomb in its memory.

And now, he had his prize back, and all he could think of was revenge.

He didn't want control. He didn't want power. He didn't want an empire. He was going to let his ship be destroyed and his Jaffa be killed and everything he had ever worked for blasted into ash and dust just so he could settle the grudges he'd carried with him for five thousand years.

The gantry trembled. A distant rumble sounded through the bay, and then another, louder.

"It begins," said Kafra. "Hera's ships are upon us."

Two Royal Guard had lifted the Casket into a glider's lift. Carter saw the platform rise, hoisted up into the glider's belly on sliding rails, until it locked seamlessly into the hull. The glider spread its wings, and there was a dull, rising screech as its engines fired.

"Kafra, this is insane," Carter whispered. "Please, help me stop this."

"I cannot. He is my God."

"You know that's not true." Around her, pilots were climbing into the lift platforms of their fighters, being drawn up and swallowed by the insectile hulls. "All your men will die."

"Then that is their destiny."

"To hell with destiny!"

"What would you have me do?" he snarled. "To rebel against

my God, as your Teal'c did? I am dying, human. Allow me to do so with some scrap of honor!"

The Jaffa flight leader was being lifted into his ship. Carter stared helplessly upwards as his fighter sealed itself, the scythed wings rising to lock into position.

"There's no honor in this," she told him. "He's taken even that away from you."

She turned away from him. If he answered her, his words were lost to the rising din of the gliders above her head. The second flight, with the Ash Eater's Casket peeking incongruously over one cockpit rim like a stunted, golden pilot, detached from their racks and swung away.

There had to be a way to prevent the Ash Eater from attacking Hera's fleet. Carter had no preference for one Goa'uld over another — in her eyes, they were all a stain on the galaxy. But Hera held O'Neill and Daniel. There had to be a way to protect them from its appetites.

The Lure, she thought suddenly. If she could get back to the vault, draw off more of that vile toxin and get it aboard a ship, perhaps the Ash Eater could be led back to Neheb-Kau like a dog to its own vomit.

It wasn't much of a plan, she was painfully aware of that. But she had done more audacious things, in her time. As long as she acted swiftly, there was a chance.

The decision was made, there and then. She bolted.

There was a shout behind her, Kafra or one of the Royal Guard, but she was nimble, and already halfway to the access arch before the alarm had gone up. As she pounded along the mesh towards it she was already working out how to short the controls from the other side, to jam the door locked so she could have at least a few minutes to find a ring transporter and get to the Vault.

There would have been casualties among the Jaffa, during the crash. She might even find a discarded weapon.

As the thought struck her, the hatch began to slide open. She caught a glimpse of golden armor beyond it, and tried to stop in time, but the mesh was slippery with grease and smoke from the fires. She skated, almost fell, and slammed sideways into the wall as another Royal Guard stepped through to grab her upper arm.

"Hold her," called Djetec, hurrying along the gantry.

The guard tilted his helm down to her, the double serpent head swiveling. "Be ready," he said.

Carter stared at him. "You have got to be kidding!"

"No humor is intended, Major Carter," Teal'c replied. "There is a zat gun attached to my belt."

She saw it, snatched it up and spun around, letting Djetec have the first shot right in the face.

He was running fast, for an old man. He hit the ground horizontally and still moving.

Teal'c leveled the staff he was carrying and loosed off three shots in blurring succession. The first struck a guard in the chest, flinging him back into his fellows. The next two blasted into the gantry just ahead of them, shattering the mesh and sending up a cloud of fragments.

Plasma bolts sang back towards Carter, shrieking off the walls. She ducked back, firing the zat wildly towards the Royal Guard, taking one down by pure chance.

"Major Carter, we must retreat."

"No argument there." She tried to head for the access arch, but he pulled her back, pointed along the next section of gantry. "This way."

"What's down there?"

"A means of escape."

She ducked as another blast ripped through the air next to her, spattering molten metal from the wall. "Okay, I'm right behind you!"

They ran a few meters on, until they reached a support brace. Teal'c stepped behind it, took advantage of the cover it provided to aim his staff carefully, and then fired several times back the way they had come. Carter saw the shots go low, under the gantry, hitting two of the angled supports that held it level.

The supports flashed apart, and the gantry sagged. The gold-clad warriors there staggered to a halt, and began to edge back.

Their pursuit might have been halted, but their ability to shoot was not. Staff blasts were screaming through the glider bay in almost unbroken streams. Carter edged back a little behind the brace. "Which way?"

"To those stairs, and then down."

"Got it."

And they ran again.

Teal'c's preferred means of escape was one of the Khepesh scouts, a glossy machine that looked like a bulked-up death glider with an elongated cockpit and narrow, backward-swept wings. Teal'c went in first, retracting his helm as he did so, and Carter followed, locking the hatch behind her.

"It's good to see you, Teal'c," she grinned. The scout had two flight seats, set one behind the other. The Jaffa was already climbing into the front, and Carter dropped into what she assumed was the co-pilot's position, set behind and above under an angular canopy. "Again."

"It is good to see you also." He put his left hand on a red orb that took up most of the scout's control board, and gripped a curving flight stick with his right. There was a bass, throaty rumble from the back of the vessel. "Are you secured?"

"Good to go." The seat had locked restraints around her when she had sat down, and the control board in front of her had activated, streams of hieroglyphs rolling down illuminated panels. If the vessel was a scout ship, Carter reasoned, she was probably looking at the sensor feeds and recording equipment.

She decided not to touch anything quite yet. "Ah, you can fly one of these, right?"

"I do not know. I have never tried."

Half the grin slipped off her face. "That's a joke, isn't it?"

"No."

The Khepesh leapt forwards.

Carter was slammed back into the seat by the acceleration. She saw gantries and metal walls and broken death gliders whipping past the viewports on either side, a few plasma bolts cutting bright trails through the air ahead of her, and then the launch tube was a solid rectangle of flat black expanding to swallow her up.

The walls of the tube flickered past her, and then they were soaring out over the Ash Eater's homeworld.

Carter grimaced. The scene around her was utterly hellish.

She was racing over an endless sea of black dust under a roiling, thunderous sky. The air was thick with ash, blasting against the viewports so fast and so continuously that it looked like static on a screen, and great heaps and dunes of the stuff rose wherever she looked. There was nothing solid below her at all, nothing jagged or edged, just mounds and dunes and huge, shallow craters.

Above that mournful landscape, the battle between Hera's fleet and Neheb-Kau's few pitiful wings of fighters was at its height. Death gliders were ripping through the dust-laden air in screaming curves, spitting cannon fire at each other while great Al'kesh bombers raced below them, raising vast roostertails of ash. Explosions chased the bombers along the ground, fountains of dust and smoke, flashing detonations as pieces of Neheb-Kau's broken Ha'tak were found and atomized where they lay.

Teal'c turned the ship, sent it arcing away from the destruction, between two mounded hills and over one of those vast craters. Her sensor boards lit up as she went over, and although she couldn't read the glyphs, the graphics showed, just briefly, a wireframe representation of the feature.

The crater was bizarre; a shallow cone maybe three kilometers across with a deep hole at its heart, according to the graphic. It was a strange sight, unsettling in its regularity. Looking out over that appalling landscape, she could see that the planet was pocked with them.

Her first thought was volcanism, but that must have been a very long time ago.

"The range of this vessel is short," Teal'c was saying. "But it will enable us to reach the nearest Stargate."

"That's great, but we've got to pick up the Colonel and Daniel first."

He glanced back. "They are here?"

"They're with a Goa'uld called Hera. I think they hitched a ride."

"Hera..." Teal'c's voice displayed little emotion. "A minor System Lord, whose domains lie far from Earth. A manipulator and a seductress. What is your plan to rescue O'Neill and Daniel Jackson?"

"I'm still working on that part."

The scout began to rise. Carter felt it angle back, saw the ground tip away, the thick soup of cloud above surge down at her. Teal'c was taking them up and out of the atmosphere, accelerating as he did so, leaving the dead world and its shroud of ash in their wake. The clouds battered at them as they punched through, dragging at the Khepesh with thick ropes of fog, but the ship was moving too fast to be held back. Seconds later, they were in an altogether cleaner kind of darkness.

The pure blackness of space surrounded her, dusted with stars.

Carter saw an immense wheel turning slowly above her: Hera's fleet, in perfect circular formation. At the centre was a huge square of complex white machinery, the base of her mountainous flagship, and orbiting it the far smaller discs of the Ha'tak motherships. Even in the meager light from the system's ravaged star, the vessels gleamed like polished bone, like fine china saucers set whirling against the pure, crisp blackness of deep space.

Around one of the marble-white Ha'taks, motes of metal whirled and burned around each other like embers above a fire. It was a dogfight, as fast and vicious above the clouds as below. The Ha'tak had already taken damage, with dark pocks marring its hull, and Carter saw one of the great towers at its circumference blossom abruptly into an expanding cloud of flame and debris. "My God. Teal'c, did you see that?"

"Indeed."

Carter gaped, watching the remains of the tower begin to tilt away, falling from the vessel towards the planet, trailing burning air. "Their shields must be down."

"Death gliders alone would not have been able to bring down the shields. Either the vessel has suffered a systems failure, or the Ash Eater is feeding from it."

"Oh no…" A horrible image had appeared in her mind's eye: the Ash Eater, hovering in the blinding heart of the ship's reactor, gulping energy while the power distribution network ripped itself apart trying to compensate…

Fire stitched a line across the Ha'tak's hull, spitting a glittering dust of fragmented metal, and the viewports in that part of the ship went out. A moment later there was a larger, more concentrated explosion, a capacitor bank or secondary generator failing under the overload and flashing apart. The Ha'tak seemed to wheel around one of its own edges, and began to slide downwards.

The ships were already dropping close to the cloud layer. The stricken vessel, if its crew failed to restart the drives in the next few minutes, was going to come down even faster and harder that Neheb-Kau's throneship.

There was a faint chirruping from Teal'c's control board. "We are being hailed," he reported.

"Maybe it's the Colonel."

"I do not believe so."

"Let's see it anyway."

One of the screens in front of her changed. Carter wasn't exactly surprised to see the shining mask of Neheb-Kau appear on it.

"Human, you have abused my hospitality and stolen my property." He settled back on what appeared to be a throne, and stroked the metal beard of his mask. "Again. I will find it difficult to let this go unpunished."

"Try." Carter tapped at the board's icons. A small, globe-shaped control rose from within the metal, and a secondary screen turned from glyph-strewn blue to pure black.

There were stars on it.

"You are valuable to me, human. Your expertise in restoring the

Casket was instrumental in the glorious destruction of Hera's army."

"Oh, I can't take all the credit for that." Carter twisted the globe, the view on her screen swung about, to show the damaged Ha'tak racing past, trailing fire. "Besides, she seems to have quite a bit in reserve."

"The Ash Eater is still growing in power."

That was probably true, Carter thought grimly. When she had encountered it, a few drops of five thousand year-old Lure had been enough to keep it trapped in an open Casket, and to draw its attention from human meals only meters away. Now it was stripping the power from entire starships.

If it continued to feed, just how powerful would it grow?

"It was stopped once. It will be again."

"By who? You? Hera, the great deceiver?" He laughed. "Human, return to my side. It is the only chance you have for survival."

Carter rotated the view again, pointing the pickup directly aft. She stifled a curse. Four death gliders were pacing the Khepesh, surrounding a broad arrowhead of dull silver metal. The God's private vessel.

"Sorry, Neheb-Kau. I'd rather take my chances with the Ash Eater." She pondered for a moment. "Actually, I'd rather *kiss* the Ash Eater."

Neheb-Kau's mask tilted slightly. "In which case, I bid you farewell."

The screen went blank. There was a moment of silence.

"He's not just going to go away, is he," said Carter finally.

"No," Teal'c replied. "He is not."

Weapons fire slammed into the scout's hull. On the screen, the arrowhead was emitting streams of plasma bolts, and Carter could see them ripping past the cockpit, twin rivers of energy.

Teal'c hauled on the controls. Carter felt the scout drop away under her, clamped her stomach muscles tight to counter the acceleration effects. Behind her, the four gliders raced in close pursuit, sending out flaring bolts from their staff cannons.

The Khepesh shook again. It felt as though someone was kicking Carter's control seat, hard, every time a bolt struck the hull. "Are they faster than us?"

"Considerably."

The clouds rose up and wiped choking billows across the cockpit. Carter felt the ship swerve violently to starboard, as Teal'c took advantage of the visual cover to try and throw the gliders off track.

She looked at the screen. The ruse wasn't working. "I think they can still see us!"

Another impact, this one sending up a sheet of sparks from behind the seats. Outside the cockpit, the clouds thinned and vanished, leaving the pocked surface of the Ash Eater's world spreading in every direction.

A great shadow, flickering with light, thundered down through the clouds to Carter's left, keeping pace with the scout. Debris was falling from it in a steady rain, burning and twisting away in long, random arcs.

Teal'c suddenly dragged the controls sideways, sending the scout heeling violently to port. Carter saw the shadow loom close, its ragged edge tearing out through the clouds, and realized that it was the Ha'tak

The gliders were a few hundred meters behind, twisting and jinking and gouting streams of plasma from their wing cannons. There was another hit, and another. "Teal'c, I think we're in serious trouble."

"I agree." He shoved the controls forwards, pointing the scout at the ground.

Carter saw black hills hurtling up at her, then she was being jammed back into her seat as the ship pulled up at the last second. She glanced down at the rear view, saw nothing but a racing cloud of dust. Then a brief flash of yellow fire, fading instantly into the distance. "One didn't pull up in time."

Above them, the Ha'tak was spinning down through the ashy air like a burning tornado. It was huge, terrifying. Carter could feel the heat of its fires through the cockpit transparency.

The scout leapt forwards, some kind of emergency thrust, then swung ahead of the tumbling ruin. Carter watched the death gliders follow, one misjudging its altitude and shattering against the dusty ground, another swept to oblivion by the falling wreck. Then a blast of plasma fire spattered the scout from wing to cockpit, and it flipped over.

The black ground whirled towards her. There was a massive, sickening impact as the ship struck the edge of a crater, flipped up again in time for her to see the vast, burning edge of the Ha'tak bearing inexorably down on them, and then everything went dark.

Utter blackness had closed around her like a fist. "What? Teal'c, what happened?"

He didn't answer. On Carter's screen, a wireframe cylinder was expanding, ring after ring.

There was a shaft at the base of the crater, a vertical tunnel a hundred meters across. Teal'c had managed to guide the scout into it at the last second, and now they were flying straight down into the planet's crust.

According to her sensor board, the shaft was perfectly regular, perfectly vertical. *Not a volcano, then.*

Without warning, the rings of light on her board vanished. "What the hell?"

The sensor feed was still pointing aft. The picture was mainly black, but there was a disc of brightening gold at its centre. For a moment the perspective was too confusing. Carter simply couldn't work out what she was looking at.

Then the view flipped in her head. The circle was the shaft, and the ship was still flying straight downwards. "It's opened out! We're in a cavern… Teal'c, level up, fast!

The entire roof of the cavern erupted inwards, a titan explosion of rock and metal, of flame and dust.

The Ha'tak had slammed with unimaginable force into the surface, so hard and so fast that it had erupted clear through the kilometers of rock surrounding the tunnel entrance. Carter saw an immense wheel of shattering white metal and fire crashing over her, spinning and splintering and shedding tons of burning armor as it fell.

The inferno whirled past, tipping over and over, the unbearable brightness of it lighting up the inside of the cavern for kilometers in every direction. Great shards of rock spun in its wake, curving fragments of eggshell stone tumbling in every direction like black comets with tails of ash and smoke. Teal'c was flinging the Khepesh around to avoid the more massive pieces, but tons of the stuff were still coming down, boulders battering the scout's hull with terrifying, drumbeat impacts.

The mothership was past them now, falling away, still spinning like a great blazing wheel. Carter held her breath, waiting for it to hit the cavern floor. She couldn't believe the size of the space they had flown into: the Ha'tak was covering kilometers every second as it fell, and still it had not struck ground.

When the light of it shrank to a whorl of yellow flame no bigger than her fist, Carter finally grasped the truth, and a sickening wave of vertigo washed up from her feet to her gut, to her head. She grabbed the seat arms hard, so hard her knuckles flared in pain.

There was no floor. The scout hung over a drop of unthinkable proportions. "Teal'c, where the hell are we?"

Above her, great sections of the planet's crust were still breaking away, tumbling down from the ragged, glowing edges of a hole the size of a small town. A fragment thumped down onto the scout's viewport, and Carter caught a glimpse of it as it slid away. A curl of gray stone, trailing something that looked like a thick, papery length of rope.

"Oh no," she breathed. Then: "Teal'c, can you hover this thing? I need to see the cavern roof."

"I do not believe we are in a cavern, Major Carter."

Neither did she, not anymore, but she didn't want to say what she was thinking. She couldn't, not yet. "Please, Teal'c."

The scout rose, slowly, the engines throttled back until they were idling. Teal'c touched a control, and an oval of light appeared in the distance. He'd activated a searchlight, and it was touching the roof of the place.

It grew as the ship rose, brightened, solidified. Carter watched it, her heart hammering, watched it picking out rounded edges, curls of pale rock, an inverted forest of drifting, tethered forms.

"Major Carter? What have you seen?"

"Teal'c, I'm sorry. I'm so sorry…" Her voice was very small, out here in the endless dark. "But I don't think we can go home just yet."

Neheb-Kau was wrong. He had been wrong about almost everything. Carter almost wished the Goa'uld was still around, so she could tell him just how catastrophically wrong he was.

Not that it would have made her feel any better. But it might have made him feel worse, if he was capable of feeling anything at all.

The Khepesh was flying under the roof. She could no longer think of the space she was in as a cavern, but somehow it was difficult to come up with another term that fitted the facts. If she thought too hard about where she and Teal'c actually were, it set her exhausted mind whirling in her skull, fascination and terror and sheer vertigo battling for supremacy within her. The concept of the fragile roof above her, and the endless tumbling darkness below, were almost too much to grasp.

She had no choice, though. The facts were indisputable — she was inside a hollow world, an eggshell-thin crust of rock over a sphere of pure vacuum as big as the Earth, and letting her mind slip away from that was doing her no good at all.

"Major Carter," Teal'c warned. "We are approaching the tower."

"Great. Slow down when you get within a hundred meters, and I'll get some more detailed readings."

At first, Carter had found the very concept of a hollow world ridiculous. The shaft had only been two kilometers deep at most, and the most basic knowledge of physics told her that a planet-sized shell that thin would shatter instantly into gravel under its own forces. Its rotation would spin it apart, the gravity of the sun would tear it to pieces. It was impossible, despite what her eyes told her.

But the further they had travelled, the more she had learned. For a start, the crust was only that thin around the entry tunnels, which were spaced regularly over the planet's surface. At other points it was almost a hundred kilometers thick, and the intervening spaces were braced by vast spars and bridges of rock, like the internal structure of a bone. This shell of a world, she had realized, was no accident. It had been designed, carefully and expertly, to hold itself in stable equilibrium for tens of thousands of years.

She felt the scout pull back slightly, deceleration tugging at her as Teal'c throttled back the drives even more. The tower her initial scans had detected was just ahead, rising like a mountain from the inside of the crust, pointing towards the centre of the hollow world. It was unthinkably vast, as wide at its base as a small country, so long that it could not possibly have supported its own weight in any other environment than this.

The Khepesh leveled out over the pitted surface of the tower and began to fly along its length. It was too huge to be seen as a cylinder. It was a flat road, an endless metal plateau, stretching away into darkness on either side.

"There," Carter said, pointing past Teal'c's seat and through the cockpit viewports. "You see that?"

In the far distance, something sparkled with a faint, silver-blue light.

"Indeed," Teal'c replied. "Is that the singularity?"

"I think so."

"So your theories are confirmed."

Carter rubbed the back of her neck. The muscles there were locked, almost numb from tension. "Pretty much. I'll run some scans of the suppression field once we reach a thinner part of the tower, but I don't think there's any doubt now. The clock's ticking."

"How long do we have?"

"Hours." Then, she thought, the wreckage of the Ha'tak would reach the singularity, be crushed into an infinitesimal speck and join the mass of the black hole that hovered, glittering with Hawking radiation, at the heart of the hollow world. When that happened, the energy from that collision, and from the untold tons of rock that had fallen from the crust and followed it down, would release a brutal flash of radiation.

It would not be nearly as much as the final demise of the black hole would cause, when it finally evaporated. But it would be enough. The sea of papery, mummified fetuses tethered over the inner surface of the crust, million upon million of them, would detect it.

And the Ash Eaters would start to wake up.

Chapter 21.

FEELING GRAVITY'S PULL

THE TROOP carriers were like great covered triremes of marble and bronze, their prows raised and decorated with *opthalmoi*. Looking down at them, Daniel could see rank after rank of Spartan Guard filing up their loading ramps, cloaked in scarlet, armored head to foot in shining gold. They carried longer, heavier versions of the hoplite staff weapons, and tall crests on their enclosed helms. They looked strong and fast and utterly ruthless.

And there were a *lot* of them. A hundred or more in each transport.

He sighed, and turned away from the viewport. "Anything?"

On the other side of the chamber, Bra'tac was hunched over a communications board, his hand resting on an indented block of silvery metal, a look of furious concentration on his face. "When I hear anything of interest, Doctor Jackson, be assured I will let you know."

Daniel nodded. And, not for the first time, felt very helpless indeed.

The chamber was part of a monitoring station, one of many overlooking one of the *Clythena*'s great hangar decks. The original plan was for the three of them to steal a ship and escape the vessel, somehow tracking down Sam and Teal'c before the Spartan guard reached Neheb-Kau's fallen starship. But that had proved impossible, given that the flagship had been put on full alert almost immediately after they had fought their way to freedom.

Maybe, Daniel surmised later, a more well-planned escape might have led to a faster exit. Perhaps doing something to conceal the injured and unconscious hoplites they had left strewn around the corridor would have delayed the alarms, and in turn led to fewer patrols and roaming pairs of Minotaurs between them and the flagship's glider bays. At the time, though, he was simply relieved that Bra'tac had turned up when he had. Daniel could have foreseen a long stay in a dark place had the old Jaffa not been tracking them.

Still, it had to be said, the escape was a mess. Hardly SG-1's finest hour. And by the time they had discovered the monitoring chamber, the first stage of Hera's assault on Neheb-Kau was already reaching its end.

There had been two hoplites manning the chamber. Both had fallen prey to Jack's accuracy with a zat gun before they could raise an alarm, and were now slumped in a side locker. Daniel had heard them start to awaken once already, and been forced to open the locker just enough to stun the pair again. He wondered how many more times he would have to do it before the way was clear enough for them to leave.

Still, the diversion had not been completely without its uses. Although all three of them would rather have been flying down to find Sam and Teal'c themselves, Bra'tac had suggested using the communications board to search for any mention of them on Hera's comms network.

It was probably the most sensible thing to do, although it still wrenched at Daniel to not be in a ship and racing to find his friends. They were so close, he thought. After so many light-years, after almost giving up hope so many times, they were only an orbit away.

And yet, for now, it was a distance that he couldn't possibly cross.

Jack was at the hatch, watching the corridor. "Come on, Bra'tac. There's got to be something."

"There is much, O'Neill. Hera's communication system has access to more channels than any I have ever known. The accursed woman listens to everything!"

"It's probably one of the ways she keeps power," said Daniel. "Most Goa'uld are all about brute strength, terror tactics. Rule by fear, you know." He sat down at the control board, next to Bra'tac. "I think Hera rules by leverage."

"She is legendary for it," replied the Jaffa. "It is said that while

Apophis will stab a man in the heart and laugh, Hera will convince him to stab *himself* and laugh!"

"She's a sneaky minx, all right." Jack glanced back. "Anything yet?"

Daniel saw Bra'tac's expression darken. "Hey," he said quickly. "Maybe I could try."

Bra'tac took his hand from the metal block. "The process requires great concentration."

"I can do concentration."

"There are many separate channels. Focusing on any one can induce fatigue, or great pain."

"Okay…" Daniel held his hand nervously over the block.

"Occasionally death."

"Maybe I should leave it to the expert." He moved his hand away, but Bra'tac reached out, faster than he could follow, and grabbed his wrist.

"Death is a rare result," he smiled, and put Daniel's hand onto the metal.

Instantly, his head was full of voices.

Daniel could hear dozens of separate speakers, so many layered one over the other that he could barely follow any of them; Jaffa voices, using the fluid, part-Greek tongue of Hera and her subjects.

Many of the voices were shouting. Some of them cursed. A few screamed, although those didn't tend to last very long. And occasionally he would hear the voice of Hera herself, deep and clipped and honeyed, exhorting her pilots and berating her enemies.

It was an insane sea of radio chatter, filling his skull, the living essence of the battle raging below them. It was the sound of people dying, in the cold and the dark.

How anyone could stand to listen to it was a mystery to Daniel: already it had set his head spinning. He lifted his hand, letting silence wash into him. "Oh my God… That's…"

Jack was looking at him from across the chamber. "You okay?"

"I think so." He shook himself. "Sorry. Just a bit intense, that's all…"

He got up. As he did so, an edge of memory caught at him, like a fragment of dream. In amongst all that babble, a word that made no sense. "Why would they be talking about swords?"

"Swords?" Bra'tac shrugged. "I do not know."

"Do Jaffa use swords?"

"Some do, in close combat. It is an old skill, mostly forgotten."

"Okay." Daniel went back to the viewport. The first transport was taking off, the air beneath it rippling with heat distortion as the slablike vessel slid towards its launch chute. "One of the voices was talking about a khepesh, that's all."

"That's a sword, right?"

He glanced across the chamber at Jack. "Egyptian, yeah. Kind of like…" He drew in their air, an elongated G. "I guess the word means something in Goa'uld, too."

"Indeed it does," said Bra'tac. "Be silent, both of you."

He placed his hand back onto the slab, and closed his eyes. A few seconds later he opened them again and smiled widely. "There have been reports of a Goa'uld fast yacht in combat above the planet's surface, only minutes ago. Apparently, it was pursuing a Khepesh before it broke off and allowed its escort of death gliders to take over."

"Hold on…" Jack checked the corridor again, then ducked back through the hatch and closed it. "A yacht chasing a sword?"

"Yacht as in private starship. Could be Neheb-Kau," said Daniel. "Which means he's making a break for it and leaving his crew to take the heat."

"Figures."

"The Khepesh… Is that a class of ship, as well?"

Bra'tac nodded. "A short-range reconnaissance vessel. Fast, but fragile."

"Doesn't ring any bells," said Jack.

"They are outmoded, and seldom used," Bra'tac replied. "I do not believe Hera's fleet contains such craft. And if Neheb-Kau was attacking one of his own fleet, does it not suggest the vessel was stolen?"

Daniel grinned. "That sounds like Sam, all right. Can you find it?"

"Not directly. But I can set a communications channel to access only that class of vessel." He took his hand from the slab and began pressing glyphs on the control board. A few moments later, the angular metal frame above it filled with light, a flat panel of holographic data.

Hieroglyphs and Greek characters coursed down it. A holding pattern. "Can you hail them?" Daniel asked.

"I am attempting to. There is some interference…"

"What if it's not them?" said Jack. "Just say 'Sorry, wrong number' and hang up?"

"In essence," Bra'tac replied.

He touched a glyph, and Teal'c's wide, golden face filled the panel.

Jack's face split in a huge grin. "Teal'c, you son of a gun! We've been looking all over for ya!"

"It is good to see you, O'Neill."

"Likewise! Is Carter there?"

"Indeed. Daniel Jackson, Master Bra'tac." He tipped his head. "I am pleased that you are here also."

"We kept your room just how you left it," said Daniel, smiling. "So where are you?"

"That is rather difficult to explain."

"Well, give it a shot!" Jack glanced back over his shoulder. "We're using someone else's phone, and she's gonna get cranky if we run up too much of a charge…"

"Major Carter can tell you better than I." A smile played over his lips. "I have already mentioned how pleased I am to see you all, have I not?"

"You have," said Daniel. "But trust me, we're not going to get tired of hearing it."

The screen blinked, and Sam's face appeared. "Hey," she said.

She looked frighteningly tired, and there was something in her eyes Daniel didn't like at all. A haunted, hunted expression. His smile faded. "Sam? Where are you?"

"In the planet," she replied. As she said it, she looked back over her shoulder, above her head, as if keeping watch for enemies.

Jack squinted at the screen. "Ah, don't you mean 'on'?"

"No sir. We're under the surface."

"You're buried?"

"No… We can fly out any time, sir."

"Then put your foot down and get the hell out of Dodge."

She shook her head. "Colonel, I'm sorry, but we've got a new problem. What we found down here changes everything…"

"Sam," Daniel said warily. "You're, ah, scaring us a little here… What have you found?"

"Well, to put it simply…" She took a deep breath. "This isn't really a planet. It's an egg, and it's going to hatch into about a billion Ash Eaters."

It took several minutes for Sam to explain exactly what she had found under the nameless planet's surface. Even when she had shown them some of the data she had captured using the scout's reconnaissance systems, it was hard to grasp.

All that was really clear was that something had to be done about it.

At first, Jack had been unable to see the urgency. "Carter, I hear you. Hollow planet, lots of Ash Eaters, black hole. I get it. But seriously, what's to stop us bugging out and leaving them in peace?"

"Sir, I don't think you quite understand. The singularity isn't there just to give the planet gravity. It's been evaporating slowly over tens of thousands of years. The Ash Eaters have been dormant inside the planet for all that time, just ticking over on the Hawking radiation it gives off as it shrinks."

"So?"

"So, they knew it was going to evaporate at a measureable rate. Sir, Neheb-Kau did get something right. He told me that the Ash Eaters were once a highly advanced race, and the evidence is right here. But they didn't eat their own civilization and then each other until there was only one left. They retreated, voluntarily, into this giant egg, and then went into a dormant state."

"I guess they must have left one outside." Daniel rubbed the bridge of his nose. He felt as though his spectacles had been on his face for a year, grinding through to the bone. He wondered if the others were as tired as he was. "You know, it's not often we come across one of these ancient legends that isn't true. Normally they pan out, you know?"

"Maybe the Ash Eaters set up the lie themselves."

"Okay, Carter." Jack spread his hands. "Simple answer: what happens if we just leave?"

"Simple answer? Worst case scenario is that the gamma radiation released when the Ha'tak reaches the singularity wakes the Ash Eaters, or even just some of them. A lot of rock went down with it, and the surface is unstable now. There's a kind of suppression field running through the crust to keep the atmosphere from falling into the planet, but that's being stressed too, and it could fail any time."

"Best case?" he said hopefully.

"The singularity reaches a natural flashpoint in about thirty years."

"How far away are we from Earth?"

"Not far enough. Sir, I've seen one of these things in action. You can't stop them. They will feed off any attack you subject them to. Hit them with a hammer or a bullet and they'll just absorb the kinetic energy. Drop a nuke on them and they'll suck up the fireball."

"Okay, I get it."

"I did some calculations, based on the absorption rates of the one that took out Neheb-Kau's ship. At full strength, a dozen Ash Eaters could shut down the *sun*."

"I said I get it!" He turned away from the screen. "Oh man. Using a black hole as an alarm clock. Now I've heard it all."

"Yeah, and it's going to go off early," Daniel muttered. "Is this our fault? I can't even remember."

"Colonel," Sam went on, "I think there is a solution. But right now I have no idea how we could bring it off."

"Spit it out."

"If we could somehow bring enough destructive power to bear on the planet, in a precisely calculated way, we could send the Ash Eaters into their own black hole."

"Would that destroy them?" Bra'tac asked.

"I'm not sure. But at the very least it would trap them at the event horizon. And the extra mass of the planet would give us a couple of centuries to come up with a more permanent solution."

Daniel threw a glance at Jack. "Hey, Sam? How much destructive power are we talking about?"

"That's the problem. A lot. The planet is held stable around the black hole by gravitational tethers — the towers. We'd need to take some of those out, and they are *big*. I think the entire nuclear arsenal of Earth might make a dent in one, but I can't guarantee it." She blinked. "Daniel, what are you smiling about?"

"Because we know someone who's got a big drill."

"Excuse me?"

"The Auger," Jack said. "Hera's toy. She said it could punch a hole a thousand kilometers into solid rock. You reckon that could do the trick?"

"Ah, it sounds good, sir. But how are you going to get her to let you use it?"

"Well, she fears the Ash Eater as much as anyone," said Jack. "It's why she came out here, to drill a hole and bury it. If she learns there are millions of them…"

"Getting Hera's attention without inviting death will be difficult," warned Bra'tac. "Neheb-Kau has escaped her, the creature she fears most has destroyed one of her starships, and you have evaded capture aboard her own flagship."

"He's right," said Daniel grimly. "If we set foot on the pel'tak she'll have a Minotaur on us before we can say word one."

Jack made a face. "I really don't like those guys."

"I'm sure they speak highly of you, too."

"We would never reach the command deck," Bra'tac offered. "Hera has ordered her guards to shoot on sight. Unless we make our case first, we cannot succeed."

"Pythia," said Daniel. "She seemed pretty level-headed. Bra'tac, could you get a message through to Hera's Oracle?"

"I can."

Jack folded his arms and puffed out a long breath. "Okay, let's do it. But I don't like going cap in hand to these people, not one damn bit."

The Oracle's reaction to Bra'tac's message was swifter than anyone had expected. Within less than five minutes there was a flash of voltage from the hatch controls, and the door slid aside. Hoplites shouldered in, staff weapons already leveled and open.

Daniel stood with his hands raised, with Jack and Bra'tac just behind him. Jack had demanded to stand at the group's head at first, but Daniel had reminded him that, for whatever reason, many of Hera's flirtations had been directed towards him. Besides, if the message failed, and the hoplites did start firing, it really wouldn't make any difference who was in front.

So he stood, very still, trying not to look at the lethal energies coursing between those glittering spear-blades.

After a few seconds, Pythia entered, her scarlet gown rustling in the silence. She gazed wordlessly at Daniel, then at the screen. "You are Samantha Carter."

Sam still had the channel open. "I am."

"You will present your data to me. If I determine it to be unsatisfactory, you will watch your friends die, in this room. There will be no appeal and no delay. Do you understand?"

"I'll patch it through," Sam replied, very quietly.

Her face vanished from the screen, replaced by the data she had collected.

The Oracle watched it in silence. When she reached the end of the sequence, she simply said "Again."

After the second time, she made her way to a chair and sat down.

"It's real," Daniel began.

"Be silent."

"Pythia, there may not be much time —"

"Be *silent!*" She covered her face with one hand, just for a moment, a brief weakness that she shook away almost instantly. "The rest of the data. The shell's full structure, fracture points, analysis of the suppression field. Do you have this?"

"I do," Sam confirmed.

"Send it through."

"No."

Pythia turned to the screen. "Send it to me or your friends —"

"What part of 'No' don't you quite grasp, Pythia?" Sam's face was set hard. "You'll allow us safe passage onto your ship. I'll be carrying the data with me. You'll get it when we meet."

Jack stepped past Daniel. "C'mon, lady, what do you think we're trying to do here?"

"The Goddess will not allow this."

"She will," Daniel said gently. "Pythia, if this works, it's the end of her nightmare."

"And if it does not?"

"Then I guess it won't matter, will it?"

The woman held his gaze for a moment, then looked back to the screen. "Very well. Bring your craft to within fifty kilometers of the *Clythena*. We will take control from there and bring you aboard." She reached out to a control, and the screen went dead. "And Daniel?"

"Uh, yeah?"

"If this plan of yours kills us all, the Lady Hera will be *very* displeased."

They watched the Khepesh come in, up through the shielded floor of the same hangar deck the troop transports had left from. Daniel thought back to when he and his shipmates had been remotely piloted into the *Clythena* in much the same way. It seemed like an eternity ago, although it probably hadn't been more than a few hours.

Jack gave a low whistle when they saw the state of the scout ship. "Bra'tac? I thought you said that thing was fragile?"

"With any less a pilot at the helm, it would be."

Far below them, on the landing gantry, the Khepesh was settling itself into a clamp. A hatch opened in its flank and two figures clambered out — one small and clad in a stained white cotton shirt and jeans, the other larger and dressed mainly in black. Both paused for a moment, obviously surprised by the dozens of scorch marks and craters melted into the hull of their vessel, and then carried on up the gantry towards the squad of hoplite waiting for them.

"Those are your friends," said Pythia quietly.

"That's them." Daniel watched her from the corner of his eye.

She lifted a hand to the transparency. "You travelled far for them."

"It's what friends do."

"I know. For Hera, I would…" She trailed off, and then straightened, suddenly all business. "We must go. Soon it will not be safe here."

Alarm klaxons began to sound as they reached the corridor that lead to the pel'tak, the dull ringing of some huge and distant bell. "What's that?" Daniel asked, a knot of worry forming under his ribs.

"The lower decks are being cleared," Pythia told him. "The Auger releases terrible energies as it is fired."

"You can control it from the pel'tak?"

"Of course. There is a shielded control module within the Auger itself, but anyone outside of that would be fatally irradiated."

"That doesn't sound good," said Sam, emerging from the junction.

Teal'c was at her side, and a dozen hoplites at their back. Daniel grinned. "Hey guys."

"Hey." She was smiling, but he could see that she was just a wisp of herself. The journey had been long and hard for all of them, but only Sam and Teal'c had spent a day shut away with the Ash Eater, locked into a flying tomb and surrounded by the dust of unnumbered corpses. For all Hera's seductive menace, Daniel couldn't help feeling that he'd had by far the easier time of things.

He reached out to her.

"Save your displays of affection," Pythia snapped. "The Goddess awaits us."

Sam gave the other woman a sour look. "Well, we wouldn't want to keep her waiting, would we?"

Pythia stalked off, and opened the hatch that lead onto the pel'tak.

Hera was waiting for them, up on her throne. Her face was pale, unsmiling. Pythia had reported back to her from the monitoring chamber, while they had waited for the Khepesh to be brought aboard, and the news had obviously affected her.

Four Spartan Guard had joined her pel'tak crew, and stood grimly to either side of her throne. A Minotaur was directly behind her, massive arms folded, brass horns lowered.

"Well," she said, as they filed in. "I see you have some new friends, Pythia."

The Oracle dropped to her knees before Hera. "My Lady."

Hera got up, and walked slowly down the steps of her podium. "Daniel," she purred. "Of course you could not stay away. Still looking for someone to scratch that itch?"

"Well, you do have *something* I want."

"So I have heard." She moved past him, to where Teal'c and Bra'tac stood. "The First Prime of Apophis," she said, looking up at Teal'c. "And *another* First Prime of Apophis. I wonder if he makes wiser choices now?"

"No choice Apophis makes is wise," growled Teal'c.

"I shall be sure to inform him of that. And you," she said to Bra'tac. "You evaded capture aboard my flagship for many hours."

"It was not difficult." The old Jaffa kept his gaze fixed, looking clear over the top of her head. "Your vessel is large, and your men are ill-trained."

"I shall be taking that into account, I assure you." She tilted her head quizzically at him. "Perhaps, if you were to train them in place of my *Lokhagos*…"

"I no longer serve false gods."

"He said that too, at first." She turned away from him. "Daniel, you do keep most remarkable company."

"I like to think so." He rubbed his neck, ever so slightly embarrassed. "Hera, I don't know how much time we have —"

"Indeed. There is a time for slow examination, and a time for haste. You strike me as a man who knows the difference. Which of you has the data?"

Sam put a hand up. "I have."

"The woman. Of course." Hera held out her hand. "Why am I not surprised?"

Everything Sam had collected was stored in a small, green crystal. Daniel watched her place it carefully into Hera's palm.

The Goa'uld took it, moved to a nearby console, and leaned across its operator to slot the crystal into a gold cylinder. "Decode this," she whispered.

"My Lady." The operator's hands roamed over his control board. Hera stood back, watching him, until the viewport at the front of the pel'tak faded from the black of space into a pale blue screen, coursing with data.

For the next few minutes Hera stood in silence, watching what Pythia had watched: the inside of the hollow world, the singularity at its heart, the forests of Ash Eaters, curled like dusty maggots tethered to the interior of their gnawed-out world and drifting slowly on their umbilicals, their backs to their ticking black hole. Dormant, dead, utterly inert, but awaiting the first flash of radiation which would awaken them, send them out, mindless and voracious, to strip the galaxy of energy just as Ra's demon had stripped Greg Kemp and Laura Miles and all the countless victims of the Pit of Sorrows.

"One was enough," Hera breathed. "Just one, enough to strip a world…"

"Setraxis?" Sam asked.

"Yes. Ra had called a summit of the System Lords. I was at his side. Neheb-Kau unleashed the Ash Eater on us…" She turned to look back at Daniel, her expression haunted, horrified. "It was like a storm. He loosed a storm on us."

"Ra got it into the Pit of Sorrows, though, didn't he?" he asked. "Couldn't we use the same method he did?"

"There was no method." Her voice was bitter. "It was caught in a transport beam, by sheer fluke. Ra used a Ha'tak's weight in naquadah merely to keep it there, while Neheb-Kau's ka'epta were tortured into building the Pit for him."

"Hera," Sam said, moving over to the console. "That one must have gone into the singularity with the ship it destroyed. But the others will wake unless we send them there too."

"Yes…" The Goa'uld nodded. "Show me."

Sam studied the console for a moment, then pressed an icon. The image on the screen changed to that of a sphere, its surface split into triangles. "Each of these apexes marks one of the gravity tethers. The system is in equilibrium now, but if we hit the three I've highlighted, the planetary crust will collapse into the singularity."

"Why those specifically?"

"Because as the tethers shear, there'll be a gravitational torsion, like a rubber band being snapped back."

"I know what gravitational torsion is, human," Hera frowned. "But a 'rubber band'?"

"Carter?" That was Jack. "I get the 'rubber band' part…"

Sam made an exasperated noise. "Look, if we do this right, the planet will start to shift out of its orbit as the singularity and the crust try to move against each other. If the right tethers are cut, the whole mess will eventually wind up crashing into the sun, too. Which will then collapse and make the singularity even bigger."

"And the bigger it is, the longer it lasts?"

"Bingo."

"I hate your language," Hera muttered. "I really do. Operator?

Upload this information to Auger control. Tell them to initiate charging immediately."

"By your will."

"Pythia?"

The Oracle stood. "My Lady."

"Go to my sister. Make sure she is safe, and ready. With the lower decks evacuated, *Clythena* will not be able to flee should this plan fail."

"Sorry, what?" Daniel stared at her. "What do you mean?"

She smirked at him. "Forgive me, Daniel, did you not realize? *Clythena* is no Ha'tak. It cannot be operated purely by the pel'tak crew — if the hyperdrives and primary thrusters are not continually manned, they cannot function."

"So if anything goes wrong, we're stuck here."

"Yes." She touched Pythia on the arm, then watched the red-clad woman hurry away. "But you believe your plans to be flawless, do you not?"

"No plan is flawless," Teal'c intoned.

"No mortal plan, perhaps." Hera trotted back up to her throne, and settled into it. "Operator?"

"Your will is in motion, Lady. The Auger is charging, and the targeting co-ordinates set."

There was a shiver in the deck, a faint vibration. Daniel felt the flagship start to turn around him. "We're moving."

"The Auger has taken control of Clythena's maneuvering thrusters," said Hera. "We are being positioned over the first target point. In eleven of your minutes, the Auger will fire its first pulse."

He turned to the others. "So I guess we just kick back until then."

There was a sound from behind him, a whistling scrape of blade on blade. He turned to see the ceiling iris open and the transport rings drop. "What the hell?"

Hera was on her feet too. "Guards! Unauthorized transport on the pel'tak!"

Light flared down into the rings, solidified into the shape of a man. Daniel peered through the cage and saw that the man was holding something.

He opened his mouth to shout a warning, but never got to utter it. A hellish, impossible explosion hammered out from the transporter, flooding the pel'tak with intolerable light and unimaginable sound.

The force of it drove Daniel to his knees. Distantly he could hear screams and shouts around him, but he couldn't see. His brain felt as if it was on fire, every neuron screaming. He was dimly aware that he had his hands clamped over his ears, his eyes squeezed shut, trying to block the sensations out, but they were flooding in through the skin.

A few more beats of his leaping heart, and the light faded.

Daniel tried to scramble to his feet, but the assault had deadened his nerves. He looked up, squinting through watering eyes, to the podium.

Hera was standing to one side of the throne. There was a man next to her, robed in black, old and hook-nosed, his left arm wrapped brutally around her head. He was holding what looked like a black metal cobra in his right hand, the tail of it coiled around his forearm, the fanged head at Hera's throat.

"Stay on your knees, scum! Or your Goddess dies!"

"It's Djetec," grated Sam. "Neheb-Kau's vizier."

"Friend of yours?"

"What's the word that's the exact opposite of 'friend', again?"

"Silence!" The man dragged Hera back a few paces. His grip on her looked agonizing, and there was fear mixed with the fury in her gray eyes. "The asp holds toxin. Attack me and she will be dead in seconds. Do not test my resolve!"

The guards were on their feet, reaching for their weapons, and the Minotaur was rising too. The sensory assault must have even affected the giant warrior.

"Spartans! Leave the pel'tak, and take that monster with you. Jaffa, take up your weapons and cover the humans and *shol'va* in your midst. They do not hold your Goddess in as high regard as I…"

"Fool!" Hera hissed. Daniel saw her watching helplessly as her soldiers moved away. "Your death is assured!"

"Hold your tongue, witch!" He wrenched her head to the side, drawing a cry from her. "This is the day your rule ends. This ship, this fleet, and the Ash Eaters now belong to the mighty Neheb-Kau!"

Chapter 22.

RAY OF LIGHT

THERE WAS a change in the light coming from behind O'Neill. He half turned, still on his knees, to see the graphical globe of the Ash Eater planet had been replaced by a very different view.

Once more, the golden mask of Neheb-Kau looked serenely back at him.

This time, however, the mask's surroundings were very different. Instead of the gloomy black and gold décor of his own pel'tak, Neheb-Kau stood inside a chamber that was all white and steel and the flickering, shifting panels of data screens. It made him look strange and out of place.

Not that it seemed to bother him. He was standing alongside his First Prime, while Jaffa warriors in gold armor and double serpent helms moved back and forth behind him. Some of the Jaffa were carrying equipment, ornate items of technology in gold and crystal. In contrast, his First Prime was very still, leaning on his staff weapon in order to keep upright.

The wound that had disfigured the man last time O'Neill had seen him looked as if it was trying to take over his whole face. What little actual skin still showed between the blisters looked pale and damp, like the underside of some rotting fungus. His eyes stared out from the mess, desperate and dull.

O'Neill had seen that look before. The man was dying, and he knew it.

"Hera, my dear," said Neheb-Kau brightly, in his strange, high voice. "Thank you so much for welcoming me aboard this vessel."

Djetec hadn't let Hera move. He was still holding her up on the podium, with the asp at her neck. Six hoplites stood at the base of the steps, their staff weapons aimed outwards into the rest of the pel'tak. If it hadn't been for them, O'Neill would have simply rushed the podium. But the hoplites were loyal to their Goddess, and clearly saw Djetec as the lesser threat. While he lived, at least, so did Hera.

But the clock was ticking. And every nerve in O'Neill's body was jumping, urging him to move, to attack, to shout. To do anything but stand and listen to Goa'uld snarling at each other.

"Do not 'Dear' me, you vile fool!" Hera hissed.

"Forgive me. I forgot — you are not *dear* in any possible sense of the word…"

Despite her position, Hera chuckled. "Where does your obsession lie, Neheb-Kau? With the Ash Eaters, or with me?"

The eyes of his mask glowed for a moment. She had struck a nerve. "Your life is in my hands, Hera. Keep a civil tongue in your head, or I shall have Djetec remove it from you."

Carter had risen to her feet. "Neheb-Kau, what are you doing?"

"Ah, human! It is good to see you again. I hear you have seen wonders since our parting. And it is you I have to thank for revealing the true glory of this world to me. Although I would have expected the Lady Hera to have used more secure forms of communication…" He stroked his metal beard. "And to think, when I first discovered the Ash Eater, I had no idea that the rest of its race hung just below my feet. Imagine what I could have done, had I known!"

"Yeah, I can imagine," said O'Neill, getting up. "Every time some girl went off with the guy next to you because he didn't have a face that was dripping right off his head, you'd sic a bunch of Ash Eaters on her, right? Turn her planet into dust, switch off her sun?"

The mask dipped slightly. "I see your infestation problem has not improved, Hera."

"It gets worse all the time."

"Nevertheless, the human fool has a certain vision. Stifled by quite startling stupidity, but vision nonetheless. I will indeed have an Army of Ash Eaters at my command, and the galaxy will tremble before me."

"The Ash Eaters are a plague!" Hera screamed. "You can't control them! Nothing can control them!"

"The loss of your ship would suggest otherwise."

"You are truly insane. When you tried to assassinate Ra with that demon, did you even stop to think of the millions it destroyed? Of the System Lords it killed? *Did you?*"

"Is that why you betrayed me to Ra, Lady?"

O'Neill whirled to stare at her. "You were the one who ratted him out?"

"Would you have not done the same?"

"You know what?" He turned back to the screen, took a few steps towards it. "I would, yeah."

"Then you are as much a traitor as she, and you will die as she dies. Thrust into the Pit of Sorrows, with the first Ash Eater I draw from its sleep."

"Buddy, there aren't going to be any Ash Eaters!" O'Neill spread his hands. "Don't you get it? The one Ra took from you is in the middle of a black hole right now, and in about seven minutes the rest of 'em are going to be there too!"

"Really?" Neheb-Kau stepped back, and lifted his ravaged hands. "You still think the Auger will fire and crush the planet below? Human, *where do you think I am?*"

"Oh my God," Carter whispered. "Colonel, he must be in the Auger control room."

"Operators," hissed Hera. "To your posts!"

"Stay where you are," Djetec snarled.

Hera laughed. "Ignore this fool. If I die, his life is forfeit."

As the pel'tak staff rose hesitantly back to their control positions, O'Neill ran to the console Hera had used earlier. The operator was just sliding back into his seat.

"Is the program still running?" That was Carter, moving up to the other side of the console. O'Neill glanced back to see that Bra'tac and Teal'c were already working their way back to the podium, and Daniel had taken his place in front of the screen.

The operator shook his head. "No, my Lady. Neheb-Kau has locked the guidance interface."

"Send guards. Dig him out of there."

"All the transporters are locked out too, my Lady." The man's face had gone white. "And the lower decks are cleared. No-one can reach him."

"You see, Hera? There is *nothing* you can do. I have spent five thousand years researching and improving our technologies, while you spent your time cavorting with slaves and bedding your way up the ladders of power. I was able to transport directly here from my ship, use my devices to lock out your pathetic guidance program. The Ash Eaters will serve *me*, not fall prey to your fear and ignorance!"

"Then you have doomed us all," said Hera. Her voice was very different. She sounded as if all the strength had left her; all the Goa'uld superiority and seductiveness and the sneer of cold command had ebbed away in the face of that final revelation, leaving a tired, frightened young woman to face the horror alone. "Everyone will die, Neheb-Kau. Including you."

"Only those who oppose me will die, Hera."

"No. Once again, you meddle with forces you do not understand, and they are your undoing. It is a pattern with you, is it not? To lose control of what you seek to master?"

"What do you mean?" He moved closer to the screen, the golden mask filling the picture. "Explain!"

"The Auger is halfway through its initiation cycle. It cannot be shut down, not from the pel'tak, or the control room, or anywhere." O'Neill saw her glance up at Djetec, and smile. "Since you have blocked its guidance program, it will unleash its energies back into the ship. The Auger will either fire into the planet as I commanded it, or it will detonate and destroy this vessel."

"What?" O'Neill turned back to the podium, aghast. "Oh, come on!"

"There is nothing *you* can do, Neheb-Kau," she smiled. "Release the guidance lock, or die in fire."

"Never!" he howled.

The screen went dead.

"Communications locked out," said the operator.

"It is over," said Hera. "Daniel?"

He ran back to her. "What can we do?"

"There is a word you use. I think it has something to do with a game, developed by the Asgard, and bestowed upon you as a gift long ago." She smiled. "Checkmate."

"Back on your knees, all of you!" Djetec barked. "My master will defeat your technologies! He will reset the guidance and use your Auger to free the Ash Eaters."

"You really are one deluded son of a bitch," O'Neill told him.

"Indeed," said Hera. "And Djetec? I admire your loyalty. But this cannot be allowed to happen. It is time to remove your advantage."

She reached across to him, and slapped the head of the asp hard into her own neck.

O'Neill heard the hiss as it struck, and Djetec's horrified cry.

The pel'tak exploded into chaos. The hoplites swung their weapons around to him, control operators leapt from their posts and rushed up to the podium as Djetec pushed her violently away.

Hera stumbled, gabbed the side of her throne, and sank down at its side. "Kill him," she choked.

Djetec lifted something from his robes, a fist-sized metal sphere. It spun from his grip as the first staff blast took him in the throat, hurling him backwards to slide, in a bloodied, smoking heap, across the podium and into the rear wall of the pel'tak.

Two hoplites ran after his corpse, stood over it, and began firing again.

Hera turned her heavy head towards Daniel. "Human, come to me…"

There was a bellow from outside, a pounding. O'Neill tried to ignore it. "Carter? How long?"

"Six minutes?" She shrugged. "Maybe less."

He nodded, then ran up the steps. Daniel was already there, kneeling next to Hera.

"Why?" he whispered.

"Checkmate," she replied, and smiled. Her eyes were wide, the pupils expanded. Sweat beaded her pale brow, plastering golden hair to white skin. "If *Clythena* explodes, the Ash Eaters will be freed. My sister…" Her breath caught in pain.

"There's gotta be a way down there," said O'Neill.

"Of course there is. Djetec used this transporter, and hoped to return. It must still be active." Her eyelids fluttered. "Hoplites will arm you. Go to him. Unlock…"

"Lady, no…" A hoplite leaned over her. "Neheb-Kau should fall by our hand!"

"Can you remove his technologies?" She smiled weakly. "They go first. Follow them."

Daniel had taken her hand. "Hera…"

Her eyes glowed, once, the light in them dull and fluttering. They went wide in sudden, unexpected wonder. "*Thalassa*," she breathed. "*Akouō thalassa!*"

Silence fell across the pel'tak.

The hatch crashed open, and the Minotaur hammered through, Spartans in its wake. O'Neill put a hand on Daniel's shoulder.

He stepped away. Daniel got up too. As he did so, the Minotaur dropped to its knees where he had been. Its huge hand fumbled for its own neck armor. There was a click as a control gem was pushed in, and then the brass head split apart, separated, the horns swinging back and down over its shoulders, the metal helm becoming blades and leaves and vanishing. Beneath it, the Minotaur's scarred, bald head looked surprisingly pale and vulnerable.

The monstrous warrior reached out, fingertips brushing a strand of hair from the dead woman's forehead. And then, with tears streaming from its eyes, it threw back its mighty head and howled in disbelieving, animal grief.

The spear felt good in O'Neill's grip. He would have preferred his MP5, but the hoplite weapon was an acceptable substitute, lighter than the standard staff and wickedly bladed. He flipped the priming control with his thumb experimentally, and the spear blades snapped apart. Sparks coursed between them, eager for release. "Carter, what time you got?"

"Four minutes, sir." She was regarding her staff weapon rather uneasily. "They'll be waiting for us, won't they?"

"With any luck, they'll only be expecting that Djetec guy." He glanced around, to where the others were bunched around him, a circle of spears facing outwards. "All right people, weapons hot. Operator?"

The console slave nodded to him. "In her name," he said, and touched the transporter control.

"Actually," O'Neill muttered as the rings came down, "I was thinking more in terms of saving our asses. But that'll do."

White light sizzled down around him, blocking out the pel'tak, the mourning Spartans, the small pale body of Hera being borne away. When it lifted, a Jaffa in gold armor was turning towards him.

O'Neill jammed the spear between two rings and thumbed the trigger. There was a whooping snarl, a kick of recoil, and the Jaffa was spinning away, trailing smoke. O'Neill dragged the spear back as the rings lifted, ducked and rolled aside as a plasma bolt ripped through the air towards him; he heard the rest of his team scatter, firing their own weapons as they spread out.

He saw another Jaffa ahead, running around a curve of wall. The man dropped to one knee and fired again before O'Neill could get a shot off. He dodged back as the bolt splashed molten metal off the deck, then came out low, blasting the Jaffa onto his back.

There were no more in sight. He got up, checked quickly behind him. "Everyone okay?"

"Looking good, sir." Carter was cradling her spear. "Easier to aim than the other ones."

"Give me bullets any day."

All the talk of a control room had made him expect a space that was small and confined, but once again his expectations were confounded. It was a like a corridor, huge and high-ceilinged, its walls curved, with a railed gallery around the outer edge. Metal buttresses supported the gallery, and there were thick, angled viewports ranged along the opposite wall.

He peered through the nearest, down into a dizzying cylindrical shaft. "Ho boy."

"This place must go right around the Auger," said Daniel. "What's the betting the guidance controls will be on the far side?"

"Symmetry and our lousy luck says even," Carter sighed. "Sir, I'd suggest two teams."

"Agreed. Carter, Bra'tac and Daniel head thataway. Teal'c, you're with me."

There was no time for more. He turned, leveled his spear, and charged.

Almost immediately, another gold-armored Jaffa was coming at him. He threw himself aside as a blast screamed past him, used his own momentum to spin completely around and loose off a shot on the rebound. It took the warrior in the shoulder, flipped him into the shot Teal'c had fired.

O'Neill cursed as more bolts splashed the viewports beside him. There were two Jaffa up on the gallery.

Teal'c darted forwards, fired up twice. The shots hit the rail, sending the men back. O'Neill used the respite to run again, but as he set off a shot whined down to explode right next to him, the blast kicking him against the viewport. He felt his head connect hard with the transparency, and sparks flared in his vision.

He fell back, pulled the spear up as he did so and fired directly upwards, taking the man who had fired in the chest. The blast continued right through the Jaffa and into the ceiling. What was left of him crashed backwards.

O'Neill scrambled up. Teal'c was ahead of him, running, then leaping, hurling himself into the air to grip a buttress and swing himself up one-handed. He twisted, whirling the spear around behind him and triggering it as he opened his other hand. The recoil threw him forwards, back down to the deck. The shot, high enough to get over the balcony, blew the golden warrior clean off it.

They hit the ground roughly at the same moment. One in a messy, tumbling heap, one in perfect landing, head down, spear held out in his right hand, its long grip behind his shoulders.

"Show off," said O'Neill.

Teal'c dipped his head, then rose, and continued on. O'Neill followed him, risking a look sideways through the viewports. He saw flashes on the far side of the Auger, bright sparks of yellow light flicking back and forth.

The corridor opened out ahead, opposite the transporter platform as Carter had predicted. There were two Jaffa there, each on one knee and already firing. Both got two shots off before they died. Teal'c and O'Neill jumped over their bodies as they fell.

The guidance area was big, bigger than the pel'tak. There was a second gallery above the first, extending out into a platform, and the deck below must have jutted a considerable distance into the Auger. The platform, typically for something built to a Goa'uld sense of scale, must have been ten meters above the deck.

O'Neill paced under it, spear leveled and crackling.

From the other side of the chamber, a Jaffa flew backwards and rolled to a smoking halt. Bra'tac emerged at a run behind him, with Carter and Daniel darting out a moment later.

Teal'c touched O'Neill's shoulder, and pointed up at the platform. O'Neill nodded.

There were ladders up to the first gallery. He chose the nearest and climbed as fast as he could with the spear still in his right hand. One day, he thought as he ascended, the Goa'uld would get around to fitting their staff weapons with a sling so they could do more than one thing at a time, and then Earth would be in serious trouble.

He clambered up onto the gallery, and stepped to one side so Teal'c could join him. On the far side, Bra'tac was already there, stalking towards the steps leading up to the platform.

Carter caught his eye, and held up two fingers in a V-sign. He nodded, and padded up the steps, keeping low as he reached the top and peering over the floor level.

There was a viewing screen on the inner edge of the control chamber, a huge glassy panel stretching from the deck to the vaulted ceiling. The platform overlooked it, and the railed edge was lined with consoles.

Neheb-Kau was there, hunched over a bank of controls, his mask retracted and his ruined head snapping left and right as he prodded and stabbed at the panels. His First Prime, Kafra, was behind him, staring over the rail at the screen.

On it, a graphic of the Ash Eater planet was overlaid with streams of crimson hieroglyphs. Red light from it washed back over the platform, bloodying them both.

As O'Neill climbed the last step, the First Prime turned to look right at him.

He didn't move.

O'Neill frowned, and leveled his spear. Carter had been right: without the heavy club at the other end, it was easier to aim.

He fired, and the blast screamed blindingly away into the ceiling.

Neheb-Kau spun around, his right hand outstretched. O'Neill caught a glimpse of the glowing gem in his palm before a ripple of distortion hurled him back into the outer wall.

More bolts whined onto the platform from both sides. O'Neill opened his watering eyes to see the barrage strike an invisible curve around Neheb-Kau, extending far enough back to encompass his First Prime and half the platform. A personal force shield, he realized: Apophis had used one too, on occasion, although his was smaller, less powerful. Neheb-Kau had been tinkering with that, too.

"Fools," the Goa'uld spat. "You waste your final moments on this?"

O'Neill forced himself up. The ribbon pulse had hit him like a truck. "Just shut the damn locks off and let it fire!"

"And see my children destroyed?"

"Your *children?*"

"Of course. Did you not see them? My unborn children, in their millions, sleeping below, waiting to be born!"

"So you're content to die," Carter said, stepping as close to the shield as she could. O'Neill saw her brush its surface with her fingertips, a crackle of voltage following her hand.

"Our deaths will be their birth-scream," the Goa'uld replied, his lidless eyes glowing with rage and fervor. "And my legacy to them will be the galaxy, fat and ripe for them to suckle on!"

"Now that's a damn nasty image," muttered O'Neill.

"Kafra," Carter called. "Do you want this?"

"What can be done? The guidance controls are locked."

"Locks have keys." She put her spear down. "Please, Kafra."

He looked at her strangely. "I cannot undo what my master has done. I cannot steal the dreams of a God." O'Neill saw his gaze flick back to Neheb-Kau. "*Not alone.*"

"We can," O'Neill told him. "Hell, we do it all the time."

"That is what I had hoped," said Kafra. And he smiled.

At the last moment, Neheb-Kau must have realized what was happening. He whirled, robes flying, and raised his hand to Kafra, but the Jaffa was already lurching forwards.

Once-powerful arms spread, and wrapped around the God.

"No!" screamed Neheb-Kau. But he was already being hauled off his feet. His arms flailed, clawed hands scrabbling at Kafra's armor, at the boiling skin of his head, but it was too late. They both knew it.

Kafra ran with him to the rail and jumped.

"Carter!" yelled O'Neill, over the sickening sound of their impact. "Go to it!"

"Already on it, sir." She was at the consoles, deactivating the gold and crystal devices clamped to every panel. He ran to her, helping to lift them free.

Daniel appeared at the rail, watching the screen. "Still a lot of red, Sam."

"Give me a minute." The devices were gone now, and she was tapping frantically at the panels.

"Ah, I kinda think we're out of minutes…"

"Some people," she said flatly, "are always in a rush."

The icons on the screen went blue, and vanished upwards.

Light, intolerably bright, flooded the platform.

"Holy crap!" O'Neill ducked away from it, shielding his eyes with his hand. The screen was blocking most of the light coursing down beyond it, but enough was spilling past to be painful.

"Sorry people," Carter said, wincing. She worked the controls again. "Didn't have enough time to get the blinds down."

The light was dimming to less searing levels, as the viewports on either side of the screen began to darken from the top down. O'Neill squinted over the rail, still with his hand cupped over his eyes, watching a river of pure white glare thundering past the viewports.

The Auger was firing. Its energies seared downwards in a vast beam, through the centre of the ring and into their target.

On the screen, the graphic had changed to a full view of the Ash Eater planet. The beam was a dot of livid white at the centre, growing, the black clouds edging away from it as if unable to withstand the brightness of it, the purity. A sphere of brilliance was growing down there, matter flashing into energy, the raw tunneling power of the Auger chewing effortlessly through the thin crust of the hollow world and ripping into the tether beneath.

He turned to Carter. "Nice work."

"Thank you, sir. But it wasn't all me."

He nodded, and followed her down from the platform.

Kafra lay on his back, under the rail, blood pooling around him. Neheb-Kau was a sprawl of silk robes a few meters away. Carter ran to the First Prime, and knelt beside him.

"He died free," said Teal'c. "And with honor."

The Auger beam shut off, its thunder turning to silence.

O'Neill felt the deck beneath him tilt fractionally. He let out a long breath. "Guess we're moving again."

"Next target," said Carter. She was still kneeling. "He got me out of a lot of trouble back on Neheb-Kau's ship, sir."

"He got us all out of a lot of trouble right here." He put a hand to her shoulder, then moved away.

Daniel was standing below the platform, gazing up at the screen. "Would you look at that," he murmured.

O'Neill followed his gaze, and blinked. "Wow."

The planet had a hole in it.

Under the spiraling, roiling clouds, the cavity carved by the Auger was growing. The crust was caving in, thousands of tons of rock shattering away from the hole's ragged edges and tumbling inwards, drawing the clouds with them as the atmosphere followed them down. Ash and dust must have been sieving down too, mountains of it, the whole nightmarish landscape falling in on itself.

"The suppression field must have given out," said O'Neill.

"Hm?"

"Carter said that the air was kept out of the centre by a field. Look at those clouds."

Daniel grinned. "I'm impressed. Hey Sam?" He turned, and froze. "Oh hell."

While they had been watching the screen, Neheb-Kau had gotten up.

He was in dreadful shape. One side of his head was a crimson ruin, one eye obscured or gone. His left arm hung limp by his side, the robes there clinging and sodden with blood.

His right arm was up, and the ribbon device was pulsing fire into the side of Carter's skull.

O'Neill snapped the spear up and fired, but the blast whined off the Goa'uld's shield. "God *dammit!*"

The awful face turned towards him. "Be fair, human. You have taken everything from me. I merely take one thing from you."

"No," said O'Neill.

He thumbed the spear's control, and the weapon fell silent in his hands, the spear blades snapping shut.

Neheb-Kau smiled. "Good boy."

"You wish." O'Neill drew his arm back, and hurled the spear, straight and true, clear through the shield and into Neheb-Kau's black heart.

The Goa'uld staggered back, a look of utter shock on his broken face. His mouth worked. His right hand came up, touched the spear-shaft emerging from his sternum as if to confirm its unbelievable existence, then rose to O'Neill. But the gem in the centre of the ribbon device was dark and cold.

Neheb-Kau sank to his knees, twisted, and fell.

There was a flicker around him as the shield failed. O'Neill was already running to Carter, and felt wisps of voltage brush him as he charged through it.

She was in a heap, but struggling to lift herself, her eyes blinking rapidly. As he dropped down beside her, she glanced around at Neheb-Kau, saw the spear sticking out of him, and then turned to stare at O'Neill.

"You've got to be kidding," she gasped.

"Wasn't even sure it would get through." The shield Apophis had used would allow slow-moving objects through too. He had tried a bow and arrow, once, and it had almost worked.

"Nice guess."

He helped her up. Behind them, the Auger erupted into searing life again.

When they reached the transporter platform, there was a small army of hoplites waiting for them. O'Neill counted at least twenty, along with a handful of Spartan Guard and a pair of hulking Minotaurs. They parted as the team approached.

In their midst stood Pythia, her mournful face streaked with tears. And at her side a small, pale woman in a white dress, with sandy-gold hair and gray eyes.

"Look who's back," O'Neill said warily.

Daniel was next to him, helping Carter along. "Ericaceae."

"That name no longer has meaning." The woman's steely eyes narrowed. "There is only Hera."

"Guess having a backup has its uses."

She walked slowly up to him, tipped her head back to fix his gaze with hers. "You succeeded."

"Looks that way."

"The planet is collapsing. Within hours, it will be no more."

He shrugged. "Sounds like a result. So what happens now?"

"What indeed?"

He heard running footsteps. From around the opposite side of the transporter came two Spartans. "My Lady!"

"Report."

"Neheb-Kau lives!"

O'Neill gaped. "What?"

"The host is gone. The Goa'uld lives, for now." She looked back over her shoulder at the Spartan. "It's name will not be spoken again."

"It's still alive? Jesus… What does it take to kill you guys?"

She smiled grimly. "We shall find out, over time. A *very* long time." She turned to Daniel. "The Spartan Guard tell me that you honored my sister, in her last moments. For that reason, and that alone, I will spare you."

"Ah, okay. Thank you…"

Then her expression went very cold, and very hard. "But seeing you reminds me that she is gone, and I will not be pained in such a way. So you will take the vessel you stole from He Who Will Not Be Named, and you will fly it out of my flagship. If you do not, I will kill you. If I see any of you again, *I will kill you*. Do you understand?"

Later, as Teal'c opened the hatch to the Khepesh and climbed inside, O'Neill stood on the mesh decking next to it and marveled. "You're sure this thing's still airtight?"

"It got us here," said Carter. She could stand unaided now, but O'Neill still wanted her back under Doctor Fraiser's care as quickly as possible. "As long as it gets us to the nearest gate, I'll be happy."

"You and me both." He glanced up, towards the monitoring chamber. Two figures stood there, looking back down. One tall and dark, the other smaller and blonde. He suppressed a shiver. "I'm done being under the same roof as these guys."

"Really? Hera seemed okay."

"You think?" said Daniel, his eyebrows raised. "Well she didn't put you in a cell, in the dark, in the —"

"Daniel," O'Neill cut in, warningly.

Bra'tac was at the hatch. "Do not be fooled, Major Carter. This time, Hera's motives were not incompatible with our own. That is all. It would not be wise to risk her hospitality again."

"I don't intend to," she said, and went into the ship.

O'Neill stayed where he was for a moment. "You know, Daniel… I was gonna ask."

"Hm?"

"What did she say? At the end, there?"

"Who, Hera?" Daniel put his hands into his pockets and fixed his gaze on the ship's battered flank. "She said she could hear the sea."

"Right." A beat of silence. Then: "Was that her, do you think? Or did the host get a look in?"

A smile ghosted across Daniel's face. "Does it matter?"

O'Neill looked at him, sadly. "No," he lied. "It doesn't matter at all."

Epilogue

STARLIGHT

THE UNIVERSE is never still.

A fixed point in space is a functional impossibility. Every object, from the smallest subatomic particle to the greatest galactic cluster, moves both in relation to every other and according to its own frame of reference. Each is inextricably linked to the rest of the cosmos and yet utterly separate from it, joined by the unbreakable chains of gravity and quantum probability and separated by the lightspeed limitations of information transfer.

There are no shared reference frames. There is no now. A man and a woman — for the sake of argument, we shall call them Jack O'Neill and Samantha Carter — might look at each other across the interior of a failing Goa'uld scoutship, and believe that they might see a future. But it is an illusion. They see each other not as they are, but as they *were*, when the light that moved from him to her and back again first began its journey. They rotate in a shared orbit, but are doomed to be separate, one from the other, forever.

As it is with humans, so must it be with suns. The universe operates on the same principles at all scales, although the connections between the very large and the very small are hard to define. Two shivering atoms live in each others' past just as definitely and irrevocably as two people or two stars, and yet they might whirl around each other so closely that they could be mistaken for the same object.

It is a complicated dance, an intricate, interwoven ballet of orbit and vector, of mass and radiation, of probability and gravity and the great, endless spinning of the galaxies themselves. It is vast and unfathomable and beyond any living mind to comprehend.

In fact, the only entities capable of truly appreciating the universe in all its unutterable complexity are those that have been designed specifically for the task.

A machine hung fifty million kilometers above the nameless star's northern pole. It had been there for some time, watching events in the system unfold with what, in a living creature, might have been called intense interest.

It had seen the Pit of Sorrows break out of hyperspace and be snatched up by Neheb-Kau's golden claw. It had observed the battle, the shattering of the Ash Eater homeworld, the destruction of Hera's Ha'tak. It had watched the remaining ships accelerate away, leaving only vast shoals of debris in their wake.

Fragmented ships and broken corpses, turning over in the nameless star's meager light, some falling into the singularity, others tumbling away on long orbits. From its vantage point, far above the system's ecliptic plane the Sentinel watched them all, tracked them all, compared their paths and their powers to its own expectations, and found the similarity acceptable.

The Sentinel was far from home. Its creators, a race whose name and nature had been carefully excised from its memory almost ten thousand years previously, had constructed it with one purpose in mind — to watch, coolly and without error, the rise of one potentially dangerous and destructive species. There were, in all probability, many such devices in the universe, simply because there were many species that required observation. If this was true, the Sentinel had no real evidence. It largely kept itself to itself, circling in a high orbit around a planet that the species in question referred to as Earth.

There were no technologies comprehensible to humans that would ever have detected the Sentinel, so it had remained safe and unmolested in its orbit for many thousands of years. For most of that time it had done nothing but observe, and send its observations off through subspace in discrete data packets. It had stopped getting return data centuries before, but it kept sending. It had no desire at all to do anything else.

Little had happened on the world below of any particular note: the humans had occasionally been swept by mass conflicts and virulent pathogens, but that was of no great consequence. Primitive atomic weapons had been detonated near its surface, although they had hardly warranted a mention in the Sentinel's reports. The large-scale modifications to the planet's biosphere were of no interest to the machine at all.

However, a small variance in temperature between two patches of Egyptian desert had been enough to send the Sentinel into a pattern of behavior that it hadn't even known it was programmed for.

Possible evidence of an Ash Eater was a red-flag condition for the Sentinel, one of a list that it was only able to access when one became apparent. This was of no concern to the machine, since it was built to be curious about humanity, not itself. But although the anomaly, recently exposed by the collapse of a rock shelf in western Egypt, was accompanied by certain quantum fluctuations that matched the phase-signature of an Ash Eater, the Sentinel needed to be sure. So it began to plan.

The machine was patient in the way only an artificial intelligence can be, and subtle beyond belief. It spent an age — several hundredths of a second — running countless simulations of its possible actions, refining and evolving the scenarios until it knew, to within an infinitely small set of tolerances, exactly how best to manipulate the initial conditions.

In the end, it hadn't really needed to do very much at all.

Its first action was to modify the flight-path of the TIAMAT satellite, in order to bring the anomaly to the attention of humans who might be in a position to investigate it further. This resulted in some of those humans ceasing to operate, but the Sentinel cared exactly as much about that as it did about how many grains of sand were displaced by their footfalls. But when the Pit of Sorrows first broadcast its message to Ra's primary Stargates, so as to warn him, no matter where he might be, that it had been compromised, the Sentinel knew it had been right to act.

The machine did not have direct access to any Stargates, but it was listening in on Stargate Command. It was listening in on everybody. It always had been.

The Sentinel's next action was to contact the Asgard. The machine had been sharing information with the creatures for some time, and they with it: a beneficial, if trust-free relationship of which the humans were thankfully unaware. The Asgard knew that the people of Earth would not welcome being spied on so thoroughly, so when they gave the Sentinel's telemetry to Stargate Command they simply said it had come from one of their probes. Had the Sentinel been blessed with emotions it might have found that slightly insulting, but the lie served its purpose. It sent certain humans off in pursuit of the Pit of Sorrows.

This too was largely according to the Sentinel's simulations, and to the plans of the Asgard. They didn't want to be personally troubled with the Ash Eater problem — they had far bigger fish to fry. But both they and the Sentinel knew that human beings cannot stay away from any new situation, no matter how lethal it might be. They are simply incapable of leaving well enough alone. So they had merely wound the SGC up like toy and let it go.

Meanwhile the Sentinel had effortlessly overtaken the Pit of Sorrows on its journey, and was there when it arrived. It hadn't been previously aware of the Ash Eater homeworld before that time, but that was not a matter of concern. Its creators had been, and once it was time for the Sentinel to know, it knew.

After that, it was merely a matter of letting the simulations play out. The Sentinel hadn't even needed to contact the Asgard again, which it was prepared to do should more direct intervention become necessary. All that was required was to take up a suitable vantage point and watch the pieces move across the board.

As a purely artificial construct, the Sentinel was not capable of satisfaction, but the patterns of information moving through its core became calm and repetitive in a way that could have been thought of as ever so slightly smug.

All — *almost* all — was as had been planned.

After thirty thousand years the Ash Eaters were gone from the universe, finally revealed by the actions of the humans and Goa'uld in orbit around their world and trapped within the event horizon of their own singularity. One day, far into the future, the black hole would evaporate and free them to feed once more, but by that time the humans would have been made dust in far more conventional manners — by age, by war, by the great cataclysm that still lurked, unseen, in their future. It was very unlikely their species would survive long enough to encounter the Ash Eaters again.

Even now, that timescale was expanding. The singularity was growing, spiraling slowly inwards towards the dead star and dragging out a thin wisp of stellar material as it approached. The two would, the machine calculated, eventually become part of a stable pairing, one feeding off the other until the mass of the star could no longer resist its internal energies. Then it would flash into sullen, stunted supernova, feeding the singularity the last of its corpse until only the black hole remained. A parasite and its host, like the Goa'uld themselves. An abusive, devouring relationship that could only end in death.

And yet...

There was a discontinuity. The patterns of matter and energy around the nameless star were not *exactly* as the Sentinel had calculated them to be. There was, in one small area, an error that could not be explained.

The matter stream between the star and the singularity had a hole in it.

The machine's calm state was disturbed by this. It was an observer by nature, but it had recently been required to predict as well as observe. In all other respects, its predictions had been correct, but this small dark spot in the stream was enough to force the Sentinel to re-evaluate its capabilities. The discontinuity might even, it decided, be evidence of a fault.

One that had to be investigated.

The Sentinel chose to act. It engaged its primary motor systems, accelerating without effort to a tenth of the speed of light, and arced down towards the matter stream. The journey took almost half an hour, an eternity to the Sentinel, but its patience was limitless. It watched the discontinuity with, perhaps, a billionth of its possible perceptions during the trip, and tracked the course of every other significant piece of matter in the system with a few percent more. Nothing except the shadow in the stream failed to match its predictions.

The nameless star and its parasite singularity were both vomiting radiation; the star in all directions, the black hole in twin wispy polar jets as it rotated. The energies they spewed out would have been lethal for organic life at such a range, but the Sentinel was made of stronger stuff by far. The machine was able to draw within a few hundred kilometers of the matter stream before it even needed to engage any protection at all.

Finally, as the Sentinel slowed to a holding position just above the stream, the cause of the shadow became apparent. It wasn't a hole, or a shadow. It was a welter of black, hairlike quantum filaments, a roiling cloud of null-energy reaching languidly out into the stream and feeding on the particles streaming past it.

The Sentinel looked more closely. And yes, there in the heart of the black field was Ra's Ash Eater, the occupant of the Pit of Sorrows; forgotten in the battle, untouched by the collapse of its homeworld, unconcerned by the imprisonment of its species. It hung, inert and lifeless as ever, with its reflexive feeding-shroud sweeping out around it — ash-gray, fetal, curled and blank-eyed and uncaring. Dead, and yet voracious. Turning slowly in the turbulence of the stream.

The Sentinel watched it for a long time. It sent out a small, high-priority data packet to its long-dead masters.

And then it spun, slowly, activated a superluminal drive array that even the Asgard could not have comprehended, and went home.

About the author
PETER J. EVANS

Peter J Evans' first novel, *Mnemosyne's Kiss*, was published in 1999 under Virgin Publishing's science fiction and fantasy imprint, Virgin Worlds. Evans later co-wrote the Judge Dredd novel *Black Atlantic* for Black Flame, which was re-printed as part of the *I Am The Law* Judge Dredd Omnibus, and the five part *Durham Red* cycle, also for Black Flame.

His latest projects have been the Stargate Atlantis novel *Angelus* for Fandemonium, and a script for the latest series of Stargate SG-1 audio dramas for Big Finish. He is presently working on a new novel, but if he says any more about that terrible things will happen to him.

During daylight hours Evans does something terribly complicated involving navigational radar. He lives near Croydon in southern England, and rather wishes he didn't.

STARGÅTE SG·1.

STARGATE ATLÅNTIS™

Original novels based on the hit TV shows **STARGATE SG-1** and **STARGATE ATLANTIS**

Available as e-books from leading online retailers

Paperback editions available from Amazon and IngramSpark

If you liked this book, please tell your friends and leave a review on a bookstore website. Thanks!